OIL &
CHOCOLATE

Nikki Kwiatkowski

Cover designed by Karis Drake

This book is a work of fiction. Names, characters, places, and incidents either are products of the author's imagination or are used fictitiously. Any resemblance to actual persons, living or dead, events, or locales is entirely coincidental.

Nikki Kwiatkowski

Visit my website at www.NikkiKAuthor.com

Printed in the United States of America

First Printing: July 2021

ISBN-13 978-1-7332165-3-1

To my husband, Chris. Your encouragement, as well as working from home, made this possible.

To my son, Lochlan. Your temperament, and love of long naps, definitely made this possible.

To my parents, Angie and Raymond

As always, with loving memory, to Kevin

CONTENTS

Chapter 1 11

Chapter 2 17

Chapter 3 24

Chapter 4 29

Chapter 5 39

Chapter 6 47

Chapter 7 51

Chapter 8 59

Chapter 9 62

Chapter 10 68

Chapter 11 76

Chapter 12 83

Chapter 13 89

Chapter 14 94

Chapter 15 104

Chapter 16 111

Chapter 17 118

Chapter 18 126

Chapter 19 135

Chapter 20 138

Chapter 21 145

Chapter 22...151

Chapter 23...157

Chapter 24...165

Chapter 25...174

Chapter 26...182

Chapter 27...187

Chapter 28...195

Chapter 29...203

Chapter 30...210

Chapter 31...217

Chapter 32...220

Chapter 33...231

Chapter 34...240

Chapter 35...248

Chapter 36...261

Chapter 37...264

Chapter 38...272

Chapter 39...278

Chapter 40...285

Chapter 41...291

Chapter 42...305

Chapter 43...315

Chapter 44...320

Chapter 45...328

Chapter 46...335

Chapter 47...340

Chapter 48...347

Chapter 49...351

Chapter 50...354

Chapter 51...361

Chapter 52...367

Chapter 53...378
Epilogue...387

CHAPTER 1

Briar walked down the sidewalk with no destination in mind. The first thing she had done when the bus dropped her off in Argent Falls was find accommodations. A twenty dollar a night hostel was far different than the mansion she used to call home; however, in the last two years, she couldn't even call it as such.

She had to admit, Argent Falls had a sleepy and cozy feel. It was far enough away from major cities, but not so far that it was forgotten. The population sign when the bus pulled in read 13,082, although, as Briar continued down the streets in the quaint downtown area, already a good distance from the hostel, she found that all of those 13,082 people seemed to know each other.

A smile came to her face for the first time in a long time. Maybe it wouldn't be so bad. Maybe she could call this place home for a little while.

Across the street, a little past where the shops and boutiques ended, a sign caught her attention. *Help Wanted.*

That was the second thing she needed to do. Find a job. At seventeen, never having worked before, she knew what her odds would be; however, the three hundred dollars she had in her pocket wouldn't buy her too many nights and meals at the hostel.

An even larger sign got her attention as she scurried across the street. Hayden Auto Body and Restoration. Though Briar knew nothing about cars, she was certain that, if given the opportunity, she could easily learn.

The second she pulled the door open to the entry and waiting area, the smell of something she couldn't place took over her senses. Rubber? Grease? It smelled every bit what one would expect from a mechanic shop.

The front counter was empty. The only person around was an old man in a corner chair, fast asleep with a newspaper on his lap.

Briar glanced over the desk where a greeter, cashier, or someone should have been. There was no bell or anything to get someone's attention. There were glass windows lining one side of the room that showed a massive garage. In the distance, she could see men working, but they didn't seem to notice anyone beyond the cars.

Just then, the door behind the desk swung open, and a man backed into the room. "Yeah, yeah, boss man! I got it."

From deep inside the garage, as the door closed, "Stop calling me that shit!"

The man that entered stopped with widened eyes as soon as he saw Briar. He pulled a small rag from his back pocket and began wiping a dark substance from his hands. "Uh, can I help you?"

Briar didn't want to beat around the bush. It was already the middle of June. She knew that school would be starting in two months or so. It would be much harder to work and save up money then.

"I saw the help wanted sign in the window," she told the man.

He gave her the exact expression that she expected, eyes that nearly fell from their sockets and a jaw dropped straight to the floor.

"Uh," the older man began. He shook his head and was overcome with a fit of laughter.

While that was another reaction Briar anticipated, it still hurt.

"Look, kid. Not to sound…uh..." He fought for the correct wording.

Briar coldly interrupted him. "Judgmental? Sexist? Ageist?"

The man who's name she didn't know, nor did she think she'd ever know at this point, narrowed his eyes at her. Normally, she would never have spoken to an older adult like that, but her world had changed. She couldn't let people push her around or treat her like a stupid child. If she did, she'd get sucked up in all the cruel evils and crumble.

"I just meant," he began again. "The job requires certain qualifications."

12

She figured as much, but decided to hold her head up and ask anyway. "Are you the owner?" When he looked surprised, "Could I speak to the owner first."

Just then the door behind him opened and two younger men walked through. They immediately caught Briar's attention. The older of the two looked to be in his mid to late thirties with shaggy reddish hair pulled back in a pony. It was the other one, with messy spiky hair as black as night and crystal clear cold blue eyes, that made a chill run down Briar's spine. She had to quickly take her eyes from him and back to the older man who looked ready to throw her out.

"Benji, everything okay," the dark-haired man asked the old one.

Not that it mattered, but at least Briar had one name to put with the three faces.

"Yeah," Benji sighed and shook his head, a smile quickly forming. "This kid wants to talk to the owner about the job posting in the window."

All three of them directed their attention to the girl on the other side of the counter. The way they looked at her, scrutinizing her, made Briar exceedingly uncomfortable, so much so that it felt as though her heart might beat out of her chest.

This had been the most forward thing she had done in her life, but judging by their looks, it was also the dumbest. She had to find a way out, but she wasn't going to look like a fool either.

"If you don't want me speaking to the owner, that's fine." She flung her finger from side to side gesturing toward the three. "Your chauvinistic attitudes speak volumes."

Just as she turned to leave, "Do you have a degree from a college or technical school?"

Briar spun back around. It was the youngest looking of the three, the dark haired one.

"The posting is for a mechanic. What qualifications do you have?" His eyes quickly flitted from hers all the way down to her feet and back up. "Can you even change a tire," he scoffed.

The redhead nudged him. "Dude, don't be so hard on her."

The dark-haired man ignored him and drew his attention back to the girl. "We need another mechanic with a rather impressive résumé, not someone we have to teach shit to. Got it?"

Briar blinked rapidly for a few seconds. "You're the owner?"

He crossed his arms in annoyance. "Yeah."

That surprised Briar. She wouldn't have taken any of the three men before her to be the owner of the establishment.

Attempting to take the high road, and not sound like a whiny brat. "Well, thank you for clarifying, Mister…"

His whole body tensed at the word and both of the other two chuckled.

"Dexter Hayden," he growled.

"Dexter Hayden," she repeated softly. "Well, thank you all for your time."

There. That wasn't as bad as Briar thought.

"You know, Dex," the redhead began. His words weren't directed toward Briar, but for some reason she thought that she might be part of the conversation. "We could use a receptionist."

Dex tore his eyes from the girl about to leave and glared at Rusty, silently asking him what the hell he was doing.

"Think about it," Rusty softly said, hoping to quell the vicious beast before him. "She could answer the phone and—"

"We have an answering machine," Dex interrupted.

"And she could actually greet people and handle the desk."

"The bell in the shop lets us know when someone enters."

Rusty shook his head. "Yeah? And how often are you under a car when that shit goes off. I'm all for someone else handling that."

"Uh," Benji quietly interjected. "He's not entirely wrong."

A strange feeling ran through Briar. Was that…Hope?

14

Dex's eyes tore from Rusty and Benji to the girl, now closer to the door than before. She was young, too young. While Dex knew that she had to still be a teenager, everything in her energetic green eyes screamed that she was well beyond her years. She had a dangerous combination about her.

Her blonde hair was haphazardly thrown into a ponytail and a few pieces clung to her neck from the warmth and humidity outside. Not that he should have noticed, but she had a sweet and whimsical look when it came to her body; although, he had to wonder why she was wearing a hoodie in the middle of June.

His eyes fell on her face longer than they should have. She wore too much makeup, at least, too much for Dex's liking. Then he saw it. He had to give her credit. She did a hell of a job covering it up. On the side of her left cheek, he saw the scratch breaking through the surface of her pristine makeup.

"What's your name," Dex found himself asking.

"Briar."

He had never met anyone with that name. It was unique, different, and he couldn't help but think that it was beautiful and fitting for her.

He shouldn't have asked, but his curiosity got the better of him. "How old are you?"

"Seventeen."

"Fuck," Dex hissed under his breath, suddenly feeling sick to his stomach. Had he really just checked out a seventeen-year-old?

Briar didn't hear whatever it was he mumbled, but a moment later, the other two men left so that it was only Dex, herself, and the sleeping man in the far-off corner.

Briar didn't know if she felt more or less comfortable without the other two there. Something about Dexter Hayden, or Dex as they called him, was a little disarming. His eyes were captivating. She had seen blue eyes before, but his were something else entirely.

After spending a lifetime around stuck-up rich kids in suits and ties, the beautiful art etched all the way down to his wrists on both arms intrigued her. The only time she had seen guys like him were in movies.

Briar wasn't stupid. She saw the look of disgust that came across his face when she told him her age. Even though she found him gorgeous, she was well-aware that he was far too old for her, and the last thing she wanted. She didn't need a guy in her life, not now, maybe not ever. No, what she needed right now more than anything, was a job.

CHAPTER 2

Hope.

That's exactly what that feeling was when Briar got back to the hostel that afternoon. When she first encountered Benji, she was certain that she looked like an idiot even walking into that place. If she ever got the chance, she'd have to bake something for Rusty. If it weren't for him, that piece of paper in her hands would never have been.

Dex hadn't asked her any more questions beyond her name and age. All he had done was hand her an application and tell her to return tomorrow. She didn't tell him, but she'd be there first thing in the morning. He didn't know how desperate she was.

She began filling out the form, but knew that she had little to add. More than half of it was prior work experience and references. She was all but certain that Dex wouldn't be calling any of her references. As bad as she felt doing so, she had to lie.

Another piece she had difficulty with was her phone number and address. She once had a phone. Not anymore. That was one thing she left behind, albeit, after wiping it clean.

Phone Number: Not Applicable.

She needed a local address, and though she thought for a moment about putting down the address to the hostel, she quickly decided against it. Dex probably lived in Argent Falls all his life. He'd know it. Maybe he'd ask too many questions. Maybe he'd feel pity for her. She couldn't bear the thought of either.

Though she had taken her computer with her, currently it proved pointless, as the hostel didn't have Wi-Fi.

She looked over to the middle-aged woman on the bed next to hers. She had recently taken some pills and looked to be slightly drowsy. She seemed nice enough, having introduced herself earlier as Olive. Briar couldn't help but wonder what her story was. Why was she staying in a place like this? Did she need a new start? Was she alone? Was she running too?

"Excuse me," Briar asked before Olive could drift off to sleep.

"Mhmm?"

"Could I borrow your phone for a moment? I just need to look up an address."

"Sure, baby." Olive's frail hand tossed the phone in Briar's direction, no questions asked.

Briar immediately pulled up the app for maps. She zoomed in to their location and began panning outward. When she found what appeared to be a nice subdivision she zoomed in until the street appeared. Oakcrest Drive.

A quick internet search left her with several numbers to choose from. *Address: 1074 Oakcrest Drive.*

The application was complete. All she could do now was hope and pray that Dex wasn't the coldhearted jerk that he appeared. If so, she'd just have to start over tomorrow.

✳ ✳ ✳

Olive was still asleep when Briar woke. She glanced at Olive's phone. 5:38. It was far too early to be awake, but lately sleep hadn't been her friend. In her sleep, she couldn't control her thoughts. She dreaded sleep. It made things appear in her head that shouldn't be there, things that needed to go away so she could move on.

The best thing about being awake so early was the fact that she didn't have to wait on one of the several communal bathrooms.

This was a different life for her, but it was hers, and in this life, she was prepared to fight. As difficult as it was going to be, she had to stand up for herself, because she knew there wasn't a chance in hell anyone else was going to.

She didn't leave home empty handed. She took several garments, mostly things that would be too expensive to come by, like jeans and shoes. Thankfully when she was out in search of a job the day before, she came across a cute thrift store. It would be a far cry from the designer fashions her father used to buy her, but in the last two years, she had been lucky to get any new clothes.

While she generally didn't wear much makeup, that was another thing that was too expensive to leave behind. Though the scratches and bruises were healing nicely, they were still there, still a constant reminder; therefore, when she got ready to leave that morning, she found herself plastering more crap on her face than usual.

When she was done, she looked in the mirror. There wasn't much she could do with her hair aside from washing and drying it. Plus, it was too warm for much more than a ponytail.

Overall, she thought she looked...Cute.

Briar knew she needed to eat, but rather than spend an outrageous amount of money on a proper breakfast, she swung by a little donut shop. Two dollars for a donut and black coffee was about all she could afford. Until she started earning money, she had to stretch that quickly fading three hundred dollars she had come to Argent Falls with.

As soon as she walked into the shop, "We're not open yet," a gruff and raspy voice called out.

"Perhaps the door should be locked then." Briar clamped her mouth shut as soon as she said it. Pissing off the owner first thing in the morning was probably not the best way to get hired.

Dex walked around the counter until he was a couple feet in front of Briar. He hadn't realized the day before just how small she was. His 6'3" frame towered over her 5' and some inches.

"What are you doing here?"

Briar held out the application. "You told me to come back tomorrow. Today is tomorrow," she said sweetly, hoping he'd overlook that first comment.

Dex took the paper from her but didn't look at it right away. His eyes narrowed curiously on her. He could see it, sense it, instantly. The hope and desperation that poured from those sparkling green eyes was all too obvious.

It wasn't until her eyes fell from his and she glanced nervously to the floor that he knew he had stared too long.

Clearing his throat, Dex brought the paper up.

Briar Stone.

She hadn't given him her full name the day before.

"What's this," Dex asked, holding the paper up and pointing to a very specific spot.

"Not applicable? That means that–"

"I know what it means, smartass. What teenager doesn't have a phone," Dex scoffed, mildly annoyed by her sarcasm.

"Apparently, this teenager," she said, emphasizing the word. It strangely bothered her with being called a kid and a teenager.

Something about her struck him. Against his better judgement, he knew she needed a break. Looking at her, she belonged in a little café or boutique somewhere, not with a bunch of greasy mechanics.

Dex turned and began walking toward another door, a different one than the one that led to the garage. When he didn't feel her presence behind him, he glanced over his shoulder. "Coming?"

Unsure what to say, Briar simply followed. Her heart raced at the idea that this might be an interview.

Dex opened the door and turned on the light. It was a large office and that was putting it mildly. A long couch spanned across the far wall. Another wall was lined with massive filing cabinets. There was a desk and computer, and also a refrigerator and coffee machine.

Dex didn't say anything at first, just simply watched as Briar glanced curiously around the room. It was then, in the bright office lights that he was able to fully look at her.

She wore slim fitting jeans and a too clean pair of Converse. He rolled his eyes. Typical teenager. She didn't wear a hoodie today. Instead, she had a rather nice long-sleeved button up, slightly patterned with an array of wrinkles. Again, he found that she wore too much makeup; however, deep down he wondered if it had anything to do with the scratch on her face. It had either healed more since the day before, or she had put something extra on to cover it better.

Briar looked around once more before drawing her attention back to Dex, who seemed to be watching her carefully. She generally didn't have a hard time looking people in their eyes when communicating, but he was proving to be the most difficult. There was something dangerously enchanting about his eyes, and it both frightened and intrigued her.

"Do you have your social security card," Dex asked, jumping past a whole array of questions Briar expected.

"No. Why would I–"

"I need that for tax purposes. Also, if you want direct deposit, I need your account information. Otherwise, I can cut you a check every Saturday afternoon," he went on. Dex saw how uncomfortable Briar became and quickly stopped, instead asking, "Is there a problem?"

"I just assumed…Is this…Are you going to interview me," Briar finally managed.

"Can you answer a phone?"

She rolled her eyes at the absurd question. Through gritted teeth, "Yes."

"Okay then."

"Wait, that's it," she gasped. "That's all you're going to–"

21

Dex held up his hand, interrupting her and silencing her. "You do realize if you continue, you're talking me out of hiring you?"

Briar held up her hands and a small smile lit up her whole face. "Understood."

Dex had to look away. She was cute. He'd give her that.

"So, all that information," he asked as he went to the desk and began to fumble for more papers.

Briar picked at a button on her shirt. "Well...I know my social security number, but I don't have the card." When all he did was groan, she knew that her next comment wasn't going to be much better. "Also, I don't have a bank account. Where would I go to cash a check around here without a bank account?"

"Are you fucking kidding me right now," Dex snapped.

Briar's eyes widened in fear and he immediately regretted his words. Something about her reminded him of a wounded wild animal.

Dex ran a hand through his hair. If only Rusty hadn't made the suggestion. If only she didn't look so desperate. If only he was as big of an asshole as he projected.

"Look," he started, more carefully this time. "I'll pay you in cash this week. By the end of next week, you better have either gone to the local bank or set something up online. Got it."

"Got it," Briar immediately answered.

From outside the room more voices were heard. Both Briar and Dex turned toward the half open door to see Benji and Rusty shuffling in.

Dex began making his way from the office. "I'm not going to sit you down and show you a bunch of shit. Figure it out on your own and try not to screw up."

Startled, Briar blinked a few times, registering what he just said. "Um, okay." Before Dex could exit the room, "I just want to say thank you."

Dex turned to face Briar, his expression softer than she had ever seen, that is, until she continued speaking.

"This means a lot, and I'll do a good job. So, thank you Mister Hay—"

Dex took a step forward. He was so close, and while Briar's brain told her to retreat, she found her feet frozen in place. Eyes that, for a moment, had looked at her so kindly, now descended frosty bolts of lightning upon her.

"Dex," he growled. "Just Dex."

All Briar could do was nod, making a note to only call him Dex in the future, never Mister Hayden. Something about that was bothersome to her, but she couldn't quite say why.

CHAPTER 3

Needless to say, but by the third day Briar was confused as hell. When she asked Benji how to do the bills, he brought up a blank document on the computer at the front desk and the most simple and basic template. He told her that they would *jot down* what to type in and the cost and she could fill in the document. That wasn't even the most absurd thing. Then he told her to print out two copies, one for the customer and one for the shop. Also, have the customer sign the one for the shop. That didn't seem too difficult, until the next part. Then, then he told her to clear the document and start over for the next customer!

After going through the office, she was only further appalled by the organizing. At first, she thought the job would be pretty boring and basic, simply answering phones and scheduling appointments, which was a whole different story. The scheduling consisted of a large desk calendar and handwritten notes.

Even more strangely, when she looked up Hayden Auto Body and Restoration, she was floored by the reviews. Some of them were written from people halfway across the country. Obviously, they had business and their work was spot on, but everything outside of the garage was a disaster.

Rusty strolled from the garage and to the employee restroom. Moments later, he emerged and entered the office, grabbing his sandwich from the fridge.

Of all the men that worked at the garage, Rusty, Benji, and very rarely Dex, were the only ones Briar had come into contact with. Of those three, Rusty was so far the nicest, which is why she didn't hesitate asking him for help.

"Are you on your lunch break," Briar asked before Rusty headed out from the office.

"Yup."

"Would you mind hanging out for a minute? I had some questions."

Rusty raised a brow, but in the end didn't think too much into it. Rather than leave the office, he sauntered across the room and plopped on the sofa. "Shoot," he said through a bite of sandwich.

"Well, I wanted to begin with generic services and prices. For instance, I know an oil change is thirty-two dollars, but that's because there's been nearly a dozen in the last three days. I'd like to know the most common services, especially the ones that have a flat rate across the board. Also, what about tire prices? Is there a book or database that you order from," Briar rambled.

Rusty swallowed too soon, not having chewed enough, and began to choke a little. Once he finally recovered, "What the hell are you doing?"

"I'm trying to make the organization and record keeping run a little more smoothly," Briar said with a shrug.

Rusty looked her over, her naïve innocence was definitely going to get her into trouble.

"And Dex is cool with that?"

Briar thought for a moment. "Why wouldn't he be?"

Rusty took a large bite of sandwich to account for why he wasn't answering that question. There was no doubt in his mind that if she changed things up too much, Dex was going to go through the roof.

Rather than deterring Briar, "What all was it that you needed to know?"

* * *

An odd sound pierced through Dex's ears when he entered from the garage. Laughter. Even more strangely, it was coming from his office.

He hovered in the doorway. Briar was relaxed in the office chair with a clipboard while Rusty was sprawled on the couch, telling some ridiculous story. Then Briar laughed again, and the sound was so unfamiliar to Dex that he couldn't help but stare.

"Hey, man," Rusty said from across the room.

Briar spun in her chair, only to come face to face with a pair of emotionless, yet serious, blue eyes.

Dex entered the office and made his way to the refrigerator, withdrawing a sports drink. "You about done with lunch," he asked, his words directed to Rusty.

Rusty eyed Dex with suspicion. Something about the tone in his voice threw him. Then he watched Briar. As soon as Dex entered she went silent and tense.

"I was just spending some time with Briar. Didn't want her feeling left out," Rusty finally said, as his eyes flitted between the two.

Briar gave him a sweet smile and turned back to the computer. The look on Dex's face was something far from a smile.

"Rusty, can I talk with you privately," Dex asked through clenched teeth.

Rusty sat back with a smirk. "I'm not done with–"

"Now."

Rusty chuckled to himself as he rose from the couch and slowly followed Dex from the office. "If you need anything else, don't hesitate to ask," he called back toward Briar.

With a great deal of enthusiasm, "Thank you so much!"

Dex didn't say a word until the office door was closed. "Outside."

Both men then walked out of the reception area and through the front doors and to the side of the building.

"Are you sure this is far enough. I was thinking something along the lines of Oymyakon," Rusty joked. When Dex cocked his head to the side, not understanding, "It's the coldest inhabited place on earth? You know what, never mind. What's this about?"

26

"Don't," Dex growled.

Rusty laughed. He knew what it was about, but sensed that Dex was uncomfortable saying it. "Use your words," he pressed.

Dex ran a hand through his dark hair and his eyes met Rusty's, full of humor.

"She's a kid. She's half your age," Dex pointed out.

"First of all, she's not a kid, and I suppose you're right. I tend to like my girls of drinking age."

Dex sighed. "This isn't funny. Aside from her age, she's also an employee."

Rusty ignored Dex and tapped his forefinger against his cheek. "You have to admit, she is—"

"Stop," Dex warned.

Rusty began laughing, leaving Dex further confused. "Dude, you're too easy to fuck with. I'm going back to work," Rusty said, shaking his head and turning to leave.

"I'm serious," Dex called out. "I don't want you in jail."

Rusty turned and though he was a distance away, Dex could easily see the smirk on his lips and the playful glimmer in his eyes.

"Last time I checked, age of consent for our state was sixteen," he said with a wink.

Dex was at a loss for words, and was thankful that Rusty hightailed it after that unnecessary and inappropriate comment. Rusty was thirty-four and loved playing the field. Age didn't matter to him at all; however, Dex was nearly certain that Rusty was being truthful when he commented that he preferred girls of drinking age. Regardless of Briar's age, he didn't like Rusty flirting with her. After all, age aside, she was an employee.

When Briar left work after the first week, with more than three hundred dollars pay, she couldn't have been happier. That, with the money she still had left would buy her another three weeks at the hostel. Despite that, deep down she knew it wouldn't be enough to get her by once school started. She needed to find another job.

When school started, she wouldn't be able to work very much at the shop, except for Saturdays. What she really needed was an evening or night job. Maybe she'd ask Rusty. So far, of all the people, he had been the most helpful.

Briar spent most of Sunday huddled on her bed and tinkering on her computer. She hoped by the end of the following week to have something to show Dex. What she was doing was simple enough; however, it would save a lot of time with billing and improve the business's organization.

Sure enough, by Thursday night, or early Friday morning, depending how one considered it, Briar was at a point where she thought that she'd be able to share her work with Dex.

The only problem, ever since Rusty helped her out that day, Dex had barely spoken two words to her. If she were being honest, she had no idea how to show him what she made when they had a difficult time even saying the simplest greeting.

CHAPTER 4

Briar didn't say anything Friday morning. Despite having two cups of black coffee, Dex was being extra Dex. That was the only way she saw it. She had to assume that was just who he was, a moody tattooed gruff beast.

Shortly after lunch, Dex and Benji passed through the waiting area and Dex was taken aback when he heard his name called out.

Briar stepped from around the desk and hesitantly, yet confidently, made her way toward Dex. When they were only a couple feet apart, "I have something I'd like to show you. It's something I've been working on."

"Can it wait," Dex sighed.

Briar tried to hide her disappointment, but both Dex and Benji saw it immediately. It was at that moment Dex knew that her eyes gave everything away.

"Go ahead," Benji interjected. "I got this."

Dex shot Benji a glare, but it didn't register to him. Instead, Benji clapped Dex on the shoulder and went about his original task.

Dex raised a brow at Briar, a signal she took to mean for her to continue.

"It's on the office computer," she informed him. "But if you like it, I can put it on the one out front as well."

Dex had no idea what she was talking about, but followed behind her to the office. Once there, Briar excitedly motioned for him to take a seat in the chair in front of the computer, to which he did.

He didn't know what he was looking at. It was just a plain white screen with several different buttons to click on. Briar stood next to him and took control of the mouse.

He couldn't help thinking that this was the closest he had ever been to her. After spending all day in a garage, smelling nothing but fumes, and oil, and smoke, and who knows what else, the scent from her was breathtaking. He didn't know how to describe perfumes and shampoos, but all he knew was that it was the sweetest and most subtle scent. It somehow reminded him of a crisp spring morning.

That thought alone made him snap back to reality and whatever was on the computer screen. He didn't think thoughts like that. Ever.

"This is just the home screen. If you click on this, this is for bills," Briar began.

"We have something for bills," Dex pointed out.

Briar shook her head and when she did, her ponytail brushed against Dex's shoulder. That's how close she was.

"Yeah, I'm well-aware of the bills," Briar grumbled.

Dex ignored the comment and let her continue.

"So, when you click on this. There's your bill. You put in the customer's name, but if they're in the system it will begin to come up gradually. Oh! No need to put in a date. There's an automatic date and time stamp when you hit save. Also, when you hit save, it automatically prints out a receipt for the customer."

Dex stopped her for a moment. "What about a copy for us?"

"Seriously?" It was a rhetorical question and before Dex could reply, "If you want a hard copy, I can make it print out two. You should know when it saves, it's backed up here." She clicked again. "I'll find a better way to organize this in the coming days, but all of your saved receipts will be here by last name, then first, then the date."

Dex sighed but said nothing. He didn't like change, but so far what she was saying wasn't too horrible.

"The best part, no more typing and erasing," Briar exclaimed.

Now she had Dex intrigued. "What do you mean?"

"I have dropdown boxes and the prices are automatic; however, if a change needs to be made, you can still do that manually."

Dex pushed her hand from the mouse and Briar sucked in a sharp breath from the slight bit of contact.

"Sorry," Dex mumbled. He quickly turned his attention back to the computer and began looking at what she had just explained.

Briar took that moment to step aside, putting just enough distance between them. Something so little and insignificant should not have disarmed her, yet here she stood, unable to take her eyes off his hand that moved the mouse from side to side.

"Where did..." Dex began slowly.

"Oh, Rusty helped me with that."

Dex's attention went from the computer screen to Briar, and she suddenly realized why she had such a hard time talking to him. Dex was something else entirely. When he looked at her, she felt frozen.

Briar knew that she couldn't think like that. A crush on someone so unavailable in so many ways would be the dumbest thing for her right now.

"What do you mean," Dex asked. He knew Rusty still spoke with Briar, but he didn't think they spent any time together. Unless they were spending time outside of work. That thought alone caused an eruption within him.

"That's what we were talking about last week. When he came in for lunch, I asked him if I could ask him a few questions about the business."

For some strange reason, Dex felt a little relieved. Then he recalled his conversation with Rusty. He couldn't figure out why Rusty would screw with him like that.

"Anyway, I guess I could have asked you, but..." Briar let her words trail off.

Dex pushed his chair back a little and spun it in her direction so they were better facing each other. "But?"

"Uh...Well...You're just busy, so–"

Dex quickly interrupted her. "You can say what you want. No consequences."

Briar's uncertain eyes flew up to meet his, and for once, they didn't hold the angry storm she was used to seeing. Feeling bold, "You just haven't been the most welcoming here. I know you didn't want to hire me–"

"But I did."

Dex saw the slightest amount of pink come to her cheeks in that moment, and it was only then he realized that she wore less makeup than she had in the past. Her face looked more real and pure. She definitely had that natural beauty thing down.

Briar opened her mouth to say something, but Dex immediately cut her off. He already knew what she was going to say.

Why?

He still wasn't sure why. She looked like she needed a chance. Though she tried to hide it, he had seen the desperation on her face. He'd never admit to it, but he also liked the little bit of spunk and attitude that rolled off her like a fog.

"So, the home screen," he began, clearing his throat, which had recently gone dry. "What are the other things?"

Briar leaned back in, but careful to keep a better distance. "If you click here," she began pointing at the screen.

Dex clicked where she told him, and his mouth fell open.

"These are all the tires that you sell. I made it so that you can add them individually or as a set. All of the prices are from the most recent orderbook you had."

To say that he was impressed was putting it mildly. She made it so simple that even Benji would be able to do it.

"When did you find the time to do all this, and how do you know how to do all this," Dex found himself asking.

"School. The school I used to go to was very forward with technology and classes reflected that," she replied, intentionally skipping the first part of his question.

"Is that a way to say you went to some rich kid school," Dex scoffed.

"If you must know," Briar began. There was now a hint of annoyance in her voice. "Yes. I went to a private academy."

Briar didn't expect the chuckle that came from Dex, but damn was it a nice sound.

"You do all this here?"

She wasn't sure how to answer that, wondering if Dex would be upset that she did a task not asked of her on company time.

The truth was always best.

"Umm…Actually, no. I don't sleep a lot. I needed something to keep me busy," she admitted.

Dex tilted his head to look at her, a million questions coming to his mind. Something about her wasn't right. Normally, he wouldn't have cared, but that was the frustrating part. For some hellishly unknown reason, he cared, and he wanted to know more.

"Ahem," came a voice from the doorway.

Briar was the first to look up. Dex didn't need to. That one small noise was enough.

"What the hell are you doing here," Dex groaned, spinning the chair around to face Lexi.

Dex had to give it to her, she looked good in her cutoff shorts and some fancy frilly blouse. After he raked his eyes up and down her body and back to her eyes, Lexi's whole face lit up. One thing he didn't like about Lexi, she knew she looked good. It was always better when a woman was beautiful but didn't know it. That was not Lexi.

Despite what she looked like, Dex was already pissed. He didn't like her coming to his work. It had nothing to do with the fact that he was possessive and worked with nothing but guys. In fact, lately when it came to Lexi, her flirting with other guys didn't bother him as much as it used to. The thing with Lexi, she never knew when to quit. She couldn't come by just to drop off lunch. No, she had to stand around and talk for all eternity. Dex didn't have time for that when he was working.

"It's Friday."

Dex was more than annoyed. That was her answer?

"Thank you for telling me something that I could have gotten from a fucking calendar," he snapped.

Without invitation, Lexi made her way farther into the room. "It's date night. I tried calling, but you weren't answering your phone. I see now that you were busy."

Dex didn't like what Lexi was insinuating and suddenly fought to ignore Briar's presence, knowing it wouldn't be that easy with Lexi.

Lexi extended her hand to Briar. "Hi, I'm Lexi. Dex's long-term girlfriend."

Dex rolled his eyes at the introduction. Unlike himself with her, Lexi found every woman a threat.

Briar took the woman's hand and shook it. "Briar."

"Oh. That's a strange name," Lexi giggled.

For some reason, Dex wanted to point out that it wasn't that strange just to shut Lexi up. He didn't want her talking to Briar, knowing that anything Briar said would only get twisted in Lexi's head. What Dex didn't expect was for Briar to have a response.

"My mother was a fan of *Sleeping Beauty*. One of her names was Briar Rose."

Dex tried not to have an outward reaction. Knowing that extra piece of information did something to him, but he wasn't sure what that something was.

"Then your middle name is Rose? How cute," Lexi exclaimed, not for one second meaning that.

"No. My middle name is Eden," Briar corrected. She realized it wasn't necessary, but she felt the need to.

The forced smile finally faded from Lexi's face. "Well, that doesn't make any sense then."

At that point, Dex rose from his chair and began rubbing at his temples. "Who gives a shit?! Damn Lexi, it's just a fucking name," he yelled.

"I see someone is having a bigger attitude than normal," Lexi hissed.

"Yeah! Because you always do this. You come in here and talk nonsense. Get to the point and leave."

"Speaking of leaving," Briar boldly interjected. "I'm going to get back to work and leave you two alone."

Dex wanted to tell her how unnecessary it was. She hadn't finished showing him everything on the computer, but judging by the look Lexi was giving him, he knew she caught on to what Briar said. He needed to deal with her first.

No sooner than Briar closed the door, Lexi was on him like a vulture. "*Work*?!"

"Yeah," Dex calmly answered with a shrug. "She's the receptionist."

"You never needed a receptionist before."

Not wanting to deal with Lexi at work, Dex gave in to what he knew would inevitably be the end of the conversation. "Look, I'm busy. I'll pick you up at seven, yeah?"

Lexi shoved her finger at his chest. "You better be taking me somewhere nice." She spun on her heels and stormed toward the door. "And don't you think for one minute that this *issue* won't be brought up again," she added.

Dex didn't think it would be as easy as it was. He fully expected a much longer fight from her. The dinging of the entry bell told him that she had indeed left.

He had to walk past Briar to get back to the garage, and though she appeared busy with some papers in front of her, he paused for a moment and interrupted her. "I'm sorry about Lexi."

Briar looked at him with confusion. "Why? She seems nice."

Dex blinked a few times. Was Briar in the same room as him?

"She's also very pretty. How long have you been together," Briar asked, hoping that she wasn't overstepping any boundaries.

Dex was baffled out of his mind, in disbelief at how nice Briar was being.

"Two years," he finally answered.

He wanted to add on *too many*, but decided not to. The conversation already seemed inappropriate to be having with someone he had known for less than two weeks. He didn't need to explain that Lexi was supposed to just be a few hookups and that was all. How he got sucked into whatever they were was beyond him.

Briar shuffled her feet. It wasn't her place, that much she knew, but she felt like she had to say something. Dex must have sensed her uncertainty.

"What," he let out, clearly annoyed.

"I just…I think you were a bit of an arrogant jerk to her."

Briar allowed her eyes to meet his and she saw a bit of surprise in his cold stare.

"I'm sorry, what?"

"You were rude. She just–"

Dex interrupted her immediately. "I don't recall asking your advice when it comes to women."

She definitely overstepped.

"I'm not a good boyfriend," Dex continued. "She knows that. She deals with it."

Before Briar could say another word, Dex stormed past her and to the garage.

That should have been the point where Briar let it go. After all, Dex was her boss. One wrong move and he would fire her. Oddly, she didn't think he would. In all honesty, he had no business hiring her in the first place. Despite his gruffness, she didn't think that her next indiscretion would land her jobless.

She hadn't run the system she created by him, and she thought that he appeared pretty impressed by it.

36

Though she didn't know much about relationships, after the way Dex spoke to Lexi, a sweet gesture couldn't hurt.

* * *

The clock on the wall already read several minutes past five, and most of the guys were already wrapping up.

"Did you ever get a call about that Bentley," Rusty asked.

"No, not yet," Dex answered. Throwing himself into work had cooled him down after his conversations with Lexi and then Briar.

"I hope you get it, kid. That would be one hell of a restoration," Benji added.

Just then the door from the inside popped open and the looks on Benji and Rusty's faces told Dex who it was immediately.

"I just wanted to say I'm out for the day," Briar called out.

Dex acknowledged her with a nod.

"Have a good evening," Rusty responded. "Don't get in too much trouble," he added with a wink.

When Dex's eyes fell on her, Briar couldn't help but hesitate. In two weeks, she already knew that it didn't take much to piss off Dexter Hayden.

"Oh, also…" She bit her lip. Maybe secretly she did want to push his buttons. "I placed an order for you at the florist. You need to pick it up before they close at six."

Dex's mouth fell open. From the corner of his eye, he could see Rusty shaking, attempting to hold in his laughter.

"Why the hell did you do that," he shouted at Briar.

"We agreed earlier that you were a jerk to—"

"We did not agree on anything!"

"Really," Briar asked, feigning innocence. "I must have misunderstood. Anyway, be there before six." Before Dex could yell or curse anymore, she pulled the door shut behind her.

"Damn," Benji hissed.

Now Rusty didn't hold back and let out a full-on roaring belly laugh. When he was finally able to catch his breath, "Dude! When was the last time you gave Lexi flowers? Have you ever given her flowers? She's going to think you're going to propose or some shit."

Benji didn't laugh much, at least not like Rusty, but he did add his amusement.

"I have to say, she's ballsy," Rusty continued. Dex still stared at the closed door in disbelief. "Maybe I should try my chances with her after all."

Dex ignored him. Rusty made stupid comments like that all the time. After what Briar mentioned earlier, it didn't seem like Rusty was anything more than a vessel of information to her.

"You know, I like her," Benji said with a few nods. "I'll have to tell Liam to look out for her once school starts."

Liam was Benji's eighteen-year-old son, a star football player and every teenage girl's fantasy.

Dex busied himself with wiping some oil from his hands. "You should. Wouldn't hurt for her to meet some people her age," he added dryly.

CHAPTER 5

Dex didn't look up when he heard the bell of the shop's main door. The quietness and soft footsteps told him who it was. She was always early.

"Good morning," Briar said with almost a whisper.

She walked past the receptionist's desk to the office, the strong scent of coffee already beckoning her. Dex didn't say a word. Perhaps he hadn't heard her; however, the little she knew about him, he was probably ignoring her.

After pouring herself a cup of coffee, Briar was about to make her way back out when something caught her attention. On the desk, near the office computer, was a vase of flowers. She hadn't known Lexi's favorite, so when she called in to the florist, she went with sunflowers. Sunflowers made everyone happy. Why they were in the office of a mechanic shop and not with Lexi was a different story.

Dex could see Briar pause through the open office door. After taking a moment to look at the arrangement, she turned to face him, not expecting him to be watching her every move. Their eyes were locked together, hers a mix of confusion, his unemotional and withdrawn.

They said nothing, as they weren't quite in normal speaking distance. It was then that Dex took a moment to look her over. For the first time, she wasn't wearing long sleeves. Instead, she had on a solid light blue polo. In the distance he could tell that the detail above her left breast suggested that she paid too much for it. As his eyes dropped farther down her body, it was apparent that the shirt was a size too small. If she were to reach upward, a couple inches of midriff would definitely show. He found her faded ripped jeans to also be quite snug.

39

As she got closer, he could tell that, once again, she wasn't wearing as much makeup as she had in the past. He had to assume that, along with a shirt showing her arms, meant that whatever happened to her before she came into his shop had healed.

He didn't want to know her business, and he wouldn't ask. Maybe she had a drunk for a father and he beat her. Maybe a boyfriend roughed her up. Those thoughts alone bothered him in a way they shouldn't. He shouldn't bother himself with her or her past.

He didn't want to know. He found that he repeated that to himself far more often since he had first met her than he should have.

Once Briar was about two feet from Dex, as that's as close as she'd allow herself to get, she finally spoke again. "Good morning."

"You said that already."

When she met his eyes this time, they were more unreadable than ever. The intensity behind them was something she had not encountered before. He never said much, and that only fed her curiosity to know more, to know what he was thinking.

"What makes you think you still have a job after yesterday," Dex asked. He wouldn't show it, but he found humor in her widened and shocked eyes.

Briar's heart pounded a little harder. "I was just trying to help, and–"

Dex laughed, really laughed. "I don't need help from a *kid* when it comes to *women.*"

Briar found that comment annoying. She was on her own in the world. A kid, or child, or teenager, or any of those other titles implied immaturity. Ever since her mother, and now her father, she had matured a great deal.

"Just because I can't vote, can't smoke, can't drink…That doesn't make me an ignorant *kid*. I'm sure I've been through more in life than you could imagine." At that she immediately snapped her mouth shut. She shouldn't have vomited all that.

Dex stared at her. She had to go and pique his interest once again. His day hadn't even started and already he had to remind himself: *He didn't want to know.*

Before Dex could say anything, could yell at her, tell her to get out, "If I'm fired, fine. I'll go as soon as I get paid for this week. I do still get paid. You can't withhold wages just—"

"Calm your tits." Once the words fell from his mouth, realizing what he just said, he bit on his fist in annoyance. "Sorry," he mumbled. "Look, you're not fired."

"Oh…"

Briar sipped on her coffee. It would be so much less awkward if some of the other guys would hurry up and show; however, the clock on the wall told her they still had a good ten minutes of awkward.

"I'm almost done," Dex informed her, as he scribbled a few things down. "Then it's all yours."

"Hey, Dex…" The tiny voice inside her head told her not to.

Her sweet voice tore his attention away from what he was writing, and he looked up at her.

"I was just curious," she slowly began.

"I have a feeling that's going to always be a thing with you." At his words she stopped speaking and her cheeks reddened several shades deeper. He already knew what she was going to ask. "Go on."

"Well, how did it go last night? What happened?"

He hated that she wanted to know, that she acted like she cared, or maybe truly did care. He didn't want to talk to her about Lexi.

"The flowers in the office should tell you," was all he gave her at first.

"She didn't like them?" Briar sighed. "I'm sorry." She shook her head and sipped on her coffee. "I thought all women liked flowers."

Dex watched her carefully. She genuinely did care. He hated that she had such a naïve sweetness about her. It only made her youth stick out that much more.

"I wouldn't know. I didn't give them to her."

Briar gasped and gave Dex an incredulous look. "What? Why?"

"If you must know, when I showed up, she was acting like a raging bitch. So, I left," he concluded simply with a shrug.

Relief washed over Dex when he heard the bell to the shop for a second time and Rusty came dragging in. Generally, he went out drinking on Friday nights. Sometimes that made Saturdays a little difficult for him.

"Are you hungover or still drunk," Dex joked.

"Ha. Ha. Very funny," Rusty said with a yawn. "I wish I was one of those. No. Instead I'm sleep deprived. Apparently, my sister and her husband finally decided to split, and she ended up dragging her ass to my place for the night, along with those little demons she calls children."

Briar could feel her heart race after that comment. It wasn't the comment at all, but it was what it did to Dex. It was different from his laugh earlier. This one was so melting that it sent sparks through her whole body. Then she had to make the mistake of looking up at him, and that smile.

No wonder he rarely smiled. If he were to smile, he'd have women falling at his feet. It was irritating how such a rude and beastly man could have such a beautiful laugh and gorgeous smile.

* * *

Briar couldn't help but feel off all day. She drank several more cups of coffee, but she still felt tired. She had to try to get more sleep. Lately, when she closed her eyes at night, there was an improvement. It simply didn't help that the hostel had people coming and going at all hours of the night.

"Good afternoon, Hayden Auto Body and Restoration," Briar answered.

It was a strange call, and she had to assume that Dex would want to know right away.

42

When she rose, her knees felt extra weak and gooey. Something wasn't right. Maybe it was too much coffee. As soon as she relayed the information to Dex, she'd have to get some water in her.

"Dex," she called through the door to the garage.

Dex rolled out from under a nearby car and gave Briar his full attention. As soon as she told him a man called about selling *some old car*, he sat up on his creeper and began wiping off his hands.

She fought to remember what kind of car it was. "Uh…something like a 1930…"

Dex bolted up and headed toward her, his pulse racing with excitement. He had been waiting weeks to hear about that piece of junk. He had so many plans for it, and was certain that he could get it beyond its original glory and bring a nice profit in auction.

Once he got to the reception desk, Briar handed him the note with the man's number.

Dex couldn't help but notice how pale Briar looked. The color from her face had just faded. He watched her carefully as he took out his phone and started entering the number.

"Don't mind me," Benji said, trudging in from the garage. "Just need to take a leak."

Dex wasn't paying attention to Benji; however, Benji didn't seem to be in too much of a rush, as he paused and looked at Briar as well.

Something wasn't right. Her eyes blinked several times, and they didn't seem to be focused on anything.

"Briar, are you okay," Dex asked.

She looked up at him, her eyes filled with horror. "What…"

He stepped closer, knowing that something was seriously wrong. "Do you need to sit down? You don't look too good."

"I can't hear…Your voice…through water…dizzy…"

"Oh, shit," Benji began. "She's going to–"

Dex didn't think. All he did was react.

43

"Faint," Benji sighed.

Dex held her seemingly dead weight against him. He leaned down enough to get one arm under her legs, lifting her up and into his chest.

"What the fuck do we do," he screamed, beginning to panic. "Call 911."

Calmly Benji strolled over. Dex couldn't believe how calm he was. "She breathing?"

Dex looked down, but he could already feel it. "Yeah."

"Get her to the couch. Elevate her legs."

Dex quickly did what Benji told him. A million things were running through his head, and though her wellbeing and getting her to wake up was the most important, he couldn't help but register other things. She was so small and frail. She couldn't weigh more than a hundred, maybe a hundred and ten pounds. When he placed her on the couch, he was very careful, feeling like she might break in his arms.

While Benji rustled in the fridge, Dex grabbed a nearby box and placed it under her feet, elevating her legs by at least a foot.

"Now what," he asked Benji.

"First, take a deep breath and calm down."

"I am calm," Dex growled. He wasn't. Not even a little bit.

Benji shook his head, ignoring Dex. "Remove any restrictive clothing."

"What?!"

"Oh, get your damn head out of the gutter! I meant, make sure her shirt isn't buttoned too tight around her neck."

Dex undid the first two buttons of Briar's polo that had been buttoned all the way up.

"Here," Benji said, handing Dex a stack of wet paper towels.

Dex dabbed them across Briar's forehead and down her cheeks. As he did, her dark lashes fluttered just a little, and a small moan came from deep within her chest. Another moment passed before she sucked in a breath and her eyes finally opened.

Briar stared up at Dex, who was dangerously close to her face. Something must have registered to Dex, as he quickly removed his hand from her face.

Briar grabbed at the wet paper towels he left there and pulled them away. She was lying down. Why was she lying down? Why was Dex looking at her with such intense concern? She quickly flung her feet off the couch so that she could be in a sitting position, and a familiar feeling came back to her.

Dex grabbed her shoulders and steadied her. "Whoa. Take it easy."

"What happened," she finally managed to ask.

Dex was about to answer, but Benji stepped in instead. "You fainted, sweetheart. Thankfully, Dex was there to catch you. Otherwise, you'd be in a lot worse shape."

A low rumble went through Dex. Benji could have left it at fainted.

He looked back up to Briar, her eyes already heavily set on his. Their faces were so close that he could see just a few freckles sprinkled across the bridge of her nose and across her cheeks. It was something he would never have seen had he not been in that proximity to her.

Briar's eyes flickered across Dex's face. He didn't have a single line. She knew he was young, but looking at him now, he couldn't be more than thirty. The only thing that made him look older was the dark stubble across his jaw. For some reason she wanted to touch it, run her hands across it. Then her eyes had to settle on his lips, and for a moment, just a brief moment, the silly girl in her had to wonder.

When her eyes fell from his to something lower, Dex quickly pulled his hands from her shoulders and rose from his knees to his feet. He couldn't look at her. He was certain that her eyes had gone to his lips, and while she might have just been evaluating his features, in his mind it brought a completely different thought.

Dex ran his hand through his hair. He didn't know what the hell just happened. All he knew was that he was so captivated, so lost in her, that he didn't even notice Benji leave the room.

That couldn't happen again. She was beautiful and kind. He'd give her that. Under no circumstances would he ever allow himself to get that close to her again. All those insane thoughts that raced through his mind in those few moments had to be squashed and forgotten.

Sensing a bit of awkwardness, "Thank you."

Dex turned to face Briar. "For what?"

She shrugged. "Helping me, I guess. I don't know what happened. I've been feeling strange all day."

"We close in a couple hours. Rest here until then."

He didn't want to. He shouldn't. Maybe he wouldn't have to.

"Do you have someone you can call to come pick you up." When Briar shook her head, the tiny gentleman part in him won over the asshole. "I'll take you home then. You can even take the flowers with you."

"No," Briar shouted.

That, he did not expect.

"You can't walk home. Not after–"

"I just haven't been eating well or getting much sleep. I'm fine. Really," Briar stressed. There wasn't a snowball's chance in hell that she was going to let Dex take her *home*.

Dex ignored the comment. He already had too many questions. Why wasn't she eating better? What were her issues with sleeping? As much as he didn't want to know, a small part of him suddenly needed to. He'd have plenty of time when he took her home at the end of the day.

"Look, I have a few things to take care of. Feel free to get whatever you want out of the refrigerator that isn't branded with someone's name, and get some water in you. Got it?"

Briar bit at her lip and nodded. "Yeah. Thanks."

"Just rest," he added before heading out.

Briar watched him carefully. There was a customer picking up a vehicle that he began to deal with. She took that moment to grab a pen and piece of paper and quickly scribble something on it.

CHAPTER 6

Enraged. Seething. Irate. Livid. Fucking pissed off.

That's how Dex felt when, not even an hour after leaving her, he returned to an empty office, only to find a scrap of paper resting against the flower vase.

Thank you for your help. I'm feeling much better, but I think I should head out. I'll see you Monday.

- Briar

He couldn't think straight. He hated the effect she had on him. He hated that he cared that she was okay.

What was so wrong with getting a ride home?

Worst of all, he didn't know how to make sure she really was doing well. He wouldn't see her until Monday. She didn't even have a number that he could call or text.

"Don't get involved," he grumbled to himself as he grabbed a folder from the desk.

Her paper was on the top, and he couldn't help himself.

* * *

Argent Falls was a pretty laidback and quaint town. Some places were nicer than others and it did have one or two shady spots, especially near the bus station and hostel where the town got drifters from time to time.

Briar lived in one of the nicer and more upscale parts of town. Dex couldn't imagine why she wouldn't want him taking her home. Perhaps she had very traditional parents and it would be too hard to explain why an older tattooed brut was dropping off their sweet and innocent daughter.

As he turned onto Oakcrest Drive, he realized that he should keep driving through. Showing up at her house would probably only embarrass her; however, there was a part of him that didn't care. She had made him worry. Her embarrassment for his worrying was an even trade.

He stopped on the street. The mailbox in front of him read 1074.

He took a deep breath, attempting to calm down. All he would do was make sure she made it home and was feeling okay. He just needed to put his mind at ease.

It was a nice house. Older. Victorian. The sidewalk up to the house was in need of repair. It looked like it had been there for the last fifty years.

The landscaping along the way was simple and clean. For some reason, when he thought of Briar, he thought there would be more flowers.

Whimsical ivy ran down the side along the front door that he was quickly approaching. There wasn't a doorbell, just an ornate knocker. Dex grabbed it, and thought for one last time if it was the right thing to do. He had only known her for two weeks, and even though he was her boss, he didn't think that he should care that much.

Against his better judgement, he went ahead and lightly tapped the knocker three times. He instinctively took a step back when a high-pitched yapping thing flew against the other side of the door.

Dex heard a voice on the other side, but it didn't belong to Briar.

"Muffin, get back girl. If you bite my ankle, I swear I'll use this cane!"

Just then the door swung open, and Dex tried to hide his surprise.

"Yes," the elderly woman greeted. She looked him up and down and eyed him carefully.

Dex was confused. He had seen the woman throughout town before. That often happened in a small town. He didn't know her name, but she had been around for quite some time.

This had to be Briar's grandmother.

"Hi, ma'am. I know you don't know me, but–"

"You're the boy with the car shop," she interrupted. Proudly confident that she knew everyone in town.

Dex couldn't help but smile. "Uh, yeah. I'm sorry to bother you, but I just wanted to make sure Briar made it home okay."

"Come again?"

This time Dex spoke louder and slower. "I wanted to make sure Briar made it home."

The elderly woman then raised her voice. "I'm not deaf or hard of hearing! I don't know what the hell you're talking about!"

Dex was taken aback and a sorrowful expression came across his face as he looked at the confusion on the woman before him.

"I know that look," she began, shaking her finger. "And no! I ain't got no Alzheimer's. My mind is sharp as a whip. I just don't know who you're looking for."

"Briar? Briar Stone?"

"It's a peculiar name, I'll give you that. You can also repeat it as much as you want. I still don't know anyone by that name, and I do believe I know everyone in this town," the clearly annoyed woman huffed confidently.

"So, you don't have a granddaughter or someone living with you," Dex continued.

He couldn't help but glance at the metal number above the doorframe. It read 1074, same as the mailbox.

"Listen here. My youngest granddaughter is a lawyer in Seattle. That would be a no."

Dex refrained from using the string of curse words coming to his lips.

49

"Not to point out the obvious, but instead of showing up to her doorstep, especially if you're not sure you're at the right place, couldn't you just text her? That's how all you young folks communicate now anyway."

Dex clenched his teeth. If she had a phone, he would have.

"I'm sorry. I must have messed up the streets or something. Sorry to bother you," Dex apologized, forcing a smile.

The woman shook her head and mumbled something, then closed the door.

Dex stood there for a moment, replaying what just happened again. He was at the right house. He was certain.

What he realized now, which didn't quell the storm of emotions continuing to brew, was that she had never put her real address to begin with.

CHAPTER 7

Come Monday, Briar took her time getting to work. She didn't want to be the only one there with Dex.

He had been so kind to her on Saturday. Well, at least as kind as he could be. After all, he didn't let her drop to the floor. That said something.

She felt bad for running out. Even worse, it was payday.

When she entered, Rusty was walking by with a cup of coffee, headed to the garage.

Rather loudly and upbeat, "Hey! How are you feeling?"

Though Briar focused on Rusty, from the corner of her eye she could see Dex watching her. "Much better. I got some rest Sunday, and I feel great," she lied.

She felt okay; however, it was impossible to rest well in that place, especially left alone with her thoughts and memories.

Rusty gave her a thumbs up and headed out.

Briar didn't want Dex to think anything was wrong, or that she was ignoring him. While she still had his attention on her, she gave him a small smile and a simple wave as she headed to the office for a cup of coffee.

Dex rose from behind the counter and followed her. He stepped beside her and grabbed him one of the disposable coffee cups as well.

Of course, she was the first to speak. "Good morning, Dex."

All Dex did was grunt in return.

Briar sighed. "Are you mad at me?"

Dex gave her a curious look. Oh, she had no idea. "Why would I be mad at you?"

"Well, I just left work on Saturday. I didn't even put in all my hours."

He had to admit. He was more than angry when he came in and found her note, but the worst of it was when he tried to be caring and concerned, only to find out that she lied to him. It was a lie that chipped away at that innocence she had about her.

He shrugged. "No worries. You left a note."

He could have asked her, called her out on it, but he had a feeling she'd only lie to him again. For once, he wanted the truth.

Looking at her now, Dex wasn't sure what to believe when it came to her. The sick part of it all, she had a magnetism that drew him in and made him want to know more, starting with why she lied about where she lived.

Briar seemed to be satisfied with his answer, and took her leave to the entry desk.

That's just what Dex wanted. He didn't want her to think that he was upset. He sure as hell didn't want her to think that he cared. There had already been an awkward moment or two between them, and he didn't want her thinking that his concern went beyond anything more than concern for another human being.

* * *

It was easy keeping Briar later than the rest of the guys. After all, he still had to pay her, and Dex took his time in doing so. Once she left, all that needed to be done was lock the front door.

He felt like a creep, a stalker. He just wanted to know what she was hiding, and she didn't seem like the type of person to open up willingly in conversation. That thought alone had him silently laughing to himself as he followed her down the street. He was such a hypocrite.

Thankfully, the town was bustling. It was after five in the evening and it was still summer break. If he stayed far enough behind, she wouldn't notice him.

The more they walked, the more concerned he became. After thirty minutes, he saw exactly where she was going.

The bus station.

That didn't make any sense. She couldn't possibly take the bus into Argent Falls every day just to work at a mechanic shop.

Dex leaned into a tree and crossed his arms. Briar Stone was definitely a mystery to him.

Then she did something that caused his heart to drop. She crossed the street, going away from the bus station. Instead, she headed toward the old rundown hostel. He continued to watch, hoping that his eyes were lying to him. The only people who stayed there were drifters, prostitutes, druggies, convicts…The list went on with all the unsavory people.

That could not be where she was going. He kept telling that to himself, far longer than he should have, far after she disappeared behind the dilapidated door.

✳ ✳ ✳

Briar stared at the clock. It was already ten minutes after eight. Dex was always the first one in, so it came as a shock when Rusty had to open the shop up and Dex was still nowhere to be found.

"Is that normal," Briar found herself asking Rusty.

He shrugged. "Can't say that it is. Something major must have come up."

Briar tried not to express too much concern. She had seen the way Benji looked at her and Dex the other day. The last thing she wanted were any speculations and rumors. Therefore, she changed the subject.

"Mind if I ask you something?"

"Nah, I've got some time," Rusty replied, and leaned over the reception desk.

"School starts in about six weeks, and I won't be able to work here much, except on Saturdays, and maybe a couple hours after school," Briar began.

"Usually seniors can opt for a work program. That is, unless you're behind on classes and have to take a full load," Rusty informed her.

Briar wanted to laugh. Behind on classes? Yeah, right. The only reason she didn't graduate a year early was because she was one semester away in one class.

"Depending on the requirements, I might be able to do that. If my transcripts from my old school come through nicely. I should be able to graduate in December."

Rusty gave her a funny look. "I don't think they do that here."

She didn't care to explain it to him. She had already emailed several schools before leaving home. While technically she would graduate in December, there was only a ceremony in May. She couldn't care less about a ceremony.

"Anyway, that work thing. You'd get out of school at 1:30, but you have to log so many work hours a week."

That intrigued Briar. "Oh, that would be nice; however, it would still be a significant cut from what these last couple weeks have given me."

Rusty wanted to ask why a seventeen-year-old, still in school, needed a full-time job, but he had a feeling it wasn't any of his business. It's not like Briar offered any information; therefore, he had to assume she didn't want to go into too many details.

"I was just curious if you might know of any places that would have evening work. Preferably not past midnight, but enough that I could add another twenty hours a week?"

It didn't take Rusty long to think about it, and he snapped his fingers once it came to him. "Chêne would probably be your best bet."

"Chêne," Briar repeated as a question.

"Yeah, off Second Street. It's a bar. Well, the only bar if you don't count that little pub joint." He saw how uncomfortable she got at the mentioning of a bar. "It's not too bad, not like the rough and rowdy ones you're probably thinking. Sorry, it's called Chêne Bar and Grille. The bar is half of it, but it has a nice little restaurant part as well."

"Do you think they're hiring though?"

Rusty waved his hand, brushing her concern aside. "Doesn't matter. Dex could get you in."

Briar arched a brow and tilted her head to the side, not understanding how Dex could get her a job at a bar or restaurant, whatever it was.

Rusty forgot just how new to the town Briar was.

"Dex is part owner of Chêne," he clarified.

Briar's eyes widened in surprise. "Seriously?"

"Long story. Sandy's wife, ex-wife, was a real winner, if you know what I mean. Anyway, a couple years ago Dex ended up having to help him out when he was going through his divorce. Like I said, long story," Rusty quickly concluded.

There was one more thing that Briar was curious about, and now seemed to be the best time to ask it. She hadn't asked Dex, because randomly asking a person for their age could have several different reasonings and meanings. At least that's what she always thought.

"Exactly how old is Dex?" When Rusty leaned in and gave Briar a skeptical look, she knew he was wondering why she was asking. "He just seems really young to be doing this and to be part owner of another establishment," she quickly added. She grew uncomfortable from having even asked the question to begin with.

A smirk came to Rusty's face. For some reason, he had the feeling that wasn't the only reason. Rather than give her a hard time, he simply answered. "Twenty-five."

"Oh…"

"Were you expecting older?"

"Actually, yeah."

It was a strange feeling, and she couldn't explain it, but something inside her felt a slight bit of relief knowing that he wasn't too much older than her. She was also very conscious that she was in no position at all to be thinking or feeling what she was.

"Well, speak of the devil," Rusty exclaimed, just as the door swung open.

Briar looked up, already knowing who had walked in, and she wished she wouldn't have. Though Dex's face looked tired, he still looked gorgeous. His jeans were covered in old bleach and oil stains, and he wore the same brown work boots as always. Today, he had on a simple and fitted black t-shirt, high-lighting muscles Briar was oblivious to in the past. Once she began skimming over the ink dripping down his arms, she had to look away. It was a dangerous beauty about him that made her forget. Forget the past. Forget her circumstances. Forget the slight age difference. Forget his role in her life, her boss.

"What happened to you," Rusty asked as Dex made his way through the room.

"Didn't get a lot of sleep," he replied with a voice hoarser and raspier than his usual.

Once he was near, Rusty slapped him on the back. "Ah, Lexi kept you up?"

Dex glared at him with eyes drained of all emotion. He ignored the comment.

Briar tried not to have a reaction to what Rusty just said, but she hoped like hell Dex wouldn't answer it, confirming why he was sleep deprived. That was another thing she had briefly forgotten, the fact that he was in a very serious relationship.

Changing the subject, "You two appeared to be having an important discussion."

So far, Dex had only looked at Rusty. He couldn't look at her. Lexi wasn't the one he lost sleep over. It was the mysterious little liar whose eyes he refused to meet. All night he couldn't help but wonder what the hell happened

56

to her, and wonder what parts she told him were the truth and what were only more lies. That only frustrated him even more because he knew that he shouldn't care, shouldn't be bothered with her. She was no one to him; however, when he thought that, then his chest hurt, and his stomach felt sick. It was a never-ending, screwed-up cycle that made sleep impossible.

Briar was thankful that Rusty didn't mention what the last part of their conversation had been about.

"Briar was looking for evening work, especially once school starts. I told her you could put a good word in at the bar."

For a moment, Dex's eyes skimmed over Briar then back to Rusty. "She can't work in a bar. She's only seventeen."

That stupid reminder squashed Briar in more ways than one.

Rusty laughed uncomfortably. "That's right. I forgot."

Not to be deterred, Briar chimed in. "But you said it was a restaurant and bar, correct?"

Rusty nodded.

"I'm sure working the bar is where the money is, but I could work as a waitress."

Rusty thought. "That is true."

"No."

Both Rusty and Briar looked at Dex. He didn't even bother considering it.

Rusty felt strangely out of place. Lately Dex was more moody than usual. Rusty had his speculations, especially since that day he and Briar talked in the office, but he wouldn't dare say anything, knowing that Dex would fly off the handle.

"Well," Rusty said, clapping his hands. "I better get out there before Benji starts complaining."

Dex didn't say another word to her once Rusty went to the garage. Instead, he headed toward the office to pour a cup of coffee.

Briar was thankful that at that time a customer came in to drop off her keys for some repair work. Though it was only five minutes of her time, it was enough to remind her of her place and take her attention away from Dex. That is, until chilling words came from the office doorway.

"Briar, we need to talk…Privately."

CHAPTER 8

Meanwhile...
Two hundred miles away.

"Mr. Burrows," Portia said slowly through gritted teeth. "It's been two years since my husband's death. At what point will his estate be settled? He left everything to me!"

Jeff Burrows, the late Grover Stone's lawyer, shuddered as the distraught woman's fist came down on his desk.

"Correction, he left you a portion of the money as well as the mansion and all physical assets." He flipped through some papers. "I believe there was a boat, and a villa in—"

"I don't care about a damn boat!"

Jeff closed the folder. He had to assume Portia Stone squandered away a good portion of what her husband left her and was getting desperate.

"What about all of his late wife's money? I know he didn't spend what she left him, and there was a two-million-dollar life insurance policy when she died," Portia pointed out.

Jeff rubbed at his temples. The first year after Grover's death, Portia had been satisfied with everything he told her, then a few months ago, she found documents that she wasn't supposed to know about. This ended up making Jeff's life a living nightmare whenever she came in.

"That money is tied up," he repeated for what felt like the hundredth time.

"But I get everything. I should have control of that."

"These documents were drafted to perfection. No one can touch that money except for Briar."

"She's a child! A stupid child! You can't possibly think–"

"Apparently her father put quite a bit of faith in her maturity. I did try to tell him to increase the age, but he insisted that she have something to set her up for college."

"Three million?! What fucking eighteen-year-old needs three million dollars?!"

"I'm sorry Mrs. Stone, but in terms of that account," he paused, and momentarily flipped open a folder, making sure the information he told her was correct. "Yes. Briar will receive three million once she turns eighteen. The rest she'll be able to receive once she's twenty-one."

"And how much is that?"

"Eleven," Jeff said quietly, already knowing that she was about to blow a gasket.

"You're out of your damn mind if you think that a twenty-one-year-old will be responsible."

For a second, Jeff wanted to desperately ask her just how responsible she had been with the monthly checks she was receiving on behalf of her husband's death; however, today wasn't a day in which he wanted to die.

"She ran away. You know that right? Doesn't that mean she's giving all this up?"

"Yes, you have informed me of that, but I must make it clear, Briar doesn't know about this. Her father never wanted her to. He didn't want her to give up on school or college because she'd be well-off. Had you not come across those papers–"

"You fool! You think I wouldn't eventually wonder what happened to all those millions?!"

"Mrs. Stone, if this is all, I do have another meeting momentarily."

"She ran away! For all you know she could be dead somewhere!"

60

That comment alone shocked Jeff Burrows. "Well, I certainly hope that's not the case; however, as her stepmother, I would expect for you to have more compassion toward your missing child. If you are concerned by the fact that she ran away, and you think she might be in danger, as you have informed me over and over throughout this meeting, then I suggest you call the police."

That didn't bode well with Portia. Rather than speak with Mr. Burrows any further, knowing the result she was expecting wasn't possible yet, she snatched her purse from her lap and stormed from his office, making sure to slam the door with all her might.

Leo bolted from his spot in the waiting room and rushed toward his mother. "I take it that didn't go well."

"No, Leo. It didn't."

Portia waited until they were outside of the law office building and in the confines of their car before she went off.

"You know this is all your fault. She wouldn't have left if you wouldn't have–"

"You told me I could do whatever I wanted. You didn't seem to care until now," Leo interrupted.

Portia let out a heavy sigh, knowing that her son was right. "It would just be much easier to deal with her if I knew where the hell she was."

Leo pulled out of the parking lot. "So, what do we do now."

"Find her," Portia said with a darkness brewing in her eyes. "We find her no matter what, and then we'll deal with her."

CHAPTER 9

Dex closed the door behind Briar shortly after she walked into the office. She stood in the center of the room, uncertain what she should do, and even more uncertain what Dex had to say behind a closed door.

"Have a seat," he said, motioning toward the couch.

Briar didn't say anything, but did as he told, thinking along the way what she could have done that would warrant this. She was a little relieved when Dex sat in the chair at the computer and not on the couch beside her. Without meaning to, she absolutely had a reaction to him when he entered earlier that morning. She needed to have some physical distance from him.

Dex watched her carefully. She couldn't meet his eyes and only one word could be used to describe her right now. Uncomfortable.

"I'm not one to pussyfoot around something." He winced as he said it. Correcting himself, "I'll get straight to the point. Why did you lie about where you lived?"

Briar forced herself not to have a vivid reaction. She could play this off. She knew she could. "I'm sorry? I don't understand what—"

"I know you don't live at 1074 Oakcrest Drive!"

Rather than trying to defend herself against that outburst, "How…"

"I went by your *house* on Saturday."

Dex wished there was another way to bring it up, but there wasn't. He knew she'd ask questions and he would be honest and direct.

Briar swallowed heavily. "You did? Why?"

"Oh, I don't know, let's see…" He paused for dramatic effect and pretended to think. "You almost hit the fucking floor, and after telling you I'd take you home, the moment I leave you alone, you disappear."

Briar's eyes fell to the floor. Her brain was quickly trying to catch up to what he was saying, but something was still stuck on the fact that he had come to her house, or, at least what he thought was her house.

She had to say something. He was waiting for her to say something.

"Umm, Dex," she began, her throat feeling dry and closing up.

"I followed you yesterday," he quietly admitted, sensing that his yelling was doing neither one of them any good.

That's when Briar's eyes shot up to meet his and he thought his heart might stop right then and there. Her face lost all color and went a ghostly white. Her eyes, her green eyes that he found to be so bright and bewitching, turned dark and cold, looking at him with such hatred, masking what she was really feeling. Embarrassment.

"You followed me?"

Dex could have kicked himself for how this was coming together. The only thing he could do was play it down.

"You lied about your address. That's a pretty big fraction when it comes to a job application."

Briar was so hurt and upset. She didn't want anyone knowing about her living situation. She didn't want anyone asking questions. She didn't want anyone knowing why she was running, what she had gone through, the loss, the pain. She didn't want anyone knowing anything.

She shot up, unable to sit a second more. At this point, she'd welcome being fired. She'd find another job. She knew she could. "You mean infraction! You asshole!"

Dex was taken aback, and quickly stood as soon as she did. He couldn't recall ever hearing her say a vile word. Before he could say anything, she was on him like a vulture, and he knew one thing. Regardless how she had been in the past, regardless what she was running from, right now if given the opportunity of flight or fight, she was going to fight.

"You want to talk about infractions! Why did you follow me? What was the point? You shouldn't have even gone to the address to begin with!"

"I went because I wanted to make sure you made it home okay," he answered as calmly as he could. He was supposed to be the hotheaded and temperamental one.

"Why? You just met me. Why would you give two shits about what happens to me?!"

"Because you're my employee," he stressed, hoping that was a good enough answer, because that's all he had in him.

Briar shook her head and a sickening laugh fell from her beautiful lips. "So, why the hell am I here?"

That was an inevitable question that he knew was coming. It was something that had plagued him all night.

"Where you're staying isn't a good environment," he began.

"To which I'm trying to fix," Briar stressed. "If I can get another job, like at Chêne, I could maybe get a room, or tiny apartment, or something, before school starts."

"And then what?"

Briar shook her head. "That's none of your concern. Once I graduate early, in December, I'll be gone."

That comment gripped at Dex. He wanted to know what it meant. There were so many things he found that he wanted to know about Briar Stone.

"I don't like you staying there."

"I don't care what you like. Right now, it's my only option."

Without thinking, "Lexi works at a salon with a lot of girls. What if you stay with her? Or someone else looking for a roommate?"

Briar's eyes softened. Dex knew it was the wrong thing to say, especially without talking to Lexi first.

"I can ask her," he added.

64

Briar's voice was softer, her words not as sharp. "I just don't see why you care."

Shaking his head, "No kid should have to live like that."

He didn't know what he said, but suddenly her lips were tight, and her eyes were narrowed, full of annoyance.

"Can I go back to work now? Assuming I still have a job?"

"Why would you think you didn't?"

Still aggravated and upset with the conversation that had taken place, but eager to get away from Dex, "I did just yell at you and call you an asshole."

Dex fought the smile coming to his face. He wouldn't admit it, but there was something cute and disarming about her calling him an asshole.

"Go," was all he said.

Briar walked past him without looking at him. She just couldn't, not right now, not with him knowing what he did. It was only when she reached the door that she refrained from opening it.

"You know…You don't have to watch your mouth," she told him, not bothering to turn around.

Dex faced her, even though she wouldn't look at him. "What do you mean?"

"Several times you've tried to correct yourself. I'm not a child. I'm also well-aware that you like to use the word fuck as a verb, noun, adjective, ad-verb…The list goes on I'm sure."

Thankful that she couldn't see him, Dex truly smiled. "I don't know what the fuck half of those are."

He couldn't see her face, but he was certain that she was smiling.

After a heavy sigh, her hand still on the doorknob, "If Lexi, or one of her friends, has space for an extra person, I'll think about it."

Briar would never know the amount of relief that went through Dex with those words. He knew that any place, with Lexi or any of her friends, would be better than that wretched place she was at now.

＊ ＊ ＊

"I'm sorry, Dex," Lexi began calmly through the speaker. Somehow Dex knew that wasn't going to last. Lexi had meltdowns over chipped nails. "You're going to need to redo this conversation, because so far, all I've heard is that you've lost your damn mind!"

There was the Lexi he knew.

"Lexi, you know that isn't a place for a young girl."

"She seems to have her shit figured out. If she's fine with it, leave it alone," she huffed.

"She's tolerating it because that's all she can come by," Dex stressed.

"I get it. This is just like with Sandy."

Dex didn't understand why she was bringing up Sandy. "Sandy helped me, so I helped him. This is not like that."

"I know! This is weird! You've known the girl for a couple weeks and here you go with that damn savior complex of yours!"

"Lexi…"

"No, Dex. No. Not me. Not my friends. You really need to sit back and think about what you're asking. She's a stranger!"

Dex rolled his eyes as Lexi ranted away, making Briar seem like some axe murderer. Finally, when he had enough, "Alright, I have an engine overhaul." Whenever he mentioned anything about work, Lexi got bored.

"Whatever, Dex. Just leave the girl alone. You've already given her a job. That's enough."

"Yeah. Okay. Later, Lexi," he said, quickly hitting the red button.

Dex leaned into the side of the building and ran his hand over his face and along the stubble of his jaw. Lexi was right, that much he knew. He just couldn't ignore something inside him. There was a pull that he couldn't ignore.

He hated when Lexi told him he had a savior complex. He hadn't been capable of saving himself. He was in no position to save anyone else. That didn't mean he couldn't try to help, to help make someone's life better.

CHAPTER 10

Dex was surprised when, after locking up for the day, Briar didn't put up a fuss and followed him. It was a strange situation, but at the end of the day, after having thought about it, she had succumbed to his suggestion. If only Lexi had done the same.

"Nice truck," Briar mumbled as they approached the impossibly clean black Silverado.

Dex acknowledged her with a grunt and hit the button on his key fob, unlocking the truck. He went to the passenger side first and opened the door, which seemed to surprise Briar. She just stood there, staring at him.

"Problem?"

Briar quickly shook her head. "No. Nobody really opens doors anymore. I think my dad was the only one."

She climbed in the truck and Dex found himself closing the door with more force than necessary.

Once he was in the driver's seat, he pulled on his seatbelt and couldn't help but ask. "So, I remind you of your dad?"

Briar flung her head in Dex's direction, her eyes growing wider by the second. "No! Oh my gosh, no. Absolutely not."

When Dex didn't say another word, and began driving down the town's streets toward the hostel, Briar sank back in her seat and bit at her thumbnail. She had to wonder now. Is that what Dex saw her as, simply a child in need of help? The thought sickened her.

Days ago, when his face had been so close to hers, she thought of what it would be like to kiss him. She hadn't thought about physical contact with any guy in a long time. Now, the first guy that triggered these foreign thoughts was completely and totally unavailable.

"Why are you taking off your seatbelt," Briar asked, once Dex turned off the engine.

"To help you get your things?"

Briar shook her head, hoping to hide her sadness. "No. It's okay, I don't have much. Really, don't."

It wasn't meant to be an intimate gesture, and maybe he should have thought first before allowing an instinct to take over when he reached for her, but she looked like she was about to combust. He wanted to steady her, to let her know everything was okay.

Briar looked down at his hand on top of hers and momentarily forgot how to breathe. It was calloused and warm. The touch alone sent her whole body into an endless ocean of flames.

It was bad. She couldn't.

Dex cursed himself when Briar yanked her hand from beneath his like he had just electrocuted her. He shouldn't have touched her. He remembered how she withdrew when he had barely brushed her hand from the computer mouse in the office. He made a mental note to never do so again. She was like a feral cat, despising the smallest forms of human contact.

"Sorry, but you should know, I know what it's like in there. You don't need to be embarrassed."

When she looked up at him, her brows furrowed, no doubt a million questions running through that inquisitive mind of hers, he realized once again what a bad idea this was.

"Just stop." Briar flung the door open and jumped out. Before closing it, "I'll be back in two minutes."

Dex didn't protest. He let her go. He only meant to be helpful, but he wouldn't push her. She was leaving, that was enough.

✳ ✳ ✳

"Hey, baby. What's the rush," Olive cooed from her sleepy state in the bed next to Briar's.

"I'm leaving."

That felt good to say. Adrenaline raced through her blood. While she was nervous and scared at the idea of living with Lexi, a woman she didn't know, and one who didn't seem too fond of her at first, there was a rush of excitement at getting to live somewhere safe. She'd have a real kitchen and she wouldn't have to share a bathroom with a whole slew of strangers.

Maybe, just maybe, she'd be able to sleep.

"Where are you going," Olive asked, now attempting to sit up.

"A friend's house," Briar lied.

She and Lexi weren't exactly friends but maybe in the future they would be. Then her inner demons rose, reminding her who Lexi was. If things were going to work out, she had to pull in the reigns quick on her developing crush on Dex.

"I thought you didn't know any folks around here?"

"I don't. I didn't. I met her through my work. She's my boss's girlfriend," Briar forced herself to admit.

"That's sweet of her," Olive sighed.

Briar slipped her arms in the straps of her backpack and zipped the final zipper on her suitcase. "You know, Olive, if you ever need anything, I work at the Hayden mechanic shop. I'd give you my phone number, but I don't have one yet."

Olive smiled sweetly. "Thank you, baby. That's nice of you."

Briar looked into Olive's eyes. They seemed despondent, void of life and direction. It hurt to admit, but somehow Briar knew she probably wouldn't be seeing Olive again.

It wasn't until she said goodbye and closed the entry door behind her that a weight lifted from her. She knew she had gotten lucky. She had gotten lucky from the moment she saw the help wanted sign in the shop. She wasn't about to ruin that.

Despite Briar not wanting him to come inside with her, once he saw her exit the building wearing an overstuffed backpack and dragging a suitcase, he jumped out of the truck.

She was already halfway to him, but he met her anyway and pulled the suitcase from her. He lifted up on the backpack and she wiggled free from it, mumbling her thanks.

"You good," he asked her after he threw the items in his backseat.

Briar nodded.

Dex didn't say anything else, and it seemed that Briar welcomed the silence. He wasn't quite sure what to say. From the moment he walked into work that morning, nothing had gone as planned in his sleep deprived mind. For an already known reason, he had a feeling that tonight wouldn't be much better when it came to sleep.

"Wow," Briar let out once they pulled up to the apartment complex.

The Argent Park Complex, though directly across the street from the park itself, had only recently been built within the last five years. It was a cold and simple tall building, and though it was one of the more expensive options in terms of apartment living, it was also leaps and bounds better than some of the town's older options.

"This must be new," Briar speculated.

Though she was right, Dex wondered why she thought so.

"Well, everything else in the town is so quaint and homey. This is very city-ish," she responded with a shrug.

It was by no means an apartment building in New York City. There were only accommodations for thirty tenants and their families. The top four floors were where the tenants lived, whereas the bottom two were filled with amenities.

Briar didn't bother arguing with her bags. She knew how that would play out; therefore, she allowed Dex to take the both of them himself.

"What floor," Briar asked, just as the elevator doors began closing.

"Six."

"Wow, top floor."

The building overall was simple enough, simple but clean. Walking down the hall felt cold with the grey walls and darker grey floors. Truth be told, Briar had never been in an apartment building. She didn't know why she expected a flashy and bustling hotel, or something out of a sitcom.

Briar followed Dex to a door with the numbers 604. For a second, she expected him to knock. Instead, he flipped through his keys and brought one to just above the handle.

Based on the little Dex said, she knew he and Lexi weren't living together, but she assumed that they were serious enough to have exchanged keys.

Dex entered first and turned on the lights, dropping Briar's bags by the door. He held open the door and motioned for her to follow.

It wasn't what Briar expected when she walked in. While the place was clean, extremely clean, it was very minimal. There weren't a lot of pictures or trinkets. The dark grey couch only had the matching pillows that it came with. The only bright thing in the room was the area rug which contained hints of blue.

Dex allowed Briar to take in the open space, knowing that an unpleasant conversation was about to take place.

Briar fell in love with the kitchen. It was far bigger than she expected and just like everything else, clean and put together. She didn't imagine that much took place within its confines.

She shouldn't have stereotyped, but she had to say, she expected more décor and color when it came to Lexi. There wasn't even an ounce of pink.

The realization hit her hard, as though she swallowed a brick.

When she spun to face him, her eyes laced with fear and uncertainty, he knew that she knew. She wasn't an idiot. There wasn't one feminine thing in the place.

"I'm confused," Briar said, a complete understatement. "Why aren't we at Lexi's?"

Dex tried to form a hundred different sentences in his head, but none of them sounded right or appropriate. Instead, he walked around her and into the kitchen.

Too many questions ran through Briar's mind as Dex calmly opened the refrigerator and took out a beer. He leaned back into the counter, took a long sip and brought his eyes to a face that seemed to have a permanence of curiosity plastered on it.

"Lexi lost her shit," he finally said.

Briar felt like someone had thrown an icy bucket of panic on her. "So, you brought me to *your* place?"

He hated the tone in her voice, and he especially hated the way she was looking at him. He had done a lot of stupid things in his life, but this was one of the most bizarre.

"I'm not some sick fuck, alright," he began. He ran the hand not tightly gripping his beer through his hair.

"I didn't say you were."

"But that's what you're thinking."

"You don't know what I'm thinking," Briar countered, now with more attitude in the tone of her voice.

Dex sighed. "I did ask Lexi if she, or any of her friends, any at all, would be interested in—"

"And she freaked out," Briar interrupted. "As she should have. I'm a stranger in this place. No one owes me anything."

Dex hated the look on her face. Somehow he felt like he was losing her, like she was slipping into an invisible darkness. He'd wake up tomorrow and she'd be gone, onto another place, living in the same conditions. It sickened him. Maybe he did have a mild savior complex.

"I know Lexi doesn't like me," Briar went on.

"Lexi doesn't like anyone. Hell, she doesn't even like the people she calls friends." After thinking for a moment, hoping to lighten the conversation, "Half the time she doesn't even like me."

73

Without thinking, "I'm pretty sure whatever conversation you had with her today didn't help."

Dex didn't say anything, but from across the room, Briar was certain that the corner of his mouth rose more on one side than the other, finding humor in what she said.

"I appreciate you caring, or whatever this is, but we both know that I can't stay here. Not even for the night," Briar finally said, all her hopes fading with the words.

He shouldn't have asked something he knew the answer to, but he did so anyway. "Why?"

Briar swallowed heavily. There were so many reasons, but some she couldn't bring up. It was awkward enough as it was. "First of all, you're my boss."

Dex shrugged and ignored her. "Look, I didn't tell you earlier because I knew if I did, you'd never leave that place."

Countering, "Who's stopping me from grabbing my bags and going back anyway?"

"No one." It was the truth. As much as it would bother him, if she decided to leave and go back to that dilapidated hostel, he wouldn't stop her. He couldn't. He had no right to.

Briar looked down at her feet and debated. "And you're comfortable with this?"

"Hell no."

She brought her eyes back up. "Then…"

Dex sighed and drained the last bit of his beer. "After this morning, you looked so hopeful. When you left the hostel, it's like a light turned on inside you." He paused, wondering where all those words were coming from. He didn't say things like that. "I just didn't want to disappoint you."

"So, lying to me is better?"

"I didn't lie to you."

74

"A lie of omission is a lie," Briar confidently pointed out. She wasn't going to argue with Dex. "I'm sorry. I don't feel comfortable staying here." She moved toward her bags.

"Right, because staying with a bunch of strangers is better. Going to sleep in a room that smells like cat piss, listening to screaming and slamming doors, watching your roommates shoot-up in the middle of the night, all that is more comfortable."

Briar paused and stared at her bags. She hadn't cried in some time, but now tears stung at the back of her eyes. She wouldn't cry. She had been in worse situations where tears were inevitable. This wasn't one of them.

Dex knew she was thinking about it. She'd have to be crazy to go back to that place. Though it was called a hostel, it might as well have been called a crack house.

Several more seconds passed, but Briar didn't move, didn't reply. Dex waited, let her battle with her own thoughts.

"If I stay, just for the night, will you do me a favor," she softly asked, only barely turning enough so that he could see her face.

"I thought this is doing you a favor."

Briar shook her head, still very much confused. "No. This…I don't know what this is."

Neither did he. "What's the damn favor?"

Briar's eyes met his and something in his gut no longer felt right. Something about her, just looking into her eyes, he knew whatever she was going to ask, the answer would be yes, because it meant she'd be here, safe.

"Put in a word for me at Chêne."

"Oh! For fuck's sake!"

CHAPTER 11

Briar knew that Dex bringing her to his place wasn't some sick plan and more of an impulsive last-minute decision. She knew this because he was completely unequipped to deal with guests for too long.

Though he had a two-bedroom apartment, the second bedroom was an empty room with a few things for working out.

The bathroom situation was odd as well since there was only one. She would have skipped showering altogether, but it was the middle of summer and, though they were in the northeast, it was still hot. She smelled and looked gross.

Just like with every other part of the house, the bathroom was immaculate. She hadn't ever imagined where Dex lived or what it was like. It was rude to judge, but based on his line of work, she never imagined that his place would be so clean. Maybe that was why it was. After spending all day covered in grease and grime, it must feel comforting to come home to something like this.

It felt weird showering in the same place that Dex used; however, that thought didn't disturb her as much as thinking about where she had showered the last few weeks. Even after a shower there, she still felt disgusting.

She looked in the cabinets for a hairdryer, but quickly gave up on that challenge. She ended up rubbing her hair with the towel as much as she could and then brushed out all the tangles she created.

When she exited the bathroom and walked back toward the common area, a familiar smell hit her.

As soon as he saw her, "It's too late to cook something, so I ordered pizza. You really need to eat."

Briar could feel her stomach twisting and turning, both from a mix of hunger and the fact that Dexter Hayden had been nice and thoughtful all day. Given, he still got irritated and cursed a lot.

"You cook," Briar asked in disbelief.

With a straight face, "No. Every day when I get home, the elves downstairs have me a feast prepared."

Briar's cheeks reddened with embarrassment. "Sorry. I just didn't think most twenty-five-year-old men living on their own actually cooked more than microwavable meals. It was a stupid assumption."

Dex slid the pizza box across the counter once Briar sat down on one of the stools. Of course, he cooked. There was no way he was going to live off frozen stuff. That part of her comment wasn't what caught his attention.

"How do you know how old I am?"

Briar had just taken a bite of pizza and tried her best not to choke. She wasn't able to answer him until after she finished swallowing like a normal human who knew how to eat. "Rusty mentioned it in passing," she lied.

Dex let it go. He was exhausted from the night before and craved sleep. "Obviously, I don't have a bed for you, so—"

"The couch is great," Briar interrupted.

Dex nodded to the couch. "I put you a pillow and a blanket."

Briar mumbled her thanks as she continued to inhale the pizza. Dex didn't recall seeing her eat lunch, and he found himself wondering how many meals she skipped because she didn't want to spend the money.

When he collapsed on his bed, it felt better than the night before. He'd never know why he had been so bothered by her staying there. Maybe it was because he knew she was young, and had so much life and potential. If he could do just a little something to protect that, he would.

That would have been fine, if that's all it was; however, something about her and her presence did strange things to him. For the first time in a long time, he felt.

✳ ✳ ✳

The smell of dark and bitter coffee upon waking meant that she hadn't been dreaming. It also meant that even though she didn't get the best sleep. She did get more sleep than she had in a very long time.

Briar sat up and patted her hair down, still uncomfortable that a stranger was seeing her first thing waking up. Once she thought about it, she really couldn't consider Dex a stranger. Aside from Olive, who had rarely ever been a hundred percent coherent, Dex, Rusty, and Benji were the only people she knew in Argent Falls.

She looked over to the kitchen and more smells began to take over her senses. Thankfully, Dex appeared to be busy; she took that moment to rummage through her suitcase and quickly head to the bathroom.

Upon looking in the mirror, she decided that one of the first things she needed to splurge on when she finally did was a hairdryer. Going to bed with damp hair made it a rat's nest the next morning. After putting on a clean shirt for the day, she yanked and pulled until she had it in an acceptable ponytail.

She splashed her face, noting that she was out of face cleaner as well. Makeup wasn't a splurge that she needed; therefore, she was very frugal with what she had now that the bruises were absent, only putting on a little blush and mascara for the day.

"Good morning," Briar said after she was ready to start the day.

She hadn't paid Dex much attention when she woke that morning, but she could see now that he was already dressed, ready to head to the shop.

"Have a seat," he told her.

She wanted to ask if he needed any help, but before she could, he was already grabbing two plates. Instead, she did as told and took a seat on one of the barstools. At least, that's where she assumed she should sit. Between the open concept kitchen and living room, off in a secluded corner, was a formal dining space; however, it looked like it didn't get much use.

Dex placed a cup of black coffee in front of her and moments later a plate.

Apologetically, "We're running a little late this morning, so that's all I had time for."

Briar stared down at the food. Was he being serious? Did he know that most of her breakfasts recently consisted of a fifty-cent donut?

When Briar didn't take a bite and continued to stare at the food, "It's not poison."

Briar looked up and smiled sweetly. "I know. Thank you."

In front of her was a mountain of cheesy scrambled eggs with peppers, two slices of crispy bacon, and a piece of toast with a slab of butter. It was only once she took her first bite that she realized just how hungry she was.

Dex stood at the island and ate. The stools at the counter were too close together in the small space. The distance between them made it feel less suffocating.

"This was really good," Briar mumbled as she took her last bites.

Dex came around the island to the counter to grab Briar's plate.

"I can clean up."

He shook his head. "Just go get ready. We need to leave soon."

Briar wanted to point out that she was ready, but she had a feeling Dex didn't want her helping him. She went and shuffled around some of the contents of her suitcase, better organizing them for later.

She had grown used to walking, but with the July heat, she had to say, it was nice getting a ride to work. The thirty-minute walk from the hostel had left her a sweaty mess by the time she arrived each morning.

If Briar thought anything would change after the night before, she was very mistaken. Dex was still Dex. While he didn't completely ignore her, he wasn't overly friendly either. Neither of them spoke about their situation, and Briar had to assume Dex was uncomfortable by it and didn't want any of the guys knowing.

* * *

"You're really going to take her to talk to Sandy," Rusty asked as he threw some tools into a drawer, wrapping up for the day.

"That's what she wanted," Dex sighed.

"And just how long do you plan on…Whatever this is," Benji chimed in.

"Hell if I know. I thought Lexi would have–" Dex was interrupted by a fit of laughter from Rusty.

"Dude, no offense, but she's such a bitch. She wouldn't help her dying mother. I don't know how a one-night stand led to two years."

Dex shrugged. Lexi was nice at first, but lately she was extra moody. He knew it had to do with the progression of their relationship. However, as more time passed, her changes in attitude only reaffirmed what he knew in the beginning, marriage wasn't their thing. It might not even be his thing at all. Above all that, Dex thought he was still too young for marriage.

"Speaking of Lexi," Benji began, interrupting Dex from his thoughts. "Have you told her about another woman staying with you?"

Dex didn't say anything. Up until now, he hadn't given it much thought.

"You didn't," Rusty exclaimed. "Holy shit, I want to be there for that. I bet the whole town will burn when she finds out."

"Stop being so dramatic," Dex scoffed.

"Yeah, that's exactly what you should tell her when she turns into Grendel or something," Rusty laughed.

"I don't know boy, I think you're playing with fire," Benji added.

They weren't telling him anything he hadn't already thought to himself; however, he was aware that Briar had plans, plans that didn't include sticking around Argent Falls past December.

Rusty bent the bill of his cap. "Wait, question. Where did she sleep?"

Though he knew Rusty asked the question jokingly, he didn't like that he had. "On the couch."

"Really," Rusty said, drawing the word out, making it seem like Dex was lying.

"Stop being such a fucking pervert."

Rusty threw up his hands and laughed.

Dex was relieved when everyone left, and it was just him. He took his time, knowing that Briar was waiting for him. He messaged Sandy earlier in the day, and Sandy was looking forward to meeting Briar. He hadn't told Briar that. He knew she wanted another job, and waitressing at Chêne wouldn't be too bad. Thankfully, she wouldn't be able to work the bar area.

Just as he expected, Briar was over the moon when they pulled into the parking lot and she saw where they were. He had to give her credit, though she was struggling, she was trying her best to make the most of the hand she had seemingly been dealt in life.

It was no surprise to him that Sandy fell in love with Briar immediately.

"That's it," Briar gasped.

"If Dex says you're good, you're good in my books," Sandy said, followed by a deep laugh. "You can come in tomorrow as soon as you finish at the shop, or maybe boss man over here can let you go early." Sandy's attention went to Dex and Dex nodded at the suggestion. Going back to Briar, "Rita can show you the ropes. I'd hate for your first night to be a Friday or Saturday. We get pretty crowded then." Sandy went on to tell Briar about Rita, his girl-friend.

Dex was tempted to make his way to the bar for a quick drink. The after-work crowd was already beginning to arrive. However, he found himself captivated with the conversation between Briar and Sandy. Briar didn't seem to have a problem talking to anyone. That both impressed and bothered him.

CHAPTER 12

As promised, the following day, Dex gave Briar off a few hours early. The restaurant part of Chêne didn't start serving dinner until 5pm and he could tell she was a little nervous about her first day; therefore, around 2pm, he told her to get going.

There was one major problem when it came to living in a small town. Eventually, in time, everyone knew or knew of everyone else, and word traveled fast. Dex knew that, but today fifteen minutes before closing, he was made sure of it the hard way.

"Dexter fucking Hayden!"

Dex hit his head on the open hood of the truck he was working on upon hearing the sharp screech throughout the garage. It was enough to give the white bellbird a run for its money; however, this sound came from no bird.

Dex stepped around the truck to face Lexi, now standing in the middle of the garage. "To what do I owe that wonderful greeting?"

She stomped toward him in heels that were far too tall. Her eyes were a mix of something he had never seen.

It had only been two nights. The only people who knew about Briar were Rusty, Benji, and now Sandy, but none of those were the sorts to gossip; however, the look in Lexi's eyes told him that's probably what this was about.

"Don't play dumb with me!"

At that, Rusty rolled out from a nearby car. Dex didn't see Benji, but he could only imagine that he was enjoying the show as well.

Dex said nothing. He still didn't know what this was about, and he had no intention of showing his cards.

"I got a call from Jennifer about an hour ago," Lexi began, pausing for dramatic effect.

"Okay?"

"Jennifer, my friend. The same Jennifer that works at Chêne. She was on her break and called to tell me about a *delightful* new girl," Lexi spat.

"Okay?"

"Okay? That's it?! What the hell Dex?! You got her a job there too?!"

Dex closed the hood of the truck. "I don't see what the big deal is."

"It's a big deal when a couple days ago you asked me to take in your little stray puppy. You already gave her a job here. You don't need to keep helping her," Lexi stressed.

Dex still didn't see how putting in a good word for her with Sandy was that big of a deal to Lexi. It impacted her in no way.

"Look, Lexi. Why don't we go inside and talk," Dex suggested. He had a feeling that he knew where the conversation would ultimately go.

Lexi gave a sick laugh. "Why? You don't want me embarrassing you in front of your friends."

Dex was going to try to keep his cool, but Lexi had a way of pushing his buttons in the worst ways. He didn't want to say it, but he wasn't the one who was going to be embarrassed if she continued.

"I mean, is she that damn poor that she needs all these handouts?"

"Lexi, just stop," Dex said calmly.

"Well, with two jobs now, I'm sure she'll be able to afford to get out of that shithole," Lexi said with a sneer.

Dex didn't answer her, only stared at her with icy eyes. He crossed his arms and raised his brow, waiting for Lexi to continue her rant.

"Oh my gosh," she gasped. "You ended up finding some poor sucker to take her in, didn't you?"

He didn't think, only let the words fall out. "If you consider me a poor sucker, then yeah."

The whole garage fell silent.

Lexi's eyes grew wide and her jaw nearly fell to the floor. Dex braced himself for the worst, but was strangely surprised.

"What," Lexi managed. Her voice was so low and soft that Dex barely heard her, barely recognized it at all. "She's staying with you?"

"Yeah," he confirmed.

Dex was pretty sure what followed could have been the equivalent of Tsar Bomba. To say that Lexi exploded was as much of an understatement as you could get.

He let her get it all out, call him every name in the book, and some names that didn't even make any sense. She yelled until she was exhausted and out of breath.

Watching her have this particular meltdown should have been enough for him to end it. He thought about it, but he had to see it from her point of view. He had done this.

He should have thought about what helping Briar would do to his relationship with Lexi. Lexi was insanely jealous. It didn't matter how he spun it.

✳ ✳ ✳

Dex answered the door at the knock. As soon as he saw her, "Shit. Please tell me you didn't walk here this late."

"It's only 10:30," Briar pointed out.

Dex wanted to tell her that a single woman all alone had no business walking home at that hour no matter where she was, but he didn't want to come across too strong. He had a feeling that Briar was used to that and more.

"But no. I didn't walk. Rita gave me a ride."

It was enough to put Dex's mind at ease.

"Did you eat?"

Briar rolled her eyes at his concern. "Yes."

She excused herself and grabbed her pajamas folded on top of her suitcase. Moments later the bathroom door closed and Dex heard the shower start.

This was good. He didn't know how things would play out once school started, but right now, her working at Chêne was actually a good thing. It meant he wasn't around her from when he woke up to when he went to sleep.

After cleaning up the kitchen, Dex decided to head to bed. It was after eleven, later than he usually went to sleep. Just as he headed down the hall, the bathroom door swung open and Briar backed out. Dex had to sidestep so they didn't end up colliding.

When Briar saw him, she jumped. "Sorry. I didn't expect you to still be awake."

"Going to bed now."

"Oh, umm…Okay."

She had her clothes balled up in her chest and she put her weight from one foot to the other. What she didn't do was leave.

"Was there something–"

"I was wondering if you wanted to hear about my evening," she quickly asked, her cheeks burning with just a glimmer of pink.

Dex wasn't an idiot. Talking could be just as dangerous as touching; however, when Briar looked up at him, full of apprehension and expectation, he easily agreed.

He sat on one of the barstools while Briar sprawled on the couch, covering herself with her blanket.

The first night she had worn what appeared to be a men's t-shirt and sweatpants, but last night and tonight, she wore shorts. They weren't too short, but enough to call attention to her legs. Dex was relieved that she chose to use the blanket.

He had never heard her talk so much. Most of their conversations were short and clipped, largely from his attitude. Something about listening to her, so full of excitement, pulled at an organ deep within, causing a pounding throughout his whole body.

"I know I'm rambling, and we both need to get some sleep."

Remembering what she told him that day she fainted, "Are you sleeping any better?"

The small smile that remained from talking about her first day of work quickly faded. A darkness Dex had caught glimpses of returned. It was still too soon to ask.

"Yeah. I mean I know I can't sleep on a couch forever, but this one is pretty comfy," she said, attempting to deflect from the issue as to why she wasn't sleeping well.

Before Dex could think of a response, his phone dinged in his pocket. It was late, nearing midnight. He couldn't imagine who would be messaging him. Maybe Rusty went out drinking in the middle of a workweek.

Briar watched as color drained from Dex's face when he looked at his phone. It had to be a long message, or he was reading it over and over.

Lexi: I'm sorry for the way I acted. I'd like to come over for dinner Sunday. With you and Blair.

Lexi could be manipulative and conniving. Dex knew that better than most people, which is why he didn't understand the text.

Lexi wasn't one to apologize, ever. He hadn't bothered contacting her after their fight earlier, and that was more than six hours ago. Generally, she'd go days without speaking to him, waiting for him to say something first.

Secondly, she went from a raging bull in a china shop to wanting to have dinner with both himself *and* Briar.

It was Briar's name that made him most suspicious of all. Lexi knew her name. Mistyping it made it seem like Briar's name wasn't worth remembering.

"Is everything okay," Briar asked.

Dex brought his eyes from the screen of the phone to Briar's.

"Yeah. Uh…Lexi just wanted to come to dinner on Sunday."

"Oh…" Briar couldn't let Dex think that she was disappointed. There had been a few times recently where she forgot about the fact that he had Lexi. "I don't think I'm working, but I have a lot of odds and ends to do. I'll be scarce."

Dex hesitated. He shouldn't have told her about Lexi's text to begin with. "No. Uh…Lexi wants to have dinner with the both of us."

CHAPTER 13

Both Briar and Dex allowed work to consume them the next couple days and didn't see much of each other except in the morning and only rarely at the shop.

The car, from the call Briar informed Dex of on the day she had fainted, arrived. It kept Dex completely occupied that Friday and Saturday when he wasn't working on vehicles for his customers.

Briar stayed later than required that Saturday night, helping clean up the restaurant part, which closed at ten. The bar was overwhelmingly crowded, but Sandy, nor Rita, wanted her having anything to do with that area.

When she did finally get back to Dex's apartment, there was a tiny note above the handle of the door.

Called it an early night. The door is unlocked.

Dex was relieved when he finally heard the door open and close. The apartment was so quiet that he heard her every movement. She did as she had every night. Take a shower and go to bed.

He hated that she was burning her candle at both ends. There's no way she would be able to work half of what she did once school started. She also needed accommodations better than his couch. Though she had threatened to go back to the hostel on the first night, she never mentioned it again. He had to think that she felt safer and more comfortable on a couch rather than that place.

Dex flung himself on the bed, exasperated. Tomorrow was Sunday. He gave Lexi a simple *sure* in response, to which she sent a string of cutesy emojis. He avoided talking with Briar about it. Why harp on it and ruin several days when you can just ruin one? Without a doubt, he knew that by this time tomorrow, it would be a ruined day, especially if Lexi had anything to say on the matter.

✻ ✻ ✻

"I've got to go to the grocery store for a few things for tonight," Dex informed Briar over breakfast.

There was a sadness that washed across Briar's face that she quickly masked.

"Would you mind picking up a few things for me?"

"Like what," he hesitated.

Briar picked at the last bits of her pancake, thinking. "What kind of desserts does Lexi like?"

"Fuck if I know," Dex scoffed. When a smirk came across Briar's face. "Shit. Sorry. I mean, I don't know."

Briar twirled her fork at him and laughed. He wanted to tell her how beautiful her laugh was but quickly caught himself, remembering that he shouldn't get comfortable enough to say things like that to her.

"I told you. It's fine. On a serious note. I wanted to make dessert. It's the least I can do."

"Can you bake?"

Briar didn't know if most girls her age baked, at least, not how she did. She had several recipes in mind, but realized that Dex might ask questions, and it was a part of her past she didn't want to talk about. It was nothing bad, she simply didn't want to become too familiar with him.

She quickly thought of something easy that required little to no skill.

"Well, I can read the back of a box of cake mix and follow directions."

That made Dex laugh.

"Just get me a box of chocolate cake mix and some Snicker's."

Dex began loading the dishwasher. "You know, you could just come along if you wanted."

Briar was thankful that he was facing away from her, because she saw right away that he didn't mean to suggest that. Every muscle of his back tensed after those words came out. She didn't need to see the panic that was more than likely showing in those crystal blue eyes.

Backtracking, "Err...It's your day off. I'm sure you have–"

"If you could drop me off at the thrift store, that would be great," Briar interrupted, not wanting to hear Dex finish what he was saying.

Dex turned to face her. "Thrift store?"

Briar rose from her stool and stepped to the side. "In case you haven't noticed, I'm wearing clothes from when I was fifteen. They don't exactly fit."

Dex's expression hardened. He wished she wouldn't have done that, because his eyes were immediately drawn to her body.

Her jeans could stand to be a size bigger. They were so tight he didn't know how she got them buttoned. Her shirt was also too small. He could see the smallest amount of skin between the top of her jeans and the hem of her shirt. His eyes trailed upward, and the tightness of the shirt made her...

He turned immediately. *Fuck.* He had seriously just checked her out. He rinsed another plate and put it in the dishwasher.

"Yeah, I can do that. Just be ready to go in thirty minutes."

Briar was a little disappointed when Dex shut down after breakfast. He dropped her off at the thrift store as he said he would, but the only thing he told her was when he'd pick her back up. Something told her not to get her expectations up for the rest of the day. She had a feeling that a dinner with Lexi and Dex wasn't going to be as simple as a dinner should be.

Dex sensed that things were off. Even though it had only been a few days with her around, things were like a rollercoaster. It was like neither knew what

91

to say and once things felt comfortable, one of them did or said the wrong thing, and made it awkward.

Ever since he looked at her, really looked at her, that morning, he hadn't been able to think straight, which made talking to her even more difficult.

Briar heard Dex let out a groan from the kitchen.

"Don't worry, I'll have this cleaned up by tonight," she informed him.

Currently, she was making a mess in his living room with organizing her new clothes into piles.

Once upon a time, she would easily spend seven hundred or more on a dress she wore once. Now she had a mountain of clothes for barely a little more than a hundred dollars. Apparently, Sunday's were half price on t-shirts, making them only a dollar each, and she hit the jackpot when she found a rack of vintage bands and cartoon characters. She was also able to find several pairs of jeans, and a few dresses, all under ten dollars each.

She decided to wash the dresses first, as she planned on wearing one that night. She didn't want Lexi to think she was some homeless filth.

"Here," Dex said, handing her a bag of several packs of hangers.

Stupidly, "What's this?"

"They're called hangers. Most people use them for clothes. You can put them in the closet of the spare bedroom. Unless you plan on washing all this shit just to cram it in a suitcase."

Briar glared at him, wondering how he managed to be sweet, and yet an asshole, all in one breath.

"Thanks," she mumbled. Attempting to keep the conversation going, "Dinner smells great."

Dex shrugged, "It's just a roast in a slow cooker. Didn't feel like going out of my way cooking."

Briar stood, a small pile of dresses gathered in her arms to take to the laundry room on the first floor.

"Well, I'm sure Lexi will love it," she said with a smile.

Dex honestly didn't care at this point. Lexi was up to something with wanting to do this dinner. In his gut, he knew he had some thinking to do after this was all said and done.

CHAPTER 14

Dex picked up the bowl of batter and twirled it around. It was way too thick. "Not to be rude, but I think you did something wrong."

Briar bit her bottom lip to keep from laughing. "What makes you think that?"

"Cake batter should be a lot thinner," Dex pointed out.

Briar chopped the Snicker's into smaller chunks. "Who said anything about a cake?"

Dex watched her curiously, but stepped back, giving her space. Only when she asked where to find a cookie sheet did he say anything.

Briar took a small amount of dough in her hands, flattened it, then covered a piece of candy inside it. She rolled it into a ball and slightly pressed it when she placed it on the cookie sheet.

Dex looked over from the sink. "I have to say, I'm intrigued."

"It's not much. Cake mix, oil, and eggs. Boom. Cookies," she said, placing the last one on the sheet. She slid the sheet into the upper oven and set a timer.

Briar began cleaning her area. She paused and looked to the table. "Do you have a tablecloth?"

Dex scoffed. "No."

"What about candles?"

"Do I look like a guy who has candles?"

Briar smiled and grabbed her things to take to the sink. "No. I guess not. It would feel more welcoming and homier."

"Too romantic," Dex grumbled.

"I don't think so."

"Well, I don't have any. So tough shit."

His raised voice startled Briar and the heavy and slippery bowl along with the spoon and spatula inside, fell into the soapy and full sink, sending water and suds flying. Dex flew back and let out a curse word.

"Sorry!"

He shook his head and dusted a few suds off his mildly wet t-shirt. Briar immediately handed him a nearby dry dishtowel; however, when he looked at her, she wasn't much better.

Dex took the towel from her, but instead of using it on himself, he reached for her cheek. It was the smallest amount of suds, probably not even enough for her to feel.

Briar held her breath as Dex wiped her cheek. He was so soft, and though the towel was rough against her skin, something about it, about the gesture, felt nice. Then, just before his hand dropped from her face, his thumb lightly brushed her cheek, and she was certain that her heart stopped. When their eyes met, something in his was no longer cold and angry. His gaze fell to her lips, and as soon it did, he pulled back.

"I need a new shirt," Dex growled and stormed out of the kitchen.

He didn't know what the hell just happened, but whatever it was created a dangerous feeling inside him.

Once Briar heard his bedroom door shut, she let out a breath. She couldn't help but bring her fingers to the same spot he just touched. For just a moment, she felt his warmth against her cheek, and that was a feeling she couldn't easily forget.

The cookies were already out of the oven and cooling by the time Dex returned. Briar only glanced in his direction for a second, but noted how incredible he looked. He had on a nice black button-down shirt, untucked from a pair of dark washed jeans. It must have been his best pair, as there were no oil stains. He had the sleeves of the shirt rolled up and pushed above the elbows so that the images painted up and down his arms were still visible.

That small glance was enough to create a tumultuous storm within Briar. For the first time, she was really, honestly, truly, jealous of Lexi.

Just then there was a rhythmic knock on the door. Briar's eyes widened as they met Dex's from across the open space.

"She's early," he grumbled.

"I haven't even changed," Briar hissed.

Dex shrugged. "You look fine."

Briar glared at him. She did not look fine with dishwater covering her t-shirt.

As Dex made his way to the door, Briar darted to the spare room to grab a dress. By the time she went across the hall to the bathroom, she could already hear voices.

Lexi seemed strangely normal as she gave Dex a hug and kissed him on the cheek. She walked around him and toward the living room, taking a minute to peek in the kitchen.

"You made cookies?"

"No. Briar did."

"Oh…So, the two of you cook together. How quaint." Her voice was laced with disdain.

Dex's mind raced with thoughts. He had a feeling he and Lexi had run their course, and how she acted today was going to make or break it.

He wanted to address Lexi's comment, to clarify, but something told him that she was looking for a reason to start a fight. He wasn't going to do that, not with Briar around.

"It smells good," Lexi told him once he didn't say anything back.

"Everything is almost ready. You're just a little early."

Lexi spun to face Dex, her eyes narrowed, watching his every breath and every movement. "I hope I wasn't interrupting anything."

If she thought he was going to react, she had another thing coming. He was good with keeping his emotions covered, hidden away.

Dex made his way past her and into the kitchen, busying himself with getting the plates and glasses out. "I don't have any of that fancy wine shit you drink. Want a beer?"

Lexi rolled up her nose. "Definitely not."

Dex was glad that she declined. A part of him didn't want Briar to feel left out, like she was beneath them because of her age.

"Well, hello there," Lexi's voice rang out.

Dex immediately drew his attention to the hallway and for a split second, he forgot how to breathe.

"Hi, Lexi," Briar said rather shyly.

"Cute dress," Lexi complimented, although Dex knew just by her tone that she didn't mean it.

Lexi looked to Dex, and he could tell that she was watching for a reaction. He had to be honest, this was one time where concealing it was proving to be difficult.

"Isn't she adorable, Dex," Lexi asked suspiciously.

Dex didn't know how to answer. No. She wasn't *adorable*. She was fucking beautiful.

Briar's yellow dress hit just above her knees and had a crew neck cut with dainty cap sleeves. A thick piece of yellow and black plaid fabric ran along her small waist, tying at the back into a bow. She had a simple pair of flats on her feet, just a solid black. Her hair was tucked and pinned in all different directions making for a messy bun, with only a few pieces pulled down in the front, framing her face.

Dex wasn't a thesaurus, but he could have found a hundred different words to call Briar. Adorable was not one of them.

Lexi's brows were raised, and she stared at Dex. He couldn't believe her. She really wanted a response from him.

Dex addressed Briar with a shrug, and nonchalantly, "The dress looks nice."

Briar gave him a tight smile and mumbled what he assumed was thanks. Though she tried to hide it, he knew she was disappointed. He was as well, but there was no way in hell that he could say what he was thinking, whether Lexi was there or not.

At a square table, the seating arrangement was uncomfortable. Lexi sat to Dex's right and Briar sat to her right, directly across from Dex. He planned on making it a point not to look up throughout dinner.

When Lexi was comfortable in her chair, she leaned over and kissed Dex on the cheek. "Baby, thank you for cooking for me."

Dex gave Lexi a skeptical look, to which a smirk appeared on her face.

He barely got to finish his first bite of food when Lexi's attention turned toward Briar. "So, tell me a little about yourself."

Briar swallowed uncomfortably. "There's not much to tell," she answered with a shrug.

"Where do you call home? How did you end up in little old Argent Falls?"

Those were questions Dex didn't know the answers to, and he assumed there were reasons why. The biggest one being that it wasn't any of his business to pry. The few weeks he had known Briar, he was well-aware that she didn't talk about anything before Argent Falls.

Her response hit him hard.

"I don't call anywhere home." Briar knew she had to say something else quickly, before Lexi rephrased the question. "I just got on a bus and ended up here. That's about it."

She could have given more details. There were several places she had looked into; however, Argent Falls High School said they would accept all her credits from the academy, ensuring that she could finish her schooling by December.

"Do you have family somewhere?"

Dex could have kicked Lexi under the table for continuing to pry.

"Simply put, no."

"I'm sure your parents miss you," Lexi went on, under the impression that Briar was a runaway.

Briar didn't want to be rude, but Lexi's questions were triggering thoughts and emotions that she didn't want to deal with, at least not now, while at dinner with Dex and his girlfriend.

"I wouldn't know. They're both dead," she responded rather sharply.

"Lexi," Dex sighed.

"How was I to know? I thought she just ran away from home," Lexi went on, as though Briar wasn't even there.

Briar quickly changed the subject. Although Dex had told her that Lexi worked at a salon, she pretended differently. "So, Lexi. What is it you do?"

Lexi perked up at the chance to get to talk about herself. "I'm a hairstylist."

"That sounds like a fun job," Briar added.

"It can be demanding, but it is rewarding getting to make people beautiful, better versions than when they walked in."

Briar fell silent, unsure what to say to a comment like that. Dex tried not to make a sound, but internally he was cursing like a sailor at how stupid and narcissistic that sounded.

Lexi went on. "I must say, I do love the color of your hair."

"Thanks."

Unsatisfied, "What's your natural color?"

Briar looked up, surprised. "This is my natural color."

Lexi giggled. "No, it isn't. Trust me, I know. That shade of ash blonde, and the tips ever slightly lighter…No."

Briar was trying really hard. Dex had helped her greatly, and if he wanted her to get along with Lexi, she'd try; however, it seemed like Lexi wasn't playing fair.

"Well, it's the same as my dead mother's so…"

Dex slammed his fist down just hard enough to cause ripples in their glasses of water. "Damnit, Lexi!"

Lexi shot him a look but soon fell silent.

With Lexi not saying a word, no one said a word. It was the most awkward meal imaginable.

When Briar was done with her plate, she took it to the kitchen and brought back with her the plate of cookies.

Dex took one first, but upon finishing it, said nothing.

"I thought you hated chocolate," Lexi pointed out when, a moment later, he went back for a second.

Dex looked up to see Briar's eyes on his from across the table. Looking at her, but addressing his words to Lexi, correcting her, "I never said hate."

Lexi turned to Briar, "You know, I must say, I am a little envious."

Dex recognized the calculating look in Lexi's face. Dinner was over. This was it.

Briar chuckled. "I can't imagine what of."

"Well, for starters, my boyfriend of two years has never once allowed me to stay the night, but after two weeks, he brings in a homeless woman."

"Lexi, stop," Dex growled.

"I'm just making an observation," Lexi cooed innocently.

Dex rose and grabbed his and Lexi's plate and headed to the kitchen. If he had hoped she would follow, he was mistaken.

Lexi made sure that her words were loud enough so that Dex could still hear. "Blair, sweetie," she began, addressing Briar like a child. "If you could go take a walk, play outside for a bit, I'd like a private moment with Dex."

Dex concluded that Lexi was right about one thing. Briar needed to leave. She didn't need to be around for the conversation about to take place.

He couldn't take his eyes from Briar, knowing how uncomfortable this entire evening must have been for her.

Briar pushed her chair back and put on one the best fake smiles she could manage. "Absolutely." She took a few steps away from the table. She told herself to let it go, knowing that Lexi expected a rise out of her, but she couldn't. Very calmly, "Oh, Lexi, dear. It's Briar."

Dex bit his bottom lip, holding back the smile that threatened to break through the surface.

Only once the door closed behind Briar, did Lexi rise from her chair and make her way toward Dex. That's when Dex exploded.

"What the fuck was that?! You were a bitch the whole time! I don't get it! Why did you even want to do this shit?!"

"Oh, shut up, Dex! I wanted to see how the two of you interacted."

Dex shook his head and laughed. "I knew it couldn't be something as simple as dinner with you."

"I saw the way you looked at her the moment she came out," Lexi screamed at the top of her lungs.

"Yeah! I looked at her because you said she looked adorable," he clarified.

Lexi let out one loud laugh. "That is not at all what I saw."

"Then go get your fucking eyes checked."

"Look how defensive you are," Lexi pointed out.

"I'm not defensive. I'm pissed. You insulted her. You made inappropriate questions and comments."

Lexi crossed her arms and stomped her foot like a child. "Why do you care?!"

That question was the easiest one yet. "Because she's a person."

Lexi then went somewhere far darker for Dex, and a sick feeling prickled every bone in his body with the question she asked.

"Excuse me," Dex asked, unsure he heard her correctly.

"You heard me. Are you fucking her?"

"You're insane," he spat in response.

She waved a well-manicured finger in his face. "And you're not answering."

"No! Hell no! I've never so much as touched her."

He thought back to the kitchen, and that time in his truck, and that time he held her when she fainted, and that time with the computer mouse in the office. He had touched her, but not in an intimate nature. Although now thinking about it, he realized that for the shortest of moments, he wanted to kiss her in the kitchen, and that thought scared him in so many ways.

"But you want to," Lexi added, as though she could read his mind.

"No," Dex growled back. "She's seventeen."

"And legal in our state," Lexi scoffed. "You act like you're ancient. You're eight years older than her. That's nothing. Do you honestly expect me to believe that there's no sexual tension between the two of you?!"

"Yes," he bellowed at the top of his lungs.

Lexi grew quiet. "I could feel it. It rolled off the both of you like a fog."

Dex twirled his finger around at his head and leaned toward her for effect. "You're fucking delusional, making all this bizarre shit up in your head."

"Then she means nothing to you?"

Briar knew it was wrong. She shouldn't have stayed plastered to the door to hear that conversation. It was sick and hurtful in every way, and she could no longer hold back from a few tears spilling over.

She stepped away from the door and made her way to the elevator. Though she knew it, she didn't want to hear Dex's answer. The truth was, she didn't mean anything to anyone. Dex wasn't a miraculous exception.

Dex crossed his arms and glared back at Lexi. He didn't know what game Lexi was playing, but he wasn't going to entertain her anymore.

Lexi stepped forward and brought her hands to Dex's arms that remained pinned across his chest. She appeared to be feigning a calmness.

Very softly, "Dex, let her go."

"I don't know what you're talking about." Truly what did that mean? Briar was free to go wherever; he just hoped it wouldn't be back to that hostel.

"I'm asking you to make a choice. It's either her or me."

Dex took a step back and dropped his arms in disbelief. "You're giving me an ultimatum? If I don't kick her out, we're done?"

Lexi seemed pleased with herself and nodded.

After what she was saying truly sank in, Dex stepped back toward her, towering over her. Lexi blinked rapidly, the smug look on her face fading once the smirk appeared across Dex's lips.

"Oh, Lexi. This was one game you should not have played."

Dex brushed past her and went to a cabinet in the kitchen. He pulled down a nearly full bottle of Scotch whisky from the top shelf. He wasn't a big drinker. He was good with an occasional beer or two after work; however, he decided this called for celebration.

It took another second for his ominous statement to register to Lexi. "Wait," she screeched, spinning around as Dex poured himself a small glass. "Are you fucking serious? You're choosing her over me?"

Dex looked toward her, his eyes drained of all emotion. "No, Lexi. I'm not choosing *her* over *you*. I'm just not choosing you."

CHAPTER 15

Briar didn't know what time it was when she got off the elevator and drifted down the hall to the door numbered 604. She wasn't sure what to do. Knock? If the door was locked and Dex and Lexi were in his room, they wouldn't hear her anyway. Ultimately, she decided to simply try the door, relieved when it opened easily.

She was surprised when she walked in. The kitchen was clean, spotless. Dex liked things clean, but she assumed he was busy with other things after she left.

Briar froze when the living room came into view and a dark figure sat in a chair by the window to the balcony, highlighted by the glistening of a nearby floor lamp.

He didn't turn to her, only took a sip of the amber liquid in an almost empty tumbler. "You really need to think about getting a phone."

Briar took a few steps forward. She glanced behind her to the clock on the oven. 10:27. She had been gone for more than three hours.

"They're expensive and right now I don't have use for one."

Dex turned to face her and his heart cracked a little. Though the room had little light, he could see the smudges of mascara as she neared him. He hated to think that something Lexi said would have made her cry.

Briar noted that Dex's appearance had not changed. He wore the same jeans and the same black shirt.

"Where were you?"

Briar sat on the small couch, not the one she slept on, located adjacent from Dex. "The park across the street."

Dex nodded, taking the final sip of alcohol, and placing his glass on the windowsill near the balcony doors.

"Look, Dex…I wanted to apologize."

Dex's eyes met hers immediately, a mix of confusion and anger. In the dim light, the magical and crisp blue appeared darker, like the deepest depths of the ocean.

When Dex didn't say anything, only continued staring, "I know I might have been a little short with Lexi. There are just things I don't like talking about…And…I don't know. I just don't want to be the cause of any problems between the two of you. After thinking a while, perhaps it might be best–"

Dex interrupted her, swiftly cutting her off before she could say what he already knew she would. "It's fine. Everything is good."

Briar's shoulders relaxed a little and she took a deep breath. "Well, tomorrow is Monday. I better get cleaned up and go to bed."

She looked over to the other couch. Dex already had a pillow and folded blanket back on it. Without saying anything else, Briar rose to go grab her pajamas from the spare bedroom before taking a quick shower.

"Briar," Dex began, forcing her to stop and turn. "You looked nice today."

Briar forced a smile. "Thanks, but you already said that."

Dex got up from his chair, grabbed his glass, and started toward the kitchen, pausing when he got within a foot of Briar. "No. Earlier I said the dress looked nice."

That comment echoed in Briar's head long after all the lights were out and she was bundled up on the couch, attempting to sleep. She felt like a silly girl, reading too much into it, but something about the way he looked at her, just for a second, made her feel beautiful.

The next week flew by. Each night Briar found herself feeling more and more exhausted; however, she kept reminding herself that once school started, her income would easily be cut in half.

"Where are you going this early on a Sunday?"

"Chêne," Briar replied, giving no other information.

Dex knew she was lying. Both the bar and restaurant were only open for dinner hours on Sunday, from five to ten.

"Do you need a ride," he asked, curious as to where she was going.

"No. It's really pretty this morning. I think I'll walk," Briar said with the most innocent smile. "But, I get off at eight. Since that's the middle of dinner, I don't think Rita will be able to–"

"I'll be there," he interrupted, perhaps a little to eagerly.

Then, she was gone.

Briar knew that Dex was suspicious and curious. She simply didn't have time to explain to him, and lately their conversations were going beyond surface level. If she told him what she was doing, there was no doubt that he'd probably want more of an explanation.

"Good morning, Rita," Briar exclaimed, bursting through the kitchen doors, full of excitement.

"Girl, I do not know where you get that energy."

"Trust me, it's all an act," Briar joked, now reaching for an apron.

"Are you going to be good in here? Alfred comes in sometime between one and two to start prepping a few things for tonight."

"I'm a little rusty, but I should be done before then. The hardest part for me was always the crust."

Rita laughed, making her curls bounce. "Better you than me. I'd buy those frozen, already made, ones."

Briar smiled and began bouncing around the kitchen. She had been in the kitchen before and made mental notes about where everything was, but it was still confusing actually working in the space.

"Trust me, you're going to love this."

"Coming from you, I have no doubt. Now, if you'll excuse me, I need to go get my nails done."

Briar had to admit, when she propositioned Rita and Sandy, she thought they'd shut her down immediately. It took some convincing, and ultimately, she had to use the mommy card; although, she made them swear not to tell anyone.

The dough for the shell came first. She needed several batches, but her mother always insisted that when doubling or tripling a recipe like that, there was a greater chance of mistakes. Therefore, Briar started with six separate bowls and started down the list of ingredients tattooed in her memory.

By the time Alfred arrived, the tarts were just coming out of the oven. It had taken Briar longer than anticipated. Normally, she could have done it from start to finish in about three and a half hours. This time it took her nearly five; however, she had to factor in that she had six, as opposed to one.

Alfred's voice came booming from across the kitchen. "Damn, that smells good!" When he walked around to see the tarts cooling, "When can we cut into one?"

"Sorry, they need to cool, and they're for dinner tonight."

"Don't you need to at least sample it before it goes out?"

Briar laughed as she prepped another peg rack to go into the industrial dishwasher. She brought down the doors and the roaring of water took over. Raising her voice, "You do have a point!"

To say that she was excited was putting it mildly. She hadn't baked in a long time. Those stupid cookies she made didn't count as baking.

It was bittersweet, as she immediately missed her mother and all the classes she had gone through when she was younger. Before her father died, he promised to send her to a basic chocolatier program for a summer, but that never happened. Thankfully there were free workshops online that she was able to come across, but all of the good ones were ridiculously expensive.

After she finished cleaning up, Alfred allowed her to help him, just as long as she stayed away from the grill.

* * *

Dex arrived around 7:30. He didn't plan on eating there, but maybe he'd have a drink. The normally packed bar and all its surrounding tables was generally at only half capacity on Sunday nights.

He chose a table in the corner and as soon as he sat, found himself looking past the partitions toward the restaurant's side. It was too crowded for him to find her, and he quickly looked away, hating himself that he had arrived early.

He was jolted from his thoughts with a slap on the back.

"What can I get you," Sandy bellowed.

"Nothing."

Sandy sat on a stool across from Dex. "Why do you look like your goldfish died?"

Dex lifted his eyes so that Sandy could see his unpleasant glare.

"I'm just messing with you," Sandy laughed. "I take it you're waiting on Briar." He motioned his head back toward the restaurant, but Dex didn't look.

"Yeah," was all he gave Sandy.

"I've got to tell you, she's something."

Coming from a man in his fifties, Dex didn't find that comment as annoying as some of Rusty's, even if Rusty was joking.

"Well, don't get too used to it. School starts soon," Dex pointed out.

"Are you sure you don't want something," Sandy asked again.

"Positive."

A grin came to Sandy's face and a moment later, he was gone. Dex appreciated that. He didn't want someone bragging, telling him how great Briar was. She made him painfully aware of that on a daily basis.

Dex was startled when a plate came down in front of him and Sandy returned to his seat.

Dex looked down at the plate and back to Sandy. "What the hell is this?"

Proudly, "It's a chocolate tart."

108

"I meant, what is it doing in front of me." He pushed the plate away. "I don't like chocolate."

"Stop being such a little bitch and try it," Sandy insisted.

Dex looked at the plate. Honestly, it was far too pretty and composed to be served in a bar and grille restaurant. The piece of chocolate pie, or tart, as Sandy called it, Dex didn't get the difference, was elegantly adorned with a perfectly placed arrangement of raspberries and mint, like something out of an overly difficult looking cookbook.

Dex ultimately took a bite, expecting to taste a plain piece of chocolate pie. His eyes shot up to Sandy, a wide grin already spreading across his face.

"Good, isn't it."

Dex didn't want Sandy getting a big head, and only nodded, going back for another bite. It was beyond good. It had a flavor or a spice he couldn't quite place, making his senses come alive.

"That crust, it's perfect. None of that graham cracker shit. And not a single crack in the chocolate," Sandy went on.

"Okay, okay. I get it. It's good," Dex admitted.

Sandy leaned in. "You should tell your girl that."

The next bite must have gone down the wrong way, because Dex thought he might choke to death, to which Sandy only laughed. "Excuse me?" He should have further corrected how Sandy referred to her; however, the next comment surprised him even more.

"Briar. That's hers," Sandy informed him, motioning to the half-eaten piece of tart. "She asked Rita and I a few days ago if she could make a dessert one day."

"How did you even know..." Dex's comment faded.

"After she told us about her mom...Err...I just think...I figured that–"

Dex's eyes narrowed. "What about her mom?"

Sandy held up his hands in defeat. "Nope. Sorry. I wasn't supposed to go there."

Dex was more than annoyed. He didn't know anything about Briar's mother except for the fact that she died. He had to admit, he wasn't the easiest person to talk to, but he assumed she'd tell him things before Rita and Sandy.

"She's good with baking, I'll give her that," Sandy went on. "But the girl can't cook a burger to save her life."

"Yeah?"

"Yeah. She tried the other night after hours. I thought Alfred was going to have a meltdown when she kept pressing down on it with the spatula," Sandy laughed.

"I don't see what the difference is," Dex said, holding up another bite of tart.

"Trust me, there's a difference. I could make you the most perfect medium-rare steak, but when it comes to that?" Sandy pointed to the almost clean plate. "Not a chance in hell. That right there requires a whole different skillset."

CHAPTER 16

Briar walked out of the office, morning coffee in hand, to find Dex at the front desk like always first thing. Rusty and Benji had now arrived, laughter filling the air. Briar liked seeing Dex smile and laugh; it was rare.

Rusty slapped Dex across the back. "Ever since you got rid of Lexi, your whole attitude has changed."

Benji let out a grunt. "And there haven't been any more Tornado Lexi touchdowns around here. Makes a much more peaceful space."

Briar froze, sensing that she entered the conversation at a bad time.

"Anyway, we're going to get started," Rusty concluded.

Briar didn't say anything at first, simply sipped her coffee. It had been a couple weeks since Lexi came over for dinner. Briar made it a point not to ask about her after that night, and Dex never mentioned her.

Just as Dex stood to leave, Briar found her curiosity stopping him.

"You and Lexi broke up?"

Dex stopped and turned to face Briar. "Yeah."

"I'm sorry," Briar whispered. "I figured she might be upset at dinner. I hope–"

Sensing where Briar was going, Dex interrupted her. "I broke up with her."

Briar's eyes widened and she felt her heart racing. Hearing that piece of information messed with her thoughts. Immediately, she wanted to ask why. Instead, "Oh. I didn't know."

Dex leaned against the counter. "And I didn't know you were making fancy desserts at Chêne," he replied, changing the subject.

He found it sweet that her eyes quickly dropped from his and a deep shade of pink appeared across her cheeks.

"Uh…Yeah. Sometimes."

Dex wanted to ask more. He wanted to know what she told Sandy and Rita. He wanted to know more about her than anyone else, and that thought alone should have been disturbing. That thought should have deterred his next words.

"There's a café a couple blocks over. They're only open for breakfast and lunch. Want to go later?"

Briar couldn't believe what he was saying, asking.

The terrified look in her eyes was enough to cause Dex to rethink his wording. It wasn't a date, but he couldn't tell her that because then she'd think that he thought she had assumed it was.

"I can see if the guys want to come too," he added.

The terror faded and a simple smile came to her face. "It's whatever."

That wasn't exactly the answer he hoped for, but at least she wasn't looking at him like he was about to murder her. Dex also had no intention of asking anyone else to join. He wanted to get to know more about Briar Stone.

* * *

Shortly after ordering their sandwiches, Dex decided to dive right in.

"I'm curious how you convinced Sandy to hand over his kitchen to you," he bluntly began.

Briar twirled the straw in her tea. Dex could tell that she was thinking her response carefully, and he couldn't help but wonder if she was going to make up some lie.

She sighed. "My mother is, was…" She shook her head not knowing how to say it anymore. "Ingrid Vera Norberg." Whatever reaction she expected

Dex to have simply wasn't there, meaning he had no idea who her mother was. "She was a pastry chef." Briar left it at that.

Dex chuckled. "No. There's more. She was really good, wasn't she?"

Though there was sadness in Briar's eyes from the memories, there was also a light that Dex rarely saw.

"Yes, Dex, very good. She judged competitions, had her own television show…She could do it all. She was a world renowned pâtissier and master chocolatier." Sensing the confusion on Dex's face, Briar clarified. "She could make any pastry and all those fancy ridiculously expensive chocolates…And I wanted to follow in her footsteps."

"I think you're doing a pretty good job."

Briar scoffed. "No. This wasn't how it was supposed to go." When Dex didn't press for more, Briar decided to give him more. "I think I could make cookies before I could read the recipes. My mother taught me everything; however, starting at age seven, they began putting me in classes for a more formal training."

"Sounds like a lot for a kid," Dex pointed out.

A smile came to Briar's face as she remembered. "It was, but I loved every minute of it."

"Did you quit, or…"

"My mom died in a car accident when I was eleven. That was a bit of a setback, but I still pressed forward. Even though she wasn't with me physically, I wanted to make sure that everything she had given me, taught me, lived on. My father made sure of that as well, up until he died."

That was the worst moment for their food to arrive. Briar was telling him so much, and he wanted to know more. He wanted to know how the strong young woman before him got to be in the situation she was in.

"When did your father die," he asked, assuming it was recently.

"About three years ago, when I was fifteen."

Dex took a bite of his sandwich and thought about what she was telling him. That didn't make any sense. Had she been homeless for years? If her mother was such an important person in the culinary world, didn't they leave her anything?

Before Dex could ask, "That's when my stepmother took over the finances completely." She shrugged. "So, no more culinary classes. I found a lot of free trainings and recipes online, but it was nothing compared to what I had. There's actually a one-month chocolatier program online that I've been looking at, but it's one of the pricier options."

Dex wanted to know more about her stepmother, but with the way she introduced that piece of information, and quickly brushed over it, he sensed to wait.

"You should do it."

"The training is nearly a thousand dollars, and that doesn't even include the list of supplies needed," Briar pointed out.

"Shit."

"It's fine. That was one thing my mom and I never got around to. I wish I had some more of the basics under my belt before–" Briar cut herself off, surprised by how much she was revealing to Dex.

Dex smiled. "You already started, you might as well finish."

Briar looked away. She wanted to tell Dex so badly how gorgeous his smile was, but that would be crossing a line. "Well, there's an intense two-year chocolatier program in London that I'm applying for, but I won't know anything until December. Even then, I might not get in."

At that moment, Dex knew why she was so frugal with her money. That's why she was eager to graduate. That's why she said she wouldn't be around Argent Falls long.

Briar surprised him with her next words, through a mouthful of food. "Now you."

"What do you mean, now me?"

She swallowed, now completely at ease with their time together. "Well, you know all about my story. I want to know yours."

"I think you're missing a few years there," Dex pointed out, and he regretted it immediately.

There was that look in her face he had seen from time to time, a dark storm of something hidden and buried.

"That's for another time."

He had to simply take what she'd give. He finished his sandwich and sat back in his chair, arms crossed in annoyance, annoyed that she wanted to know about him, and knowing he was a hypocrite for feeling that way. "Fine. What about me?"

"You're awfully young to have a business of your own and to be part owner of another." Briar hesitated. "Are your parents involved."

"Dead."

Briar winced, realizing she should have found a better way to ask. "I'm sorry."

"Actually, I'm not sure if that's entirely the truth." Did he really need to tell her everything? "My dad died when I was eighteen, so yes, he's dead. I don't know the woman who gave birth to me."

Dex paused when the waitress brought by the check. He saw Briar's eyes go to it, but he reached for it right away and placed his credit card on top of it, sliding it near the edge of his side of the table.

"My mom, right? That's what I'm supposed to call her?"

Briar watched the pain flicker in his eyes. "You can call her whatever you want."

Dex clenched and unclenched his fist under the table. "She was a horrible excuse for a mother. She never wanted that, and though I was young when she left, I remember her telling me that. She hated me, from the moment I was born until the day she left my dad and I."

"How old were you?"

"Five or six."

"Crap. I'm–"

"Don't be sorry," Dex interrupted. "Trust me, it was for the best. Aside from the fact that my dad really didn't know what the fuck he was doing."

The waitress grabbed the credit card and gave Dex a stern look.

"I made it through school alright, but I spent most of the time with my dad at the shop."

"Ahh...I see now. You inherited the shop from him."

Dex nodded. "Actually, he got it from my grandfather." Dex continued his story as they left the café and slowly walked back to the shop. "By thirteen I could do anything that someone with a degree could do. My favorite part has always been our restorations. That was what that call was about some time ago."

"That old car you're working on," Briar asked, fully knowing how consumed Dex had become with it.

"Yeah. 1930 Bentley. I probably paid too much for it, but when I'm done, I'll make a decent profit."

Briar didn't know about that. She made a mental note to ask Dex more about his job and what he did on a daily basis.

Knowing that their time together was coming to an end, but loving the fact that Dex was talking to her more than he ever had, "What about Sandy?"

Dex nudged her playfully with his elbow. "I feel like this is my part where I'm supposed to say *that's for another time.*"

"Touché," Briar mumbled.

Dex let out a melting laugh, but saw that Briar found no humor at all, which made him want to know all the more what she wasn't telling him, what had happened between fifteen and now.

"Sandy was a friend of my dad's," Dex began.

"If you don't want to, you–"

"Stop. It's not that much of a story. After my dad died...Well, I wasn't like you with your mom. I didn't give a shit about anything, and I turned to drugs. Anything and everything. And do you know where they're easiest to come by?"

116

"The hostel," Briar sighed.

"Yep," Dex said with a pop.

Briar looked up when Dex stopped. They were already back at the shop.

Dex leaned against the front of the building and ran a hand through his dark and messy hair. Briar's attention went there immediately, and she couldn't help but wonder what it felt like.

Dex rolled his head toward her and she found herself blushing, curious if he could read her thoughts.

"Long story short, after about nine months of fucking up, Sandy stepped in. I've been clean ever since, with no intentions of going back down that road. With the bar and grille? Sandy went through a bad divorce a couple years ago. Now that's a really long story. Anyway, I had the means to return the favor, and that's how I'm part owner of Chêne," he concluded with a shrug.

"Wow…"

Dex gave a light chuckle. "Good enough?"

"Yeah."

Dex pushed off the wall, and brushed by Briar to the entry doors. "Lunch break is up."

"Hey, Dex," Briar called out, walking toward him. "Thank you."

He narrowed his eyes as she got impossibly close. For a second he thought she might hug him, but whatever aura he was projecting must have made her come to her senses.

"For lunch? No problem."

"No. For…For everything," she corrected. Her voice was so soft, almost a whisper.

Dex let her go in first. Something about those simple words immobilized him. Even worse, there was a feeling deep inside, a pounding he fought to ignore.

That one hour had been such a mistake.

CHAPTER 17

Briar was surprised when Rita asked her to come in to work early, first thing in the morning, on a weekday, knowing that she worked at the shop with Dex. Dex didn't seem bothered with it, and even dropped Briar off on his way to work.

When Briar walked in, Rita sat at one of the first tables with two coffees in to-go cups.

"Good morning," Briar hesitated.

The inside of the place was close to dark, the only light that of the morning sun streaming through the windows.

Rita stood, grabbed her purse and both cups of coffee, and met Briar as soon as she walked in.

"I'm confused. Did you want me to bake something?"

Rita giggled. "Oh, no, sweetie. We're going to Gannonview for a little shopping trip."

Briar hesitated. Gannonview was a city about thirty minutes away. From the little she knew from fellow waitresses, it was far larger than Argent Falls, and held a great deal more when it came to shopping. Many of them took a trip on the weekend.

As Briar followed Rita to her car, nervously picking at the lid on her coffee cup, "What is it you're looking for in Gannonview?"

"Well, I'm not exactly supposed to say anything until I make sure you're in the car and we're on the highway."

Briar's eyes went wide with how that sounded. "Uh…Rita…I–"

"School starts next week, yeah?" Briar nodded. "Dex thought you might want some nicer things, than what you can get at the thrift store. While we do have an array of shops here, Gannonview has much more to choose from."

"That's nice of him," Briar started, now understanding why Dex was so easygoing about giving her the day off. "But the thrift store is so much cheaper. I'd rather not, if you don't mind."

"You and I both know there are certain articles of clothing you don't buy at a thrift store." Rita opened the door and raised her brows in a stern motherly way.

Briar sighed and got in.

When Rita started the car and began driving, "I wouldn't worry too much on spending."

"I just need to budget and save right now. There are other things more important to me than clothes."

"Sweetie, you're not paying for anything today," Rita finally told her.

Briar's attention shot toward Rita, but she didn't say another word. There was a sly grin of knowledge plastered across her face.

"Rita…"

As if she couldn't take the pressure of a secret for more than two seconds, "Look, he just gave me five hundred dollars and told me to do this for you!"

Briar's jaw dropped in her lap. "Rita…Could you please call Dex. I need to talk to him right now," Briar insisted.

Rita shook a finger at Briar. "Nope. He has a lot to do today."

Rita quickly snapped her mouth shut; however, Briar thought the comment over very carefully.

"How do you know what he has to do today," Briar groaned, already sensing that Dex was doing something other than working in the shop.

"I've already said too much."

"You've hardly said anything. You know I can't take that money," Briar said, her head turned toward the window watching the large oak trees pass.

"Just let the guy do something nice for you," Rita insisted.

It was too much. What Dex was doing was way too much. He had given her a job, technically two, a place to live where she didn't have to worry about her safety. Above all, even though he got irritated with her, he had given her his friendship. That was more than enough.

The rest of the drive was done in peaceful silence for the most part. Briar was lost to her thoughts, and Rita must have sensed that.

"What about this one," Rita asked, holding up another dress suitable for the upcoming fall weather. Briar looked it over. "I think Dex would like it…"

Rita chuckled when Briar shoved it back on the rack and made her way toward a wall of jeans. Briar thumbed through the jeans, looking for her size.

"I have to finally ask," Rita hesitated.

Briar made a noise of frustration, and rose with two pairs of jeans in different washes. "Please, don't."

Rita ignored her. "What's the deal with you and Dex?"

"Nothing," Briar quickly answered. "Nothing at all."

Rita sifted through another rack of dresses, carefully watching Briar. "I haven't been with Sandy long, but he seems really close with Dex and talks about him often. This all seems out of character for him."

"He just feels sorry for me."

A smile came to Rita's face. "No. I've seen the way he looks at you when he comes to pick you up. I don't know what he feels for you, but it isn't pity. I am curious though as to how *you*—"

"Okay, I'm going to go try these on," Briar blurted out before Rita could finish. Despite having a moment to collect herself, she knew without a doubt that Rita would bring up Dex again.

Rita was right about one thing. There were certain things you didn't want to touch in a thrift store. Undergarments were a huge no.

Though Briar felt comfortable around Rita, as she was a mixture of a much older sister and motherly figure…Scratch that. She was more like an eccentric and cool aunt. Putting that aside, the last thing she wanted was someone with her when she was picking out bras and underwear.

The look on Rita's face when they entered the store said it all; however, she was able to keep her opinion to herself.

Briar picked out simple and comfortable things, knowing without a doubt that no one would be seeing those articles of clothing for a very long time.

"What do you want," Rita said, answering her phone. "Mhmm..." She looked toward Briar, a smile already forming. "She's picking out panties at the moment. Let me ask her."

Briar's face turned an inhumanly shade of red. Who did Rita just tell that to?

"Dex wants to know your favorite color." Rita held out the phone, but Briar shook her head. Rita spoke into the phone, "Hold up, I think I embarrassed her." She held the phone out once more.

Briar finally snatched it, took a deep breath and turned away from Rita, feeling as though her face might burst into flames any second. "Hi."

Dex was further surprised at the voice coming through the speaker. "Briar, hey. How's it going?"

"Umm...Fine."

At first, he thought Rita was just being her quirky self, but Briar sounded so uneasy and he had to wonder if what Rita said was the truth, which would make sense with how Briar's short and clipped words came out.

Dex wanted to die right then and there. He did not want to think about Briar shopping at some lingerie place.

He kept it brief and to the point. "Favorite color?"

"Why?"

"Damnit, Briar. Just pick a color," Dex huffed.

"It depends on—"

"Briar..." He rubbed the back of his neck. "Fine, how do you feel about pink and purple?"

"Teal," she finally answered. "No, on pink and purple."

"So, blue-green shit?"

Briar rolled her eyes. "Yes, Dex. Blue-green *shit* would be a way to describe teal."

He cut the conversation after that; however, when Briar hung up, she was certain that he was smiling just as much as she was.

"Now that was cute," Rita said, taking her phone back.

Briar shrugged it off. Had Dex not sounded like he was rushed, Briar would have poked and poked until he told her what he was up to. Rita's presence was also enough of a deterrent with continuing the conversation on the phone.

* * *

After managing to get into the apartment building and on and off the elevator, Briar didn't have much left in her when arriving at Dex's apartment. With her fists clenched tightly around the handles of various bags, Briar lightly kicked at the door with her foot.

Moments later it opened, and if Dex wouldn't have immediately reached out to help with the bags, she would have dropped them, not because they were heavy, but seeing Dex dressed in the way he was turned her muscles to mush.

"Thanks," Briar managed. She brushed past Dex and into the living room, setting the few bags she still had on the couch.

Dex did the same with the remaining ones. "Damn. You went all out."

Briar looked at him with immediate concern. "I bought practical stuff, aside from a couple dresses that Rita suggested. I even got a new backpack and supplies as well. A lot of the stuff was on sale too. It's not like I–"

"Briar, I don't care."

"Just so you know, I intend to pay you back one day."

Dex scoffed and looked over the bags. "That's not how a gift works."

"I know, but it's not like you're my parent. You shouldn't feel–"

"No," he interrupted her, irritation coming across his face. "I'm not your fucking parent."

Briar wondered what it was she said that pissed him off.

"Come on," Dex growled, heading down the hallway.

Briar followed, remembering why she felt so lightheaded when Dex first opened the door. Wearing a tank and a pair of basketball shorts, he was showing more skin than she had ever seen. She was well-aware that he had tattoos covering his arms, but he also had them surrounding a large portion of his left leg. The tank was so tight across his back that she couldn't help but let her eyes trace every line of every muscle. He was big, and gorgeous, and everything about the way he looked right now screamed dangerous.

Briar had only known one kind of dangerous. Dex was a different kind entirely. Dex would never hurt her physically, but without a doubt, she knew if she wasn't careful, he could end up emulsifying her heart.

Dex opened the spare bedroom, and without stepping in, motioned for Briar to go first. She stepped around him, full of curiosity, and her heart nearly exploded when she looked into the room.

Her hands came up and over her mouth by what she was looking at. Instead of emptiness and a few pieces of workout equipment, there was an actual bedroom. There was a simple dresser along the wall with the closet. On another wall there was a desk. Directly across from the door was a twin sized bed, covered in a teal paisley fabric.

Briar spun around to face Dex. He had only taken one step into the room, no more.

"Dex," she whispered. That was about all she could get out, as she thought she might burst into tears.

"You can't stay here an entire semester and sleep on the couch." Motioning toward the desk with his thumb, "There's more."

When Briar got to the desk, she froze upon seeing the two items that meant so much. Dex was just being nice, extremely nice, and thoughtful; however, this led to Briar's undoing.

Dex became anxious when Briar didn't say anything, just stood at the desk. "It's not an iPhone or anything, just some cheap Motorola shit," he began, attempting to downplay the gesture, especially if it was freaking her out. "Also, with school and work, I'm sure we'll be coming and going at all hours, so a key seemed pretty logical."

Briar heard him, for the most part. The pounding of her heart had made its way to her head, making it impossible to hear or think.

Against her better judgment, she knew what she wanted to do. Maybe she should have thought first. Dex didn't seem like an affectionate person.

Dex held his breath and tensed. Briar's dainty body was pressed to his and her arms wrapped around his torso. It took a second to register. She was hugging him.

He clenched and unclenched his fists before bringing his arms around her and returning the gesture. This was different than when she fainted. He could feel her, really feel her, her breathing into his chest, her warmth. He slid his hands down so that they rested on her hips. She still felt so small, so breakable.

Briar knew only a few seconds had passed, and though she didn't want to break away just yet, the longevity of a first hug shouldn't last this long. Time was up. It would soon be going past awkward. When she felt Dex's hands slide down from her back and lightly dig into her hips through her clothing, she knew one of them needed to break away.

Very quickly, she pulled herself up on her tiptoes and gave Dex a swift peck on the cheek, upon doing so, immediately taking a step back. "Sorry about that…Umm…Thank you, for all this," Briar said, her eyes falling to the floor, not wanting to see how Dex was looking at her.

"No problem," Dex said rather calmly, pretending as though they didn't have some kind of moment, and hating the fact that Briar felt the need to apologize. He raked his hands through his hair as dark as night. Briar still hadn't looked up at him. "Anyway, I need to head out. I didn't get a lot done at the shop with that restoration today. So, I probably won't be in until late."

Briar nodded. "Yeah, sure."

With that, Dex turned and left. His head was messed up six ways from Sunday. First there was the hug, her body pressed against his, the heat from her soaking into his palms. His hands could still feel her delicate warmth. Then she had to kiss him. He shook the thought away. It was just a kiss on the cheek. Hell, guys had kissed him on the cheek before.

There was something different about her. Whatever passed between them was messing with his head. Did she know how she messed with his head? For a brief moment of time, he forgot everything, and all he could wonder is what she'd taste like on his lips, what her body would feel like beneath his…

"Fuck," Dex hissed.

He looked at the time on his phone. It was already after one in the morning. He had thrown himself into work for hours. He needed to get home or *tomorrow* would be a hell of a day.

He hated what Briar was able to do to his thoughts. He couldn't think of her like that. Her age was one of his issues, but even if that wasn't a problem for him, he knew he wasn't the type of guy that deserved a chance with someone as kind and beautiful as her.

Worst of all, right now he hated how, after more than seven hours, his cheek still seemed to tingle from her lingering kiss.

CHAPTER 18

"How do I look," Briar asked hesitantly.

Dex turned with two cups of coffee, almost dropping one.

She was too beautiful, too breathtaking. It pained him to think of all the idiot boys she'd come into contact with.

When Dex took too long to answer, "It's the dress, right? It's overdoing it on the first day. I'll be right back."

"Briar, stop." Dex walked toward her and handed her a cup of coffee, their fingers brushing with the exchange. "We're already running late, and you need to eat something."

"I'm too nervous to eat, and I already told you, I can walk," she said, quickly beginning to chug the molten lava of caffeine.

"It's your first day, I'll take you."

Briar rolled her eyes. "Are you going to make me hold a sign and take my picture? Are you going to cry when I get out of the truck? Did you pack me a lunch with a sweet note? Did you—"

"Damnit! It's just a fucking ride."

"Fine, Dex. I'll eat a muffin and we can go." Briar made her way past him into the kitchen. Upon seeing the time on the oven, she began stuffing the blueberry overloaded goodness. With a nearly full mouth, "You never answered."

Dex rubbed the back of his neck, lately feeling more frustrated. "Answer what?"

Briar held out her arms and twirled around. "How do I look?"

126

Did he really have to answer that? If he told her what he really thought, things would get awkward fast.

"You look nice." He watched as the expectant look on her face washed away.

Briar finished off the remainder of her coffee, washing down the muffin. "I have to get my bag and then we can leave."

Dex knew he should have left it alone, but he couldn't stop himself from reaching for her wrist when she walked past him, heading toward her room.

Briar's eyes immediately shot down to the contact. Dex's hand was much larger than her own. Looking at it wrapped around her wrist, she knew he could snap it in an instant if he chose to; however, his grasp was different. He held her softly, like he was afraid if he put too much pressure, he might break her.

It was only when their eyes met, and he had Briar's attention, that Dex dropped his hand, breaking the contact that didn't seem innocent at all.

There was something in his intense eyes that Briar couldn't place. He looked like he was in pain, like there was a war in his head. She didn't expect his next words, which only created a war of her own in her heart.

"You look pretty," Dex managed, pleased when he saw Briar's eyes widen in surprise and happiness.

He still didn't know enough about her past, but he had a feeling that she hadn't heard that lately, and she needed to. He wanted to tell her so much more; however, there would always be things he couldn't and shouldn't say to her.

"Thank you," Briar said, trying her best not to combust with the way Dex was looking at her.

She figured that he meant it as a simple compliment, and she shouldn't read into it; unfortunately, her silly little heart told her differently.

The entire ride to school, her thoughts were still on that stupid compliment. It wasn't just his words. It was the way he looked at her. There had to be more that he wasn't saying. She thought back to the week prior when she kissed him on his cheek. He never said that it was inappropriate or overly affectionate, and now, she couldn't help but wonder what would happen if she pressed for something more.

Sadly, for once in her life, she wished she would have had more experience. She had never kissed a boy. What in the hell was she thinking? There was no way that she'd ever have the courage to kiss Dex, and regardless of what he said or the way he looked at her, she was all but certain that he'd never cross that line either.

Awakening Briar from her thoughts, "What time do you get out today?"

"The work program doesn't start until next week, so four every day this week."

"Okay, I guess I can—"

"No," Briar interrupted, already knowing where Dex was going. "I'm a big girl."

Dex scoffed at her phrasing. She was a hundred pounds soaking wet.

"Just because I'm small doesn't mean I'm a child. I'm capable of walking."

"You'll come to the shop after?"

Briar shrugged. "If you want me to. I won't get much time in."

Dex shouldn't have asked her. He honestly didn't expect her to work that afternoon. He didn't know how it felt to be in a new town, going to a new school, not knowing anyone. He imagined it might be draining and stressful. He didn't tell her, but he really wanted her to come by so that he wouldn't have to wait until that evening to see how her day was.

* * *

Briar wasn't surprised by how the day went. Though she had never really been a new kid, she saw how they got treated at the academy. Several of the girls looked at her like she was competition, while she was certain that there were boys giving her looks of interest. She didn't let either bother her. She had developed a tough skin recently. If she didn't make friends over the next three to four months, it wasn't going to be the end of the world. It would only make leaving Argent Falls that much easier.

"Briar, right," a boy next to her, in the one class she really had left to take, asked.

Briar looked at him suspiciously. It was a small town, therefore, a small school. She was pretty sure that by second period, everyone knew the name of the *new girl*.

"Hi," was all she said in response. Already two boys had awkwardly hit on her. She didn't want to project anything encouraging this person to do the same. The last thing she was looking for was dating.

"Sorry, I'm not some creeper," he began, leaning across his desk a little more toward her. "My dad told me about you, something along the lines of cute blonde, occasionally defiant and snappy attitude."

Briar looked to the boy speaking. Boy was putting it mildly. He was large and muscular, clean cut light brown hair, and golden eyes that reminded Briar of a dark sunset. He was one of the cuter guys she had come across.

He held out his hand, "Liam."

Briar let out a breath and took his hand, shaking it. "Benji's son."

Liam chuckled. "Yeah." He ran his hand through his hair after the handshake. "I suck when meeting people for the first time."

"Better than some of my encounters today."

"Are we that bad," Liam joked.

The left side of Briar's lips tilted. "Some more than others."

Throughout the first day lecture, Liam made small talk with Briar. At the academy, that would have been an immediate detention; however, the teacher didn't seem to mind at all.

Halfway through, Briar felt her phone go off in the pocket of her dress. That was the whole reason she had bought the dress. Pockets!

Her heart raced as she reached for it. There were only two people in her contacts, Dex and Rita.

Dex: How's it going?

Briar: As good as a first day as the new girl can go.

Dex felt a little bad for Briar. Most of her friends in Argent Falls were much older than her. She spent her summer working and hadn't done anything that a typical teenager should have done.

He knew she was in class and didn't want to bother her, so he dismissed the comment. He'd wait until later that evening.

Dex: Are you sure I can't pick you up?

Briar: It's a twenty minute or so walk to the shop. No!

Liam chuckled beside her.

"Are you reading my texts?"

He put his hands up in defeat. "Sorry. Curiosity and all."

"It's fine," Briar grumbled.

"Dex is a little overprotective, huh?"

Briar looked at Liam with a narrowed expression. She didn't intend on getting close enough to anyone in the school for them to know her situation.

"Sorry, again. My dad mentioned that you live with Dex."

Briar had a funny feeling that nothing was a secret in Argent Falls.

Changing the subject, "If you want, I can give you a ride to the shop after school. I don't usually visit my dad during work." Just then the bell rang, signaling the end of the period. "But I could make an exception. After all, it is the first day." Nodding to Briar's shoes, "And those don't look the most comfortable."

The shoes did have a bit of a heel on them, but it was nothing she couldn't manage. In her lifetime, she had worn much worse.

Liam seemed nice, and knowing that he was Benji's son made her less skeptical of his motivations. As they began to leave the classroom, Briar didn't hesitate exchanging numbers.

"Awesome," Liam said when Briar handed back his phone after putting her number in it. "I'll text you at the end of the day to let you know where to find me."

"Thank you. That's very nice of you."

"I promised my dad I'd keep an eye out for you. It's cool we're in a class together."

Aww. Briar had no idea Benji talked about her outside of work. She remembered the first time she met him, and found herself smiling. They hadn't gotten off to the best of starts.

* * *

Dex felt a different feeling running through his veins when the door from the waiting room opened and Briar stepped into the garage. Seeing her made him want to smile, and he didn't smile.

Then a person entered behind her, and a whole different feeling took over.

"Liam! What the hell are you doing here," Benji shouted jokingly at his son from far across the garage.

Liam started toward his dad, as Briar slowly headed to Dex.

"I see you met Liam," were the first words out of Dex's mouth.

"Yeah. We actually have a class together," Briar informed him.

Dex continued to tighten something under the hood of a car, not giving Briar his full attention. He shouldn't feel the way he did, but seeing her standing there for just a second with Liam, made him realize just how messed up he was.

She and Liam looked good together, like they belonged. Dex had no doubt that Briar was one of the prettier girls in her grade, and Liam…He wouldn't admit that another guy looked good, but from conversations with Benji, Liam could have his pick of the school.

"What do you want for dinner tonight?"

"Nothing special," Briar answered. Dex didn't say anything, and Briar wondered if he had a crappy day. "Do you want me to watch the desk?"

"No. I'll be out of here by six. You can go home and relax or whatever."

When Briar didn't say anything, from under the hood of the car, Dex tilted his head to face her. Her expression was serene, at ease. Above all, she looked calmly happy. He thought over his words, wondering what he just said to cause that.

He tightly closed his eyes and looked away, frustrated with himself. That was the first time he called his place *home* to her. His heart pounded, wondering what she thought of that. Though she didn't correct him, her sharp words to Lexi echoed in his head. They still haunted him.

I don't call anywhere home.

✳ ✳ ✳

"I can help, you know," Briar insisted, hovering in the kitchen. "Pasta is pretty hard to mess up."

"Yeah? I once thought bacon was hard to fuck up," Dex retorted.

"Ugh! They told you that too?"

Dex laughed. He found himself doing that more and more when he was around Briar. "I don't get it. You can do all this fancy baking crap, but you can't cook to save your life."

"It's different!" Briar cocked an eyebrow. "You know, instead of teasing me, you could just teach me."

Dex gripped the handle of the knife so hard, he thought he might shatter it. Though she was talking about cooking, that statement alone sent his mind to other places. He quickly changed the subject.

"Did you meet anyone interesting today?"

Briar popped one of the raw mushroom slices in her mouth. "Not really. Well...I mean, there's Liam."

"He's a good kid."

Briar watched Dex carefully as he began making a creamy white sauce. "He seems nice. I like him."

Dex looked up and waited for Briar to quit tinkering with the hair tie on her wrist. "So, you two hit it off?"

Briar searched Dex's eyes, but they gave nothing away. She twirled her hair and finally pulled it into a ponytail. "I think he'll be a nice friend to have."

"That's all?"

Briar chuckled. "Yeah."

"I mean, you just met him and you'd rather he give you a ride than me. That says something," Dex cautiously pointed out.

Briar hopped down from the stool across the counter and entered the kitchen. She held out her hand for Dex to turn over the whisk. She rolled her eyes at his reluctancy. "I can stir a sauce." When he finally handed the instrument to her, "It says that I didn't want to be a bother to you. I also know that I can't expect you to take care of everything for me. It was just a ride from school."

Dex threw the mushrooms into a skillet. "You're not a bother."

"Regardless, don't get any ideas with Liam and I. Dating is the last thing I'm worried about, and I also know how guys are with fresh meat."

"Oh, yeah?"

Briar gave him a quick glance and just the smallest chuckle before she turned her attention back to the sauce. "Yeah. Trust me, Liam wasn't the only guy that talked to me today. Thankfully, he was the only nice and normal one."

Dex gave Briar his best *what-the-fuck* look, to which she ignored, changing the subject.

He made a mental note to never ask her about the guys at her school ever again. If he did, he was pretty sure he'd end up at some horny teenager's house, which would only result in jail time.

CHAPTER 19

Meanwhile…

Two hundred miles away.

Portia sipped on her third glass of vodka while Leo sat nearby, tinkering away on a computer.

He let out a sigh. "I still can't find anything."

"Did you get her phone back," Portia asked, gulping down another swallow of the fiery liquid.

"Yes. It was restored back to factory settings and she took the sim card with her."

"What about her friends," Portia pressed.

Leo hated that she asked the same questions over and over. He had come into contact with several of Briar's so-called friends. Most of them said how she had become distant since her father's death. The ones that she did still talk to on a daily basis informed him that she simply fell of the face of the earth. They hadn't heard from her in months.

"Mom," Leo sighed. He walked to the bar on the other side of the dining room and poured himself a drink. Though he was only twenty, his mother didn't care. "I've looked into everything. All of her social media has been disabled or deleted. No one knows anything."

Portia slammed her empty glass down on the table, clearly frustrated. "She can't just disappear. Anyone can be found today. She has no family, no money. I don't understand it! I thought she'd come crawling back after a day."

"Maybe something did happen to her."

Portia let out an evil laugh. "I can only pray." She stood and walked to the massive glass windows leading to the patio. "Sadly, right now she's only missing. I can't get the money with her being classified as *missing* or a *runaway*. I need her dead body found."

"And if she's alive?"

Portia turned to face her son. He knew the look in her eyes well. She held that look for many years when it came to matters concerning Briar.

"Then she won't be for long." Her voice was raspy and broken from the alcohol.

Leo didn't want to point out the obvious, already knowing that's what had gotten his mother stirred up. "Is this about her birthday coming up?"

"Yes," Portia growled. "I don't think she knows about the money, but we need to find her before anyone else."

Leo lit a cigarette. Portia had long given up on her objections to them.

Portia glared at her son, but it wasn't the smoking that she found annoying. "You just had to go there."

"You never cared when I hit her," he said with a shrug, blowing out a breath of smoke.

"You just better be thankful that she ran away and didn't go to the cops."

"Lawyers would have taken care of it," Leo pointed out.

"Yes, you little dipshit. I would have had to spend a fortune to keep you out of prison because you couldn't control a sick urge for that trash," Portia screamed.

"Okay, okay...I'm trying to help you here," Leo groaned, taking another drag of his cigarette. "I'm trying to help the both of us."

"I just can't believe she'd give up on that fancy education."

"She only had one or two more classes. She could have done those over the summer at the academy," Leo pointed out.

Portia glared at him. He knew what she was thinking. Briar would have done that, had he not been the one to screw up.

"Wait," Leo gasped. "You're right. She wouldn't throw her education away. She's too smart for that. I also don't think she'd be satisfied with a GED."

Portia walked back to grab her glass from the table. She didn't need another drink, but she was going to indulge in one anyway. "What are you saying?"

"I might need some money for a bribe."

At that, Portia loosened the now closed cap and poured just a pinch more. "Stop being a cryptic little shit and tell me what you're thinking."

"If Briar enrolled in a school, she'd have to get her papers transferred from the academy here for her records."

Leo felt relief when his mother turned, a very full glass in her hands, and a smile plastered across her face. "I don't care how much. If those documents were transferred, you find out where."

CHAPTER 20

"Homework," Dex asked from the kitchen.

Briar sat up on the couch and stretched. "Nope. Working on something for you," she said sweetly.

Dex grunted in response.

"School here is easy. I've got A's in all my classes. Not that you need to worry about my grades anyway," Briar pointed out. She didn't like when Dex was concerned in ways that pointed out their age difference. "Dinner smells great," she quickly added, changing the subject away from school.

"It's just stew."

He always said it was *just* something, but the fact that he cooked nearly every night was something that Briar found insanely attractive.

"Well, when you get to a stopping point, I'd like to show you something."

Dex turned the burner on low and put a lid on the pot. He pressed himself into the counter and watched Briar from across the open space.

At first it was strange having her on his couch. Then it was even weirder when he turned the extra room into her bedroom. Now? Now she belonged there. There were still times where they got too close for his liking, but he managed to tamp down any inappropriate thoughts as soon as they reared their ugly head.

Briar couldn't help but stare as Dex strolled toward her on the couch. He wore a cleaner pair of jeans and a fitted white t-shirt. He always looked incredible to her, and when he had on a shirt that tight, clinging to his shoulders and abs in the way it did, Briar had to fight with every thought imaginable to keep from touching him.

When Dex sat on the couch, Briar placed the laptop on the coffee table and scooted closer to him, making sure to keep just enough distance so they wouldn't touch.

"A website," Dex asked, quite stunned.

Briar laughed, and he hated it. He hated how chillingly beautiful that laugh sounded.

"It's not that hard. Trust me."

"I'm curious about this academy you went to."

Briar waved a hand. "Richie Rich school. Enough said."

More than anything, Dex hated how she hadn't opened up to him further. He still didn't know what happened after her father died, or how she ended up homeless when it appeared that she once had it all.

Briar rambled on. "The phone you gave me takes decent pictures, not the best; however, if you like this, I can get Liam to take better ones with his phone."

Dex rolled his eyes. He was glad that Briar had a friend, but…No. There didn't need to be a but. Briar had a friend her own age. That's something she needed.

Dex nudged her shoulder and Briar rocked from side to side. "Looks good," he finally said.

Briar went silent and tense. She felt warm all over, but sitting that close to Dex was unnerving. Her brain shouted at her to stop, to rethink what her heart was begging for.

"What's wrong," Dex asked, feeling a change in Briar.

Her mesmerizing green eyes met his, and he became painfully aware how close they were.

"I've never really done this," she quietly admitted, her face growing pink with embarrassment.

"It's really good."

Briar shook her head. She had a hard time thinking straight with the pounding of her heart. Dex had to be deaf not to hear it. "I'm not talking about the website."

Dex tilted his head, evaluating her. He had never seen her look so nervous and uncertain. "Then what are—"

His words were lost the moment Briar wrapped her arms around his neck and pulled herself up and into him, crashing her lips against his.

Dex didn't move; his mind had officially shut down. A second more and Briar realized what a mistake it was, getting no reaction from Dex. She pulled her face away, though left her hands around his hard and tense neck, their faces only a breath away.

Though it was difficult, they made eye contact, and each saw something in the other that hadn't been there before. Anger. Lust. Passion. Desperation.

Knowing that she'd probably never get the chance to touch Dex again, Briar brought her hands from around his neck and trailed down his chest. "I...I'm sorry," she sighed. Her eyes widened when she pulled her hands away, only for Dex to grab her wrists and pull her toward him, on his lap.

His lips came down on hers and it was different. Now he was very much into the kiss.

Dex's hands trailed from Briar's shoulder blades down her back, lightly digging into the flesh beneath the clothing. When his hands made it to her waist, he pulled her body farther into his, already painfully aware that her position on top of him was causing a growing physical response.

As Dex lightly bit at her bottom lip, Briar parted open for him, wanting, needing, so much more from the kiss. His tongue slowly slid inside, and she couldn't have stifled the moan of pleasure if she had tried. She pushed her chest against his, needing to feel every part of him on her, and dug her hands in thick dark hair she had only ever dreamed of touching.

Dex tangled their tongues together, greedily taking every breath from her. He brought one hand to the side of her face, lightly brushing along her cheek before tightening his grip and holding her into place, deepening the kiss to a barbaric level.

His other hand toyed with the area just where her shirt met her jeans, and slowly he dipped beneath the shirt. At first it was just his thumb feeling the skin of her waist, but when she moaned and rocked into him at the smallest amount of contact, he brought his entire hand under her shirt, gripping at her waist and sliding upward from the small of her back.

She rocked into him once more and he knew she could feel what she was doing to him. The pressure of her body, the heat rolling off in waves from between her legs, gave him an erection that was about to rip through his jeans.

Needing a breath, Briar pulled back, only slightly breaking away. "Dex," she breathed, her chest heaving against his.

When Dex looked into those eyes, the gravity of the situation hit him like a semi. Those were eyes that worked for him, lived with him; eyes that belonged to a seventeen-year-old high school student. He had just put his tongue down her throat, and currently, she was sitting on his very hard and prominent dick.

"Fuck," he hissed, shoving Briar off his lap and back to her side of the couch, swiftly standing.

He turned from her and attempted to adjust himself, desperately needing his body to calm down. He ran his hand through his hair in frustration, and when he did, there was a flash of Briar on top of him, digging and pulling at his hair.

He slammed his fist into the wall. "Fuck!"

Briar rose and cautiously walked toward Dex, who now seemed unable to look at her. She reached out for his arm, but her touch might as well have been lava melting his skin off, as he yanked away from her at first touch.

When Dex finally gave Briar his attention, there was a madness in his eyes she had never seen before. It went beyond angry.

"What's wrong," Briar asked, not understanding what happened. One minute his hands and mouth were all over her, and now he looked at her like the most disgusting thing he'd ever encountered.

"That," he screamed, gesturing toward the couch. He rubbed at his forehead. "That did not just happen!"

"Did I do something wrong?"

"Shit," Dex growled, remembering what she said before everything went to hell. "When you said you'd never...Damnit, Briar! Please tell me that wasn't—"

"My first kiss?"

"Fuck!"

Growing more confused and upset by the second, "Fine! I won't tell you that."

More curse words continued to fly out of Dex's mouth, and Briar backed away, letting him get out his frustration in the best way he knew how.

Suddenly, Dex became eerily calm. "This is my fault. I'm the adult. The second this started, I should have stopped it, not encouraged it."

Though his words hurt, rage was all Briar could feel. "Are you fucking kidding me right now?!"

Dex's eyes widened. He didn't know if he had ever seen her blow up like that.

"I'm not some stupid *child!* I knew what I wanted," she screamed.

Dex shook his head, he didn't want to, couldn't, believe that. "I have to go."

Before Briar could come up with anything further to say, her mind frozen with the loathing and fury rushing through it, Dex grabbed his keys off the counter, storming toward the door and slamming it behind him.

Briar couldn't stop the tears, feeling completely dejected.

✳ ✳ ✳

He should have gone to the shop to get his frustrations out, but alcohol had a much better way of making him forget. Thankfully, Rusty needed to get away from his sister, and was up for keeping Dex company.

"Are you going to tell me what this is about," Rusty finally asked, after an hour of small talk and three drinks later.

Dex glanced up with an unreadable expression, then back to his glass, twirling the liquid before taking another sip, trying to burn the taste of Briar from his mouth.

"I'm all for having a drink, but it's Tuesday," Rusty pointed out.

Dex rubbed at his eyes. "Things are just messed up."

"Need to be a little more specific," Rusty laughed. When Dex shot him a glaring look over his glass, "It's Briar isn't it."

"I don't want to talk about her," he growled.

"I'm not going to sit here and talk about feelings and shit with you. Shoot it straight. What happened?"

Dex sighed. His body still felt hers, which only made him want to claw at his skin. "We kissed," he admitted.

"Are you shitting me?!" Several patrons looked over, including a scowling Sandy from behind the bar. "You look like you've been put through a meat grinder, and you're drinking your ass off like it's the worst day of your life…All because of a kiss?"

"There are some lines that you don't cross."

Rusty shook his head and took a long swig of his beer. "If it's just her age, I'm going to tell you right now, you're being a little dramatic. She's not some kid you preyed on."

"The fact that you have to say that makes me feel disgusting."

"Cut the gentleman shit. We both know you're not," Rusty scoffed.

Dex motioned to one of the girls for another drink, knowing that he should have just stuck with beer like Rusty.

"She's too innocent," Dex blurted out.

143

Rusty narrowed his eyes and thought Dex's words over. He let out a breath, the comment registering. "She's inexperienced with guys," he asked, not wanting to use certain words.

Dex rubbed the back of his neck and waited until his next drink was in front of him and the waitress left. "She's never even kissed a guy before."

Rusty sucked in a breath. "Ah. Now that changes things a little."

Dex refrained from giving too many more details. He didn't vocalize his thoughts, but they were still there. Just a kiss wouldn't have been so bad. As soon as Briar pulled away and apologized, he should have brushed it off. Instead, he went too far, taking too much. The most haunting part was how good she felt, and even now, against his better judgment, he still wanted to feel her.

Rusty groaned, looking down at his phone. "My sister needs me to pick up some cough syrup before Walgreen's closes."

Dex gave him a nod.

"Let me take you home." It wasn't a question.

"I'm fine," Dex said. He wasn't. He knew he wouldn't be driving.

Rusty tried insisting to no avail, and ultimately gave up. He threw several bills on the table. "Just do me a favor." He waited until he had Dex's drunken attention. "Don't do anything stupid."

CHAPTER 21

Stupid.

Guilt made people do stupid things.

Alcohol made people do stupid things.

Dex was stupid to continue the kiss.

He was stupid to have gone to the bar.

He was stupid to get drunk.

He was stupid for entertaining Hannah once Rusty left.

* * *

Dex handed Hannah his keys before excusing himself to the restroom. He stared in the mirror at the sink, washing his hands, and an all too familiar figure appeared from the doorway.

"What the hell do you think you're doing?"

Dex shut off the faucet, shook some of the water from his hands, and wiped over his face. "Not tonight Sandy."

"You're seriously going to take home one of your ex's coworkers?"

Dex braced himself on the sink. He shouldn't have had that last drink. It was messing with his head, and he couldn't think straight.

"If you need to get laid, fine. Go home with Hannah. Don't take her to your place," Sandy insisted.

"So, now you're telling me where I can and can't screw?"

Sandy gave Dex such a sad look that Dex was forced to look away. "You're drunk, but we both know what you're doing."

"Yeah," Dex spat, growing agitated.

"Briar doesn't deserve that. She deserves better."

"No shit." He knew that, but he didn't know how to tell her, so instead, he'd show her.

Dex brushed past Sandy and through the hall, back toward Hannah. She was already waiting for him at the door.

"You good?"

Dex pulled her into him and pressed his lips to her neck. "I'm better than good."

Hannah let out at giggle and pushed the door open. Dex didn't find whatever that noise was cute, but by the time they got back to his apartment, he intended for her to be making other noises.

* * *

Briar remained huddled on the couch, tinkering away on her laptop. The clock in the bottom corner hit two in the morning.

She desperately wanted to text Dex, even if it would probably go unanswered; however, she was unsure what to say at this point. She didn't like the way he stormed out, and too many horrible thoughts ran through her head. She picked up her phone. There couldn't be much harm in asking him if he was okay.

Just as she clicked on his name from her past messages, there was a rattling of keys at the door, followed by a string of high-pitched giggles.

The door flung open and two connected bodies stumbled inside.

Briar closed her computer and pulled it to her chest, not believing what she was seeing in the dimly lit space.

Dex stumbled and hit the switch near the door, flooding the place with light.

Hannah pressed Dex against the door and fisted his t-shirt, pulling him downward and covering his mouth with hers. She let out a squeal when Dex grabbed her ass and pulled her into him, grinding their bodies together.

Hannah pulled away in a fit of tipsy giggles. She had a drink or two, but nothing compared to Dex. She took him by the hand and made her way through the unknown apartment. "Bedroom?"

Just as she asked the question, she froze, locking eyes with an unexpected someone on the couch.

"Uh…Dex?" She turned around, but Dex wasn't looking at her. He was glaring at the woman on the couch.

"The bedroom is down the hall."

Briar didn't speak. The guy in front of her was a stranger. He looked straight through her with eyes of glass. Just seeing his movements as he entered, Briar knew he was drunk. Kissing her was so terrible that his only option was to get drunk and bring home some random girl.

"Who is this," Hannah asked, only mildly concerned.

Dex never took his eyes from Briar. "My roommate."

"Really? If there's something else that I should–"

Dex cut Hannah off. "No. She's like a little sister."

Briar felt like throwing up. She hadn't eaten, simply put the stew Dex made in the fridge, so there wasn't anything to come out of her, but she was pretty sure that she was going to throw up.

"Nice to meet you," Hannah said, taking Dex's hand and dragging him down the hall, not even bothering to exchange names.

A strange combination of feelings ran through Dex with each step they took toward the bedroom. He hated seeing the hurt look on Briar's face, but with the hurt, he saw a hatred forming. That would be for the best.

As much as he wanted to help Briar, to keep her from living on the streets, he couldn't have her thinking of something more with him. Breaking her heart, having her see him as just another player, someone incapable of real attachment and commitment, that was what he needed to do. He was certain that tonight would stop anything from happening between them ever again. Briar looked like she didn't want to be under the same roof as him, much less touch him.

When Briar heard the bedroom door shut, a thud, and squeals and giggles from the woman in the neon pink dress, she lost it. She scrambled off the couch toward the balcony and yanked open the doors. She slammed them so hard behind her, she had to turn to make sure the glass hadn't cracked.

Briar fought to catch her breath, her head and heart an explosion of every bad feeling there was.

He could have done a million other things. He could have told her she was too young, as he often implied. He could have said he wasn't ready to move on. He could have told her he didn't have even the slightest romantic interest in her.

He didn't have to bring home some one-night stand. He didn't have to have his tongue down her throat, dragging her to his bedroom, when Briar could still smell his cologne on her.

Tears poured down her face. She told herself that it shouldn't hurt. She had only known Dex a couple months. They had no relationship, no attachment. What she couldn't tell herself was that their kiss meant nothing, because to her, it meant everything. For the first time in a long time, she had felt normal. Then he had to ruin it.

Briar gripped onto the railing and coughed. Not much came out. All she had in the last six hours was a glass of water.

Her knees felt too weak to stand anymore, and as much as she wanted to go inside and hide in the confines of her room, buried in her covers, she couldn't subject herself to that, knowing what they were doing, what she would hear.

Dex collapsed on the bed. The alcohol had done a number on him.

Hannah crawled on top of Dex, running her hands over every inch of his still clothed body. She straddled him, kissing at his neck and trailing her fingers down his well-defined abs. She grinded into him, searching.

"You don't know how bad I've wanted this," she moaned, beginning to tug at his shirt.

Dex lifted himself just enough for the shirt to come off and then fell back. She didn't need to tell him that. He knew. Most of Lexi's friends and coworkers had given him fuck me eyes during his time with her. While he might not have been the best boyfriend, he wasn't one to cheat, but he wasn't with Lexi anymore.

"I was so excited when I heard the two of you broke up. She's such a bitch anyway." Hannah lowered herself and nibbled on Dex's ear. "I promise you, I'm going to be so much better than her."

Dex desperately wanted her to stop talking. The more she talked, the more he thought. When he thought about breaking up with Lexi, someone else entirely came crashing through his thoughts.

Hannah slipped her hand between her legs, rubbing at Dex's crotch. After a few seconds, she paused. "Umm…Dex? You're not…I mean…"

Dex wiped his hand over his face. He didn't need her pointing it out. He already knew he wasn't going to be able to go through with it.

Hannah tugged at his belt. "I'll start with my mouth, then–"

Dex lightly pushed her off so that she tumbled to the side and onto the bed. "Fuck no."

He attempted to sit up and that's when he was absolutely certain he drank too much. Before he knew it, he was leaning over the bed, the whisky burning ten times more on its way up than it had on its way down.

Hannah flew off the bed. "Are you serious?!"

Dex already felt a headache coming on. "Just go home."

"Look, maybe when you've sobered up a little, we can try to–"

Annoyed and slightly embarrassed, Dex interrupted her. "Alcohol isn't the reason I can't get it up. It's you," he coldly replied.

Hannah stumbled backwards in her heels. Her jaw dropped with what he just said to her. "You bastard!"

✳ ✳ ✳

Briar pulled her head from her knees and looked through the glass doors. She could hear screams that sounded more like wailing.

Soon, Dex and the woman, fully clothed, appeared. Briar couldn't hear what they were saying, but the woman grabbed a book from the coffee table and hurled it at Dex. It sent a glimmer of satisfaction through Briar. Perhaps it would have been better had she actually hit him with it.

Briar wiped at her eyes, already feeling her lids puff up. She'd wear dark eye makeup when she got ready for school, which looked to be in a few hours. No one would see that she had spent the better part of her night in tears.

Finally, the door slammed, and when Briar looked through the glass doors, she saw Dex chugging a bottle of water.

Briar didn't think he could see her on the balcony in the darkness beyond the glass doors, but he had, and he looked at her with such hatred.

His mind told him to look away, but he couldn't. As soon as he left the room, he knew he'd be throwing up all the water he had just put down, and only partly because of the alcohol still running through his veins.

He could feel it. Hate.

He absolutely hated himself for how he chose to push Briar away.

CHAPTER 22

"Damn! You look like shit," Rusty screamed as he entered the shop.

Dex didn't know if Rusty really screamed, but it sounded like he did. How Dex managed to get to work before opening was a miracle.

Aside from being extremely hung over, and dealing with that, Dex also had to deal with the fact that he hadn't seen Briar that morning. He knew she didn't leave for good. Her suitcase and all her belongings were still there, including her laptop. Despite waking ungodly early for the way he felt, Briar must have woken earlier and left for school. He wasn't sure what time anything happened the night before, but she couldn't have gotten more than three or four hours of sleep. He knew that was his fault.

"What the hell do you think you're doing," Dex bellowed.

Rusty dumped Dex's coffee out and went into the office. Dex heard the refrigerator open and close with Rusty returning, a bottle of red liquid in his hand.

"You need to drink something without caffeine. Hydrate yourself," Rusty insisted, tossing the bottle at Dex.

"Yeah. Thanks, mom."

"Want to tell me what happened before Benji gets here," Rusty asked. "Like, how the hell did you make it home last night?"

There was no point in lying. Dex was sure her loud mouth would travel around town anyway. "Hannah."

Rusty went silent with the one-word answer.

"Ouch," Dex screamed, now standing from the stool and rubbing the back of his head. "What was that for?!"

"For being an idiot! Dude, please tell me you did not take her home and sleep with her."

"Well…" Dex hesitated. He hoped the alcohol would keep him from remembering anything, but it hadn't. "We didn't have sex."

"But you took her home," Rusty clarified, shaking his head. "Why?"

"I wasn't thinking," Dex admitted.

The truth was, he had thought; however, fueled with regret, guilt, lust, and alcohol, he hadn't made the best decision when it came to setting Briar straight about their situation.

Rusty wanted to ask him about Briar, but there was a dark and stormy cataclysm written in Dex's eyes that told him not to go there.

* * *

Briar sipped on a bottle of water at a lunch table alone. She strangely didn't mind being alone. Liam had told her that she could join him and his friends; however, his table consisted of the entire Argent Falls varsity football team. Alone was definitely more comfortable. Little did she know, that would change today.

When the girl sat in the chair directly across from Briar, Briar was taken by surprise. She had seen the girl before. She was in the calculus class that Briar was a teacher aide for. Overall, she was generally quiet and paid attention. If Briar had to lump her into a clique, she'd have to say this girl was more on the side of gothic rebel, rather, that's the vibe she got.

The girl had black hair, although looking at her eyebrows, Briar knew her original color was much lighter. She also had a few streaks of bright purple throughout. Her eye makeup was a bit overdone, the jet black making it difficult to see her eyes; although, Briar couldn't say much about that today. Hers was darker than she had ever worn, except for the few times she had to cover bruises.

The girl wore a purple and black plaid shirt with pants that had several pockets and decorative chains. Her feet completed the look with a dainty pair of combat boots.

After Briar stared for a moment too long, the girl finally spoke, a quirky smile forming on her lips. "I guess you're the girl who stole my sister's boyfriend."

Briar choked on her water. It definitely wasn't the greeting she was expecting.

"I'm sorry? I don't know what you're talking about."

The only guy she said more than a few words to was Liam. Liam never gave her any indication that he was seeing anyone, and though he was sweet, he never crossed any lines by flirting. They were absolutely and positively strictly friends.

The girl extended her hand and laughed, seeming friendly. "I'm Alyssa. I believe you know my sister, Lexi?"

Briar's eyes widened. Seriously? First of all, Argent Falls had to be smaller than 13,082. Secondly, the day after she kissed Dex, this?

Alyssa laughed. "I'm just messing with you." She leaned in and her voice dropped. "I thought it would be a funny introduction. Sorry if it wasn't."

"I'm...Uh...I'm Briar."

"I know. You're the teacher's aide for my calculus class. You must be really smart to have already taken that. Also, I'm pretty sure I've heard my sister screaming your name over phone calls with my mom," Alyssa rambled. "It was pretty hilarious, seeing her freak out with Dex inviting a homeless girl..." She stopped and thought. "Sorry, I shouldn't have said it like that."

"I didn't steal your sister's boyfriend," Briar clarified.

"I know. It was a bad introduction. Anyway, I'm sorry it took me so long to say something, but would you like to eat with Jordan and I," Alyssa asked, nodding to a nearby table with a redhead dressed in a strangely not so similar fashion to Alyssa.

"Wait...I thought..."

"You thought I'd hate you because of my sister," Alyssa laughed. "The opposite. My sister's a bit of a nutjob. At least this year at Thanksgiving, I won't have to listen to her describe her perfect engagement ring." Alyssa finished the comment with a gagging sound.

Had they been friends, Briar would have pressed on. Dex didn't give serious vibes when it came to his relationship with Lexi. Had they been thinking about marriage, or was it all one sided? Briar shook the thought. Lexi was the second to last person she wanted on her mind, and Dex currently held the top spot.

"So, want to sit with us?"

Briar nodded and grabbed her bag and water bottle. She should have eaten something, especially after missing dinner the night before, and leaving early, skipping breakfast; however, her stomach didn't feel hungry, and her mouth was still dry and sore from crying the night before. She really didn't have the effort for much more than a sip of water.

After weeks of settling in at the school, adjusting to being alone and just getting through to December, she finally felt a happiness she didn't expect. Alyssa and Jordan were extremely nice and welcoming, even admitting that they were a little hesitant about approaching Briar.

It was the highlight of a day that started off horribly.

✳ ✳ ✳

Shortly after lunch, Dex's phone went off. After ignoring the call once, due to messy hands, he decided to answer it on the second string of rings.

He wiped his hands on a nearby rag and pulled the phone from the back of his jeans. It was a local number, however, unrecognizable to him.

"Hello?"

"Is this...Mr. Dexter Hayden," a soft-spoken woman asked.

"Yeah."

"Hello. This is Georgia Webber. I'm the nurse here at Argent Falls High School."

Dex's mind went blank, and though he had mostly recovered from his hangover, short of a headache, he suddenly felt sick. Why in the world was the nurse at Briar's school calling him of all people?

"What's this about," he asked.

"Briar Stone? You're listed as her emergency contact. I regret to inform you..."

Dex wasn't sure he was hearing things right. His heart skipped a beat hearing that Briar listed him as her emergency contact; however, it dawned on him that the call then meant that there was an emergency.

Benji was helping a customer at the front desk when Dex stormed through, rushing to the office to grab his keys.

"I'll be back later," he hollered at Benji.

"Whoa, boss. Is everything okay?"

Dex didn't turn as he sprinted toward the front door. "Briar passed out at school. I have to go pick her up."

When Dex got in the truck, his headache and tiredness disappeared and all he felt was worry. Despite the school being a short drive away, a twenty minute or so walk for Briar, he didn't bother following one speed limit.

The receptionist scanned his driver's license and had him sign in before giving him a visitor pass to proceed.

After seven years, he still knew the school well.

He opened the door to the nurse's office and was greeted with the familiar voice of Georgia Webber. She looked like she was nearing retirement; however, Dex was positive that she wasn't the nurse when he attended school.

"Hello," she said in a quiet and meek voice. "You must be Briar's guardian, Mr. Hayden?"

Dex grit his teeth at that. "Dex," he corrected, extending his hand, still heavily smeared with oil.

As he shook the school nurse's hand, a familiar laugh from behind one of the curtains hit him like a ton of bricks.

There were three small rooms, all with a cot and a chair. They weren't even rooms, more like little inserts covered by a curtain.

"She's right over here," Georgia said, pointing to the only insert with the curtain pulled shut. "A couple of her friends insisted on staying," she added, shaking her head. "They need to head back to class."

Dex's stomach turned to knots when the curtain opened and he saw Briar on the bed, her knees to her chest and her back pressed against the wall. She was sipping on a bottle of water and munching on a pack of crackers.

Of all the people, she sat shoulder to shoulder next to Liam. It sent a shooting pain through Dex at how good they looked together. If that wasn't enough to screw with him, in the chair beside the bed sat a girl he had met on several occasions, Lexi's little sister.

Argent Falls was too damn small.

CHAPTER 23

"You didn't have to check me out. The nurse said I could stay there until the end of the day. Liam was going to take me back to the apartment," Briar informed Dex once they were out of the school and walking to the parking lot.

"It's fine. This way you can get some rest."

When they got to his truck, Briar reached out to open her door, but Dex's hand landed on the handle first, and she quickly pulled away, not wanting to come into contact with him.

Dex could tell she was annoyed that he opened the door for her. After last night, he was probably the last person she wanted to see.

Once Briar got in, Dex threw her bag at her feet, having insisted on carrying it.

The drive to his place wouldn't take long, but Dex had too many questions that couldn't wait. Briar seemed content on not speaking, sitting with her arms crossed and staring out the window.

Dex didn't know where to begin, none of his questions would be light topics of conversation.

"So, you and Alyssa are friends?"

Briar sighed, wishing Dex would have continued the drive in silence. "I don't know. She only asked me to sit with her at lunch today. We were walking to class when..." Briar let her sentence drift off. She didn't feel like telling Dex more than she had to.

Dex knew what she was about to say, but that was going to be a huge conversation that needed to wait until they were back home. "You know she's Lexi's—"

Briar cut him off. "Sister. Yes."

Dex clenched and unclenched the steering wheel. Speaking with Briar had never been this difficult.

Briar wanted to tell Dex about Alyssa's introduction, but decided against it. She didn't want to be friendly with him, and that was something that she would inevitably have to laugh about, and she didn't want to laugh.

As soon as they parked at the apartment building, Briar threw her door open and grabbed her bag. She could hear Dex's footsteps close behind her.

A part of her wanted to be childish. If he could be immature, she should have the chance to be as well.

Briar quickly stepped into the elevator and slammed her palm on the button for the sixth floor. Once it lit up, she rapidly tapped at the button to close the doors, not wanting to be in that tight space with Dex, even if it was only a handful of seconds.

Sadly, she didn't get that wish.

Dex's arm collided with the closing doors, shoving them back open. He didn't step inside right away, and when Briar looked up, she wished that she wouldn't have. Dex's lips were tilted on one side more than the other, smirking at her.

As much as it tore at his insides to see the hatred in her beautiful and ridiculously green eyes, a deeper part welcomed it. If she hated him, that meant she'd keep her distance, making it easier for him to do so as well. Unfortunately, that also meant that their living situation might be a bit unbearable for the time being.

He stepped inside and let the doors close on their own. A flashback from the night before came over him. He had slammed Hannah around every inch of the elevator as she licked and kissed any part of him not covered with clothing. The memory made him sick to his stomach.

Dex kept up with Briar when they got off the elevator, knowing that as soon as they entered the apartment, she'd lock herself in her room.

He reached the door first and unlocked it. Briar rocked on her heels impatiently. Dex slowly began to open it, but when Briar took a step forward to enter, he stopped, gripping the handle tightly so that she couldn't push it open.

"Let me in," Briar huffed.

"Are you going to talk about what happened at school today?"

"None of your business."

Dex closed the entry door and put his back against it, blocking Briar from the handle. "You made it my business when you put me down as your guardian."

"Correction! I put you down as an emergency contact, not my *guardian*," Briar spat.

Dex shrugged. "I don't see much of a difference."

"If you're not going to let me in, in hopes that I'll talk to you, I'm leaving." Not waiting for a response, Briar turned back in the direction they had just come.

She stopped, and for a tiny moment forgot how to breathe. The warmth of Dex's hand lightly gripping her wrist was enough to make her melt, but after last night, she couldn't. Dex was nothing more than a crack on her heart, something that should have never been there, a stupid decision because she allowed herself to finally feel. That wouldn't happen again.

She yanked her wrist from his grasp.

Dex rolled his eyes and moved to open the door. "You don't have to be so childish."

That comment struck more than a nerve and as soon as they both walked in the apartment and Dex closed the door, Briar stepped into his personal space and jabbed her finger at his chest.

"Don't you even start with that! If you want to talk about childish, we can start with your behavior last night."

This time when Briar turned, now headed toward her room, Dex didn't stop her, didn't say a word. They both knew he couldn't.

✳ ✳ ✳

Dex didn't go back to work that afternoon. Rusty and Benji had keys to the shop, and both were capable of locking it up. He also didn't bother Briar in hopes that she was getting some rest; however, shortly before five, she surprised him.

Briar stumbled through the hallway and into the common area. She was smoothing down a ponytail and twisting a hair-tie around the mess. Dex was further confused that she had changed shirts and was now wearing the black polo of Chêne Bar and Grille.

Briar didn't say anything to Dex when she walked past the living room and to an entry table. She grabbed her key and tucked it in her pocket.

"Where do you think you're going," Dex asked.

Startled, Briar spun around, only to find Dex looming over her, far closer than he should have been. Sensing her panic, he took a step back.

"I'm on the schedule tonight," Briar informed him.

Dex went around her and leaned into the front door. "You need to rest."

"No, Dex. I need to get to work. I'm running late."

Dex crossed his arms, not moving from the door. "We still haven't talked."

Briar didn't say anything in response. She'd simply have to be late, because there was no way she was talking to Dex. He'd eventually have to give in and let her leave.

Seeing that Briar was going to be stubborn, Dex pulled his phone from his back pocket and tapped at the screen, then held it to his face.

Briar could hear the faint ringing through the speaker. She couldn't imagine who he needed to call right now at this moment, when all she really needed him to do was move.

Dex smiled when the voice answered. "Hey, Rita. How's it going?"

Briar's jaw dropped. She reached up for the phone, only for Dex to pull back and put his forearm out, blocking her. It didn't help that he had about an extra foot of height on her.

"That's great," Dex said to Rita's rambling. "I was just calling to let you know that Briar got sick at school today...Yeah...I'll tell her...Of course...I'll make sure she's taken care of...Talk to you later."

As soon as Dex ended the call, "You asshole! I don't care if you're co-owner of half the damn town. You have no business interfering like that."

"I also have no business getting a call from the school that you've passed out. Are we going to talk about that?"

Briar threw her arms up. "I got weak, so what?"

"When was the last time you ate?" When Briar didn't answer him, Dex repeated himself.

"I don't know," she sighed. "Breakfast yesterday."

Dex let his head fall back into the door and let out a groan. He ran his hand down his face in frustration.

"Look, I get it. Yesterday and today were very stressful and I didn't feel like eating."

"Damnit, Briar! You can't do shit like that," Dex yelled without meaning to.

It only made Briar that much angrier. "Oh, shut up! I don't see why you're acting like you care!"

Dex stepped forward, his eyes melting into hers. "Because I do."

Those three words nearly killed Briar. Dex confused her in every way imaginable. His definition of care wasn't the one she wished for the day before, and as nice as it was to have someone who cared if she was alive, it hurt that deep down she still wanted more from Dex.

Dex didn't want to ask, but he had to. "Do you have an eating disorder?"

Briar should have known that was coming. She turned from Dex and went toward the living room, plopping down on the far corner of one of the couches, already exhausted. Dex followed and sat on the opposite side of the same couch.

"No, Dex. I don't have an eating disorder." Briar turned her head, unable to look at him. "I missed lunch yesterday at school because I wanted to finish some assignments I had been given that morning. Then I missed dinner because…" She paused, and thought carefully. Bringing up the evening and night before was too awkward. "Well, I just did. I wanted to get out of here early in the morning–"

Dex cut her off. "To avoid me."

"Honestly, yes."

He didn't expect her to outright say it, but he was glad that she could be blunt and forward.

"I didn't get much sleep either. I was just drained."

There was silence that followed. Dex stared at Briar. She looked out the glass doors to the balcony. The few times she made eye contact with him, she appeared scared and uneasy.

As difficult as it was, it had to be said. It wasn't something they could never address, pretending like it didn't happen.

"Briar, can you look at me?"

Briar let out a deep breath. She didn't want to, but she wasn't going to act like a hurt child. She turned so that her body faced Dex, and allowed her eyes to meet his.

"About yesterday," he began.

Briar could already feel a sickness making its way in her stomach.

Dex ran his hand over the back of his tense neck, already sensing how awkward the conversation was going to be. "I just need to say that I'm sorry."

Briar blinked a few times but said nothing at first. Without meaning to, her eyes fell from Dex's and to his lips. Memories of something that seemed so long ago flooded her imagination, a want and need growing inside her. She quickly brought her eyes back to his.

"For what?"

"For…Everything. All of it." It wasn't the answer he wanted to say, but it's the one he had to say.

"Okay," was all Briar said in response.

That couldn't be the end of it, that much was certain to Dex. No woman ever left something that big with an *okay*. He wished it all could have been solved, swept away, and forgotten right then and there. He hated feeling that this conversation would come back up.

When Dex said nothing more, Briar decided it was best to go back to her room. As much as she wanted to go to work, she could go with a bit of a nap before dinner.

She wasn't more than a couple feet past Dex when she stopped. Although it wasn't much, Dex got to say what he needed to, and he appeared content with it. Briar, however, wasn't.

"No, Dex. You know what, that hurt."

Dex stayed in his place on the couch. If he got up, he wasn't sure what he'd do.

"Was it so horrible?"

Dex narrowed his eyes. "What are you talking about?" He really hoped she wasn't asking what he was thinking, because there were only two answers, and he couldn't give her either.

Briar could feel her hands shaking. She knew Dex wanted to avoid the mentioning of the kiss just as much as she did, but she'd never be able to get past it if she didn't say anything. It wasn't something they could pretend never happened.

"Was kissing me so terrible that you had to get shitfaced and screw the first woman you could pick up?"

"Briar," Dex warned.

"No. I get it. You want to pretend it never happened." She shook her head and took a deep breath. "I can't do that. I'll always remember that my first kiss was so bad that the guy immediately needed to wash it down with alcohol and a cheap hooker."

163

Dex realized that he had misread Briar. He had no idea the amount of venom she had running in her blood. Though she was insulting him, he couldn't help but find her boldness attractive. If he were a dumber man, with less self-control, she had a fire that he could have thrown himself into.

There were only two ways to answer. One would hurt her even further, but the other would give her a hope that he couldn't allow; therefore, he avoided the question altogether.

"Briar, you're not stupid. You have to know that what happened between us was a mistake, poor judgment on both our parts."

Briar dug her nails into her palms. If that's how he wanted to leave it, she had no choice. "I know." She then turned back around and went to her room.

Dex's heartbeat quickened. So often, her eyes gave her away. This was one of those times. Though she agreed with him, he could tell that it was a lie on her part. She looked at him like he was a sad and pathetic man, a coward, because to her, it hadn't been something spur of the moment and random.

That was the most dangerous part of it all. He saw that it wasn't a mistake to her.

CHAPTER 24

Eventually, the days blurred into weeks, and before Briar knew it, it was already the beginning of October. Things with Dex were simple enough. They spoke, but the conversations were always surface level, generally about work and school. She noticed that he got excited whenever he could talk about his main renovation project, a ninety-year-old Bentley; therefore, she made it a point to ask about it often.

Dex had stopped trying to pry, but Briar noticed that there were times he became skeptical, and why wouldn't he be? At one point she had the perfect life, top of the line schooling, gifted and well-off parents. Of course, he'd wonder how she got to where she was. Thankfully, he never pushed for answers.

The best part of everything for Briar, finding a home in school. Despite not wanting to, she did end up making friends, Liam, Alyssa, and Jordan.

When the calculus teacher, Mrs. Reynolds, found out that Briar could do more than grade papers with an answer sheet, she asked Briar to assist her after lessons, when the students were going over the skills presented for that day. While Briar had no desire to pursue anything related to the field of teaching, she did enjoy helping her fellow classmates. At first, she favored Alyssa when it came to that time; however, as the days went on, and more students raised their hand for help, she ended up eventually meeting everyone in the class.

This also led to a strange predicament that Briar was hesitant in bringing up with Dex.

Briar handed the keys and receipt to the last customer of the day. The clock on the wall read just a few minutes shy of five.

"Are you working at the restaurant tonight," Dex asked, coming from the office with a bottle of water.

He didn't appear finished for the day. There were many days lately where he worked after hours on his personal projects.

Briar tried to ignore Rusty and Benji as they entered from the garage, preparing to call an end to the day. "No, I'm not."

"Do you need a ride home? Or are you going to stay here for a while?"

There had been a few rare days where Briar hung back and worked on homework in the office, and once she even helped Dex in the garage. She still didn't know the names of half of the things he used, and she was pretty sure she only slowed him down.

"That's what I wanted to talk to you about," Briar cautiously began. "I have a friend outside waiting for me. I was wondering if it was okay if we went back to the apartment to study?"

Dex gave her an incredulous look. "Alyssa?"

There were two times that Dex could remember of Alyssa coming over. Both times Briar asked, although he insisted it wasn't necessary.

Then Briar said something surprising. "No."

Dex saw her become uncomfortable. "Liam?"

The name now drew the attention of Benji and Rusty.

"No."

Without knowing much more, "I told you, it's fine if you have friends over. What's her name?"

Briar bit her lip and grabbed her backpack from beneath the reception desk. It shouldn't have felt awkward, but somehow it did. "Bradley."

Dex could feel the eyes of Rusty and Benji on him. He gave no reaction. "Haven't heard you mention him before."

"He's in the calculus class that I'm a teacher's aide for. He asked if I could tutor him outside of class," Briar said with a simple shrug.

Dex cringed at her wording. Though she meant it innocently enough, it sent too many other images through his mind, none of which had anything to do with calculus.

"Yeah, that's fine."

Briar was surprised. For some reason, Dex gave off this alpha vibe, and she couldn't imagine that he'd be okay with her having a boy over. "Awesome! Thanks," she quickly said, heading for the door. She was afraid if she stuck around much longer Dex would change his mind.

"Seriously?"

Dex turned to Rusty. "Yeah. If she wants a friend over for studying, I'm not going to stop her."

Rusty narrowed his eyes and looked Dex over. "I'm not buying it."

"Same," Benji grumbled. "Anyway, see you guys tomorrow." He threw his hand up and walked toward the door.

Rusty waited for Benji to leave before continuing. "You're okay with her having some dude in your apartment, all alone?"

Dex forced a laugh. "Don't make it sound so sordid."

"Sordid? When did you start using words like that?"

Dex ignored Rusty. Okay, so Briar was gradually rubbing off on him. Changing the subject, "Your shift is over. You're free to go at any time."

"I was going to see if you needed any help with the restoration."

"I'm good, but thanks."

Rusty watched Dex carefully; something about him seemed off. There was an agitation there that hadn't been earlier. "How late do you plan on working?"

"I don't know. I've had a long day. I might—"

"I knew it," Rusty screamed, nearly jumping up and down. "You jealous bastard," he laughed. "You have no intention of letting Briar be alone with some guy."

"Fuck off," Dex growled. He dropped the calm and cool act he thought he was putting on nicely. "And I'm not jealous," he added.

"Whatever you need to tell yourself to sleep at night…In a place…That you share…With someone you're *clearly* not attracted to."

"If you're done, I need to lock up," Dex replied. He was not going to engage in any further conversation with Rusty about Briar.

Things between he and Briar were fine, normal, consistent. Ever since the kiss, they managed to keep things platonic. The only time they were ever in close proximity was when they ate together or when Dex gave her rides to and from school and work.

Whatever they had going between them was nice, simple, easy. Now she had to go and invite some dumb high school idiot over.

It was like a blow to the gut when he unlocked the door and heard her laughter. In the last few weeks, he hadn't heard it much. While it filled him with happiness, it made him sick, knowing that he wasn't the one making her laugh.

Dex ran his hand through his hair, and took a deep breath. He couldn't have those thoughts.

As soon as he became visible, Briar's eyes latched to his in shock.

She and Bradley were sitting at the dining table, their chairs pushed fairly close together, with a book and some worksheets between them on the table.

Briar was confused at first. She didn't expect Dex to be home until later. When she got to the shop that afternoon, he had specifically told her that.

"Dex. Hi. I thought you had to work."

"Tired," was all he said.

He looked the boy over; however, boy was an understatement. To Dex, he looked like some college fraternity turd. More so, he looked too happy to be working on calculus.

"Hi…Uh…Mr. Hayden." Bradley politely pushed out his chair and stood. He walked around the table to Dex and extended his hand. "I'm Bradley."

Dex didn't think much of it, and didn't see why the guy would bother trying to suck up to him.

"Dex," Dex responded, taking his hand and giving it a firm shake.

168

"It's nice to meet you," Bradley said, once they dropped contact. "Briar didn't tell me I'd be meeting her brother, so—"

"What?"

At that, Briar jumped out of her chair and joined the two. She placed her hand on Bradley's arm, getting his attention, and corrected him. "He's not my brother. I said he's *like* a brother."

Briar would be lying if she said she didn't get a little satisfaction at seeing the rage that came across Dex's face when Bradley made that comment.

"Oh, sorry," Bradley apologized, though he was unsure why Dex would be irritated by being called her brother. It's not like he insulted his age by calling him her father or something.

Dex could feel the awkwardness that filled the room, and he quickly excused himself. He didn't need to be around the two of them. He just wanted to be present so that nothing would happen.

It was one of those thoughts that he shouldn't have, and yet, twenty minutes later, standing under a bitter and chilling shower, he couldn't get the image of Briar and Bradley out of his head, or the frustration that went with it.

As he busied himself in the kitchen, preparing something for dinner, he couldn't help but pay close attention to the conversation at the table.

Briar chuckled. "You didn't find the slope of the tangent line first. Where are you getting those numbers?"

Bradley pointed to something on his paper, and Briar shook her head.

"No! It's like you forgot everything from class today."

Bradley leaned forward slightly. "If I'm being honest, I was a little distracted in class."

The smile faded from Briar's face and she swallowed heavily. She should not have allowed herself to get so comfortable around Bradley.

Going back to the paper, "Okay, so first..." She began writing down an equation.

"Do you want to go for pizza after this?"

169

Briar stopped writing, the pencil pressed firmly to the paper. Without looking up to, no doubt, a flirtatious grin on Bradley's face, "I can't." She looked to the kitchen. If Dex could hear their conversation, he didn't act like it, or maybe he just didn't care. "I promised Dex I'd be here for dinner, and he's already cooking," she lied.

At that moment, Dex looked up from the island, and Briar knew that he could hear everything.

"Maybe another time," Bradley added. He went back to worksheet and began filling in the equation Briar had written down.

Briar couldn't take her eyes from Dex. Something about the way he was looking at her made her immobile. The worst part was not understanding it.

If she thought that a moment had passed between them, it was soon gone, as Dex went back to chopping carrots.

She tried her best to ignore his presence and focus on helping Bradley with the calculus assignment; however, once Dex had come out of the shower, he made that impossible.

His t-shirt was too tight, making every single one of his rock-hard muscles that much more prominent. Briar had to wonder if he knew how attractive she found his tattoos, because rather than come out of the shower in jeans or sweats, he wore his basketball shorts, and she could see every single one of them. She thought for a moment; maybe not every single one. She didn't know if he had any on his chest or back, and that only made her all the more curious.

While Bradley packed his things up, Briar went into the kitchen, curious as to what Dex was cooking; however, a good portion was already in the oven.

"I'm going to walk Bradley out really quick," she began, uncertain what to say now that she was in his presence.

"Dinner will be ready by seven, unless you have other plans," Dex informed her, pretending not to care either way.

Briar could sense that Dex had a little bit of an attitude going on, and before she could say another word, Bradley stepped in behind her.

"It was nice meeting you, Mr. Hay–" Bradley paused when the beast in the middle of the kitchen glared at him. Correcting himself, "Dex. Sorry. It's a habit, calling elders mister and miss."

Briar shook when Dex slammed down the knife and zeroed his attention on her.

"Uh, let me walk you out," Briar began, fumbling for words, as she began motioning Bradley out of the kitchen and far away from Dex.

It wasn't until they were in the hallway that she could finally relax. Dex could be intense at times.

Bradley tossed his backpack on. "He's a little touchy."

Briar found herself smiling. That was an understatement. "He's not much of a people person."

"He is intimidating," Bradley admitted.

Briar had to agree to that.

She had no intention of riding the elevator down or walking Bradley to his car; therefore, when they reached that point down the hall, Briar began to conclude their time together.

"I'll see you tomorrow then," she awkwardly started as part of her goodbye for the evening.

"Yeah, of course." Bradley shifted for a moment, uncomfortable with his next words. "There's a party Friday, after the football game. Do you think you'd want to go?"

Briar's stomach churned at the question. She tried her best to be dismissive whenever she thought Bradley might be flirting with her.

"I have to work." It was true. Friday and Saturday were the busiest days at the restaurant, and she made the most tips then. Also, Sandy didn't like her working too much during the week, claiming that it interfered with her schooling; therefore, she relied on the weekend.

Bradley hadn't bothered to press the button on the elevator yet. "Is there a day you're not working and you'd want to hang out?" Before Briar could answer, he clarified. "Doing something that doesn't involve calculus."

Briar wasn't good when it came to whatever this was. She had always been so driven and focused on her studies, that boys were never an option. By the time she was old enough to consider dating, her life was already in turmoil, and it wouldn't have been fair to drag anyone into that.

"I'm sorry. I don't think that's a good idea. I have a lot going on right now and–"

"So much that you can't catch a movie," Bradley interrupted jokingly.

Briar bit her lip and Bradley saw the sadness in her eyes.

"Ah, you're just not interested in me…In that way."

Briar felt horrible. Bradley was extremely nice and incredibly cute. He had that adorable boy next door, southern gentleman, aura about him. She didn't want to be rude, but he was a hundred percent correct.

Bradley chuckled. "I should have figured something earlier."

Now curious, "What do you mean?"

Bradley nodded in the direction they had come, Dex's apartment. "Dex?"

"No. Oh, wow. No. Absolutely not," Briar stressed.

She knew how Dex was. If a rumor got started at school, there was no telling where all it would spread, and she was certain that Dex wouldn't want the whole town thinking the things she was positive they would.

Bradley appeared quite surprised with how sincerely adamant Briar was. "Oh…"

"It's really not you, and it has nothing to do with Dex. I'm just not in a good place to think about much aside from school and work."

Bradley finally hit the button on the wall next to the elevator. "That's too bad," he said with a shrug. "You're really cute, and I wouldn't have minded spending time with you; however, with less talk of derivatives." The bell to the elevator dinged and the doors opened. Bradley hesitated for the smallest of seconds, but ultimately took a step in, hitting the button for the ground floor. "I'll see you in calculus." The sexiest grin appeared across his face as the doors closed.

It wasn't until he was out of sight that Briar allowed herself to breathe. She pressed her back to the wall next to the elevator and tugged her hair from her ponytail, ruffling it in frustration. "You're such an idiot," she whispered to herself, fully knowing that it was very much about Dex.

CHAPTER 25

The first thing Dex noticed when Briar got back was that her hair was down. He felt his blood heating as he had to wonder why.

Briar sat down on one of the stools and rested her elbows on the counter, watching Dex in the kitchen.

Unable to take the silence, "Seems like a nice kid."

Briar scoffed at the comment. "Yeah. He is."

"You do realize he didn't give two shits about whatever the hell you were saying," he finally said. Generally speaking, he was a direct person.

Suddenly offended, Briar straightened in her seat. "Funny, I didn't realize you were eavesdropping."

"I'm not deaf. I was standing right here."

"When you were supposed to be at work."

Dex turned off a burner on the stove and took the pot to the sink to drain. "I had a long day. I didn't feel like working after hours." Briar was very perceptive, and he only hoped that she wouldn't point out the obvious. It had nothing to do with work and everything to do with her having a hormonal teenage boy in the apartment with her.

"Whatever, Dex."

It was her way of dropping the conversation, but curiosity had already gotten the best of him. After placing the empty pot on a trivet, he pressed himself into the counter and crossed his arms, watching Briar from across the room. "You two look good together."

"Excuse me?"

"I can see he's really into you, and I think–"

"Well, you should rethink," she began, interrupting him. "He's just a class-mate."

Dex laughed, but it held no humor. "It's obvious that's not what he wants."

"I know! Which is why I'm careful about the signals I send out," Briar replied.

"You have no idea about the signals you send out." Without thinking about his next statement, "You're just a naïve…" Thankfully he stopped himself from saying the next word. Coming out the way it was, it would sound like an insult; however, in Briar's case, it was anything but.

When Dex looked away, Briar couldn't help herself. If he said it, she'd be forced to show one of her cracks. She didn't want him thinking she was a naïve anything. "Finish the statement, Dex," she spat out.

"Nothing," he grumbled, now busying himself with something, anything, in the kitchen.

"Say it!"

"I don't know what I was going to—"

"Virgin? Is that what you were going to say?!"

Dex cringed at the word. He did not want to think of anything sexual when it came to Briar.

There wasn't a good enough word to describe how enraged she was right now, because the word touched on such a painful memory. Unable to stop herself, needing to correct him. "You're wrong, Dex! I'm not some naïve virgin!"

She felt her throat closing, struggling to breathe. She squashed the memory, blinked back the tears.

Dex turned back toward her, wondering what she meant in that statement. Was she talking more so about not being naïve or about not being a virgin? He had to dismiss the latter. Briar very clearly pointed out a few weeks ago that the kiss they shared was her first. Now he hated how the conversation had turned, because that kiss kept replaying in his mind.

Briar hopped down from the stool, but she wasn't done with Dex yet.

"You know what? I'm well-aware of Bradley's intentions. In fact, he invited me out to a party Friday."

Trying not to show concern, "That's good. You should get out and have fun."

"I declined." Briar saw the relief in Dex's eyes as soon as she said those words, and she hated it. "Maybe I should reconsider though. After all, I'm pretty sure that going out, getting drunk, and having meaningless sex, is the mature, adult thing to do. Right, Dex?"

"Briar," he growled out in warning.

She decided at that point that she didn't need any opinion or lecture from him. He came home in a cranky mood and that's how he was going to stay.

Unfortunately, she didn't make it very far in the direction of her room, as Dex's next words completely disarmed her.

"I didn't sleep with her," he admitted. He hated to say it. He didn't want Briar having a high opinion of him. When Briar looked into his eyes from across the room, he found himself clarifying. "The girl that I brought home."

Briar's mouth fell open with a one-word question, but Dex stopped her before she could ask.

"We're dropping this. All of it," he said with a great deal of aggression.

There wasn't a chance in hell that he was going to share with Briar the details of that night when it came to what happened in his bedroom. If he went there, too many words would come out. It hadn't been the alcohol that screwed with his mind and body. It was her, and the fact that Hannah wasn't her.

* * *

It was already 7:30 and Briar hadn't come from her room. Knowing that she didn't want to deal with him any further for the evening, Dex made her plate and took it to her room, where she was quick to answer his knock.

Briar looked down at the plate. She'd be lying if she said she wasn't starving, and the baked chicken looked amazing.

"Have you already eaten," she found herself hesitantly asking.

"No."

Briar held her hands out for the plate, but after taking it from Dex, didn't return to her room. Dex didn't expect for her to join him at the table, especially not after they snapped at each other less than two hours earlier, and was pleasantly surprised when she did.

They both dug into their food, which helped with the awkward silence. Dex was aware that he needed to be the one to apologize first. He hated how irritated he got when he found out Briar was having a boy over, regardless if it was just for studying. Briar didn't strike him as a boy crazy teenager; however, if she was, that wasn't his business. He wasn't an authority figure in her life.

He also hated the comments he said when she came back in. Bradley rubbed him the wrong way, from referring to him as Briar's brother, to calling him mister and an elder.

Then there was Briar. Dex remembered what he said to Hannah that night, in front of Briar, only wanting to push her away by hurting her. It wasn't the same. Briar didn't call him her brother in front of him. That was something she said to Bradley, and had he not mentioned it, Dex never would have known that's what she thought of him.

"So, how's the restoration on the Bentley going," Briar finally asked, cutting through the silence halfway through dinner.

It was something she commonly asked. Dex didn't know if she genuinely cared, but it made his heart smile. Not once had Lexi, or any woman for that matter, asked him about work or his projects.

"Some of the exterior is going to take longer than expected with the damage. It's nothing major, but it's not something that I can just pop out. At least I'm mostly done with everything under the hood," he answered, not going into much detail, knowing it would be like Briar trying to explain her fancy baking to him.

Oddly, from there on, they were able to have a normal conversation. Briar talked to him about a few things in school; however, she was careful not to mention Bradley's name any more throughout the evening. She didn't understand why, but it appeared that Dex didn't care much for him. She figured that after their conversation at the elevator, Bradley wouldn't ask her for much help outside of school.

After helping clean up the kitchen, Dex stopped Briar before she turned in for the night. "Sorry for snapping at you earlier," he nonchalantly apologized. He didn't want it to seem like a big deal.

Briar chuckled. "I guess we can both get irritable fairly quickly, but it's different for you."

"What do you mean?"

"Well, you're used to being alone. Now you have a stranger in your space. I'm sure it's annoying at times."

"I don't think you can call yourself a stranger anymore," Dex pointed out. Briar was the furthest thing from a stranger, especially after that encounter a few weeks ago that he still couldn't erase.

"Regardless, I think I understand." Briar turned to leave on a good note. An apology from Dex was saying something. "Despite how things are," she began, not wanting to face Dex. "Thank you, for everything you've done for me."

Dex didn't say a word and allowed her to leave the room. There was nothing he could say. That statement gutted him.

He wasn't the easiest person to get along with. He didn't like most people, cussed too much, frowned and growled more than he smiled and laughed, and yet, Briar didn't seem to mind. Living with him couldn't be easy for her, which only made him want to know that much more about her past. He just never thought it would be anytime soon.

* * *

Sharp and piercing screams jolted Dex awake in the extreme early morning hours. He didn't think, only reacted, when he stormed from his room and into Briar's.

The screaming had stopped by the time he flipped her light on, and what he saw turned his stomach inside out.

Briar sat against her headboard, her knees pulled to her chest and her arms wrapped around them, tears flooding down her face.

She looked up to see Dex and immediately buried her head into her knees. "I'm sorry," she managed.

Dex cursed under his breath. He wasn't equipped to handling whatever this was. All he did know was that Briar was more upset than he had ever seen her, and yet, she was apologizing.

It was a strange instinct that came over him, but he went with it. Without thinking, he crossed the room until he sat beside her on the small bed. He pulled her from her ball of safety and into his chest, tightly wrapping his arms around her in comfort, which only seemed to make her cry more.

"What the hell are you apologizing for?" Dex was certain he heard a laugh somewhere in her sniffles and gasps for air.

"For this. For waking you."

Dex felt the cool tears on his chest and it then occurred to him that he was only wearing his basketball shorts. There wasn't a single thing intimate about their situation, but feeling her cheek pressed to his chest, her skin on his, clouded his judgement.

Dex pulled her away and looked at her already splotchy face. Tears continued to fall from faded and despondent green eyes, and he wiped away every one.

Minutes later, when Briar attempted to calm down, Dex excused himself. He had no intention of leaving her alone so soon, but putting on a t-shirt would be for the best, for the both of them.

179

Briar froze when Dex didn't say anything and walked from her room. Thinking about Dex in an intimate way was honestly the furthest thing from her mind after the nightmare that would never go away.

She still watched him walk from her room. She had been curious about his tattoos, but seeing him without a shirt for the first time, she saw that his chest and back were bare. Everything was on his arms and left leg, below the knee.

Briar was surprised when Dex returned, his upper body fully clad.

Their eyes met from across the room, and though it should have been uncomfortable and awkward, it wasn't. The look in Briar's eyes told Dex that she needed him, someone to talk to. He wasn't big on talking, but for her he'd make an exception. Lately, he was beginning to think that would always be the case. Briar was an exception.

He told his feet to stop. They could speak without being as close as they were before. Something in his body didn't respond, didn't get the message, and before he knew it, he was next to her on the bed.

Briar shuffled toward Dex, but once he wrapped his arm around her, the tears continued. She didn't want to make things weird, so said nothing. Maybe he had known, and the words would have only been unnecessary, but where they were in that moment was exactly what she needed.

"Briar," Dex sighed, feeling the wetness of her tears soaking through a spot on his shirt.

She pulled away, knowing the way he said her name was a question.

Maybe it was time to tell someone. After nearly four months, maybe she could finally talk about it. She only hoped that Dex wouldn't look at her differently. There were so many times that he looked at her like she was weak and broken. She wasn't. She was surviving.

"I haven't had that nightmare since I've been here," Briar admitted, not knowing how to start, how to blurt it out.

"*That* nightmare?"

Briar brushed her hair back and bit at her bottom lip in contemplation. She pushed herself across the bed and pressed her back into the headboard. She couldn't have Dex touching her, didn't want to feel his warmth, not with what she was about to tell him.

After taking in a deep breath, Briar finally said it aloud. "I was raped."

CHAPTER 26

Early June.

"Where were you," Leo asked, hovering in Briar's doorway.

"I had an evening class," she answered. She had to. If she didn't, he'd only leave another bruise on her.

Leo scoffed and put out his cigarette on Briar's dresser, leaving a disgusting black mark on what once was a beautiful ivory piece. "I don't get why you're doing all this extra schooling."

In hindsight, she shouldn't have responded, but she did. "By the end of the summer, I'll be done with school, graduating early, not having to do my senior year."

"And? You think that makes you special or something?"

"No," Briar snapped. "Once I'm done with school, I'm done with you and your stupid mother."

Leo's eyes darkened to night as he strode across the room, toward Briar, who was unpacking some books on her desk.

"You really think so," he laughed.

Briar turned, only to have Leo inches from her. She gasped when his hand closed around her neck. She could feel his breath upon her, the smell of smoke making her stomach churn.

"Stop it," she insisted. She didn't shove him this time. Too often she tried to push back, and it only made him hit her harder.

"After your dad died, mother told me you needed some control. I'm beginning to think I didn't do a good enough job with you."

Briar didn't say anything, didn't move. There were times that were different, when Leo's words were empty threats. She desperately wanted this time to be one of those. She still had bruises on her upper arms from days ago.

Leo loosened his grip and finally dropped his hand from Briar's throat; however, in the next second, she realized it was all false hope. His hand across her cheek stung more than ever before, and this time she could taste blood in her mouth.

He then yanked Briar by her forearms and slung her to the bed. "You'll never be done with me. I'll make sure that you always remember me," Leo spat.

It wasn't until he climbed on top of Briar and straddled her, pinning her in place, unable to wiggle free from beneath him, that panic sank in. Up until now, Leo had only done physical and emotional violence to her. She always knew he could have done so much more.

No matter what the injuries would be on her behalf, she had to fight back.

She tried her best to sling her legs upward, but Leo was too heavy on her. He placed both her wrists together and held them tightly above her head, squeezing them together so hard with one hand that she thought every bone would break.

Leo balled up his free hand and punched her in the side, causing an agonizing scream to erupt from her bloodied lips.

He brought his face down toward the side of Briar's. "Just wait, I'll have you screaming for more when I'm done with you," he hissed in her ear.

"Leo," Briar gasped, fighting for air. "Please stop. You're hurting me. Please just stop."

Briar heard a crinkling and managed to open her eyes, her sight blurred from the tears, to see Leo tear open a condom with his teeth.

"No! Leo, stop," she screamed at the top of her lungs.

She tried to pull herself up, to break free from his grasp, but her wrists were numb from the pressure he had on them, and her whole body was weak and in pain from the blows he had given her.

His hands loosened on her wrists just enough when he began to undo the button of his jeans. Briar didn't know if she'd get another opportunity, and with all her might, she pulled from him until her hands were free. She slapped his face with all her strength and continued swatting, all the while trying to get out from beneath him.

Leo was able to catch both her arms and slam them to the bed. He glared into her eyes, "Big mistake, you fucking slut."

Briar wasn't sure what happened next, as the next blow sent her vision into pure blackness. When she did come back to earth, it was only then that she realized the nightmare wasn't over.

Leo was naked on top of her, and her pants were now missing. She screamed for help, but all Leo did was laugh.

"My mom doesn't give a crap about you. She was disappointed you didn't die years ago," he said, referring to another dark time in Briar's life.

Only more tears continued down her face. She couldn't feel anymore life in her. If she had known how bad life would get, she would have sliced her wrists over and over again until she was free.

Leo ripped at Briar's panties with his free hand. "I'm so glad you're awake to remember this. As much as I hate you, I get the satisfaction of knowing that I was the first. Your little virgin cunt will always be mine."

He words repulsed her, making her want to vomit, and then there was only pain. The most agonizing pain in all her life, physical pain that ripped through every part of her body, destroying her, destroying more than just her body, destroying her mind, her soul, her heart.

✳ ✳ ✳

Dex tried not to lose it. His teeth were clenched so tight, one was sure to break at any moment.

Briar grabbed at Dex's hand, not the one she allowed him to lightly wrap around her as she told him her story, and pried at his fist.

"Please don't. I wanted to tell you, but I didn't want you to see me differently. I know you must think–"

Dex pulled his hand away from her, drawing it back into a fist, trying his hardest to keep his anger at bay. "You have no idea what I'm thinking right now."

He wanted to scream and punch something, but that's not what she needed to see. He had no idea what she went through, but what she told him was worse than he imagined. Above all, he wanted to find her stepbrother. He wanted to find him and rip his throat out with his bare hands for ever treating a woman like that. The fact that it was Briar, someone so pure, so sweet, so innocent, only made it that much worse for Dex.

"Before you can ask," she began quietly. "When his mother found out, all she cared about was Leo not getting into trouble. They took away my phone and computer and made sure I didn't leave the house until I was healed." Briar paused and shook her head. "With the way my body felt, I could barely walk, much less leave the house."

"Why didn't you go to the cops as soon as you left," Dex found himself asking.

"By that time, I wasn't sure how much evidence would be left for rape. I watch the news. I read. I know how difficult it can be to prove. I also know how the world works. Money can buy a lot of things, including one's freedom. Portia controls everything my parents left behind, which is a lot."

Dex groaned, but froze at Briar's next words.

"I'm talking millions. Leo would have had the best lawyer around. He would have gotten off. We both know that, and then where would I be left? I only wanted one thing, Dex. Out. I wanted to be free from them, from that house, from that city."

Dex pulled his arm from around her and ran both his hands through his hair and back down, down his face, pulling at his skin in frustration.

"After a few days, when I felt better. Physically," Briar clarified. "I decided to leave. Leo was out partying, and I swear Portia goes through a bottle of vodka a day and passes out by the pool. That night, I went to her room, and got my phone and laptop. I wiped my phone clean and destroyed the card. I didn't want anyone finding me. Just in case, for good measure, I left my phone behind."

Dex thought from the beginning how strange it was that a seventeen-year-old didn't have a phone. He never expected it to be the story Briar just told.

"Leaving was much easier than I thought," she concluded.

"And you just ended up in Argent Falls?"

Briar's lips turned up in just the smallest of smiles. She couldn't have been happier with her choice. "I didn't know if I'd make it through the summer with the way things were going. Considering that my academy was a little unconventional, I had already looked into high schools around the state that would accept my credits."

"Of all the places…"

"There were several. I knew I wanted a small town, and two hundred miles seemed like a little bit of distance. Trust me, if I could have gone to London, I would have, but acceptance to the program requires a high school education. That and…I only had three hundred dollars," Briar sadly chuckled.

Dex understood so much more than he wanted. There were little comments that Briar made in the past and he couldn't help but wonder. Now he knew why she worked on that program for his business during her nights at the hostel. It couldn't have been an easy place for her to get rest, and if she fought with those nightmares, no wonder she didn't sleep.

One recent comment stuck with him.

I haven't had that nightmare since I've been here.

He didn't need to ask what she meant by that. He felt it radiating from her body through his when he held her. She felt comfortable and safe with him. There was no way he was going to ruin that, to take that away from her. She needed comfort and safety in her life.

CHAPTER 27

It was like Briar could sense when Dex entered. The door opened and he veered to the left, toward the bar.

She usually got off at eight on Sundays. Sandy didn't want her exhausted for school. The only days he let her work until closing of the restaurant were Friday and Saturday. Briar insisted with Dex that she didn't need him picking her up on any days other than those. She was content with walking. Dex, however, chose not to listen, and eventually Briar gave up.

"Slow night," Dex asked, greeting Sandy behind the bar.

"Eh, Sunday. You know most people around here do the church and family dinner crap. Anyway, what'll it be."

Dex sat on a stool at the bar. "I'm good. Just waiting on Briar."

Sandy gave a smirk and threw his rag over his shoulder. "Speaking of Briar..." He held a finger up and slipped away from the bar, leaving Dex confused.

It didn't take long before Sandy returned and placed a small oddly shaped bowl and spoon in front of Dex. Dex stared at the little dish and then at Sandy.

"What the fuck is this?"

Sandy shook his head. "The dessert for tonight."

Dex hesitantly took the spoon, but found that the top of the dessert was hard as a rock.

"It's chocolate crème brulee," Sandy answered, before Dex could ask.

Dex didn't do desserts, so he never had that before. He tapped at the top again. "It's supposed to be like this?"

Sandy simply nodded.

Dex knew that Sandy and Rita let Briar make the desserts every Sunday, and there wasn't a single Sunday that passed where Sandy wouldn't make sure that Dex tried another creation.

"It's chocolatey," Dex commented after a few bites.

He didn't know what else to say. It was good. Better than good. Amazing. Decadent. He wouldn't say that, and he didn't need to. Sandy already knew. The look on his face told that to Dex.

"Eh, she was bitching about that," Sandy chuckled.

Dex arched his brow in question.

"Well, Argent Falls isn't exactly the culinary capital of the state. She has a hard time finding some of what she wants to play with. Hell, I told her we're good with apple pie and peach cobbler, but she said that's served in all restaurants."

Dex scoffed. "Food snob much?"

Sandy took the rag from his shoulder and swatted at Dex.

"I don't mind," Sandy went on. "A lot of the families who eat here on Sundays have noticed. I do have to say, she tries really hard. I know Alfred won't be doing that once she leaves."

That comment did something to Dex. He realized that Briar would be leaving in a couple months, and that thought sent a feeling through him that he hadn't experienced. He didn't even know how to describe it, or what the feeling was.

"Yeah, some fancy two-year program in London," was all Dex said in response.

Sandy reached for a beer and slid it down the bar to one of the few patrons there on a Sunday. "That's what Rita told me."

"I think that's why she's working so hard. Can't be cheap," Dex added.

"You're not charging her rent, are you?"

Dex shook his head. If he would have charged her rent, even a little, that would probably look a little better. By not charging her for anything, even buying her a phone and clothes, it looked bad for someone looking in. It wasn't a simple roommate situation. It looked like there was more, some strange and weirdly domesticated arrangement that he thought he'd never be in. Dex had never lived with a woman, and he never thought he'd do so in such a platonic nature.

Platonic might be the wrong word in describing what he had with Briar. They had kissed, and there wasn't a doubt in his mind that he wanted to again; however, that complicated things out the ass. All he had to do was keep his desires at bay for a couple more months. Then she'd be gone, and he could go back to feeling normal.

"Good. It seems like she needs someone to help with whatever burdens she's carrying."

Dex's heart stopped for a second, remembering the bombshell that Briar had thrown out there not too long ago.

Sandy continued. "You know, you can be a moody asshole, but what you did for me, what you're doing for her...You have a good heart."

Dex pushed the finished dessert across the bar to Sandy and groaned. "Don't get all mushy and shit."

Sandy laughed loudly. "If you want mushy, you should see the way you look at—"

"Stop," Dex insisted, unable to hear Sandy finish that thought. He tried his hardest not to give Briar much attention when he came to pick her up, but something about her was mesmerizing, and on several occasions, he couldn't help but stare. Ever the observant, of course Sandy would see that.

* * *

Dex handed Briar a to-go cup of coffee. There was no way she could make it to school by walking. "Why are you being so stubborn?"

"I'm fine with walking! Just go to work," Briar insisted.

Of all the days for Dex to play hero, he had to pick this one, the one day Briar desperately did not want him taking her to school.

He had a point, she knew that. The beginning of October was proving to be a rather chilly autumn for the northeast; however, that's what jackets and boots were for.

Briar couldn't tell Dex her real reasoning. Despite his gruff attitude and acting like he didn't care, deep down inside a small part of him did. He continued to show her that, sometimes without even meaning to.

Even though Briar spent another good ten minutes arguing with Dex, he eventually won.

"What is it with you today," Dex asked.

Briar hadn't said a word since they left the apartment, and now she sat in the truck next to him, arms crossed and a sour expression on her face.

"I told you that I wanted to walk today, and you just don't listen."

"It's getting colder. You don't need to be walking," Dex pointed out.

Briar said nothing, only gave a sigh of annoyance.

Dex didn't press any further. Had it been Lexi, he would have immediately asked her if she needed a Midol or whatever women now take for that stuff; however, he was truly trying to be a little more wholesome and sensitive when it came to Briar. He couldn't change overnight, but after everything she told him, he really didn't want to lose his shit with her. It seemed she had enough of that.

Briar was halfway to the building when Dex reached over and threw the passenger door open. "Not even a thank you?!"

Briar turned back toward Dex and shot one brow up more than the other.

When she didn't respond, "Okay. Not even a fuck off, Dex?"

He knew he had her at that. She tried to hide it, by biting at her bottom lip, but even with the amount of distance that separated them, he could tell she was fighting a smile.

"Thanks for the ride, Dex," Briar said in a low tone that was supposed to resemble his voice; however, it dripped in sarcasm.

190

Briar gave a small wave and slowly continued making her way toward the last of the students entering the building. No doubt about it, she was late.

She lingered outside for just a second, until she saw Dex exit the parking lot and make the turn onto the street. Finally, she was able to breathe a sigh of relief, though still annoyed that he had easily set her back an hour.

* * *

Needless to say, Dex caught hell when he walked into work and Rusty had already opened the doors and had a fresh pot of coffee in the office. It wasn't the first time, and he knew it wouldn't be the last. He'd never tell Briar, or anyone else, but he felt good getting to drop her off at school. Then, upon thinking that, the sickening feeling hit him. He was dropping her off at school. Fucking high school.

Just as he did every day, Dex threw himself into work, hoping it would drown out thoughts of Briar.

"Old lady Mable is back," Rusty called out from the reception area shortly after.

Dex rolled out from beneath a car. "She was just here last week. What the hell now?"

Rusty shook his head. "Another flat tire."

Throwing his wrench on the concrete. "Are you fucking kidding me?! That's the fifth one in two months! Where is that crazy ass woman driving?!"

From the glass windows separating the reception area and a part of the garage, Dex could see Mable glaring at him. He knew she didn't hear what he was saying; she was deaf as a post. She simply didn't like him; therefore, she was always glaring at him. She was a very strict religious woman and Dex…Was anything but.

As soon as Dex got up from his creeper, his phone went off. For a split second, he was tempted to ignore it; however, there was this ominous feeling that told him to at least see who was calling.

He stared at it, afraid to answer. Something was off with Briar that morning. Now her school was calling. She had eaten a granola bar in the truck. They had dinner the night before, and she even had seconds. Unless something else was wrong, she couldn't be weak from lack of food, as his first thoughts went to her fainting again.

"Hello," he quickly answered.

"Hello. This is an automated message from Argent Falls High. This is to let you know that…Briar…Stone…has been recorded as absent for the day. Upon her return, please send valid proof this is an excused absence."

The phone went dead.

Dex took a deep breath and bit at his bottom lip in frustration. He knew it; he just knew it. Briar was too adamant about him not taking her to school. She always put up a fuss, but something about today was different. She was a smart girl and cared too much about graduating early. The fact that she skipped school angered him. Had she simply told him that she didn't feel like going, he wouldn't have cared. It was her life. He was pissed because she deliberately lied to him.

He needed to make sure she was okay. That was all.

He called her phone three times in the next five minutes. Every single time, the call eventually ended by going to an automated message informing him that the person he was trying to reach had a voice mailbox that had not been set up.

He didn't want to appear too worried. When it came to Briar, he was already much too involved. Freaking out about her not being in school, not answering her phone, was only going to make him look like he cared too much. Playing it as cool as possible, he sent a simple text. *Call me.*

For the next thirty minutes, he busied himself, quickly fixing Mable's tire so she would go away; however, after that short amount of time, he still hadn't heard from Briar.

He thought of all the places she could be, but nothing came to mind. All she did was work or study. Not wanting a lengthy conversation with Rita, Dex quickly fired off a simple inquiry.

Dex: Is Briar at the restaurant?

Rita: No. Why?

Dex: Nothing.

Rita: You can't just ask something like that and say nothing! Why? It's a weekday. Isn't she at school?

Dex realized he probably should have just called Sandy; however, both Sandy and Rita were also too involved when it came to Briar. He didn't imagine asking either would have gone well. The only reason he went with Rita was for the simple fact that she was most likely to respond or answer.

Dex: Yeah. Forgot.

Rita: Dex! You asshole! What is going on?

Dex: Nothing. I have an oil change.

Rita: Just wait until I see you!

"Is everything okay," Benji asked.

193

Dex could feel that his brows were tightened in frustration, and attempted to soften his expression. "Yeah. I just got a call that Briar wasn't at school today."

Benji chuckled, and Dex knew why. The guys still gave him a hard time about Briar putting him down as her guardian, or rather, her emergency contact as she referred to it.

"Sometimes those teachers screw up. Want me to text Liam? Just to ease your mind," Benji went on.

"My mind is at ease," Dex growled.

"Oh, cut that shit. You worry about her. We all see that. Stop acting like such a scrooge about it."

Dex rubbed at the back of his neck in annoyance. "I can't get in touch with her, and something about her seemed off today."

"Look, it's a slow morning so far. I know you wanted to work on the Bentley, but that can wait. Why don't you go home and see if she's there? If everything is okay, we'll see you in half an hour," Benji calmly suggested.

Dex took a deep breath and contemplated. If Briar didn't feel well, obviously she would have gone back to the apartment. Right now, that seemed like the only logical suggestion.

"I'll be back soon," Dex stressed.

Benji waved his hand and mumbled something along the lines of not worrying about it. Dex didn't hear. He was already rushing from the garage and to his truck, a million different thoughts running through his mind.

Of all the things that came to his mind, he never could have expected what he encountered when he walked into the apartment.

CHAPTER 28

Dex froze as soon as he opened the door. The sounds and smells that flooded his senses were unfamiliar to him, unfamiliar to his home. He softly closed the door as the confusion sank in. The music wasn't loud, but it pierced his ears. What the hell was that?

It wasn't his type, but a second more and he clearly recognized it. Bob Dylan was one of those voices. If you heard him once, you'd know it was him with any other song.

Then there was the smell. It smelled sweet but earthy. All he knew was that it didn't belong in his apartment.

He cautiously rounded the corner from the entry and scanned the area, the sounds of Bob Dylan becoming louder with each step. His mouth fell open when he saw her in the kitchen.

The sight of Briar casually dancing in the kitchen as she dried dishes was something that would forever be imprinted in his mind.

Briar changed from the outfit she had worn to school. Now she was in an oversized t-shirt and a pair of shorts that Dex found annoyingly snug. Her light and ashy blonde hair was twirled up in a messy bun, with a few of the shorter pieces hanging around her face.

She placed a clean spatula in its respective drawer and opened the oven door, poking at something with a toothpick.

Dex glanced to the bar. Briar's laptop was open, and sure enough, an entire collection of Bob Dylan was up on the screen. The words of the particular song playing gripped at him, making him hate the way he was just looking at Briar. Unable to take it, he hit the pause button.

Briar spun around as soon as the silence cut through the apartment. "Dex," she gasped.

Dex crossed his arms and wore a hardened expression upon his face. "Care to explain what the hell you're doing."

Flustered, Briar tucked pieces of hair behind her ears. "Umm…I was baking a cake."

Dex remained standing in the space between the kitchen and living room. Briar had taken a step in his direction, but after seeing the look on his face, immediately regretted it and went no farther.

When Dex didn't say another word, only looked her up and down, "What are you doing here? I thought you'd be at work?" Apparently, it was the wrong thing to say.

Dex let out one loud laugh. Briar knew it well. He was annoyed and pissed about something.

"I could say the same to you about school. They called me, saying that you were marked absent today."

Briar huffed and rolled her eyes. She forgot that schools still did that, even high schools.

Ignoring Dex, Briar took out several trivets and placed them on the island countertop. She then grabbed a potholder for each hand and took three round pans from the oven.

"Briar…"

"I'm sorry if the school interrupted your morning," Briar apologized, though her statement was lacking in any remorse.

Dex slammed the palm of his hand on the bar. Normally it would have startled Briar, but not anymore. Dex rarely hid his frustrations.

"Damnit! I was worried about you."

Briar's eyes widened in surprise. There wasn't a soul alive who worried about her.

"I dropped you off at school and then get that kind of call. Then, I call and text you and get nothing back. I thought something happened, but no. You just wanted to play fucking Betty Crocker."

Briar felt a momentary sickness in her stomach as Dex's words sank in. Not knowing where to begin with addressing everything he said, "My phone is in my room."

Apparently, that didn't sit well with Dex. His icy blue eyes narrowed in annoyance and didn't leave Briar's for a second. She should have looked away, but it was getting harder. It didn't matter how Dex looked at her; every time he did, she found herself unable to break whatever unspoken words were passing between them.

With her eyes still on his, "I really am sorry that the school bothered you."

"That's not the point," Dex insisted.

"I know. I just…" Briar paused. So many words were running through her mind that she had a hard time forming a coherent thought much less sentence. "You don't have to worry about me, about me missing school. I'm an adult. I wanted, needed, today to myself."

Dex laughed again, though there was no humor in his voice. He shook his head. "Look, I get that you think–"

His words cut off immediately, Briar's now sinking in. He looked down to the island and the pans of warm chocolate cake. Curiously, he slowly raised his eyes back to Briar's. This time, she was looking at him with an unreadable expression, waiting for him to connect the dots.

He gripped the bar to keep from moving into the kitchen. Just looking at her made him want to be closer to her, not even in an intimate way, but just to be in her presence. "Why today," he hesitantly asked.

"What?"

"You stressed that you needed today to yourself. Why," he asked again.

Briar's eyes fell to the floor, feeling so pathetic, and not wanting to tell Dex.

"Why, of all things, are you baking a cake?"

Dex wasn't stupid. He didn't need her to answer.

"I just wanted a cake," was all she gave him.

Briar turned and went back to a few dishes that she had washed by hand. She hated a messy and unorganized kitchen just as much as Dex.

She tightly closed her eyes, pinching back any tears, and took in a deep and silent breath. The bowl in her hands was dry, but she continued rubbing the dish towel over it, unable to turn around. Dex's footsteps weren't exactly the lightest, and not only could Briar hear the increase in volume as they made their way into the kitchen, but she was certain that the closer he came, the more she could feel an invisible heat radiating off his body. It made her head dizzy and her heart beat uncontrollably.

Briar sucked in a breath when Dex's hand lightly clasped over her shoulder; it was big and warm, and most of all, it steadied her. Though she wanted to combust from being so close to him, his touch also awakened her senses and made her acutely aware of the moment.

"Briar…"

She placed the bowl to the side and turned to face Dex, already sensing disappointment with the simple way he said her name.

Dex released his hand as Briar faced him.

"Is today your birthday?"

Answering, without answering, "Can we not make it a big deal?"

Dex took a step back, disheartened that she hadn't said anything to him about it.

Briar had to turn away from Dex, hating the way he was now looking at her. She would much rather have preferred annoyed, frustrated, pissed Dex, not whatever this was now, this saddened and broken Dex.

"This is what I've done the last couple years. I like it," Briar lied.

Birthdays since her mother's death were never that good. Her father tried his best, but she knew that he often felt like he was letting her down; therefore, he simply spoiled her in gifts. The last two birthdays were the worst of all, because she was alone. Her birthday to Portia was the worst day of all; it was the day she was born, something Portia would no doubt go back in time and change if she could.

Dex cracked his neck in annoyance. "This is really what you want?"

Briar wasn't sure exactly what he was asking. "To not go to school today? To bake myself a cake? Yes."

"To be alone," Dex quickly added.

Briar felt her chest tighten. She forced a smile. "I'm used to it."

Dex rolled his eyes, hating how she did that. She wasn't stupid. Hell, she was smarter than any of the women he'd ever come in contact with. She knew exactly what he was saying, but she pretended otherwise, making him come out and be direct.

"Can I do something nice for you today?"

Briar swallowed heavily. If Dex didn't stop looking at her like that, she was pretty sure tears were about to rain down.

"You've already done so much for me over these few months, so that isn't necessary," she finally said, giving him her answer, regardless how much she didn't want to be left alone.

Dex walked to a cabinet, retrieved a mug, and began to pour him some of the lukewarm coffee from a couple hours before. He took a sip and eyed Briar carefully, attempting to read her. Finally, "I know it's not."

Briar blinked a few times, not understanding what was happening. Dex left the kitchen and went to his chair near the balcony. The memory of him sitting in it, in the late darkness of the night after that dinner with Lexi, flashed through her mind. Though he wasn't dressed up like then, now in his stained work clothes, he still looked just as melting to her.

She waited for him to say something more, but he didn't. He began to busy himself with something on his phone, and she needed to get back to her cake.

From time to time, Dex would look up at Briar. First, she banged the pans around, eventually bringing the layers of cake out to cool. Then she started making another mess with a bowl and a godawful amount of powdered sugar.

Dex was surprised that it didn't take more than a few minutes to find what he was looking for, at least, he hoped it's what he was looking for. He was certain that it would be something perfect for Briar, and if so, he'd make a mental note to thank Sandy for the idea.

Briar was startled when Dex finally said something, asking her how much longer she was going to be.

She tasted the icing. It was perfect. "Uh, the layers are cool. I just have to icing and stack them."

Dex didn't say anything, causing Briar to look up and meet his raised brow. "That doesn't answer my question?"

"Ten minutes?"

Dex took his empty coffee cup into the kitchen and placed it in the dishwasher. Briar was about to ask him if he wanted to try the icing, fully knowing that he didn't care for dessert or chocolate, but still wanting to be nice and give him the opportunity; however, just as quickly as he entered the kitchen, he disappeared from it. A moment later she heard the closing of his bedroom door.

"Definitely not how today was supposed to start out," she huffed to herself, delicately slicing the top of one of cakes so that it was flat on top and bottom.

✽ ✽ ✽

Briar was attempting to place one of the glass measuring cups on the second highest shelf, cursing to herself as to why Dex kept them so out of reach, when a large hand lightly brushed hers. The cup was pulled from her grasp and placed on the shelf.

"Thanks," Briar mumbled. Despite her height, she had gotten it down, she could have gotten it back up there.

She sank from her tiptoes and turned around. Nothing could have prepared her for the person in front of her. For once, Briar was utterly speechless. Dex wasn't dressed formal by any means, but seeing him moments ago in his work attire, to the guy standing inches away from her, took Briar's breath away.

He had on dark jeans with just a slight brown fade from the thighs to the knees. While he wore a work boot style shoe, they were clean, looking as though they were hardly ever taken out of the box. Briar scanned back up to Dex's white button-down shirt, with the sleeves slightly rolled to just below his elbows.

She quickly searched over his face, as she was staring for far too long without saying a word. He had clearly styled his hair. The black strands had the perfect intentionally messy yet put together look. Briar never wanted to touch someone's hair so badly before.

She took in a deep breath, attempting to focus, and that's when the smell truly hit her. She had gotten so used to Dex smelling like oil and gasoline, but the cologne he had on now was far from that. He smelled crisp, clean, and intoxicating. A creepy part of her wanted to grab his shirt in her fists and breathe it in even more.

Dex cleared his throat uncomfortably, awakening Briar. She could feel her cheeks heating in embarrassment.

Dex took a step back. "I can finish up here, if you want to go change."

"Change?"

"Isn't it a little cool outside for shorts," Dex questioned back.

"I didn't know I was going outside."

Dex tapped at the buttons on the loaded dishwasher. "Well, now you know."

Briar had to assume that Dex now had something up his sleeve. "That's all you're going to give me?"

He shrugged. "Yeah."

Mildly annoyed, "Well, what am I supposed to wear? I need to know where we're going. Do I need to dress up? You look like..." Briar trailed off, not knowing how to finish that sentence.

"Like I know how to take a shower? Like I own clothes that aren't covered in oil," Dex teased.

"Something like that," Briar answered quietly. She and Dex didn't have the kind of relationship where she could tell him how sexy he looked without making it awkward for the foreseeable future.

"Just wear something comfortable," Dex finally said.

CHAPTER 29

At first there was an uncomfortable silence in the truck. Dex tried to hide his reaction after Briar changed clothes. He wouldn't say it aloud, but she looked incredible. Her snug jeans were tucked into a pair of boots with just a small bit of heel, stopping somewhere in the middle of her calves. Her light blue sweater was paired with a checkered scarf of various shades of brown and tan, matching her boots, giving her a classic and chic appearance.

For some reason, Dex found her hair to be even lighter and her eyes that much greener.

Thankfully, he was driving; had he not been, it would be difficult for him to take his eyes off her.

"You can change the station," Dex said, breaking the silence.

"It's okay. I don't mind." Dex's rock had grown on her.

"Not exactly Dylan," he added.

She chuckled and picked at one of her plain and unpainted nails. "No, definitely not."

Dex had a feeling that surprising Briar had taken her off guard. She had a nervous energy about her. Attempting to keep the conversation going, "I thought you'd be into all those pop princess drama queens, the ones writing all those screwed up songs about their ex. Or maybe boy bands?"

"No to both," Briar answered, her words slightly clipped. Of course Dex would think she'd have the musical tastes of a thirteen-year-old girl. "He was my mother's favorite. She listened to him all the time, especially in the kitchen. For a while after she died, I couldn't listen to his music without tumbling into a fit of tears."

When she paused, Dex looked over briefly to make sure she wasn't crying. She wasn't. Instead, she had a soft, barely there, smile on her face. "And now?"

"I can't say that I don't think about her when I hear his music, but the pain isn't there anymore. I have happy memories with her, and that's enough. Also, I really like Bob Dylan," Briar added with a laugh.

Dex didn't say much more about her mother, and Briar took the comfortableness between them as a way to pry. Overall, Dex knew more about her than anyone; after all, he was the only person she had ever told about Leo, aside from Portia.

Knowing not to tread in the area of Dex's mother, "Were you and your father close?" He had only spoken a little of his father at their lunch long ago.

"Very," was all Dex said to that question.

Briar took his one-word response to mean that he didn't want to talk about it. Sadly, she decided to drop the conversation of all their dead parents.

Upon glancing at the time on the dashboard, Briar noticed that they had been driving for over forty-five minutes, and were now well out of Argent Falls.

Curiously, "Where exactly are we going? And how much longer is—"

"Just this shop, and about thirty more minutes," Dex answered vaguely, attempting to play it down.

Briar gasped. "We're driving for more than an hour for a *shop*?"

"Something like that," Dex answered with a slight chuckle in his voice.

The conversation was kept light for the rest of the drive. Briar was able to get Dex to really talk when she asked him yet again about his restoration. It was only then that he spoke of his dad for just a moment. He didn't give her much, but she found out that restoring cars brought their business big bucks at times. He wasn't specific, and she didn't want to snoop and ask about figures. Dex knew her parents were well off, but he never asked for specifics; therefore, she wouldn't either.

✱ ✱ ✱

"Shit," Dex breathed when he saw Briar's reaction.

Briar's jaw hung open and she quickly dabbed at the corners of her eyes. It looked different from when she had last seen it, nearly ten years ago. The building had expanded, now easily twice the size from when she visited. The sign was larger too; however, still in that beautiful scripty font she loved.

Au-delà du Chocolat.

"I thought this would be a place…" Dex started. "Sandy said a few days ago that you couldn't find everything in Argent Falls…I didn't know this would upset–"

"Stop," Briar interrupted. She dabbed at a tear or two that managed to escape. "I'm happy."

"Really? Because from where I'm sitting, you look like you're crying and in shock," Dex hesitantly pointed out.

Briar turned to Dex, her lips forming one of the biggest smiles he had ever seen, leaving him impossibly confused.

"Shocked, yes…But you do know people can cry when they're happy too?"

Dex didn't know that. Yes, he heard that. Occasionally if Rusty laughed enough, he'd get teary; however, Briar wasn't laughing. She was simply sitting there crying. How the hell was he supposed to know that she was happy. If any other person randomly started crying, sadness was the first thing he thought of.

Motioning with his hands, "So? Good surprise?"

Briar laughed and shook her head. "The best. I could hug you right now."

Dex pretended he didn't hear that. It would have been innocent enough, but he knew what her body felt like against his, and having her that close wouldn't do him any favors in the end.

"Wow. They've really expanded," Briar gasped when they walked through the doors.

"You've been here before?" Dex was only mildly disappointed.

205

Briar turned her face from Dex, unsure why her cheeks were reddening. "Yeah. With my mom."

Dex let out a ragged breath, now understanding the happy tears.

"That's a good thing," Briar quickly added. "I mean…It doesn't make me sad, it–"

Interrupting her, "I get it."

"I am curious as to why we're here however."

"Sandy told me you were bitching about not finding stuff at our market," Dex said nonchalantly, repeating himself from earlier, as if that answered her question.

"Oh. Well, thanks then. I'm sure there are a more than a few things I could use. I desperately need cocoa butter."

Briar grabbed one of the baskets from a stack near the entry, but froze the second Dex's hand clasped over her forearm. The heat from his palm went straight through her sweater, through her skin, invading her head and heart. Once she turned to face him, locking eyes, he broke the contact.

She wanted to scream. Every time he got close to her or touched her, he immediately recoiled. The only thing that was different this time, his expression wasn't laced with hatred and regret.

"You didn't give me much notice," Dex began.

Briar's face held a confused look.

"This is my present to you."

"I don't think I follow," Briar slowly managed.

"I want you to get whatever you need that will help you get through those online things, those free courses or whatever." Dex had paid attention to the little she told him at lunch that day. He remembered her telling him about a one-month program online. "If you'd rather I buy you that online course–"

"No! Absolutely not." Briar began shaking her head. "Dex, you really don't have to do this. A simple 'Happy Birthday' would be more than enough."

With a smirk coming to his lips, Dex stepped in closer. "Happy Birthday. Now go pick out whatever you'll need."

Dex took the basket from her hand and put it down on the stack, opting for one of the carts instead.

Briar laughed. "I'm not going to buy that much. I know how to restrain myself."

More than thirty minutes later, she regretted saying that. She easily had around five hundred dollars in the cart. Guilt sank into her stomach. There was no way that she could allow Dex to pay for everything.

"What about this," Dex asked, pointing to a tempering machine.

Briar choked on her spit. He could not be serious. "Absolutely not!"

"Why, I read that—"

"Because! That particular machine costs over three thousand…Wait…You looked this up?"

Briar had rarely seen Dex blush, but that's exactly what appeared to be happening.

"I was curious about a few things," he said with a shrug, pretending that her interests were of little concern to him.

"Well…That machine is for larger scale projects."

Dex didn't say anything, just stared at her, waiting.

Briar's eyebrows knotted up. "If I wanted that, you'd seriously buy it," she said in disbelief. It wasn't a question, just a statement. "Why?"

He knew how it might look to Briar. He had given her a job, technically two. He gave her a place to live, rent free. He made sure she didn't have to only wear thrift store clothes to school. From the outside looking in, it looked like he was trying to buy her, to buy her affection. In reality, that was the furthest thing from the truth.

"I know this is your thing, the baking and chocolate making. I want to make sure you have everything you need."

"Dex…"

He told himself not to say it over and over again. Something about the statement felt like he was crossing a line, and yet, the words still tumbled from his lips. "I want to make you happy." With a shake of his head, he tried to rephrase. "I mean, I want to see you happy, and if that stupid machine will help you, then why not?"

"I don't need things to make me happy," Briar sighed.

She knew Dex was coming from a different place than her dad. Her dad bought her things not to make her happy, but because a part of him felt guilty, especially after remarrying. Once he married Portia, and Briar had her meltdown, all he ever did was buy her things. He loved her, but he never bothered to ask her what would make her happy.

"I know that," Dex said, interrupting Briar's thoughts. "But will this make it easier for you?"

Briar twisted her lips and stood tall. She rolled her eyes. "I know how to temper chocolate. That's for amateurs," she only partially lied. Her tempering could use a little work.

While Dex didn't doubt that, "Is it about the money?"

Briar tried to hide her reaction. Dex had a way of always reading her face. It was a hundred percent about the money. How could he casually spend over three thousand dollars on a birthday gift.

Dex stepped closer and tilted his head to the side, evaluating Briar. He could see the wheels turning in her head. When it took her more than a second to respond, he already knew the answer.

"Ah...It's because I'm a mechanic, and you don't think I can afford that." Though he was teasing, he quickly saw that Briar felt guilty that he thought that.

"No," Briar gasped, not wanting to offend Dex. "There's nothing wrong with being—"

"Three hundred and fifty thousand," Dex interrupted.

Briar's mouth hung open and she blinked a couple times. "I don't...I don't understand."

"That's how much I profited off my last restoration when it went to auction."

Briar didn't know what to say to that. So, Dex had a little money. A part of her almost wished that she hadn't known. She came from a world of money, and in the end, it was a sad world.

She met Dex's eyes, wondering if anything would change with that bit of information, but it hadn't. Dex could be worth millions, and it didn't change anything. To Briar, he was simple, caring, helpful to everyone around him, albeit, a bit of an asshole from time to time. Most of all, he cared about making her happy.

For the first time in a long time, her birthday didn't completely suck.

CHAPTER 30

She thought that thought too soon.

Dex wanted to take her to a nice dinner for her birthday once they got back to Argent Falls that evening. The town had one extremely nice restaurant, an upscale Italian place, only open five hours every evening.

As much as Briar would have loved it, the look on Dex's face when he mentioned it, made it impossible for her to accept his offer. While he wanted to do something different, Briar knew that going to a place like that, with a person of the opposite sex, screamed date. That was clearly something that terrified Dex.

Therefore, Briar suggested they keep it simple by going to the pizza parlor, Bontà Grassa. That seemed to relax Dex. Briar wouldn't say anything, but the pizza was nearly the equivalent of a fancy Italian restaurant. It reminded her of her first night with Dex, and for some reason, made her feel a little wistful.

What Briar forgot was just how small of a town Argent Falls was.

Dex tensed when halfway through what had been a pleasant meal with Briar, a group walked in, every one of them recognizable to him.

For a split second, he held on to the hope that maybe they were just picking up; however, as they made their way farther inside, he knew that wasn't the case.

Briar shyly brought her head down, hoping the women wouldn't see them. Unfortunately, Dex stood out wherever he went. Tall, handsome, incredible hair, melting blue eyes, the female population would notice him from outer space.

"Well, isn't this cute," an all too familiar voice cooed from nearby.

Dex took a long sip of his soda before responding with a simple, "Lexi."

Briar looked up momentarily to see two faces she recognized, and one she did not. A cringy feeling ran through her. Lexi was friends with the woman Dex brought home?

"Hi, Dex," Hannah said in a rather seductive way.

Dex looked from Lexi to Hannah. The knowing way she stared back at him meant that she hadn't said anything about that night to her friend. "Hey," was all he said in response.

Hannah smiled and shook her head. She tugged on the elbow of the other girl, Becca, another hairstylist, and motioned toward an empty table several away from Dex and Briar. Not so strangely, the greeting hadn't been enough for Lexi, as she still stood before them, her attention now fully on Briar.

"Blair, sweetie. It's nice to see you."

Briar took a barely noticeable deep breath and smiled sweetly. Rather than give in to Lexi's inner, outer, and all-around bitch, "Likewise."

"You know, I hear your name quite often," Lexi went on.

Briar wanted to point out that if that were the case, she could have called her by the right name to begin with. She wasn't stupid, Lexi knew her name. Lexi wanted Briar to feel as though she wasn't important enough for her name to be remembered.

Lexi became mildly annoyed that Briar nor Dex said anything in response. "I guess stealing my boyfriend wasn't enough. You had to go and steal my sister too." Lexi let out a cackle. "I swear, it's like you're obsessed with me."

Briar gave Lexi an incredulous look, and from her peripheral vision noticed that Dex was about to blow up.

Ignoring most of Lexi's comments, Briar quickly spoke before Dex could. "Alyssa. Yeah, she's pretty great. She actually introduced herself to me, and I'm so thankful that she did. She's been a great friend."

Lexi scoffed. "Whatever. She's a gothic loser. It's no surprise that the two of you would get along."

Dex didn't know what clouded his judgment when it came to Lexi, but now, watching how she and Briar spoke to each other, he realized just how immature and snotty Lexi was.

Thankfully, Becca called out for Lexi, as their waitress had arrived.

"Well, I hope the two of you enjoy your little *date*," Lexi hissed, emphasizing the last word.

"Everything was fine until you showed up," Dex replied with little emotion.

"Oh, go to hell, Dex."

Just like that, Lexi spun on her heels and stomped off to her friends.

Briar watched Dex carefully. He didn't look up at her, only went back to his pizza.

She was confused. Maybe Dex didn't want to go into it any further with Lexi, but he still should have corrected her. It was just pizza. Definitely not a date. Though Dex didn't strike her as the type of person who cared too much about the opinions of others, shouldn't he have cared just a little about such a drastic assumption?

Briar and Dex had nice conversation prior to the arrival of Lexi; however, once that happened, they ate in mostly silence, quickly finishing the remainder of their meal and paying before the girls even received their order.

The sun had already set, and downtown was twinkling with streetlights as Briar and Dex walked toward their parking lot. It was then that Briar stopped at a little vintage shop on the corner.

Dex was about to cross the street, but noticed that Briar wasn't beside him. He didn't know what she was looking at. The lights in the shop had been out for a couple hours now, and there wasn't much to see through the windows.

Briar looked around, behind her and to her left and right. "You know what? This is a great location."

Dex was curious. "Oh, yeah?"

"Yeah. It's on one of the main streets through town, and directly across from parking."

"Maybe that's why Benny Georges has had this shop for over fifty years," Dex added.

Briar looked up to the sign above the main doors that read Georges' Antiques and Collectibles.

"Great location for what?"

Briar looked down. Hopefully some of the darkness concealed her reddened cheeks. "It's nothing. Just a silly idea."

"I'd still like to know what you were thinking," Dex asked with slight caution.

"Well, I think it would make a wonderful spot for a bakery or chocolaterie."

Dex didn't want to come across as harsh, but he was realistic. "Argent Falls has a bakery, and anything too fancy probably wouldn't float around here."

Briar rolled her eyes and chuckled. "Your bakery," she said, using air quotes. "Sells donuts and pigs in the blanket. Also, you just drove well over an hour for supplies. Argent Falls is within two hours of three major cities. If you have something that's worth it, people will go out of their way for it."

A tiny part of Dex loved her optimism. She wasn't entirely wrong. He and his father once restored the car of a CEO based out of Los Angeles. That was on the opposite side of the country.

"Good luck convincing Benny of that," he said, motioning to the street, as it was a clear time for them to cross.

Briar knew it was crazy. Maybe in an ideal world she'd be able to afford her own business one day, but she had many years of hard work ahead of her.

* * *

Briar tried to help Dex carry in the bags, but he managed with all except one. She was grateful that he dropped the idea of buying her a tempering machine.

Briar went through the bags, organizing her supplies so they'd be out of Dex's way. That's when she came across a small box that she hadn't picked out. "What's this," she asked, twirling the box in her hand.

"Candles," Dex responded with a questioning tone.

"I can see that. I didn't put these in the cart."

Dex went to the refrigerator and got a cold bottle of water. As much as he loved the pizza at Bontà Grassa, the grease and salt left him craving water all night.

"Don't all birthday cakes need candles?"

"Maybe if you're five," Briar quickly answered; however, began opening the box.

She went to the dining table, where she placed her cake before they left earlier that day. She took all but two candles from the box of twenty. In the kitchen behind her, clinking and clanking could be heard from Dex.

When she was almost done arranging the candles, Dex came to the table with several items. He set down two plates and forks and pushed a large knife in Briar's direction as he used a lighter, setting the little wicks ablaze. Briar was tempted to point out that a thinner knife would be more delicate on the cake, but left it alone.

"Just so you know, I'm not singing to you," Dex informed Briar as he lit the last candle and took his seat.

Briar couldn't help but laugh; however, she did find Dex's deep voice undeniably attractive, and for a split second had to wonder what his singing might sound like.

She crossed her left leg under herself and hovered over the table.

Dex watched her carefully, her eyes closed, and brows knotted in contemplation, as she made a wish. A second more and the moment was over. Through a soft haze of smoke, her eyes fluttered open and found his, and he couldn't stop his chest from tightening. He hated how sweet and beautiful she was, hated how she made him feel things he wished would have stayed buried in his lifetime.

"You don't have to force yourself to eat it," Briar said, placing a slice of cake on the plate closer to Dex. "I know you aren't fond of chocolate."

Without thinking, "It's starting to grow on me."

Briar's eyes fell to her own plate and quickly took a bite, unable to respond to a comment that she was clearly taking the wrong way.

"So, what did you wish for," Dex eventually asked.

Briar's eyes widened. "I can't tell you that."

"Why?"

"Here's where I'm supposed to give you the classic response, *if I do, it won't come true*," Briar teased.

"Something to do with that course in London," Dex asked, taking Briar by surprise.

A flash of disappointment came across her face as she took the last bite of her cake. "Something like that," she lied.

She rose from the table and reached out for Dex's plate, but he stopped her.

"I'll clean up," he quickly insisted, grabbing her plate instead.

Briar hung back for a moment before following Dex into the kitchen. She bit her lip uncomfortably. The day had gone so well, even despite running into Lexi; it was wonderful. She didn't want to do anything that would make it uncomfortable for Dex.

"Thank you," Briar stated rather simply.

Dex turned from his place at the sink and actually smiled. It wouldn't have been obvious to someone who didn't know him, but Briar saw it in his eyes. It was as much of a smile as he'd give right now.

Without thinking, Briar took a step forward. When Dex narrowed his eyes, questioningly, she immediately regretted the gesture and took two steps backward.

Dex closed his eyes with a long blink and took in a deep breath before opening them. "You can hug me if you want."

215

Briar tried not to freak out, but she wanted to hug Dex. Before he could change his mind, she rushed toward him and flung her arms around his torso, her fingertips barely coming into contact at his back.

"Thank you," she repeated, breathing into his chest. "Today was great."

Dex wasn't good when it came to certain forms of physical contact, but he wrapped his arms around her small frame and held her against him.

Tears almost came to Briar's eyes, knowing that where they stood now would be the closest Dex would ever allow her, squashing any wishes she might have for something more.

CHAPTER 31

Meanwhile…

Two hundred miles away.

"Whoa," Leo exclaimed, walking into the massive living room, void of all light but that of the fireplace. "It feels like a funeral in here."

Portia glared at her son from her half empty glass. "No, you idiot. If it were a funeral, well, that would be a blessing for us."

"I told you, I'm working on it," Leo stressed. He took a seat on one of the sofas.

"No. That's not good enough anymore!"

Leo groaned at his mother's dramatic outburst. "Apparently, Briar had some connections at that academy. Also, there was no one listed on her records after her father's death; therefore, you and I can't freely request anything."

"She was a minor!"

Leo shook his head. "Again, she must have known someone in that place and talked to them before all this happened."

"Did you try bribing the–"

"*That* didn't work. Like I said, I'm working on it," Leo stressed.

Portia took a long sip of her vodka. "Working on it? Screwing around with the office women isn't what I'd consider *working on it*. I've come up with a better and faster plan, one I should have gone with as soon as that filthy lawyer told me about this."

Leo eyed his mother suspiciously. In the last couple weeks, she had become even more obsessed with finding Briar and eliminating her chances of claiming her fortune.

"Private investigator," Portia finally said.

"I don't think that's a good idea. How will it look if Briar ends up dead after you hired someone to find her?"

Portia hadn't considered that. "I'm her stepmother. I care about her well-being, so I needed to find her," she laughed.

"Oh, come on, mother. We fucked up when we didn't report her missing months ago. If the daughter of the late Ingrid Vera Norberg is found dead, you know there will be an investigation like—"

"Stop," Portia screamed at the top of her lungs. "Don't you ever say that bitch's name."

Leo closed his eyes in frustration.

Portia considered herself lucky, having hit the jackpot with Grover Stone; however, she soon found out that she'd never be first, or even second, in his life. His heart would always belong with Ingrid, and he would move heaven and earth for Briar.

Shortly after Portia and Grover married, Briar attempted suicide by slashing her wrists. Grover felt so guilty that he continued to spoil Briar rotten, even when she objected. Gradually, it took a toll on his relationship with Portia. He claimed that he loved her, but she knew those were empty words.

Leo began more calmly with his mother. "Give me a few more days. I promise, we'll know where she is, and I'll take care of this. Just don't get anyone else involved," he stressed.

"I want results, Leo."

"Briar's smart, but she's not that smart. Plus, she has no money and no family. She couldn't have gotten far," Leo speculated.

He wouldn't tell his mother, but he wanted to find Briar for different reasons, reasons that had nothing to do with money.

The feeling of being in total control of Briar still sent chills through Leo. He had been with women since then. It was basic, boring. He kept his sickness in check.

It was only at night, when he was alone, that he let his thoughts go back to that day. He loved the feeling of his hand tightening around her neck, having her gasp for breath. Her screams still echoed in his head. Other women screamed in pleasure, but that didn't do it for him. It was the screams of agony and torture from her that stayed in his head. He got off knowing that he was her first, ripping her to shreds, breaking her, leaving her a bloodied and bruised mess.

No, he wouldn't tell his mother that; however, he was already anticipating when he found Briar. This time he'd take his time with her, living out every sick and twisted fantasy he had for her.

CHAPTER 32

"You're so lucky," Alyssa sighed as she scribbled down some numbers.

Briar looked up from her bowl of filling. "How so?"

"You get to leave school at 1:30 even on days you don't work."

"True, but my weekends are pretty much nonexistent. I do work at Dex's shop most days, but Sandy doesn't like me working too much and too late at the restaurant on school nights," Briar clarified.

"Have you heard from that program yet?"

"No. I won't know anything until sometime in December. If I do get in, I have until mid-January to give them an answer, and I'd need to be there by the beginning of February at the very latest," Briar babbled.

Alyssa let out a groan and Briar put her bowl down. She took Alyssa's paper and looked over the problem, soon instructing Alyssa as to where she messed up.

"Thanks," Alyssa mumbled. "You know, as much as I want you to get accepted. I'd really miss you."

Briar laughed. "Why? You can still text and email me your calculus problems."

Alyssa stuck out her tongue. "It won't be the same."

Briar turned quiet and solemn. Lately, a part of her didn't want to think about London. Though it wasn't the glamourous life she imagined, she was starting to fall in love with Argent Falls. She didn't want to think about leaving yet.

"Oh! I forgot to tell you," Alyssa said after a much-needed break of silence. "Bradley hooked up with Serena."

Briar didn't know much about Serena, just that she was a cheerleader. "That's nice, I guess."

"You don't care?"

"Why would I," Briar questioned back, utterly confused.

"I just know that he had a thing for you not too long ago. You never said much about it, but I thought–"

"No. No. No," Briar began, waving her hands. "He expressed interest, but he's not my type. Besides, I have too much on my plate to even bother with boys."

"Boys," Alyssa emphasized. A teasing and knowing grin came to her face.

Briar watched her curiously, but said nothing. Eventually, Alyssa burst into a fit of laughter. "I don't get it."

"Does Dex have anything to do with the fact that you're not bothering with any *boys*?"

Disappointment came crashing through Briar. "No."

"Oh…Wow…" Alyssa gasped.

"What now?"

Alyssa became serious. "I was just messing with you. I mean, Dex is gorgeous. There isn't a woman in town who would turn him down. But…" Alyssa paused and gave Briar a sad look. "You like him."

Attempting not to turn to a puddle of goo thinking about her crush on Dex, Briar veered the conversation away from what Alyssa was suggesting, downplaying her speculation. "I do like him. He's helped me out a lot, and I'll forever be grateful for that."

"You know what I mean! Seriously, my sister blew up when she found out about you living with him. Don't tell me that nothing has happened between the two of you."

Briar shrugged. "Sorry to disappoint you."

"Damn."

Just like that, Alyssa dropped all talk of Dex, giving Briar the slightest bit of relief, and quelling the butterflies that came to life in her stomach when she thought of all the moments with Dex that meant so much to her.

Though it seemed like it happened a lifetime ago, she still couldn't forget that kiss. There were so many times where she wanted to try again, but the way Dex freaked out that night made her sick to her stomach.

Briar and Alyssa were wrapped up in talking that neither of them heard the door open and close.

"I take it that's not dinner."

Briar jumped at Dex's voice and met his eyes across the room. They were less pissed off than usual.

"I...Uh...I'll be done soon," she stammered.

"I was joking," he said without a hint of humor in his voice. He turned his attention to the person at the bar. "Alyssa."

"Hey, Dex. We were just talking about you." Alyssa finished her statement with shooting Briar a look.

Briar was too quick to respond. "No, we weren't."

Dex watched the two as they gave each other strange looks, silently communicating to each other. He didn't dare ask.

He made his way into the kitchen. There were bowls filled with strange things he couldn't even begin to describe. The whole apartment smelled sweet and chocolatey. Lining part of the large island, he saw that Briar had her seashell shaped molds out.

Without getting too close, he leaned over Briar and peered into the large bowl that she was currently working on. He dipped his hand near the bowl, not expecting Briar to react.

"Shit," she gasped.

From the other side of the room, Alyssa burst into a fit of laughter.

Dex felt the warm chocolate from Briar's spatula plastered to his forehead. He took his index finger and swiped at it.

Holding his finger inches from Briar's face, "Seriously?"

Briar met his gaze, thinking he might be irritated, but this time, there was a sparkle in those intense and enchanting blue eyes. Without thinking, forgetting they weren't alone, she foolishly reacted.

Dex felt his throat close up, brain shut down, lungs forget how to process the simple act of breathing, when Briar's mouth closed over his finger. Her tongue swirled around the tip, and she applied only the smallest amount of suction.

Just as soon as she started, she pulled away, leaving his finger void of any substance but her.

Briar looked at Dex with wide eyes and felt her cheeks burn to ashes. She couldn't hide the horrified look on her face, and quickly looked away before Dex could freak out.

From nearby, Alyssa began to pack her things. Trying to keep her voice as even as possible, "On that note, I should be going."

Briar let the spatula fall into the bowl. She hurried from the kitchen toward Alyssa. "I'll walk you out."

It was only when the door closed that Dex could breathe. He looked down and adjusted himself, letting out a string of curse words and running his hand through his hair, as he often did in frustration.

He wasn't sure where to go from that, but he didn't want Briar to think that things were awkward. The mood was light. For some time now, things were more relaxed and stable between the two of them. He didn't want to freak out again and change that.

✳ ✳ ✳

Alyssa shrieked as soon as the apartment door closed. "Oh my god! That was so—"

"Embarrassing," Briar interrupted with a groan.

Alyssa rapidly shook her head. "No. That was hot."

"What? You're kidding, right?" Briar smoothed back her already pristine and pinned hair. "He probably thinks I'm such a weirdo. I don't know what I was thinking."

"Did you see the look on his face," Alyssa gasped. She and Briar had to have been in different rooms.

"Not really…"

"I honestly don't know what would have happened if I weren't there. The way he looked at you…Just…Wow."

Briar didn't allow herself to get her hopes up. As soon as she walked back in the apartment, she was certain Dex would have some words for her.

Alyssa shoved Briar in the arm. "I can't believe you told me nothing is going on between you two."

"Because nothing is," Briar stressed.

"After seeing that little exchange, the both of you clearly want something to be."

Briar was screaming on the inside, telling her heart to stop that pounding full of hope and desperation. Everything Alyssa continued to say, Briar was quick to shut down. Whatever Alyssa thought she saw in that moment with Dex, was wrong.

Dex made it clear long ago where they stood, and now that they were getting along rather well, Briar didn't want to do anything to jeopardize that.

Briar was both shocked and disappointed when she returned to the apartment and Dex was still hovering in the kitchen. She hoped to avoid him and any conversation for just a little longer.

Dex watched Briar as she hesitantly came into the kitchen, avoiding eye contact at all costs. He didn't say anything; he'd wait for her to do that. From the looks of it, there were a million things running through her mind, and as much as he wanted to know every single one, he was honestly too terrified to open that door.

Briar began stirring one of her more time sensitive concoctions; although, Dex standing there was a complete distraction.

"Sorry about hitting you with the spatula," Briar finally managed.

Dex needed to lighten the heavy air that had fallen around them. "I don't think you are," he countered, a teasing tone to his voice.

Briar found herself chuckling. "Maybe you did deserve it."

"Oh, yeah?"

Briar closed her eyes and took in a breath. Dex had stepped closer to her from behind. She knew because she could feel the heat radiating off him from his closeness.

"Yeah," she answered, her voice sounding more needy than she expected.

Briar yelped and bit her lip the moment Dex snaked his hand around her and pulled her back against his chest. He reached over and grabbed one of the spatulas, saturated in chocolate and brought it to her face.

"Dex!"

Briar squirmed against him, to which he began tickling her and continuing to pelt her face and neck with the gooey remains on the spatula.

"Stop it," Briar squealed, although she had a hard time fighting off her laughter, as well as Dex.

Though he couldn't see her face, Dex was content. He tossed the spatula back in the bowl and released Briar from his grasp. As soon as he took a step back, she spun around, and a wicked grin immediately came to his face.

"Satisfied," Briar asked sarcastically. She couldn't see much, except for a few drips on her old t-shirt, but she could feel the warmth now cooling on her cheeks and neck.

"I think you look good," Dex laughed.

"I'm sure I smell and taste good as well," she grumbled. "Considering you just—"

She stopped midsentence when she looked up at Dex. His smiled faded and his eyes flickered over her face. That cool and calm blue seemed to darken.

Dex bit his lip, but he could already feel a nervous sickness consuming him. His mind wasn't operating the way it was supposed to. All feeling had gone to two organs that really needed to shut the hell up in that moment. His heart and his dick.

"You do smell good," he acknowledged, bringing himself too close to her.

Briar swallowed heavily and stopped breathing when Dex, nearly a foot taller than her, brought his head down toward her. For a second, she allowed her eyes to flutter in anticipation of a kiss, which she'd welcome fully; however, what Dex did instead caused her whole body to explode.

He wasn't thinking. That was the only thought he was able to have.

At first, he meant for it to be a shock factor when his tongue licked at the smeared chocolate across her neck, but once he tasted it, he found that he had difficulty pulling away. Something about the flavor and her soft skin hypnotized him, making him unable to pull away.

Briar was frozen in place with the initial contact, but soon it turned into more. A small flick of Dex's tongue on her neck turned into contact she'd never had with a man, and it felt unexplainable. Briar took in her bottom lip between her teeth and fought to regulate her breathing.

Dex's tongue softly swirled along Briar's neck, applying the lightest suction, careful not to leave any marks. He walked her back half a step until her backside was pressed into the counter and her chest was flush against his.

Briar's arms went around Dex's torso, to his back, her nails digging in, needing something to hold onto with the sensations Dex was sending throughout her entire body. Fire ran from where his lips connected to her neck, down her chest, until she could feel a wanting heat building lower.

She couldn't fight back the small moan when Dex pushed his hips farther into her and his erection dug into her stomach.

Briar vocalizing her pleasure only further messed with Dex's head, and he couldn't help the nipping of his teeth against her neck. With that, Briar gasped, and her nails clenched deeper into his back, only slightly bringing Dex back to reality.

A single coherent thought came to Dex. *Fuck. This could not be happening.*

He should have let her go and stepped away like she was molten lava, the plague, the reaper coming for his last breath, but after what he just did, he knew how much it would hurt her.

Dex slowly pulled away, their faces still too close. Briar took a few long blinks as Dex watched her eyes fall to his lips. She didn't want to stop. It was clearly written on her face, and knowing that made being near her incredibly dangerous.

After another second, Dex pulled away entirely, putting more than an arm's length of distance between them.

Briar felt that nauseating feeling coming to her stomach. The butterflies that were once wildly dancing were being pelted to death with burning stones. Dex did a good job pretending to hide it, but she could read his face, especially his eyes, more clearly than ever. He was terrified and wrecked with guilt, attempting not to tailspin like he had done when they first kissed.

She needed to find something to say, as whatever happened between them was undoubtedly over and not moving beyond that moment. "Did it taste okay," she asked, bringing the tips of her fingers to the now clean spot on her neck where Dex's lips had just been.

Dex's eyes flew up to hers. He was nearly at a loss for words with the bold question, not fully understanding exactly what she was asking. He only replied with a simple, "It was good."

He turned and pressed himself into the cabinet of the bar, pleading internally for his boner to go away and never return for the duration of Briar's time with him. Feeling an awkwardness, "You should probably go to the bathroom and clean up."

He thought he handled it well; however, when he glanced behind him to an empty room, he had to assume that Briar saw it differently, as well she should.

There were too many times where he was close to losing it with her. This topped them all, even the kiss on the couch. She initiated the kiss, and he allowed it to continue and to progress, but this was different. He wanted to tease her. After her comment, it was only supposed to be a lick, but it tasted incredible…She tasted incredible.

He needed a release, but it wouldn't be like before. This time, the gym would have to do.

* * *

Briar finished wiping the remnants of chocolate from her cheek and forehead. The coarse towel feeling nothing close to Dex's tongue. From nearby, she could hear the faint rumbling of rock music coming from Dex's room.

Dex was the type of person that was blunt, liking to get everything out in the open and resolved. Though it made Briar nervous, remembering how their conversation about the kiss had gone, Dex calling it a mistake and poor judgment, talking about what happened in the kitchen would be for the best. It seemed like the lines between them, the ones that were so clear at first, were becoming more blurred by the day.

Needing some type of closure or explanation, even if all it would be is Dex calling it a mistake again, led Briar to standing on the other side of his door. Hesitantly, she tapped her knuckles across the thin barrier separating them. She shifted her weight from side to side, waiting for Dex to come to the door. When he didn't, she tried again, hoping her knocks came through over the music.

In hindsight, she should have left it alone, but she'd only regret her choices minutes later. Trying the doorknob and finding it unlocked, Briar slowly opened the door and called out Dex's name; however, as soon as she saw him, she became speechless and unable to move. It was a sight that she would never be able to erase from her memory. If she thought her body was heated from their encounter in the kitchen, from his touch, that was nothing compared to now. The only difference, Dex wasn't touching her. He was touching himself.

He didn't know how long she stood there, but even a second was too long. As soon as he opened his eyes, so close to a much needed release, and saw her across the room, Dex tore his hand away from his engorged cock and quickly pulled up his basketball shorts he had changed into.

"I…I'm sorry…I knocked…and…" Briar shakily began.

Dex growled and flung himself down into the bed. "Get. Out."

He didn't have to tell her twice. From his peripheral vision, he saw her disappear before he finished those two words.

It was an absolute nightmare. He didn't intend for any of that to happen. When Dex got to his room, it was with the intention of changing and heading downstairs to the gym; however, this time, it was too difficult to ignore his arousal.

He slammed his fist into the comforter. All he needed was a quick jerking off, and though the desire was still there, he couldn't bring himself to finish, not knowing what Briar just saw.

Dex had to get out of the apartment. The whole evening, from the moment he walked in the door, was something out of a horrible and twisted dream. They were too comfortable together. It was becoming too easy to forget about lines that shouldn't be crossed. Friends and roommates were all they needed to be.

Briar would be leaving in a couple months. That's what Dex kept reminding himself. If there was no other reason for not allowing things to progress, that was enough. In the end, they'd only end up hurting each other. Their lives were too different.

If Dex expected Briar to run away and hide in her room, avoiding him, he was strangely mistaken this time. She had changed from the girl feigning toughness that entered his shop months ago. Briar was much cheekier and blunt, which only helped in pushing Dex over the edge with her. It was becoming harder and harder to see her as an injured baby bird, in need of someone to rescue her.

"I'm headed out," Dex casually mentioned as he walked around the kitchen.

Briar, whose back was turned to him as she washed dishes, paused what she was doing. Not daring to look at him, "To the bar?" Her face twisted when she said that, thankful that Dex couldn't see it. The question was laced with jealousy and disdain.

"No. The gym downstairs. You should go ahead and eat without me though. I'll be there for a while."

Briar said no more. Once the door closed, she let out a frustrated breath. She was frustrated because she enjoyed their dinners together; however, she had to see it from Dex's point of view. It would be awkward to say the least. It might be that way for some time now, and she couldn't take that. There was only one way to clear the air about their actions, more so Dex's than hers, and as dangerous as it now sounded, that was talking.

CHAPTER 33

Briar slouched on the couch, flipping through the television stations. She didn't know what she was looking for, or even what she flipped through, at that point. She had already eaten, showered, brushed her teeth, done her entire nightly routine, and Dex still wasn't back. What kind of person spent over three hours at the gym?

She didn't want to think the thoughts that ultimately entered her head. After what happened in the kitchen, and what she saw him doing moments after his tongue was on her skin, she desperately wanted to believe that he wouldn't be out finding some random hookup. However, if he was with someone, at least she didn't have to see and hear it.

Though she continued scrolling through the channels, her mind was still in Dex's bedroom. She couldn't get the image of him stroking himself out of her thoughts. It was something so intimate and private, and all she could wonder about was where his thoughts were when he was doing that. That alone sent a heat rushing down her own body, and for the first time for as long as she could remember, she wanted more with a man.

Briar bolted upright when the opening and closing of the front door pulled her from her fantasies of Dex.

When he rounded the corner, coming into view, Briar's jaw dropped. Dex looked like hell.

His hair was drenched, dripping in sweat, as was his face and basically every inch of skin. His black tank and shorts clung to his body, soaking up every bit of perspiration. His skin was redder than Briar had ever seen, and he seemed to just now be finding oxygen.

Dex glanced to Briar on the couch before turning his attention to the kitchen. For once, her presence had no effect on him; however, deep down, somewhere in his barely functioning brain, he knew he couldn't wash Briar away with hours upon hours at the gym every day.

After chugging his second bottle of water, the adrenaline calmed within him, and tiredness took over. His arms and legs felt like gelatin. His chest and back burned. All the pain and fatigue was welcomed, because with it came the disappearance of his sexual arousal for Briar. He had worn himself past exhaustion, to the point where sex, or even masturbation, was the very last thing his body wanted.

"Dex," her soft voice came from the couch.

Dex turned to face Briar, his feet firmly planted in the kitchen and staying there. They could speak with half the apartment separating them. For a split second, he wanted to tell her that it was late, she had school in the morning, but he knew that would only irritate her, pointing out the years between them.

"Yeah?"

"Uh...How was the gym," Briar asked awkwardly.

Dex snorted. "Great," he lied. He loved working out, and his body clearly reflected that; however, what he did tonight was far past simply working out.

Looking away from Dex and back to the television, "Can we talk?"

Not tonight. That's what he should have said, but a part of him didn't think Briar would go there.

"What about?"

Briar's chest pounded. She didn't expect for Dex to be up for talking about recent events.

"What was that in the kitchen today?" That one question was a struggle for her to get out. A part of her already knew what the deflating answer would be, but she needed to hear it from him. *Mistake.*

Not wanting to squash her like a bug, but not wanting to give her hope, Dex was careful with his words. "I was just messing around, and it got out of hand."

He questioned his words after he said them, thinking that they sounded as best they could. From across the vast distance separating them, he could see a slight marking, a purplish-blue scratch, on Briar's neck from where he lightly nipped her toward the end.

Dex knew that if he didn't take control, the conversation could quickly become treacherous, and he hadn't just spent more than three hours at the gym, only to go to bed with a raging desire for his roommate. *Roommate.* That's all she was to him.

Before Briar could say anything, Dex began making his way as far from her as possible. He desperately needed a shower and as much sleep as time would allow.

"I'm not done," Briar insisted, rather boldly.

Dex stopped at the edge of the hallway. When he turned, Briar was faced backward, her chin on her hands that were covering the back of the couch, watching him. He could feel himself beginning to unravel the second their eyes met, and it was in that moment that he knew. He'd never be able to completely get Briar out of his system, to wash away all desire for her.

"Well, I am," Dex coldly responded, although he waited for her next question or statement.

Briar looked down, already feeling her cheeks reddening. "In your room earlier–"

"We're not going there. Forget whatever it is you think you saw," Dex insisted.

It was difficult, so difficult, but if she didn't rip off the bandage and ask, then she may never have the courage. As hard as it was going to be, she had to look him in the eyes, had to see how he'd react.

"What were you thinking about?"

Dex's eyes widened in shock, full of disbelief at the fact that Briar just asked that. What the hell was wrong with her? "Seriously," was all he could manage. His tone was more aggressive now.

The words were caught in her throat, but she had to. More than anything, she wished he'd just answer her next question, despite the back of her mind telling her she was wasting her time. "Were you thinking about me?"

That was hands down the last question Dex ever expected Briar to ask. It was too blunt, too bold. She had to know that he couldn't answer that truthfully; however, by asking, it meant that she didn't expect for the answer to be as simple as *no*.

Rather than say another word, Dex stormed off.

Briar sank back in the couch. A part of her figured that's how that might take place. Another part of her had undoubtedly read too many romance novels. If she thought she could push Dex to admit even the smallest attraction toward her, that right there told her differently.

Dex stopped at his room, adrenaline now raced through his veins once more. His heart beat uncontrollably, still bewildered that Briar would go there, would ask something so personal.

Against his better judgment, he went back to the living room.

Briar stopped breathing when she felt Dex's hands nearly slam into the back of the couch, each one inches from her shoulders. He brought his face close to the side of hers, and she could feel his heat, smell a mixture of sweat and a scent that was inherently Dex.

"Don't waste your breath asking questions you already know the fucking answer to," he hissed in her ear.

His breath sent tingles all across the skin of her cheek and down her neck. She didn't dare turn around when she felt him push off from the couch. It was only when he closed his bedroom door behind him that her brain began to function again, realizing what he just said, had just admitted, in his own way.

There was no way that she'd be able to close her eyes and not think of Dex that night.

✳ ✳ ✳

"What's going on with you," Rusty asked.

Briar doodled on a post-it while waiting at the reception desk.

"Briar?"

Hearing her name jolted her from her daydreaming. "Huh," she asked, having no clue what Rusty said prior.

He tossed a clipboard on the desk for Briar. "You've seemed out of it the last week or so. Is everything okay?"

Briar sat upright and tried to focus. It had been about that long since that strange evening with Dex, and her focus was slipping, especially when she was at work at the shop.

"I've just got a lot on my mind, school and work...and stuff." There was no way that she would say anything more to Rusty. She hadn't even told Alyssa what happened with Dex. It was too private.

Rusty leaned over the counter, suspiciously watching Briar. "Does this have anything to do with Dex?"

The mentioning of his name caused Briar to jump, which only fed Rusty's curiosity. Briar wondered if Rusty knew something. Lately she and Dex were a little awkward around each other. The first couple days were nearly unbearable, but now they were able to have conversations. Although, she couldn't help but become uncomfortable when, in the middle of a conversation, her mind screwed with her, sending vivid images of Dex naked.

Thankfully, Rusty's suspicions went in a different direction. "Is he being an asshole again?"

Briar couldn't help but laugh. "No. He's alright."

"I don't know about that. He's always been quiet, but lately he's quieter. Don't get me wrong, he can be a moody little bitch, but there have been a couple instances in the last few days where he's just flown off the handle. Figured he might be giving you a hard time too."

"Really?" Briar hadn't noticed. Oddly, Dex was much calmer around her.

Before Rusty could go on, the door from the garage swung open. Briar didn't need to turn to know who it was. She never believed all that magical crap when it came to relationships, but the more she was around Dex, the more she found it to be true. Something about his presence, she could feel it when he was near.

"Well, speak of the devil," Rusty chuckled.

Dex's eyes went from Rusty to Briar. She looked uncomfortable, and Dex had to wonder what the two of them were talking about before he entered.

"What's that supposed to mean," Dex asked, a little more aggressively than needed.

Rusty's eyes narrowed playfully and a smirk came to his face. "Oh, nothing. Briar and I were just having a little chat about you."

"Really?"

Briar quickly stood from her seat. "No we weren't," she blurted out. Feeling skittish with both sets of eyes now upon her, she excused herself to the bathroom.

Rusty waited until the door closed behind Briar. "Why don't we take a break outside. I need a smoke."

Dex rolled his eyes, but began to follow Rusty. "I thought you quit that shit."

"Dude, my sister and her kids are still living with me. You'd smoke a hell of a lot more than a couple cigarettes if you were in my position." As they walked through the front door, Rusty couldn't help but point out the wanted sign. "That's been there for months. You do know that no mechanic is going to be walking down the street looking for a job around here."

Dex shrugged, the sign not bothering him nearly as much as Rusty.

Dex leaned into the wall of the side of the building. "Aside from you needing a smoke, what's up?"

"I'm hoping you could tell me that."

"Not much. The Bentley is almost—"

"Cut the shit," Rusty interrupted, a hint of laughter in his words. "I mean with you and Briar. One minute you two were buddies, hanging out, having dinner. Now, she's jumpy around you. You barely talk to her in the shop."

"I'm working," Dex pointed out.

"You know what I mean. When the two of you are in a room together, the tension is so thick."

Dex pressed his head to the brick and looked up to the cold autumn sky.

Rusty deeply inhaled the cigarette. "Just spill already. What the hell did you do?"

Dex had very few guys to talk to. For the most part, he liked to keep his private life just that. Private. If there was one person he could mention recent events to, it would be Rusty. The only other person he shared details of his life with was Sandy, but Sandy was too protective of Briar now. If he knew what happened between them, he'd no doubt smash Dex across the head with a bottle.

"We had a moment."

Rusty didn't say anything, and allowed the words to sink in, not knowing what Dex meant. When Dex didn't give any details, "What kind of shit is that. *We had a moment?* Sounds like some wussy crap from some stupid romantic comedy."

Dex found himself laughing at that. Those were words he didn't think he had ever used when describing an encounter.

Hesitantly, and careful with his words, attempting to play it down, Dex filled Rusty in on what happened between him and Briar in the kitchen a week prior.

"I don't know why I did that," Dex concluded.

"Uh…You dumbass! You like her."

Dex shook his head. "No," he lied. "Even if I did, you can like someone without making a move on them."

"I'm actually surprised you managed for this long," Rusty commented through a lungful of smoke.

Dex gave him a curious look.

"Come on, seriously? The moment you saw her when she stood in there looking for a job, you were already interested. Now that you've gotten to know her—"

Interrupting Rusty, "Now who sounds like some screwed up romance?"

Rusty scrunched up his face. "I just don't see how that is enough to mess the two of you up for the last week."

Dex held his breath and looked down at the gravel beneath his feet. He debated telling Rusty everything. If it had stopped with that moment in the kitchen, it might have been a different story; however, it was everything that happened after.

"Dex?"

"What," Dex quickly asked, unaware that Rusty was still talking.

"Okay, you were in another world just now. What is it? What aren't you telling me?"

For a minute, Dex thought about bumming a cigarette off Rusty if the conversation were to continue.

"Wait," Rusty gasped. "Did the two of you…"

"No. Absolutely not."

"Don't freak out. I just thought…I don't know."

Dex rubbed his hand down his face. "She walked in on me," he finally admitted.

Rusty took one last drag of his cigarette and tossed the remains to the ground squashing them out with his boot. "Walked in on you," he quietly repeated, not sure what Dex meant by that statement.

When Rusty looked up, Dex made an obscene gesture with his hand, and Rusty erupted into a vicious fit of laughter.

"Glad you see the humor in it," Dex grumbled, annoyed at how ridiculously funny Rusty thought it to be.

"Dude! No wonder she can barely look at you!"

One thing Dex knew he couldn't tell Rusty, that he'd keep just between Briar and himself, that comment at the end. He didn't think Briar had changed toward him because of what she saw, and he knew for a fact that wasn't why he was a little different lately either.

It was that he basically admitted to her that she was the one on his mind during that act.

If Dex thought that talking it out with Rusty would help, he was completely wrong. He should have known better of Rusty by now. Rusty had told him long ago to go for it with Briar and, though Dex wouldn't admit it, it had very little to do with her age, and everything to do with hurting her. They were on different paths in their life, and neither path involved the other.

CHAPTER 34

Briar put in another two orders and grabbed a tray of plates for a different table. Needless to say, Fridays were crazy busy. Lately, she welcomed that busyness. It kept her mind elsewhere, away from Dex.

Eventually, the more they were around each other and talked, the awkwardness faded. Maybe it had to do with Briar helping Dex with his cars after hours. She read several books, in the little bit of free time that she had, and at least now she knew most of the tools and gadgets. Half the time it felt like that's all she was able to help Dex with, just handing him things.

Much to her displeasure, she hadn't come in physical contact with Dex since that evening in the kitchen. There wasn't even a brush of the hand when they were working together.

She told herself that it was for the best. Sadly, she couldn't tell her heart that. The more time she spent around Dex, even though it was platonic, the more she wanted something *more* with him. She never had feelings like that before, which only made her think that what she felt for Dex wasn't just a silly crush.

"Not too much longer," Jennifer laughed in passing.

Briar glanced at the clock in the kitchen. "Are you kidding me? It's only nine."

Jennifer laughed. "Yeah, I know. I was hoping to give you some encouragement. You look a little tired."

Briar didn't know if she was tired. She was too busy to think about it; however, her feet did hurt. "I've been up since before seven, at school, at Hayden's shop, and now here. I might be a little tired," Briar joked.

"I don't know how you do it. Hell, by the time you're thirty, you're going to be ready to retire."

Briar didn't admit it, but she liked to work. She didn't want to live a cushy lifestyle like her stepmother and so many other women from back home. If all went well, she hoped to have her own business well before thirty.

"Thought you might be at Liam's game. They don't have many more home games left," Jennifer added with sadness in her tone.

"He understands."

Briar didn't have many friends. She didn't have much time for them. The few she did have understood how important it was for her to work. While they didn't know everything, most importantly the wealth she came from, they knew her parents were gone, and she was left with nothing.

Just then, Alfred shoved several plates for one of Briar's tables under the heat lamps, and as quickly as her conversation with Jennifer started, it was over.

* * *

Dex arrived at Chêne a couple hours earlier than usual. Briar worked until eleven or twelve on Fridays, depending how busy it was and if they needed an extra set of hands for cleaning up.

Rusty persuaded Dex to join him for a few beers that night, as he was going more insane by the day with his sister and her kids.

"What can I get you boys," Marlee asked.

"Two Bud Lights," Rusty answered.

"They both better be for you," Dex chimed in before Marlee could leave.

"The hell, man? You're not drinking?"

Dex turned to Marlee. "Just a water."

Rusty jokingly punched Dex's shoulder once Marlee left. "What's with you?"

"Just not in the mood for anything."

"I swear, you're like an eighty-year-old, sex-deprived, senile, old bastard," Rusty grumbled.

"Well, at least I won't be showing up hungover tomorrow," Dex quipped back.

Rusty held up his hands in defeat. "I'm going easy tonight."

Marlee brought back the beers and did a poor job of attempting to flirt with an oblivious Rusty. Dex ignored them and found himself looking across the crowded bar, through the partitions, hoping to catch a glimpse of Briar. It was one of the few times he could watch her without her knowing, without her wondering why he was looking at her and what he was thinking.

Dex glanced toward Rusty, but watched Marlee tend to another table from his peripheral vision. "You know she's into you."

"Too old," was all Rusty said, although he did look in Marlee's direction.

"She's your age," Dex scoffed.

Rusty wiggled his brows. "Like I said, too old."

Dex didn't understand Rusty. To say that he was a giant man-child was an understatement. Dex assumed that someone his age would be thinking about settling down; however, Rusty still enjoyed going to clubs outside of Argent Falls and picking up any girl over the age of twenty-one.

Dex couldn't help but feel a little bad for Marlee. She looked at Rusty with hope and stars in her eyes.

"You should give her a chance. You never know."

"Whoa," Rusty coughed after a swig of his beer.

"If not, then set her straight. Don't lead her on just so you get a free beer here and there."

Rusty raised his brow and took one long sip of his beer. "First of all," he said in a hushed voice. "Don't be telling people that. Secondly, you're one to talk." With that, Rusty nodded in the direction of the restaurant of Chêne.

Dex dropped all talk of Marlee at that point. The last thing he wanted to do was talk with Rusty about Briar.

He wasn't leading Briar on. They were amicable toward each other once again, and he was going out of his way to be cautious with every signal, every comment, every breath, he took around her. So far, it was working.

It didn't matter where he allowed his thoughts to go when he was alone. Those thoughts would never turn into actions.

* * *

"Briar, honey," Rita called out.

Briar finished wiping the table and turned to find Rita, a stack of plates in her hands. She rushed over to help.

"No, no. I've got this. Could you help out at the bar?"

Briar's eyes widened. She had never been asked to help in the bar.

Rita laughed. "Not like that. A huge bachelor party just left. They have eight tables that are a complete mess."

Relieved, "Oh, yeah. Of course."

Briar spent enough time around her drunken stepmother. She had no desire to work in the bar, even if the tips were much better.

To say that the tables were a mess was an understatement. Aside from the gobs of beer bottles, and pyramid of empty shot glasses, it looked like there was a food fight with nachos and wings.

Briar couldn't help but wonder what it was with some men that when they got around friends, fueled with alcohol, they turned into animals in desperate need of housetraining.

Sandy nodded for Briar to come over to the bar where he was currently pouring a line of shots. He kicked at a newly changed trashcan that rolled toward the edge.

Briar caught it and rolled it from behind the bar. It wouldn't be empty for long.

Somewhere between then and the third table, Briar got a funny feeling. She already knew what it was. She had it more often than she cared to admit. Upon looking away from the train wreck of a table and across the still boisterous bar, she saw him.

He and Rusty were at a table against the far wall, and though he appeared to be paying attention to Rusty, even saying a word here and there, he's eyes were completely focused on her.

Briar figured that Dex was just surprised to see her working in the bar, even if it was just cleaning tables and not actually dealing with patrons. She had to squash the feeling that went through her when their eyes met.

Things with Dex were going good, normal. As much as it killed her at times, she was careful with her every word and action around him. Her head knew where they stood, it was her stupid heart that had the problem getting the message.

"Hey, sweetheart," a man at a nearby table called out, snapping his fingers in Briar's direction.

She tore her eyes from whatever staring contest she and Dex were having, and gave the man her attention. "What," she said rather coldly. Jennifer had told her long ago that when in the bar area, sweet, meek, and nice didn't cut it.

The man gave her a rather seductive look, or at least that's what Briar assumed. His expression was hard to decipher in his inebriated state. He held up his empty tumbler and shook it at Briar. "Another whiskey neat."

Briar tried to give everyone the benefit of the doubt, especially when they were impaired. She had dealt with her stepmother long enough when it came to impairment from alcohol.

Something in her had now changed. She didn't like being called sweetheart. Honestly, if Dex ever called her that, it would be a different story, but the tone in this man's voice when he said it rubbed her the wrong way.

Then there was the snapping. There had been one time prior that a patron in the restaurant snapped at her to get her attention. Rita was nearby and lashed out at him. Briar wasn't accustomed to that kind of treatment. Anytime she ate out with her father, he was always kind to the waitstaff, even tipping well above twenty percent. Now that she was part of that world, she knew it shouldn't be something she tolerated.

"Sorry. I don't work here."

The man banged his glass on the table several times, his friends egging him on. "It sure as hell looks like you work here. Look here, sweetheart. Just march your pretty ass over to Sandy, and get me another."

Briar meant the bar; however, it was pointless trying to explain that to him.

She definitely changed her mind on sweetheart after that. It was a pet name she could absolutely live without.

She took a deep breath and threw another platter of wing bones in the trash. She wanted to say that one little phrase to him, but the last time she told Portia that, she got slapped across the face. *I think you've had enough.*

Briar continued to ignore the middle-aged jerk and his table of drunken friends laughing and snorting. Their words were barely understandable to begin with. Once she was done, she moved on to the fourth table, unfortunately bringing herself closer to Mr. Whiskey Neat.

"Still waiting," his voice came from behind her.

Briar gritted her teeth. If he kept pestering her, she'd go up to the bar and get him his damn drink. Hopefully it would be enough for him to fall in a sewer somewhere.

Her whole body suddenly tensed when the stinging sensation came across her ass.

Laughter came roaring from the table behind her.

"I told you to get that pretty little—"

Just as Briar was about to turn and let the drunkard have it, his words were cut short and a massive collision rocked the floor beneath her feet.

Dex had the man on the floor under him in an instant. His balled-up fist came across the man's jaw, and Briar was certain she heard bones breaking or teeth shattering.

"Hayden, what the fuck?" The man tried to move his jaw from side to side, but winced in pain.

Dex grabbed him by the neck and held him in place on the floor. "Don't you ever do that to another woman, especially her." He lightly slapped the drunk across the face when he didn't respond. "Do you understand, Jasper?"

"Yeah, man. Yeah. I didn't know she was your girl," Jasper cried, attempting to hold his hands up in defeat. Dex's body crushing down on top of him made every movement difficult.

"Well then, this is your warning."

Dex felt large hands pulling at his shoulders, slightly knocking him off his bearing. "Nope. Not today. Most of the cops are at the game or afterparties tonight. Like hell am I calling them over a barfight."

Dex got up before Sandy could pull him anymore. Jasper followed suit, scrambling on his hands and knees until he was on wobbly feet.

As soon as Jasper was up, "Apologize."

"For real? Come on, Dex. I was just–"

Jasper's words were cut off the moment Dex's hand went around his throat. Sandy slapped at Dex's wrist.

"Knock it off. He'll apologize. No need to go all Prince Charming with anger management issues," Sandy joked, attempting to lighten the situation. He saw the rage in Dex's eyes and knew a simple joke wouldn't cut it.

Sandy glanced to Briar standing behind Dex, her face and body frozen in shock. Upon seeing Sandy's concern, she took a couple steps forward and grabbed Dex's left wrist hanging at his side.

"Come on, Dex. It's fine now."

Dex glanced to the small body at his side then back to Jasper. "Apologize," he growled.

"I'm sorry. I'm sorry, lady," Jasper cried out. He was on his tiptoes to stop from choking with the hand firmly clasped around his neck.

Briar tugged at Dex's wrist. "There. We're all good."

Dex still wasn't happy, but slowly loosened his grip on Jasper's throat, eventually dropping his hand from the man altogether.

Both Sandy and Jasper let out a sigh of relief. While Sandy knew that Dex wasn't a violent person, recalling that he had never seen Dex in a fight before, he also knew that Dex was strong and could defend himself if need be.

"Briar, why don't you go ahead and call it an early night," Sandy said.

"What?!" Briar fully needed the next two hours of time and tips.

Sandy nodded in the direction of Dex, knowing that if Briar left, so would Dex. Briar understood.

"Oh, and Jasper? Get the fuck out of here," Sandy insisted, yanking away the empty tumbler from the table. "All of you," he added to the table of encouraging friends.

Dex pulled Briar to the side. "Are you okay?"

Briar glared at him, a range of thoughts and emotions running through her head.

Dex couldn't understand the look of frustration and anger that blossomed over Briar's face.

"Just fine. Let me get my bag from the back and we can leave." After taking a couple steps away, she turned back toward Dex. "I'll find you. Just wait in the truck." She needed him out of the bar before he snapped at someone else.

As she made her way to get her things, she became further confused. While she appreciated Dex defending her, she could have handled it herself, in a less bloody way. All she had to do was tell Sandy, and Sandy would have sent the Jasper guy packing. There was no need to get physical with someone clearly not in their right mind.

Then, Dex had to go and acknowledge in front of a crowded bar in a small town that she was his. He was only responding to Jasper's assumption, putting him in his place, but that hurt her a little more than she expected. Despite how Dex looked at her when she entered the bar, ultimately, she didn't belong to him, and she never would.

CHAPTER 35

"Are you finally going to say something to me," Dex asked as the elevator doors closed, sealing them inside for a few moments.

"I'm too tired to talk to you tonight," Briar insisted.

Dex groaned and raked his hand through his hair. That had been Briar's response since she got in his truck that night.

Once the doors opened up, Briar marched toward number 604, already grabbing her key.

"You're seriously fucking pissed at me? For what," Dex called from behind her.

Briar put the key in the door but turned, facing Dex, already hovering on top of her. "That's my job!"

"You're forgetting I own part of–"

"It doesn't matter! You had no right to act like that," she cried out, interrupting him.

Dex crossed his arms and Briar could see his muscles tightening under the long sleeves plastered to his skin. "So, you didn't mind him slapping your ass?"

"Of course I minded, you idiot! That didn't mean that I was going to throw him to the ground and beat his face in."

"That's only because you couldn't."

"No, Dex. It's because it was unnecessary. I could have asked Sandy to tell him to leave, which is what eventually ended up happening. I just don't see why you–"

Dex took a step forward, and upon instinct, Briar stepped away, her back colliding against the door.

"Because I care. I couldn't take seeing another guy touch you, wanted or unwanted."

That admission messed with Briar's head too much. *Wanted or unwanted.* That meant that no guy could ever touch her if it was up to Dex, and that wasn't his decision to make.

Briar turned from Dex and wiggled the key in the door until it clicked. She twisted the knob and entered the apartment, along with Dex. It would be less embarrassing for their conversation to conclude behind closed doors.

"You shouldn't," Briar stressed, tossing her purse on the entry table. "You're not my father, my boyfriend, my lover, nothing! You're just my room-mate. You've made that clear. Therefore, your actions tonight were unacceptable. You're not in a position to behave like that."

"The fuck I'm not," Dex yelled, furious with everything Briar just said.

Briar continued farther inside and down the hall leading to her bedroom. Arguing with Dex was more exhausting than a slammed Friday night shift at Chêne.

Dex followed after Briar. Something inside him was snapping; it had been for a long time. He tried so hard to hold it together, but he had a feeling that it wouldn't last much longer.

"I'm not anyone's father and I don't plan on being for some time," Dex began, with Briar still walking away from him.

She made it to her closed door, but before she could grab the handle, she felt the soft pulling of her wrist, spinning her around. Taken off balance, she managed to catch herself by pressing her back against the door. Her breathing nearly ceased when Dex's palms came up on either side of her head, pushing against the door behind her.

He looked her dead in the eyes, his not wavering for a second, hers darting from side to side in a surprised panic as he continued. "We also know that I make a pretty shitty boyfriend."

Briar licked her dry lips without meaning to, and only then did Dex's eyes drop momentarily. She waited for him to mention the lover comment she made, but he didn't. He skipped over that, as if she never said the word; however, what came next was unexpected.

"But you know damn well that we're more than just roommates."

Briar couldn't let him mess with her head. Every time she thought they were progressing, it ended up being a mistake, or a situation getting out of hand. She couldn't let Dex's words and the way he looked at her affect her heart.

"You're right. I consider you my friend," she said in response.

Dex dropped his hands, his shoulders deflating, as he took a step back from her. "Briar," he sighed.

Briar knew that look of disappointment well. Dex was already having second thoughts about how close he had just been to her, and it hurt.

"Don't. Just don't say anything." She wouldn't cry. There was nothing to cry over. Every day she continued to fall for a guy that was emotionally and physically unavailable. No more.

"I know you think—"

Briar angrily interrupted. "No! You don't know. You have no idea what I think or feel," she added.

Dex saw a mix of emotions in Briar's eyes, and he knew this was it. He could let that string continue to unravel and finally snap, or he could do what he was supposed to. If he said the right words now, he could tell that he'd lose her for good, and that was for the best. They were already involved more than they should be.

Then there was a part of him he had never known, a part of him that felt. She made him feel.

Briar closed her eyes and sighed. The conversation was over. Dex had no response to that. Ultimately, he had given her an answer to all her unasked questions time and time again.

"I do," he said quietly.

Dex stepped forward, bringing their bodies a breath apart, towering over Briar, forcing her to crane her neck back to look up at him. Her lips parted to say something, but he cut her off before she could get a word out.

"Sometimes if feels like you're drowning. There's a massive ocean with a bottomless ending, and you're being pulled deeper and deeper. When we're close, when we touch, even accidentally, you can't keep your chest from exploding, and breathing becomes one of the most difficult tasks of your life. Even after that contact is gone, you still feel it on your skin. You miss it, crave it, wonder when it will happen again, when it will be more. There's a heat, a liquid fire, that runs through you, clouding your thoughts, leaving you wanting and desperate. You still think about that kiss, and my lips and tongue on your neck." Dex looked down to Briar's neck and could see her swallow heavily, his words affecting her.

He shouldn't be telling her the things he was, but he couldn't hold them in any longer, and as they continued to pour out, he felt lighter, relieved.

Dex wrapped one arm around Briar's waist, and steadied himself with his other against the door. He pressed his forehead to hers, her sparkling green eyes meeting his.

"Tell me if I'm wrong."

His voice was deep and chilling, pleading with her. His warm breath came across her face. There wasn't a hint of alcohol, and Briar knew that he meant every one of his words. He was completely sober. This wasn't some drunken mistake.

"I can't."

Once Briar said those words, she felt Dex's grip tighten on her waist. There was a rush that ran down her whole body, craving, wanting, needing more. If Dex dared to make a move, to kiss her, it wouldn't be enough this time.

Dex took in a deep breath. "Tell me to stop," he pled. "Tell me to stop, and I swear I will."

All Briar gave Dex in response was a shake of her head, still pressed against his.

251

Dex couldn't help but chuckle. "I don't think you understand."

Without missing a beat, "Then show me."

Dex searched her eyes. Before he could decide if he wanted to say something more, Briar brought one of her hands to his abs and slowly trailed upward along the ridges of his chest until it rested around his neck.

There was a hunger, a passion in her eyes, in her touch, and whatever held him back in the past was gone.

As soon as Dex's lips touched Briar's, she was floating. All the frustration and angst that was buried in her for so long was washed away. When his teeth lightly tugged at her bottom lip, she opened for him. The touch of his tongue against hers when he invaded her mouth sent another rush of heat through her body, this time hitting her deep, all the way through her core.

Dex dropped his hand from the door so that both were clutching around her dainty waist. He grabbed her tightly, sinking his fingers in deep so that she'd feel the pressure through her jeans and sweater.

The possessive nature in Dex forced Briar to let out a pleasurable moan and press herself farther into him. Dex took that to mean that he could take it a step further. He attempted to nudge Briar's legs apart with his knee, and not only did she comply, but as soon as his leg was pressed against her most sensitive region, she rocked forward, grinding into him. Despite the clothes between the two of them, he could feel her warmth, building between her legs with each movement.

Dex slowly pulled back from the kiss. His breathing was just as ragged as Briar's. He watched her face carefully, gauging her reaction, as he gradually slid his hands from her waist, around to the small of her back, and down. His hands cupped her ass before sinking in, squeezing, pulling her into the erection straining against his jeans.

Briar bit her lip and threw her head back, letting out a groan of frustration. She had an inkling as to where they might end up now, but so far, Dex was taking it impossibly slow.

Dex's hands continued their descent until they reached Briar's thighs. He gripped them tightly and flung Briar upward.

Briar gasped, shocked by the abrupt change; however, she caught on quickly and wrapped both her legs around Dex's torso as well as her arms around his neck, allowing her fingers to play at the base of his hair, softly digging in and moving upward.

Rolling his head from side to side, wanting more of her touch, "Damn. That feels good."

Briar dropped one of her hands and reached behind her, fumbling for the doorknob to her room. Dex spun her around so that his body was now against her door, making it impossible for Briar to get her arm around him.

"What do you think you're doing," he asked teasingly.

"My room…I thought…"

Dex gripped at the back of Briar's neck, only holding her up with one hand, and pulled her face to his, going in for a deep and slow kiss. He only pulled back far enough to speak, his lips still brushing across hers with each word. "My room. I have a bigger bed."

He felt Briar begin to tense with each step he took in the direction of his room. As much as he wanted every inch of her body, and though it felt like she wanted the same moments earlier, he knew she was inexperienced.

Upon opening the door and flipping on the lights, Dex slowly pulled Briar away, her small frame sliding down his until her feet were on the floor; however, his hands never left her body.

Briar nervously looked up at him, but before she could say anything, he wanted her to know that there were no expectations.

"We don't have to–"

"I want to," Briar interrupted. She slid her hands down his arms until her hands were clasped in his.

Dex looked down at her tiny fingers intertwined in his. It was such a small, yet intimate, gesture; however, it was enough to cause a deeper feeling within his chest. He brought his eyes from their hands to her face. Everything about the way she was looking at him screamed nervous uncertainty, and he'd continue to give her an out with every step forward.

When he first kissed her, it was all about a primal need, his body aching for hers, but something shifted. She looked at him with a trusting innocence and in that moment, he knew, it wasn't just about sex for her. As much as he wanted to shove the feeling away, it was mutual.

Briar stepped backward, pulling Dex along with her, closing the space between them and the bed. Dex's eyes never left hers, which only made her feel exposed and vulnerable, despite being fully clothed.

Once her knees hit the back of the bed, Dex guided her body downward, giving her a soft kiss as they scrambled upward towards the pillows.

Briar shivered when Dex slipped his hand beneath her sweater, partly from nervousness, partly from the first exposure to the cool air.

Dex tugged at the hem of the sweater, but didn't rip it off like the animal inside him desperately wanted. "Do you want to stop?"

"No," Briar immediately answered.

She held her arms above her head, waiting for Dex to pull the fabric away, uncovering her. She felt his cock twitch against her leg from inside his jeans, and found herself finally look down at the bulge. Just the anticipation sent a wave of excitement through her, which only moistened her panties more than they were already.

Dex's mouth went dry. He stared in awe at her silky skin, unlike his, void of all markings. She was a beautiful, untouched, canvas.

He brought his mouth down to Briar's neck, and began easing her beneath him to the comforter. Once she was on her back and comfortable, he continued downward, licking and sucking every inch of her, slowly pulling one of the straps of her bra off her shoulder. He tugged at the cup until one breast was exposed. His tongue swirled around the nipple as his hand kneaded it, his fingers lightly digging into her flesh.

"Dex," she breathed.

He pulled back. His name from her mouth wasn't one of pleasure, it was one of indecision. He ran a hand through his tousled hair and along the back of his neck. "Do you want to stop?"

Briar slammed her head into the pillow and found herself unable to suppress a laugh, startling Dex. "No. Please stop asking that."

"I just don't want to push you if you're not ready."

Briar wriggled upward from beneath Dex and rested against the headboard. She pulled the strap of her bra up, feeling strange about being the only one with so few clothes.

"It's not that…"

Dex watched as a flash of hurt crossed her face. She brushed back her dirty ash blonde hair that had fallen over her face. He didn't speak. Briar had to gather her thoughts for whatever she needed to say, confess, admit.

"Obviously, I'm not a virgin," she began.

It was a blow to the gut. It only reminded Dex of her past and what she had gone through. A wave of anger passed through him. It was worse than seeing the drunkard in the bar slap her ass.

She brought her eyes to meet his, knowing that he might very well be the one to stop things now. "However…I've never really done this…Consensually," she added, knowing that she was probably screwing up the mood.

"Would you want to—"

"If you say stop, one more time, I'm going to lose it," Briar interrupted.

A smirk came to Dex's face and he crawled toward her, pulling her down from the headboard so her head sank into his pillow.

"What you're saying," he whispered in her ear, his voice deep, rough, and sensual. "Is I'd be your first?"

Briar liked the sound of that. It made her forget. She could start over in so many ways, including right now, in this moment with Dex. "Yes," she breathed, wrapping her arms tightly around Dex's neck and pulling his face to hers.

The kiss was hungry and needy, full of passion and desire, but in the end, not enough. Not nearly enough for either of them.

Dex eased himself down Briar's body, leaving a trail of kisses, feeling her shudder beneath him the lower he went. He kissed just below her navel before sucking at the skin of her hip.

He wouldn't ask her again, but he felt like he needed her permission with each new step he took; therefore, he pulled her hand to the button of her jeans.

Though Dex couldn't see it, a smile appeared across Briar's lips. She knew exactly what Dex was doing.

She didn't hesitate in fumbling with the button and zipper of her jeans. As soon as she attempted to slide them from her body, Dex took over. All Briar felt at that point was a rush of cool air against the skin of her legs, and then there was a small plop from her jeans hitting the floor.

Dex pulled away from her so that he could see all of her. He ran his fingertips down the middle of her chest, over her flat stomach, until he reached the top of her black cotton panties. Briar shuddered when he began playing with the elastic waistband.

He brought himself up once more, hovering over Briar, and gave her the softest of kisses. "I'll be gentle," Dex promised with a whisper while nuzzling into Briar's neck.

After lightly licking the tip of her earlobe and placing another kiss on her collarbone, he descended downward.

Briar was confused at first. Dex was still completely clothed. She didn't fully understand his statement, but before she had time to think about what was happening, she felt her panties being slowly pulled down, past her thighs, knees, ankles. She didn't hear the small amount of fabric fall, but she assumed they went to the same place as her sweater and jeans.

Dex kissed one of her ankles and continued upward. It was painfully slow, and certain spots tickled, causing Briar's body to flinch. The closer he got to her center, the more she could feel the heat building within her. She was more than desperate at that point.

"Just touch me already," she breathed out as though she was fighting for air.

Dex let out a warm breath; however, mixed with her wetness, it sent a chilling sensation up her body.

"I've been touching you," he teased.

Taking a thigh in each hand, Dex spread her legs apart. Finally putting her out of her misery, his mouth fell to the mound on display for him.

The moment Dex's tongue swiped across Briar's clit, she cried out, and her hands turned to fists in the comforter.

Dex's head came up from between her legs to find Briar's chest heaving. Her eyes said it all. They were clouded with lust, begging for a release. As much as he wanted to tease her, a bigger part of him couldn't wait for her to explode in his mouth.

"That feels so good," Briar managed once Dex's mouth was back on her.

He pulled her clit into his mouth, lightly holding it between his teeth, and flicked his tongue rapidly. With every passing second, Briar's body became more receptive, less hesitant, more open to him taking every part of her. Needing to taste more of her, Dex licked up and down the entirety of her slit, sucking at the sweet juices of her arousal.

Briar let out a sharp gasp with Dex's next movement. Ever since he began devouring her, she hadn't been able to think straight, and this was dangerously close to sending her spiraling out of control.

Dex continued to press his tongue deeper through her entrance. The more he whirled it inside her, the more she bucked and squirmed against him.

Her words could barely be heard. "Don't stop. Please. Don't stop."

He wouldn't tell her, but if his tongue inside her caused this much of a reaction, he wasn't sure how she'd handle his cock buried in her.

Dex continued to push his tongue in and out of that tiny hole that tightened and pulsed with each time he entered, until finally he thought he might finish in his pants if he didn't get inside her soon. Knowing it wouldn't be long, he increased his speed, lapping his tongue against every inch of her wetness.

Briar felt it. It was a building sensation, like a tidal wave far in the ocean, quickly gaining momentum, becoming more powerful by the second, until it reached its peak and crashed.

A piercing cry erupted from her lips. Her entire body exploded, shaking and spasming against Dex's mouth, where he drank up every bit of her release.

By the time Briar came back to earth, there was a coldness where Dex's mouth had been moments earlier. She focused her eyes on Dex, little spots of white still interrupting her vision.

Dex rose from the bed, never taking his eyes off hers, unable to stop the satisfied grin from forming across his face. He pulled at the hem of his shirt and yanked it upward, once off, using it to wipe the juices dripping down his chin.

He began working on the belt of his jeans, then the button, then the zipper, until all that covered him was a pair of red and black boxers.

Briar felt her throat close up. Seeing Dex, with very little covering him, only made her realize just how big he was compared to her. As he walked around the bed to the nightstand, she took in every part of him, including the markings she found so attractive.

All she could think about was tracing up every piece of ink, and down every muscular curve.

Dex opened the drawer and withdrew a gold wrapper, and though Briar felt as though she hadn't yet recovered from that intense orgasm, her body was already anticipating what was next. She reached behind her back and undid her bra, tossing it somewhere in the direction of where her pile of clothes might be.

Dex faced Briar and slowly lowered his boxers until they fell to the floor. Her mouth fell open as if to say something, but no words came. As he watched her soft pink lips open, all he could think about was that day in the kitchen when her mouth had been around his finger. It wouldn't be now, not today, not in this moment, but he couldn't wait for the day when that pretty little mouth would be wrapped around his dick, taking in every ounce he pumped into her.

Dex ripped open the condom and slid it on. Though he needed to be buried in her warmth, he took his time, making sure that she'd feel comfortable.

Briar pulled her knees up and spread her legs open, Dex settling in and hovering over her. He kissed along her neck to her ear, then down her jaw until he reached her lips. The kiss was slow and hungry with Briar instantly parting for him.

She could smell her scent, taste herself, all over Dex. It sent a dizzying feeling throughout her, as she was still unable to believe what just happened, what was currently happening, between them.

"I can't promise you it won't hurt," Dex cautiously admitted.

Briar brought her hand to his scruffy cheek and massaged it tenderly. "I don't care," she replied, a smile coming to her face.

Dex took himself in his palm and gave a few strokes, allowing his tip to brush along Briar's wet and inflamed folds. His lips descended back down on hers, hoping the kiss would take her mind away from the initial pain.

Moving his hips forward, he slowly entered her, feeling her body tense with each inch she took.

Briar wouldn't admit it, and tried her best not to cry out in agony, but it was painful. Dex stretched her to her entirety, to the point that she felt like she might split in two.

Dex brushed his hand down Briar's cheek and into her hair. "Relax. Breathe."

She trusted him. He'd never hurt her.

Once Dex was halfway inside, he stopped, allowing Briar to adjust to him. Though she was slick and wet, allowing him to glide in easily, she was tighter than he expected. When her body appeared to relax and she let out a deep breath, only then did Dex continue.

259

Briar cried out when Dex pushed farther, filling her completely. He was slow at first, barely moving inside her. With someone as intense as Dex, she knew he was taking it easy on her.

Dex was surprised when Briar brought her hips up, taking him in, attempting to increase the speed.

"It feels good," she groaned in his ear. The initial pain subsided, and it was replaced with something far more powerful and consuming.

Dex wouldn't allow himself to turn into a raging beast full of blind desire, chasing after a quick release; however, when she told him that, he couldn't go as slow as he had been.

He pulled away, leaving only the tip inside and plunged back, the jolt causing Briar's perfect breasts to jiggle back and forth. Her once cries of anguish soon turned into heady moans.

He continued to pump inside her, his momentum growing, her pussy expanding, taking in every thrust.

Briar's arms came around his torso, clawing at his back, silently begging for more. Dex was bringing to life parts of her, sensations she'd never known. Soon he pulled her hips upward, giving him a better angle, and that did it for her.

"Oh, god. Don't stop…Please…don't," Briar wailed.

Whatever had come over her before had nothing on this. This was an all-consuming devouring pleasure that rocketed through every bone in her body.

Dex leaned forward, cradling Briar beneath him, as her orgasm ripped through her, leaving her convulsing, writhing, shuddering, against him. He thrust harder and faster when she tightened around his cock, knowing he was close.

It wasn't until she screamed out his name that he was done for. His name from her lips, full of blissful ecstasy, along with her walls clenching, pulling him inside her, was all it took for him to let himself go. Dex felt his dick pulse, beginning to fill the condom, and before Briar had the chance to come down from her high, Dex was falling along with her.

CHAPTER 36

Meanwhile…

Two hundred miles away.

"Good evening, mommy dearest," Leo sang out as he entered the mansion's living room.

Portia sat in front of a fireplace, in her pajamas and robe, sipping on a nightcap. She turned toward her son and gave him a go-to-hell look. "Do you have any idea what time it is?!"

Leo rolled his eyes, though Portia wouldn't see in the darkness. He was twenty, not twelve, and it was barely eleven. "I don't think you'll mind once I tell you this."

Portia held her empty glass up. Though Leo grumbled about it, he walked toward the liquor cabinet and grabbed the bottle of brandy that was out. "Argent Falls," he said as he filled his mother's glass.

"What the hell is that supposed to mean?"

With a smug grin, "That's where your darling stepdaughter is."

At that comment, Portia sat up straighter and took a long sip of the liquid. She was immune to the tingling burn that went down her throat. "Where is that?"

Leo fell to an accent chair across from Portia. "A few hours away."

"What is she doing there," Portia continued.

"How the hell am I supposed to know?"

Ignoring Leo, "How did she get there? Where is she living? Do you think she knows someone there?

Leo waved his hands back and forth, gesturing for his mother to calm down. "I don't know! Damn."

"Don't use that tone with me!"

"Look, that's all I know. It's a quaint, sleepy little New England town, one of those where everyone knows everyone," he scoffed. His preferences would always be the larger cities. If there wasn't a Starbucks within walking distance from any given place he was at, there was something wrong.

"When are you planning on leaving," Portia quickly asked.

"In a week or two. There are a few things I need to secure," Leo stressed.

Portia waved him off. "Already taken care of," she said, pointing to a small box on the table behind her.

"Unserialized?"

"Of course," Portia gasped. "I casually mentioned a thing or two to the gardener, nothing too serious. I told you that he was a shady fucker. Anyway, it works out in our favor. One of his cousins specializes in ghost guns, as he called them."

"Wow. I'm impressed," Leo laughed, content with the fact that it was one less task for him to take care of.

Portia leaned forward, her face now a taking on a deadly serious expression. "I expect this to be taken care of immediately."

"I just know the town, mother! I can't exactly walk into her school and gun her down. We have to make this look like she ran away and got into trouble."

"There's also a gram and a half of cocaine. If you could somehow threaten her into getting a portion of it into her system, and leaving the rest on—"

"What the hell?! You have way too much time on your hands to plot this out. She's just a dumb young girl," Leo interrupted.

"You idiot! There has to be reason and motive," Portia screamed.

Leo finally poured himself a drink. Everything was becoming too real. Could he still do it? Of course. He'd enjoy torturing Briar to her death. A sick part of him got off knowing that he'd be the only man to touch her. Her first and her last. "Okay, I get it. I just didn't know you had already done all this planning as well as execution."

Portia rose and tied up her robe. "Someone has to. The sooner I can produce a legitimate death certificate, the sooner we get our hands on the remainder of the money."

CHAPTER 37

"What are you doing," Dex asked from Briar's doorway.

Briar stopped adjusting the covers on her bed and turned to Dex, who had just gotten done with his shower after she finished hers. His hair was still damp, and fell perfectly across his forehead, flipping out just a bit around his ears. All he had on was a pair of basketball shorts, which made it difficult for Briar to take her attention away from his incredibly athletic and muscular chest.

When she brought her eyes up to his face, he smirked, and confidently leaned against the doorjamb, fully knowing that Briar was checking him out. He'd be lying if he said he hadn't done the same before he announced his presence. After her shower, she had opted for the t-shirt of his that he gave her after sex. The fabric drowned her, but she had never looked sexier in his eyes.

"I'm getting ready for bed," she stated, although it came out more in the form of a question. "It's almost midnight, and we both have work tomorrow."

The idea that tomorrow was Saturday, and they'd both be working at the shop together, made Briar both nervous and giddy. Things had drastically changed in the last couple hours, and she wasn't sure how that would affect their relationship in the days to come.

Briar's body froze in place when Dex pushed off and walked toward her like a lion stalking a gazelle. Butterflies swarmed throughout her stomach when his hand reached out and took one of hers. There were lots of things she didn't expect from Dex. That was one of them. Before she could process what he was doing, his next words hit her like a ton of bricks, making her heart thunder out of control.

"I know. I want you to stay with me tonight," he said, his words taking even him by surprise; however, it was the truth. After what had taken place between them, he didn't want Briar to feel like it was just about sex.

He tugged her forward, in hopes that she would follow, and she did.

Having her next to him, in his bed, was something new and insanely dangerous. He genuinely cared about most of the women he was with at one point or another while in a relationship, but not enough that he *wanted* to wake up to them in the morning.

He felt a tightness in his chest when, nearly an hour later, he looked over to Briar sleeping soundly beside him. There was something magical about her that pulled at his heart. She made him want to wake up next to someone, and not just anyone, only her.

✳ ✳ ✳

Upon stretching, Briar realized two things. She was alone. Dex's side of the bed was cold. Though she was slightly disappointed, it was the next realization that floored her. She always slept rather well in Dex's apartment, but all those nights were nothing compared to last night. She must have fallen asleep as soon as her head hit the pillow, and she didn't wake up once.

She rose from the covers and made her way to her room to get dressed for the day. The smell of coffee already filled the apartment.

As she stood in the mirror, fumbling to put her hair in a side braid, the nerves began to work their way up, and a thousand thoughts and questions went through her mind. Had Dex woken that morning and regretted everything now that he had time to sleep on it? They hadn't said much after the fact. Did he at least enjoy it? The soreness reminded her that she indeed had.

How would things change? Would they go back to normal? Would they be intimate again?

Briar quickly finished off with a small amount of mascara and decided that it was time to face Dex. They didn't have to be at work for a good hour, so hopefully they could talk, and clear up whatever happened or was happening.

"I didn't expect you to be up so early," Dex said as soon as Briar came into view.

Briar jumped and turned toward the voice. Dex sat casually in his chair at the balcony doors, a cup of coffee in one hand.

"I could say the same for you."

Dex shrugged. "I have you a cup of coffee. Poured it when I heard that you were awake, so it wouldn't be too hot."

Briar tried not to have a reaction to the sweet gesture. To some people, that might not mean a lot, but coming from Dex, that was something.

"Thanks." Upon taking a sip, it was the perfect temperature for her.

"I didn't make breakfast yet," Dex pointed out. "If you want, we can go to the café near the shop and grab something."

Briar watched Dex carefully, noting every little change in his features. He seemed softer than the gruff, surly, beast she was accustomed to. Above all, and despite that it was just breakfast before work, it felt like he was asking her on a date.

"We don't have to, but—"

"I'd like to," Dex interrupted.

The intense look in his eyes told Briar to go along with it. They had eaten in public together before and it wasn't awkward. Why should now be any different?

Needless to say, it was different. Something in the air surrounding them had changed. Dex walked closer to her when they crossed the street, and when he opened the door to the café for her to go inside first, he placed his hand low on her back and guided her inside.

Briar expected it to be busier for a Saturday; however, it was barely after seven. Most people were probably sleeping in.

"You can say or ask whatever," Dex said, leaning back on his side of the booth once the waitress took their order.

"What makes you think I have something to say?"

Dex gave a low chuckle. "You're nervously picking at your nails. You're looking everywhere but at me. You look like one of those cartoons with all the question marks swirling around your head."

Being called out, Briar finally focused on Dex, but looking into his eyes was the hardest thing in the world. All she could think of was how those same eyes looked at her the night before, with such a hungry passion.

Briar bit her lip and carefully thought how to respond. She kept it simple with, "I don't think this is the place for that."

"Why not?"

Briar's eyes widened, and she leaned into the table, lowering her voice. "Do you seriously want to talk about last night in a public place?"

Dex tilted his head to the side. "You could probably leave out some of the explicit details." A smile came across his lips when a rosy tint blossomed across Briar's face and she slumped her shoulders, as if she were hiding from embarrassment.

"I guess I'd just like to know where we stand after…that."

"That's up to you."

Briar let out a sigh of frustration. Dex wasn't making the conversation easy on her. Terrified to ask, she did so anyway. "Was that one of those spur of the moment, one time things?"

"I hope not," Dex answered, maybe a little too quickly.

Briar was thankful for the interruption of their waitress. It gave her a moment to gather what he was saying. Unfortunately, it was October. She never intended to stay long after graduating. She wouldn't know if she was accepted to London for a couple months, but a small part of her was pretty sure she'd get in. Last night changed a lot, and if things were to progress with Dex, no matter what, her heart would end up broken in the end.

Thankfully, Dex didn't press her any further about the things running through her head, and she was able to keep her breakfast down. Despite knowing they'd eventually talk about the night before, they were able to push it aside for the time being and enjoy a normal conversation like always.

Dex refrained from doing everything that ran through his mind while they were in public; however, last night seemed too long ago, and he needed to touch her, to kiss her.

When he unlocked the shop ten minutes to eight, he took Briar by surprise by pulling her through the entry and across the space until they were in the office. Not bothering to close the door, as they were the only ones there, he took her face in his hands and crashed his lips against hers.

At first, Briar was a frozen statue, shocked that Dex was kissing her, at that moment, in his office, but as soon as it started, it ended. Dex wrapped his arms around her and pulled her into his chest.

"I've wanted to do that since you woke up," he admitted, all the while realizing that he sounded like a lovesick puppy.

Now being out of the public, where it was just her and Dex, Briar felt a little easier in bringing up her concerns. "At the café, when you said that you hoped not…What did you mean?"

"I didn't just lose control last night. I did, but it wasn't like I hadn't thought things through, and I hope it was the same for you. I saw the way you looked at me when you came into the kitchen this morning, and to answer that question I know was, and is, on your mind, no. I don't regret a single thing." At those words, Briar looked up at him with a face full of hope.

"Why did you want me to spend the night?"

Dex tucked back a piece of hair that had come undone from her braid. "I'm not good with all that romance and relationship shit. You know that, right?"

Somehow, that confession hit her a little deeper than she expected, but she hid her reaction and simply nodded.

"I wanted you to know that you weren't just some fuck." He winced, wishing he had words that were less vulgar. He should have stopped there, but something in the last twelve hours had turned him to a bowl of pudding. "And maybe I wanted to know what it felt like to sleep next to someone I cared about."

Briar wiggled her toes to make sure that she was still on solid ground because everything he just said made her feel like she was floating. Though she thought her like for Dex might be bordering on something more, right now she knew that it most definitely was. She was falling in love with Dex.

Briar began prepping the coffee machine once Dex released her. The timing was perfect, as the bell from the entry went off. Before she finished, she could already hear Dex at the reception desk talking to Rusty, as he prepared for the day.

Dex and Rusty were just about to join Benji in the garage when Briar strolled from the office, carrying a to-go cup of steaming liquid. Dex tried not to have a different reaction around her, but felt his lips turning up in a smile.

"Here," she said, handing him the coffee.

He brushed the tips of his fingers across hers when he took it. "Thanks." He hadn't expected for Rusty to pick up on something so small, but Briar's flaming cheeks and sweet smile didn't help matters.

"Whoa! What?!"

Briar and Dex both turned to Rusty's outburst. He flung his index finger between them.

"When did this happen?"

Briar shut down, but thankfully Dex was able to play it much cooler. "What are you talking about," he asked, raising a brow, suggesting that Rusty was crazy.

"Hell no. I saw the look on your face when she walked out. Then with the coffee. Dude, you smiled," Rusty nearly screamed at the top of his lungs.

269

"I can't smile?"

"I should get back to some stuff in the office," Briar interjected.

Dex knew that he wouldn't be able to hide what was going on between him and Briar, and he didn't want to. She didn't deserve to only receive his affection and attention behind closed doors. If Rusty wanted an answer, an explanation as to why he was quick to smile when Briar appeared, he'd give it to him.

Briar felt her heart skip a beat when Dex's free hand grabbed her wrist and pulled her into him. Very sweetly, he kissed her on the cheek.

"I'll see you for lunch?"

All she could do was nod. It wasn't an intensely romantic gesture; however, it made it appear quite obvious that there was something more than friendship between them.

Rusty could see that Briar was embarrassed; therefore, he waited until the door closed behind them, and they were in the confines of the garage, before he freaked out again.

He slapped Dex across the back. "I knew it! I so knew it!"

Dex turned and crossed his arms, flattening his facial features to show no expression. "Knew what?"

"Oh, come on! After you went off on Jasper last—"

"He had no right touching her," Dex growled. It was the one part of the previous night that he did not want to think about, despite it being the catalyst for everything that unfolded.

"What happened between then and two minutes ago?"

"I think that's private."

Rusty's jaw hung open and he adjusted the bill of his cap. "Oh…Shit. *That* happened."

"Words were said, that's all."

"Bullshit," Rusty exclaimed with a laugh. "Within seconds of talking to you, you seemed less assholish compared to usual. I'm guessing last night had a lot—"

"We're dropping it," Dex sang out.

"So, are you two dating? I mean, she lives with you. That makes things serious. Being romantically involved and living together…Damn. The next step is like marriage or–"

Dex threw up his hands and interrupted Rusty's ridiculous rambling "Whoa. Stop. You've been watching too much Hallmark garbage."

Rusty groaned. "My sister, man. Do you know they're playing Christmas movies?! We haven't had Halloween and Thanksgiving!" He shook his head, walking over to a car Benji just pulled in.

Dex tried to dismiss Rusty's words, but something about them sank in more than he would have liked. Last night a lot was said, and though it was their first time together physically, it wasn't as if everything happened over-night. For months they had been getting to know each other, all while fighting an attraction that didn't seem possible anymore.

Was he thinking about marriage? Hell no.

Did he want Briar to stay for longer than she had planned? Absolutely.

Briar had too much going for her. Despite the hand she was dealt in life, she had talent, brains, drive, and a passion for what she loved. Dex knew she'd get into her program, and there was no way he'd ever stand in her way. Even if it meant breaking both of their hearts.

CHAPTER 38

Leo would be the first to admit that he didn't know where to begin when arriving in Argent Falls. It wasn't like he could walk in the high school and demand for Briar to be handed over to him.

For three days he waited for classes to end, and not once did he see her. The high school wasn't that big. He also noted that very few of the girls coming out had hair near Briar's color; however, none of them were Briar.

He wasn't a morning person, but he realized that the morning might be the best time to find out if she really was attending Argent Falls High School. At the end of the day, students all stormed out at once; whereas, in the morning, they slowly trickled in.

Leo sat in his car, bundled up in his hoodie and beanie, sipping on a cup of awful coffee from the hotel lobby, wondering how there was still a town in existence without a Starbucks.

He glanced at his dashboard. School didn't start for another forty-five minutes. Maybe he didn't need to get there that early, but three days was long enough in the small and cheery town. With the holidays just around the corner, the residents appeared more joyful. At least that's what he assumed, having a hard time believing that people were always so friendly to strangers.

Gradually, after many passing minutes, more staff and students began to arrive. Many drove, several walked, and a lot of the younger ones were dropped off by parents or came on a couple of the yellow buses. There still wasn't a sign of Briar.

Five minutes before the starting time that was listed on the campus website, Leo was ready to give up, full of frustration at having wasted three, going on four days.

Then his twisted prayers were answered.

It was the hair that caught his attention. Her hair was a strange and unique shade of blonde, unlike his yellow and straw-like tone.

She jumped from an impeccably clean black truck, but the driver must have said something to her, because she turned around and ran back. This time to the driver's side, where a window was being rolled down.

Even from far away, Leo could make out some of the man's features. He looked older than Briar, maybe college age or a little older. He definitely didn't look like another high school student.

A flash of heated anger ran through Leo's veins with what happened next. Briar jumped up on the truck's running boards and leaned in the open window. That's when the male's hand cupped the back of her head and pulled her in far longer than Leo cared to see; it wasn't just a peck.

"Fucking slut," he hissed, slamming his hand on the steering wheel of his rental.

Then he broke out in a fit of manic laughter when he realized something. He had never even kissed Briar. He'd have to fix that.

Leo quickly started the car before the black pickup could exit the parking lot. Briar was off-limits while in the confines of the school; however, Leo had a feeling that knowing a little more about her *friend* might be of use to him. Therefore, when the truck made the turn out of the school parking lot, Leo stayed close behind.

Oddly enough, Leo didn't have to follow the truck for long. They ended up near downtown, not far from the hotel he was staying at.

Leo had hoped to get a better look at the man when he exited his truck; however, he pulled up his hooded jacket before the driver's door could close behind him, blocking out a good view of his face. He then walked from the parking lot the short distance to a building with the words Hayden Auto Body and Restoration.

Shortly after, as the time continued to tick by, the town was bustling.

Leo ran over in his mind the little bit he had discovered. All of it could be condensed to not a whole lot. At least he knew that Briar was indeed a student at Argent Falls High. He also discovered that there was one person of significant importance in her life, and he appeared to work at a mechanic shop.

For some reason, curiosity was getting the best of Leo, and that's how he found himself parked near the drop-off zone of Hayden Auto.

✻ ✻ ✻

The bell and light in the garage went off, signaling that there was a person in the waiting room.

"I got the last one," Benji called out.

"Not it," Rusty laughed.

Dex shook his head, already wiping off his hands, heading into the main building.

The guy at the counter wasn't from Argent Falls, that much Dex knew. He had encountered most everyone in the town at some point or another throughout his life, but this guy looked like a fish out of water.

"Can I help you," Dex asked, all the while looking him up and down.

Attempting not to judge, but doing so anyway, Dex had to guess that the customer was on the wealthy side. He wore some kind of fancy jeans with too much embellishment, and though his hoodie seemed simple enough, Dex figured that the Brunello Cucinelli name on it meant something that suggested it was on the pricy side.

Strangely enough, the man before Dex appeared to be doing a similar assessment of Dex.

Leo immediately knew that the mechanic was the same one that dropped Briar off at school. He knew what the boys at her academy were like, and he couldn't fathom the fact that she was romantically involved with the dirty creature before him. His hair was dark and messy, eyes a chilling blue, and face a little scruffy. His sleeves were rolled to above the elbows, showing bulging arms that were heavily inked.

Briar had to be using him for protection of some kind. There was no way that she could find a person like him attractive.

"Umm…Yes. I uh…" Leo didn't know anything about cars, aside from which ones meant a better status for him. "Oil change!" That was a common thing, or so he thought. He didn't handle the maintenance of his cars.

Dex went to the computer and brought up Briar's program. "Let me get you checked in. Name?"

Leo hesitated. "George Bailey."

Dex went ahead and typed it in. "Make and model?"

"Oh." Leo pointed out the main windows, his car barely in view. "It's that white one."

Dex refrained from groaning and rolling his eyes. *That white one.* George should be embarrassed to call himself a man.

"The Camry," Dex stated after slightly leaning around the counter.

He got a little more information from George, who obviously knew nothing about cars or car maintenance.

This only proved truer when Dex turned the car on and saw that the oil-life was at seventy percent. He looked around the interior; it looked too clean, even for some rich brat. The only thing in the car was an empty to-go coffee cup. Then he saw something between the seats, a wad of folded up papers.

He shouldn't have pried, but something about the stranger was concerning. He had no reason to be suspicious; however, his gut told him differently.

Dex was even further perplexed when he saw that the papers were for the rental of the car he was currently in. Stranger yet, it wasn't listed under George

Bailey. Instead, the renter's name was Marcus Brown, and he rented it five days earlier.

Something didn't sit right with Dex. The names not matching was a red flag, and on another note, why would someone want an oil change for a rental that clearly didn't need one?

He tried to dismiss it. Marcus could simply be a friend who George was traveling with, and George, clearly knowing nothing about cars, may have thought that seventy percent was low; therefore, he'd go about the service.

"I went to take a leak," Benji began, just as Dex was finishing with the Camry. "That's an odd duck in there."

"Oh yeah?"

"Yeah. Prissy boy was asking about the help wanted sign."

At that Dex laughed. "I should take that shit down."

"That's not the weird part. He seemed pretty interested in you. He wanted to know what your name was, then he figured out you're the owner, asked how long you've had the shop…"

It was a little strange, but Dex already knew the guy was clearly not from around Argent Falls.

Rather than going back to work, Benji continued his rambling. "I mean, don't take this the wrong way, but you're a good-looking kid. I think he might be interested in you."

"Whoa. Thanks for the compliment, but don't even go there. Even if I was into guys, which is a hell no, *that* one in there is so far from doing it for me. He didn't even know the make and model of his fucking car," Dex pointed out, although now annoyed at the direction the conversation had taken.

"How much you want to bet that he'll ask you for your number?"

Dex shook his head; however, couldn't help but laugh a little. "Go to hell, Benji. Better yet, get your ass back to work."

Needless to say, after that little chat with Benji, the last thing Dex wanted to do was go back in and deal with George. Thankfully, George didn't say much. Whatever ideas Benji had gotten were just in his head. Not once did it

276

feel like George might be interested in Dex in a romantic way, nor did Dex think that George was flirting in any way during their exchange.

"Here," Leo said, handing the black card over.

Dex was just about to swipe the credit card when George had a sudden and panicked outburst.

"Shit. No. Uh…Let me pay in cash."

That took Dex by surprise, and he slowly handed the card back; however, he clearly saw the name written on it, which only sent up another red flag. Leonardo Chichester.

George, or whatever his name was at this point, tossed a hundred-dollar bill at Dex as soon as the card was back in his hands.

"I don't need a receipt," he nervously mumbled. With that, Leo grabbed his keys off the counter and tore from the building like he was on fire.

CHAPTER 39

"Rusty fucked up the computer program this morning," were the first words Briar heard when she entered the shop.

She tossed her bag in the office and went back out to the reception desk. "What's wrong," she asked Dex. "It looks fine to me."

"It's only printing one copy."

"Everything is saved. Is it really necessary to have a paper copy for yourself?"

Dex crossed his arms and glared at Briar. It wasn't the first time she was about to get on him with the number of trees he was killing. "Yes. I'll plant a tree in the spring if that'll make you happy," he added jokingly.

Briar swatted at Dex's chest, but quickly turned her attention to the computer. There wasn't a setting to select how many copies to print. She had it automatically coded to do so; therefore, something must have broken.

"When you fix it, can you print out one of everything after Mable's flat tire," Dex asked, as he headed back to the garage.

"Again?!"

He chuckled. "I'm not even going to go there. Today has just been a strange day all the way around."

"Oh, don't forget," Briar said, stopping Dex momentarily. "I work at the restaurant tonight."

"I'll drop you off."

"I was simply telling you. I can w—"

"Like I said," Dex interrupted. "I'll drop you off."

He gave her a wink and disappeared into the garage, leaving Briar to the task at hand. Even minutes later, she couldn't stop smiling, all the while realizing that she was falling harder by the day.

Ten minutes to five, Dex came back inside, tossing a set of keys on the counter. The woman sitting off to the side, bickering on her phone, finally decided to cut her call, as she made her way to the desk.

"That's the last one today," Dex informed Briar as he headed to the bathroom to wash his hands.

Once Briar checked the woman out and sent her on her way, she began quickly sorting through the stack of receipts, putting them in alphabetical order.

"You ready," Dex asked.

Not bothering to look up. "Almost. I just need to be there by 5:30."

She took Dex by surprise with a sudden outburst of laughter. He raised a brow, not understanding what was so funny about receipts. That's when Briar held up one in particular.

"Seriously," she gasped. "This has to be a joke."

Dex leaned forward and groaned when he saw the name. "He was one of the strange parts about today."

Briar's jaw dropped. "George Bailey?! Come on, Dex. George Bailey!"

Dex crinkled his brows. The name meant nothing to him, aside from belonging to the weirdo from earlier.

Briar let out an exasperated breath. "He's a fictional character from one of the best Christmas movies ever. *It's a Wonderful Life?*"

Dex shrugged. "I haven't watched many movies lately."

Briar's face fell flat. "It was made in the forties." To that Dex had no response. "I suppose both names could be common, but together, it's just too cute." She thought back to Dex's original response to the name. "Wait, what do you mean one of the strange parts, because you clearly didn't mean his name?"

"He was just different, definitely not a local. He had a rental, and wanted an oil change when he didn't need one."

"Oh…" Briar then turned her attention back to the remaining unalphabetized papers.

"It got weirder from there. The rental papers were listed for Marcus Brown. Then when–"

"Wait," Briar interrupted. She felt her stomach flip in the worst way when she heard that name. Though it was a very generic name, it hit her hard because she knew someone with it. "Did you say Marcus Brown?" She had to ask, even though she was certain that's what he said.

"Yeah. Are you okay?"

Briar blinked a few times and tried not to freak out. That had to be a bizarre coincidence. There was no way. "Anyway, then?"

Sensing that something was wrong, Dex decided to cut the conversation about the odd customer short. "He basically handed me his credit card, immediately took it back, threw a hundred-dollar bill at me, and that was that." Dex then changed the subject. "I'll take care of these tomorrow. You ready to go?"

Briar's body lost all feeling, as something ominous swept through her. Her thoughts went to the worst place imaginable. There was only one reason someone wouldn't want to pay with a credit card. It could be traced.

"Dex, did you see the name that was on the credit card?"

Dex hated that he had ever brought it up, and something about Briar's interest was concerning. "Leonardo…I don't know, Churchill?"

"Chichester." It wasn't a question; it was a statement. When Briar said that, all the color faded from her face.

"Okay, what the hell is going on," Dex growled. Briar had a strong reaction to Marcus Brown, but now this?

"Bathroom," she managed to say, storming around Dex.

Briar didn't even bother to close the door behind her. She fell to her knees and held on to the toilet for dear life while everything inside her came tumbling out.

Dex got several paper towels and dampened them. By the time he got to the bathroom, Briar's sickness seemed to settle.

Briar couldn't look at Dex when he handed her the wet scraps. She would have a lot of explaining to do, and that thought sickened her further.

Dex took a step back as Briar retched into the toilet once more.

"Just go away," Briar cried out.

"You're sick," Dex sighed. "I need to know what I can do."

"Nothing!"

Dex had never seen Briar so torn up. While the vomiting eventually stopped, it was then replaced by a fit of tears.

He managed to convince her to leave the bathroom. Now she sat pressed up against him on the couch in the office, attempting to sip on a cold bottle of water.

"What was that about," he finally asked.

Briar only shook her head. Dex would go nuts if he knew who the person was he encountered earlier that day.

"I'm not sure what's going on. That was unexpected. As uncomfortable as this is…" He paused for a second. He had no clue what caused Briar to suddenly get so sick, but his mind had to go down the list of the obvious. Like ripping off a bandage, he went for it. "I know we've been using protection, but do you think–"

"No! God no," Briar burst out, interrupting what Dex was about to ask. If she wasn't so nervous and agitated, she might have found humor in that. After all, she rarely saw Dex blush as much as he was doing now. "There's something you should know."

Dex slightly braced himself for whatever Briar was about to say. Her being pregnant, so young and so soon, would have been the worst of it. If that wasn't it, he figured he'd be able to handle what he should know.

Briar ran a hand over her face, wiping at the mascara smudges. "Marcus Brown is the name of a man who does a lot of the landscaping for my stepmother."

That admission sent a chill through Dex, and before he could connect the pieces, attempting to go back and remember a name that Briar had once mentioned, she hit him with the rest of it.

"Leonardo Chichester is my stepbrother."

Dex bolted from the couch, and cracked his knuckles.

Briar took a deep breath. "Please don't. I didn't want to tell you at first because—"

"If I would have known that, he'd be dead right now," Dex growled.

"I know that," she sighed. "If you would take a second to calm down, and let me think. I feel like something strange is happening…"

"What do you mean," he asked. He hated to tell her, but his rage wasn't going away anytime soon.

"After all these months, why now? Why did they bother looking for me?"

Dex saw a fear cross Briar's face as he repeated her questions to himself. She was right. If her stepmother had all that money at her disposal, she could have found Briar within weeks, maybe days. Why now, more than four months later?

"Shit," Briar hissed, looking at her phone. "I'm late."

"Late?"

Briar grabbed a few tissues from the nearby box and wiped at her smeared makeup. "Yes, late, for my shift at Chêne."

"Like hell!"

Briar glared at Dex, not following.

"Your demented sicko stepbrother is out there. There's no way—"

Briar walked over to Dex and placed her hands upon his chest. The tension within him seeped through. "Look, you're dropping me off and picking me up. The rest of the time I'll be surrounded by other people, including Sandy and Rita. Nothing will happen to me."

As always, Briar's eyes showed her cards. She tried to pretend she wasn't, but Dex saw the terror inside.

"Fine, but I'm coming inside."

Shortly after Dex's attack on Jasper, Briar insisted that he wait for her in the parking lot, as opposed to coming inside. While Jasper had been the only patron who dared touch her, she did get hit on from time to time. The last thing she wanted was Dex going all alpha on someone and ending up in jail.

Though it took a bit of convincing on this particular night, eventually Dex relented, and promised to wait outside.

"Handicap? Really," Briar asked, mildly annoyed, when she got in Dex's truck.

"I've been here for less than five minutes and it's after ten. Nobody who needs handicap parking is going to a bar at this hour," Dex scoffed, already pulling away from the spot nearest the entry doors.

Briar yawned. She was drained from school, work, and stress. She couldn't wait to take a shower and fall asleep in Dex's arms. "You'll also be happy to know, tonight was as uneventful as any other night."

"I don't care. The fact that the fucker is around here and came into *my* shop, should have you concerned," Dex harshly pointed out.

"You don't think I'm concerned? Of course, I am, but what can I do about it right this second?"

"Go to the police."

Briar's head fell to the seat as she gave Dex an incredulous look. "And tell them what? I feel uncomfortable that my stepbrother is in the same town as me?"

"He's a fucking rapist!"

Briar clenched her eyes shut and turned away, making Dex realize how much it hurt her that he pointed that out.

He didn't know what it was like in Briar's world. He had to assume that she had her reasons, as she told him from the beginning. People coped differently with traumatic events. Perhaps in Briar's mind, not going to the police, pressing charges, going through a trial, if one would even happen, was best for her.

However, Leo showing up was greatly hindering her ability to move on. Dex saw that as soon as his name was mentioned earlier in the day, and that was going to be a problem.

CHAPTER 40

"We seem to have hit the jackpot today," Portia's voice squealed through the phone's speaker.

"Yes, you did because you got to sit on your ass all day and drink top shelf liquor. Meanwhile, I'm over here drinking coffee that tastes like mud, in a hotel that doesn't even have room service. I had to order pizza, mother!"

"I know you've had a long day," Portia sighed, making sure that Leo could hear her sipping her drink on the other end.

"I was in that car all day, waiting and following. To make matters worse, the car's Bluetooth stopped working after I left the auto shop. I'm sure that brute doesn't know what the hell he's doing when it comes to cars," Leo whined. He flung himself on the bed. He felt horrible. His body wasn't used to so much greasy food, and for days it seemed that's all he had been eating.

"The best time will be to get her between school and work then," Portia asked.

"Yes. I waited near the auto shop for most of the afternoon, thinking that Dexter Hayden would maybe leave to pick Briar up, and maybe that's why I hadn't seen her after school. These public schools are strange. She must get out early, because she ended up at his shop before two. I'm only assuming that she must walk every day. It's only slightly problematic because despite this being a small town, people are everywhere!"

Portia popped an olive into her mouth, delighted that Briar was at least within Leo's range.

"I have no idea about the restaurant thing," Leo went on.

"Late at night would be good," Portia pointed out. "Less people about."

"If only her thug of a boyfriend, or whatever he is, didn't drop her off and pick her up."

Portia let out a sigh of annoyance. "You're certain she's living with him."

"I don't know! I wasn't going to stay there all night. Oh, and by the way, he lives in the nicest apartment complex in this shithole. It's gated," Leo stressed.

"You're just going to need to get creative. You need to make sure she has drugs in her system and on her," Portia reminded her son.

"Yes, mother. You've told me this a hundred times."

"And I'll tell you a hundred more until her body is found in a ditch somewhere," Portia hissed through the phone.

With that, she ended the call. Leo was frustrating her, and she had no desire to continue speaking with him. He relayed his information and it was late.

Above all, Portia dreaded that it was taking so long to find a stupid girl and dispose of her.

* * *

Leo was enraged when, the next day, he decided to wait at Briar's school, and things didn't go as planned.

Around 1:30, several students exited the building, most of them going to their cars; however, Briar didn't take the path he assumed. Rather, she didn't walk at all, because waiting in the fire zone was a familiar black truck.

"You have got to be fucking kidding me?!"

It wasn't until then that Leo became nervous. He had to wonder if Dexter and Briar knew he was around. They couldn't possibly know about his mother's plan.

Either Dexter was a doting boyfriend to Briar, or they did indeed suspect something, making them take extra precautions.

Leo tried to think of the ideal opportunity, but so far, it was slim. He wondered how long Briar would keep her guard up, and then, a strange idea hit him.

His mother would be furious if it didn't work out, but he was getting desperate. It seemed that the only time Briar wasn't around Dexter was when she was at school. As bad as it might come back and slap him in the face, it was all he had to work with.

Obviously, Portia wasn't happy when he told her that he had to wait until after the weekend to figure things out; however, buried in his hotel room, that's exactly what he did. Come Monday, he fully intended to put an end to this whole ordeal.

"Yes," was how the aged receptionist greeted Leo when he entered the main office.

Leo glanced at the badge around her neck. It read Geraldine. He couldn't help but cringe. To him, it was a name that suggested she had never left Argent Falls and was content in a dead-end job dealing with high school students.

Attempting to put his acting skills to use, Leo smiled sweetly. "Good morning, Geraldine. I have to say, I love your hair. Are those curls natural?"

Geraldine wasn't one for small talk. She smacked on her gum and shoved it to the side to respond. "No. Kitty Beauty Shop."

Leo was a little taken aback. The woman didn't even smile. Given, she was easily three times his age; however, he could make even the oldest and most bitter women at least smile with a nice compliment.

"Can I help you with something?"

"Yes, I'm here to pick up Briar Stone," he said, unwavering.

Geraldine clicked around on the keyboard to a computer that looked like one of the first of its kind. Leo thought of two scenarios, and thankfully, this godawful woman before him, handed him information on a silver platter.

"The only person that can check her out is Dexter Hayden."

Leo originally leaned more toward the idea of Dexter being in an accident from the beginning; however, now knowing that he was Briar's contact, made even more sense to take it in that direction. The other option was for him to admit to being Briar's stepbrother and come up with a family emergency. The only problem he ran into there was if they asked for identification, as he and Briar did not have the same last name.

"That's why I'm here, on behalf of Dexter."

Geraldine stopped momentarily. Just that one statement caused her to become wary. "Oh?"

"Yes, there was an accident at the shop, nothing major, but he wanted to get in touch with Briar immediately. He tried calling and texting, but obviously she's in class. He asked if I could pick her up and bring her to the hospital," Leo calmly finished. He replayed his words quickly in his head, wondering if he covered all his bases.

"And what is your relation?"

"To who," Leo asked, slightly confused.

A smirk came across Geraldine's lips. "To *Dexter*."

"Oh, I'm an old friend visiting for a couple days. We were hanging out at the shop and…" Leo paused. He had no idea what to say. A car fell on him? He burned his hand on something inside a car? What was hot inside a car? Instead, he finished with, "One thing led to another. I didn't see it all, but he needed to go in to get checked out."

Geraldine thought about asking the man for his name, but she didn't want to spook him and make him think that she found him strangely suspicious.

She knew Dexter Hayden, the town's mechanic. Most everyone ended up dealing with him at some point or another. More than anything, she knew that no one called him Dexter. If common folk in the community didn't call him that, there was no way that his *friends* would.

"Excuse me for a minute. Our PA system is down. I'll have to go to her room," Geraldine informed Leo.

He nodded in response while she took her leave.

Geraldine walked through one of the office hallways, turned down another hallway, and ended up in the privacy of the mailroom, already searching through her phone. She couldn't remember the number listed for Dex; however, she had the main local businesses a couple taps away.

"Hello," a gruff voice answered.

"Hi, this is the receptionist at Argent Falls High School," Geraldine announced with a soft motherly tone.

Benji groaned as soon as he heard that. "Yeah?"

"Is Dexter Hayden available," Geraldine asked, calling him by his formal name as it pertained to school business.

Benji looked behind him through the glass panels to the garage. "One minute," he said placing the phone down on the counter. He opened the side door and called out in a loud voice sure to carry across the racket. "Dex. The school is on the line."

It didn't take Dex more than a second to process Benji's words. The school never called with any good information.

"This is Dex Hayden," he answered urgently.

"Hi, this is Geraldine, the receptionist at Argent Falls High School," Geraldine practically repeated.

Dex only got a slight feeling of relief. At least it wasn't the nurse calling.

"This call might sound strange, but I need to ask, did you request for anyone to check out a Miss Briar Stone?"

"Hell no!" Dex quickly corrected himself, realizing that he was speaking to a respected elder at the school. "I mean…No Ma'am." He remembered Geraldine from when he attended high school. She had to have been the receptionist for the last fifty years.

"Then I need to inform you, there's a young man here claiming that you were in an accident and requested that he bring said student to the hospital on your behalf."

Dex was speechless. All he saw was red. There was only one person that entered his mind, and if he ever encountered him again, Leo was a dead man.

* * *

289

While Geraldine was out, Leo noted the incessant ringing of the phone at the front desk; however, it was once it stopped that he realized something was wrong. Rather than another ring, a voice came through on the speaker above.

"Geri? This is Georgia. Has my FedEx package been dropped off?"

Leo remained silent.

"Hello? Geri?"

Then there was a click and the speaker from above went silent. That's when Leo grasped that *Geri* hadn't gone to get Briar. The loudspeaker system was working all along. For all he knew, she might be on the phone with the cops.

His plan was clearly ruined, and this was something he wouldn't dare tell his mother.

CHAPTER 41

After spending so much time together, Briar could read Dex pretty well, without him saying a word. So far, after picking her up, all she had gotten was a simple *hey*. His whole body appeared tense, and his brows were more furrowed than when he assessed the most difficult tasks.

The short drive to the shop was accomplished in silence. It was only when Dex held open the entry door that he finally spoke to her.

"Office. We need to talk."

His face held a pained, worried, saddened expression. It was something inherently unlike Dex.

"Dex, you're scaring me a little," Briar blurted out as soon as he closed the office door.

He motioned to the couch. "I think you should sit down."

Briar did as Dex suggested and stared at the floor, unable to look at him when he sat next to her. "Are you…You want to end things, right?"

Dex found himself nervously chuckling, realizing what Briar must be thinking. Nothing good ever came after *we need to talk*. This was the case as well, but on an entirely different subject.

Hoping to put her mind at ease and still unsure how to express his concern, he pulled her close to him and kissed her sweetly on the cheek. He pressed their foreheads together and stared into intoxicating eyes full of questions. "No. That's the last thing I want to do."

Briar slightly pulled away, now confused. She was thankful that's not where the conversation was headed, but there was still a dark seriousness in Dex's features.

"I'm not good with words and I'm trying to find a way to tell you something without blurting it out and scaring the fuck out of you," Dex admitted.

Briar pulled away completely. "Oh! Well! When you put it like that?! What the hell?!"

"Damnit, Briar."

"Damnit, Dex," she said in a mimicking voice, not caring how childish she appeared.

Dex took a deep breath. "Fine. Okay? Leo was at your school today."

Briar clamped her mouth shut and blinked a few times in rapid succession. "I...He...What?"

Dex pressed his back into the couch, not wanting to look at the hurt shock on such a beautiful face. "I got a call from the receptionist. She didn't get his name, but gave me a description. I know it was him. He said that I was in some kind of work accident, that he was an old friend visiting, and you needed to go with him to the hospital."

"Dex," Briar gasped. "You do realize I would never have—"

"I know. As soon as you would have seen him...I know. That doesn't change the fact that he's trying to get in touch with you. From what you've told me the last couple years have been like, I can't assume that it's of an innocent nature."

"What ended up happening," Briar found herself asking, knowing that she was never paged from the classroom.

"He must have realized how fucking stupid his idea was and bolted. The lady stayed on the phone with me, but he was gone by the time she got back."

Briar nodded her head, processing.

Dex went on, giving her one final statement. "You should know, the school resource officer was put on alert. If he shows up again, it'll be serious."

Briar didn't want to get cops involved, knowing that it would end up becoming a headline story. All she wanted to do was live a normal and peaceful life; however, she wasn't naïve enough to dismiss Dex's concerns.

What Leo did sent up a huge red flag. It would have been one thing if he was honest, but the fact that he crafted such an elaborate lie also led Briar to believe that there might be something deeper in his arrival.

The silent contemplation was broken when Briar's phone went off several times.

"What is it," Dex asked when Briar sighed upon reading the texts.

Briar held her phone out for Dex to read.

Rita: Jennifer just told me that she's down with the flu.

Rita: We're already short in both the restaurant and bar.

Rita: Can you please please please work tonight?

"Just tell her no."

Briar glared at Dex. "I can't do that."

"It's a Monday. I'm sure they won't be that busy," Dex added.

"She wouldn't have asked me if they weren't in a bind."

Dex rose from the couch with Briar quickly doing the same. "I think after today—"

Interrupting Dex, "It's a public restaurant and bar. I think I'll be safe there. I'm sure Leo doesn't even know I work there."

"He knew the town you were in and that you were enrolled in the school. He knows about me. I'm sure he knows more than you'd like to believe."

Briar let out a deep breath, feeling exhausted. She wanted to put Dex's mind at ease, but already knew that wouldn't be happening. Briar wasn't going to tell him, but with the millions of dollars at Portia's disposal, she probably hired a private investigator. There wasn't a doubt in her mind that Leo knew that she worked at the restaurant.

* * *

293

"You have no idea how glad I am that you could come in," Rita squealed as soon as Briar walked through the kitchen door.

Briar couldn't help but laugh a little. Rita and Sandy were awesome people to her. There was no way that she'd let them down, knowing they needed her.

At first Briar thought Dex would give her a hard time about going in, but he dropped her off like everything was fine and simply told her that he'd be waiting in the parking lot when she finished her shift.

Dex's words earlier must have jinxed the place, as it was extremely busy for a Monday, much more than the Mondays Briar worked during the summer.

It wasn't until shortly after eight that the place finally began to dwindle down. All the families had cleared out and the only ones dining now were a few couples. Just when Briar thought she'd be able to catch her breath and go into the kitchen for a bottle of water, her air was knocked from her lungs.

She watched with nervousness as the hostess placed Leo in a secluded table along the wall. His eyes locked on her immediately and his lips tilted more on one corner than the other.

The hostess placed the menu down and turned around. She nodded to Briar and motioned toward Leo. Briar looked around, hoping there was another waitress to take Leo's order, but the only other one she could see on the floor was consumed by flirting with a table of gentlemen.

"Hello, Briar," Leo said slowly and seductively.

Briar cringed as Leo's eyes roamed up and down her body. The days were getting colder, and though she was completely covered, something about the way he looked at her made her feel naked and exposed.

Whatever fear she had, she buried it. She had to. She couldn't let Leo see the negative effect he had on her. She had to be strong and assertive, especially after his actions earlier in the day.

"What are you doing here," Briar asked coldly.

Leo laughed. "Hospitality isn't your strong suit. I'd recommend a job other than waitress and receptionist."

It was easy hiding her surprise, as there was none. If Leo knew where she attended school, Briar knew that he'd already know the places she worked, and probably even where she lived.

When Briar didn't say anything, "This is a restaurant. I thought my reasoning for being here would be obvious."

Mustering up all the confidence she could, Briar leaned into Leo's table and lowered her voice. "Cut the crap. I know you were at my school today."

Leo already had a plan in motion. He wanted Briar to know he was around. If he feigned innocence, perhaps she and Dex would eventually become comfortable. Then he'd strike.

"Did that awful woman finally tell you I was there," Leo huffed.

Briar narrowed her eyes. Leo's admission, just like that, wasn't what she expected. "No, Leo. The school called Dex because you were being a creepy weirdo."

The curious smile that came to Leo's face told Briar that her response had been the wrong one.

"Dex? The mechanic," he asked, pretending to not follow.

Briar ignored Leo's question. "That story was completely ridiculous. Why would you do that?"

"I wanted to see my sister," Leo said with a shrug. "Since we don't have the same last name, I figured…" He let that statement go, not having a good ending. "I just wanted them to call you out of class so I could talk to you. That simple."

"You could have found a better way."

"You're either working or at school. Although, seeing as you live with Dex, I'd imagine you've found other ways to occupy your time."

Briar tightened her ponytail, needing to do something with her restless hands. "What do you want, Leo?"

"Nothing. Mother and I just wanted to see how you were doing." Leo looked up to the ceiling, then to the windows, then he craned his neck around Briar, looking toward the partitions. "I see you've really fallen on hard times."

"You should know by now that I have no intention of serving you," Briar spat.

A sinister look appeared in the depths of Leo's eyes. He took out his wallet and withdrew several large bills. He tossed them on the table and rose from his seat. He stepped around so that he and Briar were toe to toe. "I'd say you've served me rather well," he whispered. "I'll let mother know that you're on your feet."

Briar ignored the sickening first part of his comment. "You're leaving Argent Falls?"

"God, yes! Why anyone would live in this dump is beyond me."

Though Briar tried not to show it, Leo picked up on the relief that washed across her face. He'd go back home for a little while, but he'd be back. Briar and Dex would let their guard down eventually.

"Oh, just so you know," he began, leaning in. He nodded toward the money on the table. "That's the most I've ever had to pay for a piece of ass."

Before Briar could think of what to say, Leo turned and casually walked away.

She closed her eyes tightly and repeated over and over to just breathe. When she thought that she might be well enough to keep her tears at bay, she looked at the pile of cash on the table. There was no way in hell she was keeping that.

Leo's sick words continued to echo in her mind long after they were spoken. Briar tried her hardest to appear normal on the outside, but she could feel Dex's eyes darting from the road to her.

He already asked her how work was, as he always did. Her response today was a simple and flat 'fine'. Dex got the impression that Briar didn't want to engage in conversation, therefore he didn't push any on the short drive to the apartment.

It wasn't until Briar was in the shower that Dex bothered to sit down and check his phone, already knowing he had unread messages. Only then did he realize that something about work that evening was not *fine*.

Sandy: Rita said that Briar declined one of her tips for the night. I wanted to make sure everything was okay. The whole situation is a little weird, and she didn't elaborate.

Dex didn't think much of it. The weird part for him was the fact that Sandy could text that much.

Dex: I'm sure it's nothing.

Sandy: That was more than a normal tip. It would have helped a lot with her savings.

Dex: Wait. How much was it?

Sandy: A grand.

That immediately didn't sit well with Dex. People in Argent Falls didn't tip like that. Every bad thought he could conjure up began racing through his mind, so much so that he was tempted to break down the bathroom door so that Briar could explain and give him some sort of understanding.

Ultimately, he waited, not so patiently, in his chair by the balcony window.

"The bathroom is all yours," Briar informed him, just barely poking her head from the hallway. She then disappeared.

Dex rose and followed after her. Much to his surprise, Briar went to her bedroom.

He watched from her doorway as she prepared her bed. Since their first night together, she always slept in his room. He couldn't think of anything he might have done that would warrant the sudden change.

"What's wrong," Dex calmly asked.

Briar turned to him and smiled, but he saw the pain beneath it. "I'm just really tired."

Dex walked across the room until they were practically chest to chest. He reached out and took her shoulders in his hands, and what she did was worse than a punch to the gut. She stepped away, shrugging him off.

Briar quickly apologized when she saw the hurt in Dex's eyes. "I'm sorry."

"If you don't want me to touch you, that's fine. I know something happened at work today." He stopped for a second. When he mentioned work, her eyes widened in surprise and her face drained of its rosy color. Even if she chose to deny it, her eyes once again told him the truth. "Briar…"

She sat down on the bed and nodded to the side for Dex to do the same, the bed sinking with his weight. Briar closed her eyes and took a deep breath, before beginning. "If I talk to you about this, you have to promise not to lose your temper."

Dex let out a growl from deep within.

"Dex," Briar said with a warning tone.

"Fine."

Briar was only mildly satisfied. She was certain that Dex would find an excuse for the yelling and cursing that would undoubtedly follow once she shared her encounter.

"Leo stopped by the restaurant tonight," she began, carefully watching Dex from the corner of her eye.

Dex's jaw clenched, tightening from grinding his teeth together, trying his hardest to let Briar talk. His fists were digging into the bed. If Briar wasn't sitting next to him, there's no doubt there would be a hole in the wall.

Briar slowly continued, surprised that Dex was trying his best not to turn into a raging monster. "He explained the whole school thing. It was stupid, but maybe in his delusional mind it made sense. Apparently, he just wanted to talk to me."

"Why," Dex snarled.

"He said that Portia wanted to see how I was doing."

298

"So, months later, after her son rapes you, now she wants to see how you're doing. Come on, Briar. You can't be that naïve." Dex quickly realized that he was allowing his anger to get the better of him, and by doing so, his words were cutting. "I'm sorry. I should have said that in a different–"

"Stop," Briar insisted. "I know you're upset because you care. I've told you before, you don't need to watch your mouth for my sake."

"Upset isn't the word I'd use." Dex watched as the faintest of smiles came to Briar's face. "I'm guessing something about that fucker being there tonight has to do with the tip you declined."

Briar finally turned to looked at Dex, her mouth agape. "How...did..."

"Sandy messaged me. A thousand dollars? Why?"

Dex felt something inside him shatter when tears fell from her expressionless eyes. He waited, but she said nothing, didn't dare to look at him again. All he could think was that she was regressing, falling back into a darkness that once was so close to being defeated in her world.

Dex rose from the bed and knelt in front of Briar, taking her hands in his. Much to his relief, she didn't pull away.

"Briar, I need to know what happened."

"Just words," she managed.

"Words can do a lot."

Briar didn't respond, so Dex simply stayed there, waiting for the tears to slow, until she could talk.

Briar must have sensed that Dex had no intention of leaving until he had the full story. Her brain told her that she was being ridiculous for letting Leo's words get to her. He had done more damage in the past, but it was the reminder that gnawed at her confidence and self-worth.

"The money..." That was all she said at first. Dex's eyes remained on hers, waiting for whatever she'd give him. "He basically said it was payment."

"Basically?"

Briar felt Dex's hands tighten around hers. She didn't want to say it. Ever since he entered her room that night, she saw a more protective part of him,

299

but that part was also very dark. She could read it in his body language and those cold blue eyes.

"Just say it," Dex insisted, fighting to keep calm.

Briar pulled her hands from his and placed them around her neck, rubbing the tension that had been there all night.

Dex finally stood and took a few steps away. Whatever Leo said to Briar must have been like a knife opening up a wound that hadn't quite healed. Worst of all, he knew why she didn't want to talk about it. She didn't think he could handle it.

It was that thought alone that made Dex realize how deep his feelings were for Briar. He'd do anything to protect her from any more pain in her life.

"It's not that big of a deal. I'm just overreacting because I'm—"

"Just. Say. It," he repeated, slowly enunciating each word.

Briar stared at the floor beneath her feet dangling from the side of the bed. Another second passed before she got the courage to repeat Leo's words that still made her feel sick to her stomach.

"I told him that I wouldn't be serving him," she began. "He said that I had already *served* him, insinuating that's what the money was for, as I was the most he ever paid for a piece of ass. Which is basically just calling me a…" Briar let her words drift off.

She fully expected Dex to fly off in a fit of anger, but he took her by surprise in the best of ways when she felt herself wrapped in his warmth.

Briar buried her face in Dex's chest. He hadn't showered yet and his clothes smelled like the shop, oil and gasoline. It was strangely comforting to her.

Dex gently cradled her head. "I can't tell you not to let those words bother you, but I can tell you that nothing he said is true. You're one of the purest and most genuine people in this damn world. He's nothing but a fucking bastard that will eventually pay for every evil he's done in his life."

300

"I just don't get why. Why now? I was doing so well. I accepted that it was something terrible that happened to me, but it was the past. I just want the past to stay in the past."

Briar's words were difficult to understand as she spoke into Dex's chest, but he heard them loud and clear, and they tore at his insides. Briar could always tell him what she was thinking and how she felt, but he realized that he'd never truly understand what she had been through.

Dex was grateful when Briar wrapped her arms around his torso, embracing the hug. He wasn't about to ask, because he could easily assume, he knew the answer, why she didn't want him touching her earlier.

"I'm sure you want some space tonight."

"Can I ask you a stupid question," Briar quickly stated, dismissing Dex's comment. She slightly pulled back, but only so she could see Dex's face. He nodded. "From the moment I met you, I found your tattoos intriguing."

"That's because you come from a different world, full of polo shirts and khakis," Dex snorted. A small part of him was happy for the change of subject, especially if it meant that it stopped any more tears from falling down the angelic face looking up at him.

Briar raised a brow, but couldn't hide the smirk on her face by how correct Dex was. "Why don't you have any on your right leg, or your chest or back?"

Dex's eyes, which once held a glimmer of amusement, turned to dark shadows.

"Oh…Was that the wrong thing…It was just something I was curious about. I didn't think…" Briar let her voice trail off. It was a stupid question to ask. It probably sounded weird and juvenile to Dex.

Dex rose from the bed. "It's getting late. I should get a shower and head to bed too."

Briar nodded. She never expected a simple question to make Dex so cold and rigid.

It wasn't until Dex neared Briar's doorway that he froze. After everything that Briar told him, and continued to tell him about her past, he could at least give her something in return. Had he not been caught off guard by the question, he probably would have lied about it; however, there was a heavy air that lingered from recent events, one that made him want to tell Briar the truth.

"To cover the past," he said, turning to face Briar. Dex leaned into the wall behind him. He didn't want to be close to Briar when he told her. "Remember how I told you I let myself go after my dad died, turning to drugs?" Briar nodded. "No offense, but I'm sure where you're from that's like weed, or maybe some rich stressed housewife takes a few Xanax."

Briar bit her lip and felt her cheeks reddening by how accurate Dex was. She only knew of one student at the academy that supposedly smoked a joint from time to time. She wasn't so naïve to know there weren't worse things out there, but they didn't exist in her world, at least not to her knowledge.

"I'm not sure I'm following." Briar was unsure how drugs had anything to do with what she thought was a simple question about the placement of Dex's tattoos.

"Cocaine, heroin, methamphetamine…If you could inject it with a needle, I was all for it."

Briar felt her heart nearly stop, realizing what Dex was saying.

Dex's eyes fell from Briar's to the floor, unable to take the look of horror behind eyes that once looked at him with so much affection. He could have glossed over his past, but that wouldn't have been fair to either of them.

"At first it was just my left arm, but when track marks started to appear, I went to the other one. Towards the end, I started shooting up in my left leg. That was much easier to hide." Dex paused, waiting to see if Briar would say something, but she didn't, just watched him carefully, the horror in her eyes now fading to sadness. "I know you must think I was this fucked up drug addicted maniac, and I was in a sense. I was addicted. I wasn't always high. I still worked and worked for my certification. I just don't remember a lot of my days. Time kept passing and I kept waking up and getting by, always needing to numb myself from the pain of being alone."

302

The one thing Dex didn't want to talk about was his mother. He mentioned to Briar that she left when he was a child, and that's all he'd say. The truth was, it still stung, realizing that his own mother never wanted him.

"After what you've been through, I know that must sound ridiculous."

"No," Briar quickly corrected. "We all cope in different ways, some of which aren't the healthiest."

Dex watched as Briar wrapped her right hand over her left wrist, her thumb lightly rubbing against the skin. Suddenly, he had to wonder what she wasn't telling him.

"Well, after about nine months of being a complete fuckup, Sandy stepped in. You wanted to know about the tattoos. The scars were never that bad, and eventually they started healing, but I still saw them. The first couple months of sobriety were difficult. I hated looking at myself in the mirror. I hated everything about me. I also always saw those scars, even if no one else could, so I covered up those places."

Briar understood. She wondered why his left leg was covered but his right completely clean. She had no idea that there was such a heavy meaning.

"They're beautiful," she said, rising from the bed and walking toward a closed off Dex. "You're beautiful."

As Briar got closer to Dex, he saw something in her eyes, something hidden. Then he remembered what she just told him, and how it seemed like she wasn't just talking about him.

He took her hands in his and flipped them over. She tried to pull away, but he held her firmly in place.

The scars were faded, but across her soft pale skin, he could see them. He rubbed his thumbs over the elevated disturbance of skin.

"Briar," Dex sighed, shaking his head.

"So, I tried to kill myself," Briar stated rather blandly. "It was years ago. After my mother died and my father remarried."

"I don't know what to say."

Dex loosened his grip and that's when Briar ultimately pulled away.

"There's nothing to say. At the time, I really didn't want to be here any-more. Little did I know, things would only get worse after my father's death. There were times that I contemplated, but I didn't want to give in. I just wanted to get out. Then I got here, to Argent Falls, and I've never been so happy to be alive."

Dex felt his chest tighten. There was only ever going to be one end to their relationship. Realizing how fragile Briar might be, he really didn't want to be that something that determined her happiness.

CHAPTER 42

Though Briar, and especially Dex, had reservations about Leo's motives, as the days went on, they had to take his word. Dex was still unsettled by what Leo did at the school; however, that was the end of it. Weeks went by, and Leo never popped up again.

"You're awfully cheery," Dex mentioned as Briar jumped in his truck.

"It's Friday before the week of Thanksgiving. That means no school for nine days."

All Dex did was grunt in response.

"Also, I'll be working at the restaurant all week. Rita said I can bake in the mornings and waitress for lunch and dinner, given that you don't need me at the shop."

"Go for it."

Briar smiled from ear to ear. "Also, tips are really good around the holidays. You know, I have enough saved up. I could probably get my own place."

Dex's face scrunched up. "You'll be headed to London in a month or two. You can stay with me until then."

Briar mentioned moving out in hopes that there would be a clear definition to what they were or weren't. This happened to be yet another time when Dex stated the finality of their relationship in his own way.

Whenever he mentioned Briar leaving for school, it broke her heart. Never once did he ever say anything about a long-distance relationship. Due to that, his next words took her by surprise.

"Sandy asked if we wanted to join him and Rita at the restaurant for Thanksgiving dinner."

"Just the four of us," Briar asked.

"They usually invite several people who don't have big families or places to go," Dex clarified. He noted that Briar's shoulders gradually sank.

"That sounds nice. I'd like to go," Briar plainly added.

Dex knew what Briar needed to hear, he simply didn't want to make it a big deal, already assuming that it was understood. "Good. Rita would give me shit if I finally had a girlfriend she liked, only for that girl to not want to spend the holiday with me."

Briar's jaw dropped. "Dex," she breathed.

"I said it. Just let it go."

Briar bit her bottom lip trying to hide the massive smile on her face and looked out the window as they neared Dex's shop. She knew Dex had a hard time with feelings and emotions; therefore, that comment was enough for her.

If Briar had been ecstatic and excitable when Dex picked her up from school, that was nothing compared to the days that followed.

She felt like her life was finally falling into place. It wasn't what she had dreamed, but at the end of each day, she was happy. She had a safe place to stay, someone that cared about her in ways she never thought possible, and as unconventional as it was, she had family.

Argent Falls was home.

* * *

"You should have called or text. I would have come to pick you up," Dex said after Briar got done explaining why she was at the shop near closing time on a Tuesday.

She was at the restaurant extremely early to finish up desserts for the next day, as well as orders for customers who would be picking up to-go meals for their Thanksgiving celebrations. Shortly after the lunch rush, Rita insisted

Briar take the evening off, as they absolutely needed her to be in tiptop shape the following day.

"I liked the walk. I got some fresh air."

"It's forty something degrees," Dex scoffed. He tossed a wrench in one of the drawers and made his way to Briar, standing at the stairs leading into the reception space. He gave her a soft peck on the lips. "Let me wash up and we can start locking up."

"Whoa," Briar exclaimed, looking past Dex, farther into the garage.

Dex followed her line of sight to a faraway corner. "Oh, that?"

"That?! Yes, that. When did you get that?"

Dex chuckled. "I've been working on it for the last month. It was originally white, but the paint got all fucked up."

Maybe Briar had noticed it before, but the blazing red suddenly stood out. "I take it you're done with the Bentley?"

"Got picked up yesterday for an auction."

"And this is," she hesitated.

"1967 Mustang GT convertible."

Dex got the car for little to nothing from an estate sale. Though the exterior needed a little extra care, the owner had treated it nicely over the years. The major issue with the interior was the upholstery, which was an easy fix.

Sensing that Briar was intrigued, "Give me a second and we'll head down and check it out."

Needless to say, when Dex went to the bathroom to clean all the grime from his hands, Briar allowed herself to roam through the garage on her own.

Aside from popping her head in and out of the garage from time to time when she did work there, she hadn't taken the time to look around and see some of the projects Dex was working on lately. She was a little disappointed that he hadn't told her about this one. He always asked her about her day, and in the past shared a great deal of his, even though he insisted that he was boring her. Perhaps that's why he hadn't said more about a new restoration.

Upon returning to the garage after cleaning up, Dex found Briar in the backseat of the Mustang, looking up to the empty metal ceiling of nothing.

"I said give me a second," Dex huffed, pretending to be annoyed that Briar ventured through the shop on her own.

Briar looked away from the ceiling, pushing aside any thoughts running through her head and took Dex in. He looked incredible as always. Teasing back, "Clearly, I didn't listen."

"Do you ever," Dex mumbled, climbing in and taking a seat next to Briar. As soon as his jean clad leg pressed against hers, Briar felt his warmth soaking through. Though the garage was quite cool, she felt like a volcano about to erupt.

Different thoughts now took over Briar's head as they sat in silence.

"You're awfully quiet," Dex pointed out. When Briar said nothing, "Ready to head out?"

With her head still pressed against the seat, Briar turned to face Dex. "I missed you."

His eyes flickered up and down her face, unable to ignore the lustful look blossoming in her green irises. Something about the way she looked at him screamed for him to touch her, but now wasn't the time or place.

"You saw me three minutes ago," he said, dismissing her words.

"I haven't seen you all day."

"You saw me this morning."

Briar's movement was quick, startling Dex. Before he could protest, which he never would have in the first place, Briar was straddling him.

"You know what I mean," she breathed into his ear.

He hated how she could do that. Contact with her, her breath on his skin, a touch of their lips, the simplest things sent his body spinning out of control, needing to have more of her. She was the most dangerous and addictive drug in existence for him.

Briar knew immediately what she was doing to Dex, and she loved it. As soon as she felt him harden beneath her, she pressed farther into him, rocking forward.

"Briar," Dex warned, closing his eyes and pressing the back of his head to the seat. "We're in a cold and dirty garage, we're not–"

"So," she interrupted.

Before Dex could counter, Briar lifted herself so that she could reach his face.

Once her lips collided against his, Dex felt the hunger and intensity bleeding from her into him. His hands that refused to touch her, in hopes of deescalating the moment until they were in the confines of his apartment, now flew to her waist, dragging her tightly against his erection.

Briar moaned into Dex's mouth. Though they were fully clothed, rubbing against him was already giving her sensations, heating her insides, making them cry out for more.

"Here? Really," were the only words Dex could get out to form a question as he momentarily broke their lips apart.

Briar nodded rapidly. "Please tell me you have a condom."

"Wallet."

Briar moved backward and began patting Dex's pocket. He chuckled. Though she was on top of him, he lifted himself and tilted to the side, withdrawing his wallet from the back of his jeans. He barely got the condom out before Briar slid away from him, her boots already falling to the floor of the car, as her hands reached for the button on her jeans.

Though he was anything but, Dex waited patiently for her to scramble out of her jeans, which proved to be not so difficult for her, despite the small space they were in. Once she was out of them, and only in a pair of black panties and her oversized sweater, Dex pulled her back to his lap.

He loved how bold and aggressive she was becoming with him. In the beginning, long before sex came into play, there were times where she appeared uncertain with her words and actions; however, lately she was more confident, surer of herself and what she wanted and needed. It drove him crazy in the best of ways.

He brought his mouth to her neck just below her earlobe, over time learning that it was an immediate weakness for her, a spot that connected to every other part of her sexual needs.

Briar rocked against him, encouraging him to go further. "You have no idea how much I want you right now."

She felt the light laughter pulsing through her neck.

Dex reached between her legs and skimmed along the thin fabric, feeling her arousal soaking through. "I think I have a pretty good idea."

When Dex slipped his hand from beneath Briar, hers quickly went to his jeans, hurriedly fumbling with the belt, then the button, then the zipper. Dex only helped her when she began to tug at both the jeans and boxers, all at once. He rose slightly until she had them pulled down to his ankles.

Dex reached for the condom, but Briar stopped him. A mischievous sparkle came to her eyes as she slid away from him.

Briar positioned herself on her hands and knees on the seat next to Dex.

His eyes widened and he sucked in a breath, already anticipating what was to come.

"Fuck," he hissed, slamming his head into the back of the seat when Briar's mouth and hand wrapped around his cock.

Her tongue, warm, soft, and gentle, teased at the tip while her hand slowly tightened around the base. It took every bit of restraint for Dex not to grab the back of her head and slam her down, until she had every inch of him, until she was gagging, until hot liquid burst from him and coated the back of her throat. Instead, he let her take it slow. It was painful for him, but he knew this wasn't going to be his release. He needed to have her tight walls clenched around him for that.

Briar moaned into Dex's cock when his fingers sank into one of her ass cheeks. Slowly she eased him farther into her mouth. When she was comfortable, she began pumping her hand and mouth around him in a steady motion.

Dex grazed upward on her ass, until he was at the band of her panties, pulling them downward. Once they were down to her knees, he ran his fingers along her thighs, higher and higher, until he felt her gasp around him.

At first, he was soft, only teasing her clit, which made her hand tighten and her mouth move faster against him. Needing to give her more, he inserted one digit, then another, attempting to finger her at the same pace that she was sucking him.

It was Dex who stopped things. He withdrew his fingers from Briar's folds and pulled her away from him.

Briar looked at him in confusion, her eyes clenched, wondering why everything came to a screeching halt.

Dex had been wrong. If she were to continue, there wasn't a doubt in his mind that he was seconds away from exploding in her mouth.

His cock throbbed when he looked at her swollen lips, coated in saliva. Maybe he was stupid for not finishing in her mouth, but there was a rational voice in the back of his head that knew how much better he'd feel inside her tight pussy.

Dex nodded to Briar. "Sweater," was all he said.

As Dex ripped open the condom and rolled it on, Briar tore her sweater over her head, leaving her in just a small bralette. She reached around to undo the clasps, but before she even touched the fabric, her arms were being pulled with her body following, until she was straddling Dex once again.

His mouth descended on hers. There was nothing sweet or romantic about it when his tongue broke through her lips, swirling around her own.

Briar felt his erection beneath her, skimming at her folds, teasing her. She tried pressing herself farther into Dex, but his grip on her waist, holding her in place, wouldn't allow it. He was definitely messing with her.

She broke away from his ravenous kiss and glared at him. "Dex…"

He gave her a playful smirk before leaning forward. She felt the movement, the heat, of his lips as he breathed his next words into her ear. "Tell me what you want."

Briar knew what Dex wanted to hear. Every time they were together, she became more confident. She wasn't timid or shy, not knowing what to do, nor was she afraid of the pain, afraid of him hurting her. She craved his touch, his body, mind, and soul. She craved the pleasure that only he could give her.

Briar brought her face to his and stared into his illustrious and hauntingly blue eyes. "I want you to fuck me," she replied, slowly enunciating every word.

Dex would be lying if he said that hearing those words from her lips hadn't taken him by surprise. Not waiting a second more, he gave her exactly what she wanted.

Briar cried out and momentarily stiffened in Dex's arms when the entirety of his cock plunged inside her.

Dex realized that maybe he had been a little aggressive. "Sorry..."

Briar's nails dug into Dex's shoulders. "Don't be. It feels so good," her lips moaned against his. She closed the gap, bringing forth a slow and sensual kiss this time as she rocked back and forth, the feeling of Dex deep inside, touching every sensitive part of her body.

Their pace was slow at first, Dex allowing Briar to have full control of her movements while he unfastened her bra and rotated his mouth from nipple to nipple, just barely swirling his tongue around them. She bucked against him with the thrilling feeling he sent deep within her.

Dex moved his hands downward, wrapping them around Briar's waist. A part of him hated how tiny she was, as he was always afraid of hurting her, breaking her. As he dug his fingers into her skin, his large hands almost covering the entirety of her waist, she arched her back, giving him full permission, full control.

He moved her back and forth, slow and deep at first, until her next words sent him spiraling out of control.

"Dex," Briar breathed, clenching her fists into his pecs. "Please. I need to come."

That was all it took for Dex to slam her into him at a rapid speed, her glistening hair falling from its confines as she bounced on his thick length.

He didn't stop, didn't allow himself to fall, until he felt her shuddering, spasming, exploding all around him, crying out his name, as her climax rocketed through her. Only then did he give in, his whole body feeling the volatile eruption hurtling through him.

As Dex held Briar in his arms, still inside her, a thought he currently had after every time they had sex lingered far longer this time. It wasn't just sex. He saw that in Briar's eyes each time, and each time it scared him. Though she hadn't said the words, and they were ones that terrified him beyond belief, whenever she was in his arms, bearing everything to him, he knew how she felt. He also knew how he felt. He was in love with her.

* * *

From a foggy and dingy glass window, seemingly obscuring the contents inside, Leo watched. Suddenly the chill of the bitter November air didn't bother him.

His body heated. Though the dirt and grime made the image blurred, he could see the scene unfolding well. The alley behind the shop had afforded him the perfect spot to keep an eye on Dex. Never did he think he'd come across this.

At first, he thought about writing the scene into his memory, going back to the warm hotel, having a drink and a smoke, and masturbating the rest of the night to Briar's writhing body, but the longer he watched her effortlessly fuck the beast beneath her, he realized he couldn't wait.

Leo looked around the deadly quiet alley behind Dex's garage. In the weeks he came by, he had yet to encounter a soul; therefore, he felt no worry in what he did next.

Once his zipper was down, he eased one hand inside his boxers, using the other to steady himself on the wall near the window.

"That's right," he began, whispering to himself. "Take this dick. You dirty fucking slut. You'll be screaming my name soon enough. I'll be your first and your last."

Leo continued to pump himself, harder and faster, never taking his eyes away from the sight of Briar riding Dex beyond the hazy glass, but he didn't see Dex. All he saw was Briar hovered above him, crying out his name as she came over and over.

He let out a gasp and shuddered violently as he reached his peak. Warm wet liquid coated the inside of his boxers, running down his leg, seeping through the fabric of his jeans.

He withdrew his hand, zipped himself up, and disappeared down the alley.

CHAPTER 43

That night, the night before Thanksgiving eve, there was a light snowfall.

It wasn't a lot. It didn't render anyone incapable of movement for the holiday.

"You can't be serious about walking to work?"

Briar twirled her hair around in a messy bun. "I need to be there early. Did you know we have reservations for tonight? I mean, who the hell makes reservations in this town. I guess a lot of residents have family coming in. I can't imagine cooking for more than a day or—"

Dex grabbed Briar's shoulders. "You're rambling."

She took in a deep breath and let it out. "Sorry. I've been up since five. I already had a couple cups of coffee. I made some muffins for you if—"

"Are you kidding me right now?"

"They weren't that hard. I put them in while I got dressed and did my makeup. I really do need to go," Briar insisted.

Dex went to the table near the front door and grabbed his keys. "I'll take you."

Briar's face held the sweetest and most innocent smile, which Dex found disturbing so early in the morning. "You're in your pajamas," she pointed out.

Dex crossed his arms. "They're sweats," he clarified.

"Dex…The sun is out. I know it's cold, but I can—"

"No," he growled.

Briar knew that tone well. It was one that meant there was no way she was getting her way in the matter. Dex had that superior savior complex. He was absolutely dropping her off at Chêne that morning, pajamas or not.

Halfway through the day, Briar was grateful that she didn't walk to work. It wouldn't have taken that much energy out of her, but after helping prep and baking a few more desserts, not to mention the insane lunch crowd, her feet were feeling it.

Briar finally decompressed and relaxed around three, knowing that they were expecting a large dinner crowd. She lounged in a booth, guzzling down a large glass of iced water and looking through her phone.

Long ago, she would have been scrolling through social media, seeing what all her friends were up to for the holidays. That wasn't the case anymore.

She read Dex's last text and shook her head.

Dex: I'll be there around 8:30 or 9.

Briar: You're not allowed in here while I'm working. I work until 10 tonight.

Dex: That's a bullshit rule you made up.

Briar: With good reason!

Dex: You're not working in the bar, are you?

Briar: No, Dex.

Dex could picture Briar rolling her eyes in annoyance. He knew that she could get hit on regardless what part of Chêne she worked in. She could be in the kitchen and get unwanted advances from some pimple faced dishwasher.

Dex knew that drunks were another story.

Dex: Good. Rusty needs to let off some steam with his sister still living with him. I'm just meeting him for a beer.

Briar: I have to go. Help needed in the kitchen.

Briar's hand shook when she continued the text, immediately deleting the few extra words she was about to add. She stared at the screen. She ended the conversation with a simple *bye*.

Her heart pounded. She desperately wanted to tell Dex how she felt, but he had a hard enough time calling her his girlfriend. There was no way she was going to throw that bomb on him right now.

If Briar thought the lunch rush was bad. It was nothing compared to when 5:00 came about. Shouldn't families want to spend time together at home the evening before Thanksgiving? Didn't they have to prepare for the feast the next day? Maybe that was the problem, their reason for needing someone else to cook for them.

The next few hours became a blur, but Briar couldn't complain when the tips started coming in. The holidays definitely made people more generous.

Briar brushed past Jennifer after delivering plates to a party of nine, which took forever.

"Hey, I'll be right back," Briar began. "I haven't peed in hours."

Jennifer chuckled. "No problem. It seems to be dying down in here, now is when the bar is going to catch it."

Briar smiled and headed down a hallway to the restrooms. She hadn't paid attention, but things must be dying down, as the women's restroom was completely deserted.

After relieving herself, Briar stood in the mirror washing her hands, taking a little extra breather and playing with the suds. She didn't realize how exhausted she was until the adrenaline began wearing off.

She heard the door open and close behind her. She shook the droplets from her skin and reached for a couple paper towels from the dispenser and dried her hands. After tossing them into a nearby trashcan, she looked into the mirror, wondering how her makeup held up.

It wasn't her reflection in the mirror that caused her heart to stop.

"Hello, Briar. It's been a while," Leo's reflection said.

Briar spun around facing him, now her heart was racing. This wasn't good. She couldn't think of a single thing to say in response, so she pointed out the obvious. "You're in the women's restroom."

He laughed like some villain in a superhero movie as he slowly walked toward her. Ignoring her statement, "I've been watching you."

Briar tried not to have a reaction. She needed to remain calm, though she was anything but. "What are you doing here?"

"Wrapping up some loose ends."

Briar pressed herself into the sink. She had nowhere to go as Leo closed the gap between them. She could try to bolt for the door, but it was behind Leo. He'd catch her before she would get halfway there.

Briar felt sick to her stomach when Leo's hand closed around her neck. Instinctively she reached for his wrist with both hands, attempting to pull him away. That only made him tighten his grip, so much so that she didn't know if she'd be able to breathe much longer.

"Leo, stop," she insisted, gasping for air with her words.

He came in close. He wasn't as big as Dex, but he still towered over her. He brought the side of his face close to hers and inhaled deeply. "You even smell like your little fuckboy," Leo spat.

A disgusting chill ran down Briar's whole body when Leo licked from her chin up to her cheek, until he was at her ear. That was too much for Briar, and she brought her hands to Leo's chest attempting to push him off.

Leo responded by slamming her into the sink, surely leaving bruises. He then opened up his coat and gestured inside. "If you don't want me to kill him as well, I'd say you go about this more willingly."

Briar glanced down and though she didn't see much, she wasn't dumb. A gun.

Then Leo's words hit her.

As well.

As well?!

Leo smirked, knowing that Briar picked up on it.

"I don't understand," was all she managed. What could she say after he dropped that on her?

"Simple. For mother to get her money, and I mine, you need to be out of the picture."

Briar shook her head not understanding. Before she could speak, Leo yanked her away, nearly breaking her wrist in the process.

He wasn't stupid. The longer they stayed in the restroom, the greater the chances of someone coming in. He stumbled across a golden opportunity to end things, and he wasn't about to ruin it now.

He dragged Briar farther down the hallway. That's when it hit Briar. *I've been watching you.*

Leo knew where they were going. He knew the back exit to the restaurant. How did he know that? For how long had he watched her?

Briar gasped like she had fallen through thin ice and was drowning in a frozen lake. In reality, Leo had thrown them into the cold night air and she didn't have on more than a button down.

Snow once again had started falling since Briar was dropped off that morning.

Leo shoved her around one of the dumpsters along the back of the building.

A million thoughts began running through Briar's head. Someone would realize she was missing soon enough. Right? She hoped that Dex would realize as soon as he walked in the bar. He told her he and Rusty were meeting around 8:30. It was nearly that time.

She felt disappointment thinking that. Dex wasn't superhuman. He wasn't some werewolf that could sense his mate was in danger. The truth of it was, he might think she was in the kitchen. He wouldn't become concerned until after ten, more than ninety minutes from now.

There wasn't a doubt in her mind. She'd be dead in ninety minutes.

CHAPTER 44

Leo slammed Briar into the brick wall of the back of Chêne. He grinded his hips into her. Briar could feel that he was getting off at being in control. It repulsed her, made her sick to her stomach.

Needing to expand on their conversation in the restroom, "What do you mean I have to be out of the picture?"

Leo laughed that horrible sickeningly sinister laugh. "You have no fucking idea, do you?"

Briar was braver than before. "If I did, I wouldn't be asking."

She felt the sting of Leo's palm across the side of her face. She tightly clenched down on her teeth, pleading with her internal self not to cry. Leo loved to see her cry.

"Your daddy left millions to you."

That wasn't the comment Briar was expecting.

"You were supposed to get three when you turned eighteen, more than triple that when you turn twenty-one. The only way mother can get it is if you're dead," Leo continued.

Briar didn't think. She didn't think about the money. She didn't need the money. She was making it on her own. All that flashed through her mind was the contentment she felt in Argent Falls, the contentment she felt with Dex. Money was worth nothing to that.

"I'll sign it all over. I don't want it," she quickly stated.

"This isn't up for negotiation. You being alive is a problem. It will definitely be a problem after I'm finished with you."

Leo thrust his hips into Briar, and she realized that death wasn't going to be the worst thing that happened to her that night.

"Leo, you're not a criminal mastermind. You'll never get away with this," she carefully began, hoping she could talk some sense into him, hoping to bargain with him. The despondent darkness in his eyes told her that it was all going to be in vain.

"I saw you with him yesterday," Leo growled into her neck.

His cologne took over the smell of grease and smoke pouring into the alley from the restaurant. It was a smell that made her want to vomit. She remembered that horrible day when that smell engulfed her.

This time she would fight. Not yet. There was still hope. Hope that someone might see them before he took her away.

If that moment should come, and there would only be the option to submit, she would go down kicking and screaming, biting, punching, clawing. She would rather die than have him take her body again.

"I watched you fuck him like the whore you are," Leo went on. He felt Briar tense and got satisfaction that his words affected her.

"What are you—"

"In the garage," Leo interrupted. "When I say I've been watching you, I mean it. I saw you suck his dick." Leo trailed a finger over her lips. "I bet you were thinking of me, weren't you?"

He gripped Briar's wrist so tightly, it sounded like the bones were breaking. He forcefully rubbed it over his crotch. "That's it, baby."

Briar felt the bile rise in her throat. "Just kill me. Just put a fucking bullet in my head and be done with it."

Leo tsked. "I see that convict has turned my sweet and innocent little sister into a piece of trash as well." He clasped his hand back on her neck, with much more force than he did in the bathroom, and that was saying a lot. "Don't worry, tonight it's going to be my dick you're riding, my name you're screaming. Then when I've had my fun with you, I'll do exactly that. Let's go," he insisted, yanking Briar from the wall and pulling her down the alley.

321

* * *

"Where the fuck are you," Dex bellowed through the phone.

"Did you search the whole damn parking lot? How do you know I'm not there," Rusty huffed back.

"One, your truck is easy to spot. Two, if you were here waiting on me, you'd be outside smoking because you're too chickenshit to go in there alone, knowing Marlee is going to ask you out again. So again, I ask, where the fuck are you?"

"This asshole demon stole my keys," Rusty screamed through the phone.

From the distance, Dex could hear Rusty's sister. "Don't call him that! He's five! He'll take that shit back to school."

A small smile came to Dex's face. He honestly felt bad for Rusty at times. "Bribe him with a cookie or something."

Rusty let out one short laugh of sarcasm. "You think it's so easy. You and Briar take these things for the weekend."

Dex's smile faded and he swallowed heavily. He hated where that comment sent his thoughts. He found himself wondering if Briar wanted kids. He shouldn't be thinking that. Though neither said anything, they both knew exactly where the relationship was headed by the end of December. At least he did.

"They're in the toilet. In the damn toilet Dex," Rusty screamed through the speaker.

Dex continued to listen to Rusty spew a string of curse words as he retrieved his keys from the toilet. Dex looked out his windshield, taking a moment to appreciate the soft snowfall. Very little had fallen, but it was starting to stick. Though the ground was white, a single footprint could erase the blanket forming. Suddenly the image of Briar dusting her desserts with powdered sugar flashed in his mind, and he found himself smiling.

"…Anyway, give me ten minutes," Rusty finally concluded, interrupting Dex's daydreaming of Briar.

322

Dex was just about to respond and cut the call, but suddenly lost his voice. It was as if he dreamed of Briar, and she suddenly appeared; however, what he saw was no dream.

Across the parking lot through a couple rows of cars, he saw her. If it were any other woman, he might have missed her, but her ashen blonde hair made her stand out with the night sky and streetlights overhead.

A male walked with her, far too close to her, making her movements jerky and forced. Dex didn't need to see the man's face to know exactly who he was.

Before he knew it, he was flying out of his truck.

"Call police and ambulance to Chêne, now," Dex screamed into the phone, still on the call with Rusty.

"Wait…What? What are–"

"Police. Ambulance. Chêne," were the only words that Rusty was left with before the call ended.

A chill came over Rusty. He didn't know what Dex was talking about, but he wasn't about to doubt him. He knew he was going to have a hell of a time explaining to dispatch what his emergency was; however, he didn't hesitate for a second with doing as Dex said.

* * *

"Will you stop shoving me," Briar insisted, attempting to shake Leo's hands off her.

He tightened his grip on her upper arm. "And risk you trying to run? Yeah, right." Then he nodded to the end of the parking lot, near the exit. "Right up here."

Leo said something about the car, maybe which one it was, but with the sharp wind picking up, she didn't hear those words.

Briar needed to clear her mind, to think of what to do. She couldn't get in his car. If she did, that was it, she'd never see another living soul.

Briar stopped walking, firmly planting her feet in place. Leo yanked hard on her arm, causing her to stumble.

"Don't try anything stupid. You're what, ninety pounds? I will pick you up and haul your ass in there myself," Leo spat in her face.

Briar felt an icy chill running down her cheek, and only then realized that she was crying. She wasn't sure if it was from the fear, or the wind whipping at her face, all she knew was that Leo loved to see her cry and she didn't want to give him that satisfaction.

"I can't." She couldn't believe she was going to beg. "Please, Leo—"

"I said, this isn't up for negotiation!"

He shoved her with such force that this time when she stumbled, she couldn't adjust her balance, and she landed on the cold snow-covered pavement.

Leo laughed. "Didn't expect I'd have you on your back this soon." He kicked her in the ribs, and brought out his gun, pointing it at her. "Get the fuck up."

Briar didn't know what broken ribs felt like, but Leo's boot did a pretty good job of making it feel like every single one of hers was shattered.

Briar attempted to sit up, finding difficulty in doing so, which only led Leo to grow more impatient.

"Come on," he screamed, waving his gun in the air.

Just as Briar looked up, she saw Leo stumble forward howling in pain as Dex's fist slammed into the side of his head. Briar scrambled out of the way, forgetting any pain that radiated through her.

"You sick fuck," Dex growled.

Dex lunged at Leo from behind, attempting to get him to the ground. Though they were almost similar in height, separated by a couple inches, Dex had a great deal more weight on his side.

"Dex! He has a gun," Briar screamed from nearby.

Before it registered, Leo fired. Ten feet away, a car window shattered.

"Get off me, you freak," Leo roared as he tried to slip from Dex's grasp.

Dex linked his hands together around Leo's chest, tightening his hold. He took his right foot and kicked at Leo's ankle, and Leo gave.

Briar couldn't do anything more than watch as both men fell to the ground face first, Dex on top of Leo. It wasn't going to end well, that much she knew.

As Dex attempted to reach for Leo's gun, Briar patted the back of her jeans for her phone. Upon retrieving it, thankful that it hadn't broken after her fall, she called 911.

Leo gripped the gun, despite Dex scrambling, trying to pry it away. The gun was his only salvation, the only advantage he had to the monster on top of him.

In the background Dex heard Briar on the phone with dispatch, no doubt being told that they already received a report for the area. He didn't know if he could keep Leo down until authorities arrived. If Leo would stop trying to fight him off and submit, he'd end up living, but if not, Dex was fully prepared to kill him.

Dex's left fist came across the side of Leo's face as he continued to fight for the gun with his other. Another shot rang out, startling everyone. With Dex's loosened grip on Leo's hand, the one with the gun, Leo quickly slipped free and brought his hand under his body, out of Dex's reach.

Dex's whole body, his chest to Leo's back, covered Leo, plastering him to the snowy pavement.

Leo couldn't shake Dex off, and being on his stomach, with the gun beneath him, made it nearly impossible to get a good shot into Dex. He could feel the knuckles on his hand tearing beneath him on the cold dark ground as he attempted to shield the gun from Dex.

Dex had gone easy on Leo. He could have snapped his neck. He wanted nothing more than to take out the monster that for so long haunted Briar, but he also knew that death was too easy. After tonight, there was no doubt in his mind that Leo would end up in prison for a long time. For a rich little brat like Leo, that was a fate far worse than death.

Finally, attempting to put an end to their struggle, Dex brought his left elbow down hard, right between Leo's shoulder blades, eliciting a painful howl from the worm beneath him.

Leo's body shifted just enough for Dex to get his right arm under Leo. He was unable to feel the gun, but he had a firm grip on Leo's wrist that undoubtedly inches away kept the gun safe, out of Dex's reach.

Somewhere in the distance, Dex could hear Briar screaming into the phone, pleading with dispatch to hurry. She seemed so far away, her words barely a whisper to Dex. All he could truly hear was the man panting beneath him.

The next seconds of sounds came in too fast.

The echo of a final shot.

Briar's piercing screams.

Gasps from the body beneath Dex.

Ringing in Dex's ears.

Then there was the pain. Dex didn't know how long it took for him to realize there was a stinging, deeper than a stinging, sensation growing more unpleasant by the second across his left side.

Upon rolling off Leo, he watched as the white snow atop the grey pavement began to bleed.

It wasn't until Leo rolled on his back and began coughing, blood slowly seeping from his lips, that Dex realized he wasn't the only one who was hit.

Unable to quickly get up, Dex saw the gun slip from Leo's grasp and he immediately kicked it away. It was clear that Leo was incapable to go after it.

Briar wrapped her arms around Dex, warm tears searing across her frozen face.

"You're bleeding! Oh my god, Dex," she cried out.

Dex softly pushed her away and forced himself to stand. It was then that the pain shot through his side. He looked down, just below his heart, along his side, and he saw the ripped fabric of his sweater, now soaked in his blood, maybe even a little bit of Leo's. The extent of the wound was unknown, but he didn't feel like he was badly injured, like he couldn't breathe, like he was dying.

Before Briar could say anything else to Dex, they were interrupted.

"Briar," Leo coughed from the cold ground.

The pained strain in his voice was foreign to what Briar had heard from him that evening. It wasn't until then that she gave her attention to Leo, and she shuddered at the site. Blood continued to pool from his chest, an ever-growing puddle surrounding him.

Glancing briefly from Leo to Dex, she realized what happened. The single shot, that one bullet, went through Leo and hit Dex; however, looking from one man to the next, it was clear that Leo caught the fatality of the round.

"Tell mother," Leo began, clutching his bloodied chest and gasping for air. "Sorry. I messed up."

The words made Briar dizzy, sick to her stomach. A moment longer and Leo's wide eyes glazed over, staring into nothingness, no longer able to blink. In the cold night, one more hazy puff of air drifted from his lips as he took his last breath.

Dex could see that the scene had visibly shaken Briar, and before she could collapse, he wrapped his arms around her, pulling her to his good side, shielding her from her stepbrother's lifeless body.

The sirens in the distance, growing louder with each heartbeat, let them know that it was over.

327

CHAPTER 45

The next hours, and days were such a rapid blur, until finally it became the middle of December.

Not to Briar's surprise, Dex protested the entire way about being taken to the hospital. He became even more irate at being held there for three days with what he decided was the grazing of a bullet. Perhaps most disconcerting to Dex was the fact that he had to eat hospital Thanksgiving food as opposed to Rita's.

Briar was most concerned about Dex getting into any trouble by what had taken place; however, thanks to cameras and some distant witnesses, in the eyes of the law, Dex was innocent.

Needless to say, Leo was pronounced dead at the scene. It took Briar a long time to realize that she'd never hear his disgusting words, never feel his cringy hands on her, ever again. When she left that place that she was supposed to call home, she knew that Leo would always haunt her. While the image of his dead body, and his final words, were etched into her memory, and probably would be forever, she was strangely at peace. He could no longer hurt her.

A lot was brought to light in the weeks after the accident. As Briar already knew, Portia was definitely not innocent in the matter. Thankfully, after finding blatantly incriminating text messages and pings from cell towers, investigators were quick to take not only Portia, but Marcus Brown as well, into custody. The fact that Marcus had a criminal history and was looking at more time than expected, he easily sang like a canary with the information he knew.

Briar attempted to stay out of the spotlight, and after the initial arrest, she found that the media would soon move on to something else besides what happened to Grover Stone and Ingrid Vera Norberg's daughter.

* * *

"Let me get this straight," Benji began when he saw Briar at the counter, tinkering on the computer. "Yesterday was your last day of classes. Technically, you've graduated. Of all the things you could do, you show up to work?"

Briar let out a soft laugh. "I like to work. Plus, thanks to Dex, I've really been able to save a lot."

Ever since she showed up in Argent Falls, Dex had helped her, albeit a bit begrudgingly at times.

Something about that statement made Briar a little sad, knowing what she was saving for all along.

"Yeah, Liam mentioned that fancy school of yours a while back."

That comment there was the thought that made her sad. All this time she had been saving for the chocolatier program she heard her mother speak so highly of, but over the weeks and months, the thought of leaving for Europe no longer enticed her, no longer filled her with adrenaline.

Thankfully, Benji didn't go into any more detail about her future schooling, and that Saturday went on just like any other, rather, the morning did.

Dex walked out of the bathroom after washing up, ready to take Briar out for lunch, when an older, and very well dressed, gentleman walked through the door.

"Mr. Burrows," Briar gasped.

Dex walked around the counter and took his place beside Briar. He knew this guy wasn't from around Argent Falls, and the last time someone popped up from Briar's past, it didn't go well.

"Miss Stone," he sighed with a smile. "It has been quite some time."

Sensing Dex tense from beside her, Briar introduced the two. "Dex, this is Jeff Burrows, my father's lawyer."

Dex looked the man up and down. So far, he didn't get any creepy vibes like when he first met Leo; therefore, he held out his freshly washed hand. "Dex Hayden, I'm the–"

"Owner," Jeff said, cutting him off. "I've done a bit of research." He then drew his attention back to Briar. "I'll cut to the chase. I have some matters I need to speak with you on. I have for some time."

Briar let out a breath. The last time she saw Jeff Burrows was at her father's funeral. The only other time she ever heard mention of him was when Portia was yelling at him through the phone over tedious things with her father's estate.

"Is this about Portia," Briar asked. It had been nearly two weeks since she was arrested on charges of conspiracy to commit murder.

Jeff's mouth twitched from side to side, making his mustache do a little dance. "Partly," was all the answer he gave Briar. Changing the subject, "It has been quite the drive. Is there somewhere we can grab a bite to eat and discuss matters?"

Hesitantly, Briar looked to Dex, but he gave her nothing. "Do you mind if he joins us," she asked Dex.

Before Dex could answer, Jeff cleared his throat uncomfortably. "While I am okay with discussing this in front of your…friend, I do believe that this is something you might want to know privately at first."

Both Briar and Dex's interest was piqued at that comment. While Briar told Dex about who her parents were, and in the last few weeks, the media made it even more clear, he realized there was still a lot that he didn't know. If the family lawyer thought it best to talk to Briar alone, he wasn't going to insist differently.

330

Shortly after the waitress took their orders and brought back the standard salads that everyone received with an entrée, Jeff Burrows took in a deep breath, and pushing the bland salad to the side, folded his hands on the table.

So far, they had only made small talk. Jeff asked Briar about school and her jobs, how she was doing overall. Never once did he mention the incident. For that she was thankful.

"I can see you're uncomfortable with this," Jeff began, looking around. He was glad that the café had very few patrons, as what he was about to tell Briar should have been done in his office, not in a public place.

"I'm just curious as to what business I'd have with you after all these years. The only thing I can think of is the house, now that Portia's been arrested," Briar said with a shrug.

Not one part of her wanted the house that was once a happy home for her. If it burned to the ground today, all the better.

Jeff reached inside his briefcase and withdrew a single paper, a condensed version of an extensive document. Briar was smart, but she didn't need all the legal terminology to tell her of her inheritance.

Briar quickly scanned over it. The farther she got, the blurrier her vision became, the harder her heart pounded. For the first time, she didn't understand a word she was reading.

"What…What is this? I don't un—"

"Something your father set up for you shortly before he married Portia," Jeff interrupted.

"Three million dollars," Briar whispered.

A small smile spread across Jeff's face. He didn't get emotional with clients, but this was one that tugged on his heart a little more than he cared to admit. Without saying anything he pointed closer to the bottom of the document, knowing Briar hadn't gotten that far.

Briar let out a gasp. Suddenly, nothing made sense.

"He wanted to make sure you didn't have to worry when it came to college, or whatever your choice of education; therefore, when you turned eighteen, you were granted access to the three million," Jeff began.

Briar stopped herself from saying what didn't need to be said. Everything made so much more sense now. Now she understood why Portia and Leo were so set on finding her. Leo's rambling about the money didn't fully register to her at the time. With Mr. Burrows and this paper in front of her, everything was so much clearer.

Jeff continued to go on, many of his words unheard to Briar, lost in her thoughts. "Then of course the other eleven million when you turn twenty-one," he added.

Briar looked up, a despondent look in her eyes. Never in her wildest dreams did she think her father left her anything. Portia said as much over the years.

"I don't know what to say."

"Well, now would be where I tell you that I need you to come back home to my office so we can straighten out the paperwork."

Briar nodded, knowing that would be the case, knowing Jeff Burrows wasn't walking around with three million dollars.

"However," Jeff slowly began. "I know with everything that has happened…" He let his words drift off and held up his briefcase. "We can get this moving today, that is, if you can spare the rest of your afternoon. The local inn I'm staying at has a quaint little business center that I've asked to be secured, if you want."

"Thank you, Mr. Burrows," was all Briar could say, beyond thankful that she wouldn't have to leave Argent Falls for the time being.

As soon as Dex got home, he threw together a quick chili. After receiving a text from Briar during her lunch break, informing him that she'd be out the rest of the day, he hadn't been able to keep his mind on the simplest of tasks. The last thing he could think of was cooking.

While Jeff Burrows didn't scare Dex, what the man had to say to Briar that was so important he came to Argent Falls himself, did make him nervous. Briar went through so much over the years, especially over the last few weeks. He only hoped that whatever Jeff had to say was good news.

It took every bit of restraint not to tear through the apartment when he heard the lock snap on the door.

"Something smells wonderful," Briar called out from the entry.

Finishing off the last of the dishes, Dex wiped his hands and patiently waited for Briar to come into the kitchen.

Briar held a look on her face that didn't suggest anything out of the ordinary. If Dex expected her to be distraught or in tears about something, it absolutely didn't show.

"How was your meeting," Dex asked.

Briar rolled her eyes and made her way around the bar and into the kitchen. Once she was near Dex, she wrapped her arms around him and pulled their bodies together for a hug, inhaling his scent as she did so. Though he appeared to have recently showered, and maybe it was something her mind had grown used to, and now looked for, the smell of the garage and oil somehow lingered far beneath Dex's bodywash. No one else would ever notice it, nor find it so intoxicating, but Briar did.

"Hello to you too," Briar mumbled into Dex's chest.

Dex lightly rubbed over her back. "Sorry. I don't mean to be all in your business, but—"

Briar slightly pulled away. "It's fine. I do have a few things to talk to you about," she said, putting it mildly, as though she hadn't just found out she was a millionaire. "Let me get a quick shower and into some comfy clothes. Then we can eat?"

"Sure. Whatever you want," Dex answered, placing a kiss on Briar's forehead before she bounded out of the kitchen.

Just as Dex let out a sigh of relief, Briar popped her head back around the corner. "You know, you're free to join me," Briar announced, slowly beginning to tug off her sweater.

Dex would be lying if he said that those words and actions didn't cause a building sexual need within him; however, he saw the seriousness in her eyes when she returned home. They needed to talk about something important, and the sooner the better. Then they had the rest of the night for anything and everything else.

CHAPTER 46

"You've had your shower. We've eaten. You're comfy on a nice warm couch," Dex said, pulling the blanket up over Briar and himself. "What do you need to talk about?"

Briar let out a breath and turned in Dex's lap so that she was facing him. The way he looked at her always sent butterflies through her. Though they had grown comfortable around each other given the strange circumstances of how things came to be, Briar felt like she'd always be in awe with Dex. Not a day went by where he didn't make her heart beat in a way that she couldn't imagine anyone else doing.

After Briar remained silent for far too long, simply staring into his eyes, Dex decided that what she had to say might require more time on her part. "We can talk tomorrow. I'm sure you need some rest after—"

"No! Sorry. I just…" She stopped herself and let her gaze drift from Dex, already feeling herself blushing. She shook away the silly infatuated little girl inside her and cleared her throat.

Briar knew that Dex liked to shoot things straight. Besides, she couldn't think of a good way to ease into what she wanted to share with him.

"Mr. Burrows came to inform me of my inheritance."

Dex's eyes narrowed. "Inheritance?" Nearly six months ago she was living in a drug infested hostel, now she was talking about an inheritance.

Briar sat back, distancing herself from Dex's lap. "I know. I was more shocked than yourself. Portia always made me believe that everything was dried up or left to her."

Dex slowly nodded his head. "So, this inheritance, that's why they were so eager to find you."

"As it turns out, I wasn't able to touch the money until I turned eighteen." Briar was tempted to tell Dex about the rest of what Mr. Burrows dropped on her, but decided to hold on to that until she saw his reaction.

"And I'm guessing if you were dead, Portia would get whatever was left to you?"

Briar nodded, already feeling Dex tense up. A part of her would always find his protective nature attractive.

"It all makes so much sense, but at the same time, it doesn't."

"I'm sure people have killed for a lot less."

Briar tilted her head, curiously evaluating Dex. "You didn't even ask how much?"

Dex shrugged. "Does it matter?"

"Yes, Dex. Three million dollars matters!"

Dex's eyes widened and he held in his breath, waiting for Briar to say something more. When she didn't, "What the fuck? Three million?"

Briar decided that she'd tell Dex about the rest of her inheritance at a much later point in time if three million seemed like a lot. Given her circumstances, it was a lot; however, she knew that in their prime, both her father and mother were worth infinitely more.

Once Dex was able to breathe like a normal human, and Briar gave a few more details of her meeting with Jeff Burrows, he brought up that lingering piece of knowledge that continued to keep them both holding back just enough.

"Shit, with that now, you'll be able to get a good place in London. You won't even have to work while you're going through the program," Dex exclaimed, attempting to sound as upbeat as possible, all while knowing that he wasn't really the sort.

Briar swallowed the lump in her throat and felt sick to her stomach. Her reaction to Dex's words must have been written across her face in big bold letters.

"What's wrong," Dex quickly asked.

"I didn't get in," Briar softly corrected.

"Are you serious? How the hell could you not get in? Wait, when did you find out," Dex asked a little too skeptically.

"A couple days ago," Briar began, attempting to keep her voice steady. Dex always had a way of seeing the truth in her. "I wanted to tell you right away, but I didn't know how."

"Damn…I don't know what to say. Are you okay?"

Briar let out a breath and let her shoulders sink. "I was looking forward to it," she said rather blandly.

"Maybe there's something else. Maybe you can take a break for the spring and find another school or program for the fall?"

Against her better judgment, Briar looked up to meet Dex's eyes. She hated seeing the mixture of pain and disappointment in them, hated having Dex look at her like that. "I was actually thinking of just diving head first." When Dex gave her a curious look, "With the inheritance, I thought about staying here, opening up a little shop. I'm good with computers, so I'm sure I could build an amazing website. Also, as much as I'd like to not use my parents' names to my advantage…"

Briar stopped when she saw Dex shaking his head.

"You're still thinking of that corner antique shop." It wasn't a question. "I think you should consider all your options before you invest in something in Argent Falls."

"We've been over this. It's a quaint town, an escape from larger neighboring cities. Do you know how much a store front in some of those places would be?"

337

Ignoring Briar's reasonings, "I just wish you would have gotten in. That's what you've been working toward, and you deserved for something to finally go your way."

"Who's to say it's not?"

At that, Dex pulled her back down, into his chest. A sick feeling ran through him when he realized how relieved he felt when she told him she didn't get in.

She'd be staying in Argent Falls for a little longer.

As much as Dex wanted to pull his elation from deep within, a feeling of guilt hit him like a semi.

From the moment he met Briar, he knew there was a spark in her that was slowly getting snuffed out. She was meant to do all those fancy programs she talked so highly of. She was never meant to stay in Argent Falls. She was never meant to stay with him. She was meant for something more.

✻ ✻ ✻

"So, how was your Christmas," Rusty cooed while wiggling his eyebrows.

"Fine," Dex answered, drawing the one word out longer than necessary.

"Did you get Briar anything special," Rusty pressed.

Dex closed the hood of the truck he was working on. "No. She insisted we keep it small and simple."

Rusty laughed. "Since when was Soleil d'Or Jewelers small or simple?"

Dex froze and tilted his head, carefully watching a giggly Rusty. "What the hell is that supposed to mean?"

Rusty held up his hands. "Hey, come on. Marlee told me she saw you the other–"

"Shit," Dex huffed and rubbed over the back of his neck in frustration. "Do you think she said anything to–"

"Hell no." Rusty saw the nervous and anxious look flash across Dex's face. "Wow."

"What?"

Rusty shook his head and chuckled in disbelief. "I'm guessing you didn't buy her earrings."

"No. I didn't buy fucking earrings," Dex scoffed. He absolutely did not want to have the conversation Rusty seemed dead set on pursuing.

"Not too long ago you were saying how she needed to leave this town, now you're trying to chain her to it?"

Dex shot Rusty a deathly glare.

"Sorry. I didn't mean it like the way it sounded," Rusty quickly corrected.

The damage was already done. What Rusty said was the exact reason that was holding Dex back. Given, he hadn't planned on proposing on Christmas. That was too cliché. However, maybe New Year's Day? Or maybe not at all.

All he did know, was that if he and Briar continued the way they were, he wanted to give her something permanent. He hated feeling like a commitment to her was a way of holding her back, squashing what was once her dreams of getting out and making a life of her own.

Dex wasn't generally one to believe in signs, but if they existed, he could use one.

The thing with signs, oftentimes, they're not a discreet rustle of the trees from a cool spring breeze, or the floating of a butterfly in the soft warm morning light. Instead, sometimes signs are about as subtle as a volcano raining down on screaming villagers, or a hurricane thrashing across the coast, heading inland, taking down and engulfing everything in its path.

CHAPTER 47

"Hey, man," Sandy called out as he began tending to the bar. Though the bar wasn't open yet, he had to be fully prepared for the New Year's Eve crowd later that evening. "Dropping your girl off?"

"Yeah. Thought I'd come in and say hi. I'm sure I won't even see you this evening with all the drunk partiers."

"Those drunks keep the doors open," Sandy laughed.

Dex sat down at the bar and watched Sandy pop open a box containing a dozen bottles of vodka.

"You and Briar going to hang out after her shift? Or do you have something special planned," Sandy asked with a knowing wink.

"Mother fuck. Marlee?"

"Maybe she told Rita. I've got to say, we're all over here on pins and needles," Sandy joked.

Dex turned serious. "You don't think I'm rushing things?"

"Who's to say? Hell, when I met my ex-wife, we ended up in Vegas two weeks later!"

"And look how well that turned out," Dex grumbled.

"Hey! Watch it boy. We were married for over thirty years before she lost her damn mind and turned into a greedy bitch," Sandy half joked.

Dex sighed. "I just don't want her to wake up one day and realize she could have had more."

"I think that's her decision, and it looks like she's already made clear what she wants," Sandy said with a shrug as he set the last bottle down on the counter behind him and moved on to the next box.

Something about Sandy's comment didn't sit well with Dex. "What do you mean? Why did you say it like that?"

As if it were common knowledge, "Well, with the whole school thing."

"Yeah..." Dex was surprised how well Briar took the rejection; however, she insisted that there were online programs where she could teach herself whatever skills she needed.

"I mean, if you're worth all that to her—"

"Wait, what," Dex interrupted. His eyes were narrowed and the hair on his arms shot up beneath his sweater.

"With her declining that London thing?"

"Declining," Dex spat.

"Yeah. Didn't she tell you? Apparently, they wanted her pretty bad, being the daughter of Von Nor...Whoever her mom was. They even said they'd keep her spot open in case she changed her mind."

Dex felt his heart race. He could feel the blood pumping in his head. He was hit with emotions, all of them ghastly and volatile.

Sandy went on. "I guess it wasn't important to her anymore. She found something, someone, else more important. If you're on the fence about something permanent with her, you should know, that girl really lo—"

Dex bolted from the barstool. "Can you do me a favor?"

Taken aback, "Yeah, sure."

"Can you make sure Briar gets home alright after her shift tonight."

Sandy shot Dex a wink. "Ah, got some planning to do?"

Through narrowed eyes and pursed lips, "Something like that."

✳ ✳ ✳

Briar was more than a little surprised to walk into a dark and empty apartment on New Year's Eve. When she found out that Dex wouldn't be able to pick her up that evening, she fully expected for him to be making dinner or preparing for a nice night together.

Feeling uncertain about the situation, Briar text Dex as soon as she took off her shoes which were killing her all day.

Briar: I'm home. Where are you?

Dex: Taking care of some things at the shop.

Briar didn't want to show her annoyance, but it was nearly eleven on New Year's Eve. What could be so important at the shop?

Briar: Do you know when you'll be home?

Dex: Not sure. I might just crash here.

Briar felt her heart plummet. Something was definitely wrong, but she knew how Dex was. He wouldn't tell her if she asked.

Perhaps things between them were going too perfect. Dex always insisted that he wasn't a good boyfriend, wasn't good with relationships, wasn't good with feelings. Maybe he needed space, room to breathe. Any other night, it might not have hurt so bad, but Briar really wanted to start the beginning of a new year next to Dex.

Though it had been some time since she last slept in her own bed, that night she decided to. It didn't feel right sleeping in Dex's room without him.

Briar wasn't sure when Dex came home, or even if he came home to sleep, but her senses woke to the smell of coffee brewing. Feeling hesitant, she took her time getting dressed. Normally, she'd run out, still in her pajamas, but she wasn't feeling it, not after spending the night alone.

"Good morning," Briar said, announcing herself as she came from the hallway and into the living room.

Dex sat in his chair near the windows to the balcony. He tilted his head, carefully watching Briar, though his face was void of any emotion.

"I have you a cup of coffee on the counter," was all he said.

Briar went for the cup. It was at a perfect drinkable temperature. As she ventured in the direction of Dex, something now caught her attention.

Against one of the couches was a set of brand new black and teal plaid luggage, along with a folded piece of white paper.

Briar's eyes shot up to meet Dex's from across the room. His were latched to hers, but something in the way he looked at her was different. The softness from less than twenty-four hours before was gone. Now, he looked straight through her, like she was a stranger. It was a complete look of indifference.

Trying not to read too much into Dex's demeanor, Briar pretended to be her usual self.

"What is all this? Christmas is over. I thought there were no more gifts," Briar said, attempting to sound lighthearted.

She sipped on her coffee and walked closer to the luggage.

"Just one last gift. I think it's exactly what you need," Dex dryly replied.

Briar narrowed her eyes skeptically as she reached for the paper on top of the largest bag after placing her cup on the table. At first, the airline confirmation made her a little giddy, thinking that Dex was surprising her with a vacation. It wasn't until she looked at the date and location that she felt the sickest she had in a long time.

Her heart thundered out of her chest. If it were possible for all the blood to drain from her body, that's exactly what was happening.

The flight was for that evening.

LHR.

London Heathrow.

London, England.

Briar set her cup down on the small coffee table. Her vision already blurring, partly from wanting to pass out, partly from the tears already falling down her face.

The worst part of all, it was a one way flight.

Briar forced herself to look up at Dex. Though he wouldn't show it, seeing the look on her face, the heartbreak, was gut wrenching.

"I...I don't...understand," Briar finally managed.

Dex rose from his seat and stalked toward her. "I think you do."

"Dex..."

"You fucking lied to me!"

Briar threw up her hands. "Fine. Yeah. I got in."

"Then why didn't you tell me that," Dex stressed.

"Because I knew you'd want me to go!"

An incredulous look came to Dex's face. "Of course! That was the whole reason you've busted your ass off."

"Dex..." Briar began, attempting to bring the volume down. "I want to stay here. I want to stay with–"

"No," Dex growled coldly. "You're not going to give up your future by settling here. You're eighteen. You don't know shit."

He'd never tell her the hypocrisy in his words. Had he not found out about her acceptance to the program, their new year would have started out much differently.

Feeling challenged, "Yeah? Well, you're twenty-five and you still don't know shit!"

"Wow. That's mature."

Briar waved over the suitcases. "Like this? Rather than talking to me, you're basically throwing me on a plane the second you found out."

"Why? Just why couldn't you–"

"Because I love you!"

Dex took a step backward. Every part of him wanted to reach for Briar, to hold her, to tell her the same thing, but he knew if he did what that would mean. She worked too hard, and for once, she deserved something good in her life. He'd never stand in the way of her education and training, which is why he needed her to get on that plane. The sooner the better.

Dex let out a deep breath. "From the moment I met you, I knew you wouldn't be here long, and you made that clear time and time again. The only reason you're saying differently now is because of whatever this is between us."

"Whatever this is? I just told you that I love you," Briar spat, becoming infuriated that Dex could so easily dismiss such a tremendous admission for her. "Why did you even do all this in the first place? Why didn't you just let me stay in the hostel? Why didn't you leave me alone and on my own? Why did you let me fall in love with you?"

Dex forced himself to ignore the last question. "When you came in the shop that day, I saw the bruises that you tried really hard to cover. I knew you were down on your luck. There was this fire in you, but I could see in your eyes that it was slowly fading. Whatever past you were carrying with you was extinguishing something bright and beautiful. You needed a chance. You needed someone to see you for what you were, for what you're worth."

Dex rubbed the back of his neck in frustration, fully knowing that Briar needed to hate him by the end of the conversation. It would be easier for her to leave if she did.

"As far as our relationship, it always had a deadline," he concluded.

"So, regardless? You're ending this," Briar asked, still in disbelief with the entire situation unfolding.

"Yes. You're more than financially capable of taking care of yourself, and you and I both know damn well that you're supposed to be in London, not Argent Falls."

"What if I just want to be with you?"

Dex hated that Briar still continued to press forward with them being together. If only he wouldn't have given in to temptation with her, this so-called decision wouldn't even be up for debate. She would have told him weeks ago that she got into her program and she'd leave, just as it was always intended. Now she stood before him, tears streaking her face, wanting to give up her future for him, to stay with him.

He couldn't bear it anymore and went in for the kill, knowing how much he was going to piss her off. "It ain't me, babe. It ain't me you're looking for, babe."

For some reason, it was those words that made Briar's heart shatter. It was her favorite, and Dex had to taint it.

"Bob Dylan," she whispered softly at first. Her body shook. Her blood turned to liquid fire. "You're breaking up with me by quoting Bob Dylan?! You fucking asshole!" Briar grabbed the suitcases and the now crumpled airline confirmation. "You want me gone?! Fine! Go fuck yourself, Dexter Hayden! I fucking hate you!"

Had he known something so simple would have sent her packing, Dex probably would have started with that. It would have saved them a lot of emotional discussion.

He had gotten good with hiding his feelings. It was best that Briar thought that he could so easily rid himself of her. Once she was gone, he'd allow himself to feel, to hurt.

Though it pained him to be so callous, if Briar hated him, she'd leave.

As Dex stood outside her closed door, he could hear the hangers scraping in the closet along with the zippers of the suitcases. Within a matter of hours, she'd be gone, destined for where she was always meant to go.

CHAPTER 48

"Is it really so bad in there that you'd rather sit on a park bench in the snow," Liam half joked upon getting out of his truck.

"I needed to get out of there as soon as possible. I'm sure we would have only said worse things to each other," Briar said, rising from the bench just outside the park, opposite the apartment complex.

Liam quickly reached for her bags and began placing them in the back of his truck while Briar climbed into the front.

Once he got back in the driver's seat, he turned the heat on full blast, still in disbelief that Briar chose to sit in those freezing temperatures.

"I can't believe you asked me to drive you."

Briar felt bad asking anyone, especially on New Year's Day. "If I would have asked Rita or Alyssa, they'd want to talk too much. I'd spend the next ninety minutes crying."

"That bad?"

"I guess I should have known from the beginning. He's an asshole with a savior complex," Briar sighed, only for Liam to chuckle at her words.

"That does sum him up. I hope I'm not overstepping, and I really don't want to upset you by talking about Dex, but you should know, he has been different since you." Briar said nothing, but Liam could feel her eyes on him. "He hasn't always had it easy, but he made something for himself. What am I saying? You worked for him, obviously you know how well he does with some of his restorations."

"Your point..."

"I guess," Liam began, still thinking. "Maybe he just wants to make sure that you have the opportunity to make something for yourself."

Briar fell silent. If that were the case, couldn't they have made something work? It was only two years. While that was a lot of time, she could always fly back during breaks and holidays.

The little devil on her shoulder told her differently. Dex was a jerk to Lexi. Why should she think she'd be any different? Why would he want to wait two years? Alyssa constantly emphasized that there wasn't a woman in town that didn't find Dex attractive.

He could have anyone. She wasn't something special.

As they continued to make their way out of Argent Falls, through the main streets, now quiet due to most being closed for New Year's, Briar took notice to one in particular.

"Wait. Can you stop?"

Liam's attention drew to where Briar was looking as he sat at a stoplight.

"The antique shop is open today," Briar asked.

Liam shrugged thinking nothing of it. "Old Benny probably has nothing better to do. He acted like he was going to retire to Florida to be closer to his grandkids. That was years ago."

"Could you just give me a minute," Briar insisted, already unbuckling her seatbelt.

"Just keep in mind. The airport is a ninety-minute drive, and your flight–"

"It'll be quick," Briar interrupted as she bolted from the truck toward Georges' Antiques and Collectibles.

✳ ✳ ✳

Dex didn't dare leave his room until he knew Briar had to be long gone. Once he did, he saw the little pile of things she left on the kitchen counter. The apartment key. Her phone. A plain white envelope.

Upon opening the envelope, and unfolding the piece of notebook paper, something else fell to the floor. A check.

He couldn't believe it. Briar wanted to make sure that everything he did for her was paid back. She didn't want any favors from him.

The check was written out for fifty thousand dollars. The memo was simple: *for everything.*

It was a punch to the gut. Even if she wanted to pay for half the rent and utilities, for every morsel of food, even for the clothes and gifts, none of that added up to anywhere near fifty thousand.

Without even thinking, Dex ripped the check to shreds. Then he made the mistake of reading the letter that came with it.

Dex,

I'm not sure what to say at this point, but I know "thank you" is part of it. Thank you for giving me a chance when you gave me a job and then a home. I hope this is enough to repay you for your kindness.

I'll forever remember all the good that you did for me, and I hope to pass that along in the future.

Also, I didn't get a chance to message anyone before I left. If you could do me a favor and let Rita know that I'll reach out once I have a new phone.

I hope the new year finds you well. Take care.

Briar

He was hoping that it wouldn't hurt as much as it did. He wasn't an emotional person. He never let emotions get in the way. Right?

Something about that letter tore his insides to shreds. There was nothing wrong with it, but somehow if felt cold and hollow, like Briar wrote it because she had to, had to leave with saying something.

He should have ripped up the letter and tossed it out with the check, but then there was the masochist in him that folded the letter neatly into thirds and placed it back in the envelope.

349

Dex returned to his room and opened the drawer to his nightstand and shoved the envelope far to the back along with a tiny black box.

CHAPTER 49

Six months later.

"How long is she going to ignore me or give me murderous stares," Dex grumbled when Sandy placed his and Rusty's beers down.

"She really liked Briar," was all Sandy said at first.

"All of you act like I sent your precious angel to the fiery pits of hell. It's been months, get over it."

Sandy leaned onto the table and glared at Dex. "Really? Because we all see how well you've gotten over *it*."

Rusty couldn't help but chuckle. It was clear that he already had a drink or two prior. "Sandy has a point. You've been a pain in the ass ever since she left."

"I wanted her to leave. How many times do I have to say that?!"

"Still doesn't mean your heart shares the same sentiment," Sandy said with a saddened shrug.

"For fuck's sake! I wanted a damn beer after work. I don't need the two of you going on about her, *again*," Dex growled angrily.

Maybe Rusty and Sandy had a point. He thought once Briar was gone, he'd move on. That didn't happen. The closest he came to moving on was throwing himself into work from sun up to sun down.

Women were a different story entirely. Normally if he weren't in a relationship, he'd be up for something casual, but there was still the lingering of everything that was Briar.

He didn't throw any of her things away. Her bed was still there, as were all of her baking supplies and contraptions. He wasn't saving them by any means, but something about getting rid of them felt wrong. He didn't realize the pull she had on him until she was gone, gone for far longer than he would have liked, without so much as a word to him.

That didn't mean other people didn't hear from Briar, and boy did they let him know. Liam relayed his conversations to Benji, who then let Dex know. Rita relayed her conversations to Sandy, who sure as hell let Dex know, every little detail in fact. Then, if it couldn't get any worse, even Lexi knew things about Briar's life from Alyssa, things that Dex had no clue on.

Oddly, things with Lexi were *fine*, especially now that she was seriously dating some guy named Frederick, not to be called Fred, from the local bank. Ironically, she was one of the many people who lashed out at Dex for being such an asshole and sending her little sister's best friend away. To say that conversation was a shock to Dex was putting it mildly.

Interrupting Dex's thoughts, "Marlee has a friend, and was–"

"No."

Dex didn't need to say another word.

"Yeah. I told her as much," Rusty said, taking a swig on his beer.

Not everything had gone to hell in a handbasket since Briar left; for starters, Rusty and Marlee. Rusty liked to downplay their relationship, but despite it being rather new, they were a good match for each other. She also had a strange way of turning his niece and nephew from night terrors into Christmas angels.

It also helped their relationship that Marlee no longer worked at Chêne's bar since getting her real estate license. It made it easier for Rusty to compartmentalize certain aspects of his life.

Changing the subject, "How did the last restoration do?"

"Profit of two-fifty. Not bad for a month's worth of work," Dex answered, now relaxing, grateful for no more talk of Briar or dating.

Rusty swallowed a big gulp of beer and let out a sigh Dex knew all too well.

"What..."

"I mean, that's great and all, man. Just...you don't do anything other than work."

Dex drained the rest of his first beer. "What the fuck do you call this?"

"Oh, come on. Drinks with me once a week hardly counts as a social life."

"I'm fine, okay," Dex insisted.

He was. He really was. He just thought that after six months people would get over Briar; he'd get over Briar. The truth of it was, she cast a beautiful spell over everyone she met. She made it hard to forget her and hard not to love her.

In hindsight, should he have acted differently? Absolutely. However, after hearing the things he had from the people she remained in touch with, a part of him was thankful that things played out as they had. Apparently, she was killing it and blazing through the program at the top of her class. She also had friends. Dex didn't want to hear much about that, as he knew her friends were of equal sexes.

As much as he missed her, and couldn't get her out of his head and his heart, he was glad that for once her life was going in the right direction.

Unfortunately, there was still the lingering trail of Portia Chichester-Stone.

CHAPTER 50

Another four months later.

"I'm so glad the both of you could make it over before I have to go back to London," Briar said as she sipped her coffee.

Rita and Alyssa had come to visit her for the day, the last day of Briar's testimony for her stepmother's trial. Now here they sat, in a quaint café, in a city Briar swore she'd never return to once she left.

"I can't believe you're not staying for the end. I'd want to see the look on that bitch's face when she gets that guilty verdict," Alyssa only partially teased.

"I did what needed to be done. It's been draining. Also, I really can't afford to fall behind in my lessons."

"I do love the pictures you send," Rita piped up. "Although, I started a new diet, and a daily influx of mouthwatering pictures of chocolate so far isn't helping."

"I honestly don't know how you're doing that and college," Alyssa admitted, shaking her head. "I mean, I'm only taking twelve hours and it's a bitch."

"I like keeping busy, and I figured that since I don't have to work, the college thing could help me, especially if I want to start my own business." She didn't need to tell them that staying busy also meant less time still thinking about Dex. "Besides, it's only online college."

"Only," Alyssa scoffed.

Briar chuckled. They had already discussed the trial, London, her apartment, her chocolatier classes, new friends, and her attempts at a business degree. Briar didn't know how to ease into it, so she simply asked. "How's everything in Argent Falls?" She directed her question to Rita, knowing that Alyssa was now at college about an hour from her home, in a dorm.

"He's a miserable asshole," Rita answered.

Briar's eyes widened. "I didn't ask about—"

"It's clearly written on your face what you meant," Alyssa interrupted.

"If you don't want to reach out to him first, I'll give him your new num—"

Briar was quick to cut Rita off. "Absolutely not. We could have tried to make things work, but…"

"I'm not taking up for him in the least," Rita began. "Despite not showing it, I know that Dex has struggled with being good enough. His mom walking out of his life so easily has a lot to do with that. If I'm looking at it from his side, I don't think he wanted you to be tied down or settling. You're young. You still have your whole life to settle down and fall in love."

Briar swallowed heavily, and her gaze dropped down to her coffee cup. She wouldn't tell Rita or Alyssa, but in almost a year, nothing had changed for her.

She met a lot of new people, even guys, but the thought of even so much as a date ripped her heart to shreds. What hurt the most was the fact that the person she hated more than anyone else was also the person she couldn't stop loving.

When Briar didn't say anything in response, "Regardless, I still give him shit."

It was enough to make Briar smile.

She wished she would have had more than half a day to spend with Rita and Alyssa, but an early morning flight the next day was calling her name.

As Briar stared out the window, aimlessly watching the clouds engulf the plane over and over, many thoughts ran through her head.

A part of her felt like she should have stayed to hear the guilty verdict Portia was sure to receive; however, seeing that woman, being in the courtroom, made her sick to her stomach. To this day, she still couldn't believe the lengths that Portia and Leo had gone through.

Then there was the incessant reminder of Dex. It felt nice to hear Rita call him a miserable asshole, but deep down inside, Briar didn't want that.

For the most part, Dex was a wonderful person. Though he cursed entirely too much and was a little gruff with most people, Briar knew that he was also kind, giving, protective, gentle, and the list went on. In the end, she truly wished him happiness.

What Briar couldn't get over was something that Rita said that seemed so unfathomable. After nearly a year, there was no one in Dex's life.

Briar was forced to think back to Lexi, and then the night she first kissed Dex and he brought home a random woman. Alyssa told her many times how women of all ages drooled over Dex. Briar knew all too well how attractive he was. That's why she couldn't understand what Rita told her.

It gave her a sick hope that she wanted to bury deep down and never think about. Had she had an effect on Dex the way he had on her?

He could have any woman in Argent Falls, but yet, Rita insisted that he didn't even have the slightest encounters bordering on romantic with the opposite sex.

Briar could admit, she was extremely inexperienced with men before Dex. After she left Argent Falls, she threw herself into her training and put dating on the back burner. As amazing as sex was with Dex, and the fact that it ended up becoming a daily habit, she hadn't felt the need to find it elsewhere. Sex, romance, love…That could wait for two years.

Briar shook her head and chuckled to herself. There was no way that Dex had made it a month without some kind of physical contact from a woman.

Briar was never the sort that was addicted to her phone; therefore, it wasn't surprising that she didn't bother turning it on until she got out of the shower after returning to her loft.

Her heart nearly stopped when she saw the voice message from an all too familiar area code.

* * *

"I honestly never thought I'd see the day," Marlee gasped to Rusty.

They stood at the auto shop's front counter after returning from one of their weekly lunch dates.

"Hey," Rusty greeted as Dex came in, in the middle of his conversation with Marlee. "Did you know that shit?"

Dex couldn't care less what those two were talking about, but indulged Rusty anyway. "What?"

"Old Benny is finally selling his shop," Rusty laughed. "About damn time! He's got to be pushing eighty."

Dex froze momentarily. "Wait, what? The antique shop?"

Dumfounded, "Uh…Yeah? Unless he has another shop I don't know about."

Ignoring Rusty and knowing that Marlee would have all the details, "How much is it listed?"

Marlee looked at Dex rather confused. She didn't anticipate that he'd care about that place. "Um…Well, I think it's been sold. I mean, I'm not the agent handling–"

"What the fuck do you mean already–"

Dex's interruption was quickly interrupted by Rusty. "Dude! Chill."

Marlee swatted at Rusty. She was accustomed to Dex's demeanor. "I think he had a buyer previously lined up. Nothing is set in stone yet, but I do know for a fact that there is an offer."

"How much," Dex asked again.

"Five hundred thousand." When Rusty sucked in a breath, "Considering it's commercial, and the location and square footage, that's actually not too much, even for Argent Falls."

Dex pondered for just a second while Marlee rambled on about statistics he didn't need to know.

Rarely was he impulsive. It might come across that way because he hardly ever voiced his thoughts to those around him.

"I'm headed out early today," Dex said, silencing both Marlee and Rusty. "Can you lock up?"

Rusty narrowed his eyes, attempting to figure out the rapid change in Dex. "Why?"

"There's something I need to do," was all Dex said, already grabbing his keys from behind the counter.

Rusty stepped in front of Dex, blocking him from the main door. "Whoa, whoa, whoa. What's this about?"

"Rusty," Dex warned.

Using the same tone as Dex, "Dex…"

Repeating himself, "There's something–"

"Yeah, yeah. I got that. What the hell is that something, and why did you think of it all of a sudden once you found out about Benny?"

Dex didn't feel like filling Rusty in, especially not with Marlee still standing there. He placed his hand on Rusty's shoulder and patted it. "We'll talk tomorrow."

"Why do I feel like you're going to do something stupid," Rusty sighed.

Dex finally cracked a grin, one that Rusty hadn't seen for quite some time. "Because you know me too well."

"Damnit, Dex. What does Benny's shop have to do with anything," Rusty groaned, now rubbing his forehead.

"Tomorrow," was all Dex left him with.

✳ ✳ ✳

"Mr. Hayden," Benny sighed, as he wrapped some old looking vase in newspaper.

"You said that nothing is final. Surely you'd entertain another offer," Dex reminded him. So far it had been nearly half an hour of wasted time.

"It's not so much about the money. I made a promise to this buyer that if I ever decided to sell–"

"Are they even a local?"

Benny shook his head, a saddened expression coming to his face.

"Please don't sell to some rich city asshole who's going to probably turn this place into a fucking Starbucks or McDonald's." Dex saw who he assumed was one of Benny's granddaughter's from across the shop cross her arms and send a deathly glare his way. "Apologies," Dex mumbled.

Ignoring Dex's language, "And what interest does a mechanic have for my wee little antique shop?"

Dex felt his face reddening. He would be the first to admit, this was hands down the dumbest and most impulsive buy he'd be making, and he had made a few over the years. Most of his impulsive buys, however, could be turned into profit. There was no doubt about it, he'd be sinking money into this place and receiving no return on his investment.

"I don't know yet," he only partially lied. "All I can say is that I'll take care of the place that you've taken care of the better part of fifty years."

"Let me get this straight. You want to buy this property, and then do nothing with it? Just own it?"

Dex rubbed the back of his neck. "I know that sounds stupid–"

"You're damn right it does!"

"Grandpa," the girl from nearby spat.

Benny waved her off. He then stared at Dex.

Dex hoped that he was wearing Benny down, but the old man's expressionless face gave nothing away.

Then, after the sweat began to drip down his back, waiting for Benny to say something, anything, Benny put him out of his misery.

"What's your offer?"

Dex knew he'd have to give Benny something to really consider. He managed and invested his money very well, and without thinking, he knew what was easily doable.

"Seven fifty." When Benny's eyes widened and lips parted, Dex decided to go in for the kill. "Right now. On the condition that you won't entertain any other buyers."

Benny narrowed his eyes, and a smirk came to his face, giving Dex the smallest amount of hope.

CHAPTER 51

More than a year after that.

Benji popped the hood of a car and immediately got to work with an oil change.

"Did I tell you about the girl Liam met at college," he called out to Dex nearby.

Dex truly didn't care about Liam's relationships, but entertained Benji anyway. "No. What about her?"

"Funniest damn thing," Benji began, laughing. "Well, they met here, but they ended up going to the same college."

"Okay…"

"Lexi's sister! What a small fucking world!"

Dex clenched his teeth. Coincidentally, both of those people shared one person in common, one person that after more than two years, still continued to come up in his conversations.

"That's great. She seems nice," was all Dex said.

"Little strange. Wears a lot of black. Complete opposite of her sister. I guess that's a good thing," Benji said with a shrug.

He refrained from mentioning that Liam really got to know Alyssa through Briar. More than likely Dex already knew that, which would account for the sour expression that was now plastered to his face.

"Good thing the snow finally melted," Benji went on, attempting to change the subject.

All Dex gave in return was a grunt.

Snow or sun, it didn't matter to Dex. It was another day, another change of the weather.

Though each day was different, a different task at hand, they were all the same. He worked. When he didn't work, he'd go to the gym, read a book, get much needed sleep from working too late.

Rusty still made sure to keep one night a week open for drinks; however, most of his nights were consumed with Marlee. He already made hints to Dex when it came to a particular piece of jewelry, so Dex knew it was only a matter of time.

Never in his wildest imagination would he have ever put Rusty and marriage in the same universe.

Just as that thought flittered away, he was quickly reminded of the woman who captured so much of Rusty's time and attention.

With the spring breeze and sunlight making the temperature a perfect balance between cool and hot, all the garage doors were open for the day.

It was still strange seeing Marlee in a suit as opposed to a t-shirt and Chêne apron. Dex watched as her heels clicked from the parking lot into the large garage, her steps a direct line to Rusty. Though they were some feet away from him, Dex easily picked up on the conversation.

"I thought you had a lunch with a big buyer," Rusty said shortly after Marlee kissed him on the cheek.

"I did. It's already after two," she laughed.

"Crap. I guess I lost track of time. What are you doing here then?"

"Actually, I have some business I need to discuss with Dex," she attempted to whisper.

Her words weren't lost to Dex. "What," he called out.

Marlee gave Rusty a nervous look and playfully bit at her lip. Turning and walking a few steps closer to Dex, "I was hoping to talk to you about the antique shop, or whatever it is now."

It was an empty space. That's all.

Dex had taken care of it as he promised. He even redid all the walls, and hired someone to replace the old and torn linoleum into crisp and clean wood, with the perfect amount of grey and tan so that it would fit any color scheme.

"No."

"No?"

"I don't want to talk about it," was Dex's response.

Rusty let out a breath and shook his head, knowing whatever Marlee wanted to say was a lost cause; however, she had his curiosity piqued. "What about it?"

Keeping her attention focused on Dex, "I have a couple that has been interested in the space for quite some—"

"No," Dex said, sharply cutting her off.

"Come on, man," Rusty began, although knew how pointless it was to reason with Dex. "You've been paying taxes and utilities on it for the better part of a year, and you haven't gotten anything out of it. Just let go of it."

"Dex, I really think you should meet the buyer. It's an amazing offer," Marlee insisted.

"I'm good."

"No, dude! You're not," Rusty burst out. "I know why you bought that place. I just don't get why. You're the one who—"

"Don't start," Dex growled. He kicked the creeper nearby, sending it colliding into a metal wall.

"You know what, man? I have been your friend for a long time, but this is ridiculous. You're going to end up bitter and alone. Hell, you already are. You'll probably be that gross curmudgeon at the end of the street that doesn't shower, talks too much to his dog, or cat, or fucking plant, whatever, and yells at all the kids to get off his piece of shit lawn," Rusty exclaimed.

"Rusty, calm down," Marlee whispered.

Dex crossed his arms. "You done?"

Rusty threw a wrench to the side. "Fuck it. Do what you want. Sink money into a place you're never going to do a damn thing with." He rubbed Marlee on the shoulder. "I'll be right back. This bastard is driving me to crave a cigarette." Rusty then glared at Dex but addressed his words to Marlee. "You're wasting your time with this one."

Marlee waited until Rusty left before saying another word to Dex. She was quite surprised that Dex still stood there. After the last few minutes, she thought he would have been the one to storm off.

"Dex…"

Dex's shoulders fell in defeat, knowing that Marlee and Rusty were right. He didn't know what he'd ever do with the property. He just never wanted anyone else to have it, not after seeing Briar get so excited about her dreams for it.

When Dex said nothing, "Will you at least meet my buyers. If you don't want to accept their offer, can you at least tell them that much?"

Answering her question with another question, "I'm curious. What is it? The offer."

Marlee took a deep breath and shook her head. "Two million."

One of Dex's brows shot up in disbelief. "Are you serious? I paid more than the asking price, but…It's not like it's value shot up in–"

"Apparently, this location has value to someone."

Dex couldn't believe it. Though it was never about the money to him, that was an insane offer considering what Benny asked a little over a year ago.

He walked over to a bench near one of the massive garage doors. He expected Marlee to follow, but not for her to sit right next to him. Unfortunately, she remained quiet, which only left Dex battling with his thoughts.

Finally, "You think I'm stupid, don't you?"

Marlee softly chuckled at first but then turned serious and empathetic. "I think you're holding on to something in place of something you lost."

Not wanting to have that conversation with Marlee, Dex conceded. "Fine. I'll meet them."

"I'm glad you said that," Marlee squealed.

"Yeah. Just tell me when."

He never said he'd sell, but for that kind of offer, he was curious who they were and what the hell they wanted with the property.

Dex never expected Marlee's response.

"How about now?"

* * *

Marlee glanced at the clock in the small conference room for what must have been the fifth time. "He said he'd be over shortly."

That wasn't exactly what Dex said. It was more along the lines of, "I'll get there when I get there. Let me clean up a little first."

"Are you sure you want me here," Henrik whispered quietly, although in the small space, Marlee could hear any private conversation.

Marlee looked over and waited for a response as well, knowing that once Dex walked in, it wouldn't be good, with or without Henrik present.

"Yes, of course."

"I'm in dire need of a cup of tea," Henrik complained.

"Just be here at the start. Then I'll handle the rest. There's a café two blocks down, but I highly doubt you'll find their tea to your liking."

All conversation ceased when a strong rapping on the opposite side of the door came through.

Marlee nervously wiped her now sweaty hands along her dark dress pants and reached for the door.

"Dex," she greeted, slowly opening the door for him to enter.

Dex stepped inside, already visibly annoyed with agreeing to meet with potential buyers. He had, however, attempted to look like he hadn't just rolled out from beneath a car. If someone had two million dollars to sink into a little shop in Argent Falls, he could at least show up in a clean shirt.

At first, he focused on Marlee, the only presence in the room that gave him some level of comfort. It was only when he met her eyes after she greeted him that he saw a change in her from an hour before.

She looked apprehensive and uncertain.

Marlee held out her hand toward the couple across the room on the opposite end of a long table. "Dex, I'd like you to meet our interested buyers…"

Dex turned, giving his attention to the others, and in that moment, his heart stopped beating.

"What the fuck?!"

CHAPTER 52

"Typical Dexter Hayden greeting. I wouldn't have expected anything less," Briar scoffed.

Her eyes latched on to Dex's, fully intending to watch his every action and reaction. She had time to think about how this meeting might go, and her instincts were right on the money when a second later, Dex tore his gaze from her and turned back to the door.

"Sorry, Marlee. I'm out."

Marlee nervously stepped in the doorway, although knew that she was no match for a beast like Dex.

"Dex," she began with a shaky sigh. "You promised you'd at least–"

"I didn't promise a damn thing," he interrupted. His eyes held a deathly glare that gave Marlee goosebumps.

"I think I should go for that tea now."

Dex couldn't ignore the voice across the room.

"Just one second," Briar insisted to Henrik.

"Please," Marlee begged Dex at the same time.

There was something in Dex that was a glutton for punishment. He knew he should have walked away, far away; instead, he turned and faced the couple seated at the end of the table.

Seeing her after all that time only made him angry. He could not have hated himself more than he did in that moment, seeing her sitting there, with another man.

Briar watched as Dex's attention flew to Henrik beside her, and a sick elation ran through her veins. Though Dex tried not to have a visible reaction, Briar could see it in his eyes.

So often he had told her that her eyes gave away her truths. If that were the case, he was telling her a lot right now, starting with his jealousy.

Dex figured Briar would move on in those two years. No one had ever said anything, but maybe they thought they were helping him by not telling him every detail of her life. This was definitely one he could have gone without knowing.

Henrik wasn't bad looking in the least. He was very clean cut with his short blonde hair perfectly parted and combed more to one side than the other. His soft brown eyes held a boyish sparkle of playfulness. Then, as if to put the final nail in the coffin, he was wearing a plaid button-up with a yellow cardigan.

He was the opposite of Dex in every way.

Dex didn't own anything that bright unless white counted, and he certainly would never be caught dead in a cardigan.

Dex brought his attention back to Briar. Her unique blonde hair was shorter, making her appear older, but in a good way. Her outfit was similar to Marlee's, all business; however, all that flashed in Dex's mind in that moment was a memory of Briar in his t-shirt and nothing more.

Briar was only satisfied when Dex looked down and seemed unsatisfied. She kept her hands folded beneath the table, in hopes of tormenting him for just a little longer, fully knowing what he was searching for.

Marlee and Henrik could not have felt more uncomfortable with the tension in the room. Henrik was the first to subtly make that known by taking his leave.

"Text me when you're done," Henrik told Briar as he rose from his seat. He placed a kiss on her cheek. "Cheerio, love."

"Later, Henrik."

No sooner than Henrik stepped over the threshold into the hallway, Marlee found herself doing the same, closing the door as she spoke. "I have a few papers…and…I'll be right back."

The only sound left was the clicking of the door shutting behind Marlee.

Briar rolled her eyes. "Would you at least sit down?"

Dex wasn't sure if he could sit down. Every part of his body wanted to explode with the feelings and emotions running through him.

Briar sensed the war waging in Dex's head. She always knew it would be a shock for him to see her back in Argent Falls, but this had to have really knocked him off his feet; therefore, she threw him a bit of a bone.

She brought her hands from her lap, from beneath the table, and clasped her left over her right on a stack of papers in front of her. Sure enough, Dex's eyes dropped from hers to her fingers, void of any jewelry.

For a moment, his tight and furrowed brows appeared to ease of tension. He took in a deep breath and pulled out the chair across from Briar. Though he sat down, he didn't bring himself forward, leaving a large gap between himself and the table. He clearly had no intention of staying too long.

Briar leaned in and folded her hands together, the sleeves of her blazer riding up ever so slightly. Normally Dex wouldn't have noticed, but his senses were suddenly heightened with her presence and he was noticing every little detail, including the black markings on both her wrists.

Briar saw his eyes fall to her hands again. For a fleeting moment, she thought about trying to cover them, but he had already seen it. Knowing how little Dex wanted to be there, she didn't expect him to change the subject of the shop to something personal.

"What did you do," Dex asked rather gruffly.

Disliking how the question came out, Briar answered with more sass than she would have. "They're called tattoos."

Something inside Dex started to ache, and when he brought his eyes up to Briar's he knew they were both thinking of the same memory.

It was something Briar didn't talk about, kind of like Dex with his mother, but Dex knew. He remembered the scars on her wrists, horrid souvenirs of a past she put behind her a long time ago. He wasn't close enough to her, but he was certain that the tattoos did a good job of covering the constant reminder.

As much as he should have shut up, he had to know. "I mean…What is it?"

Reluctantly, Briar flipped her hands over and held her wrists out. She didn't want to get personal with Dex yet. She wanted to stay mad for just a little longer.

One wrist was covered in generic black birds of different sizes, whereas the other had a phrase. Dex didn't want to ask, so he memorized it, making a mental note to look it up later. *Dum Spiro, Spero.*

As if reading Dex's mind, "It means, while I breathe, I hope."

Dex's eyes shot back up to hers, and each wondered if the other could feel whatever it was passing between them.

Briar quickly flipped her arms over and tightly crossed them over her chest. She forced herself to get serious. First, there was the issue of the property. Then she could think about her relationship, or rather lack thereof, with Dex.

"I'll spare hashing out the past," Briar began, realizing her careless dismissal of the past affected Dex.

Though it pained her to do so to someone she still desperately cared for, she wanted him to hurt. He hurt her once when he brought home the woman from the bar, but he destroyed her when he sent her away to London, not even bothering to try to make things work.

After a pause, without any response from Dex, "I will say, I was rather surprised when I got a call from Mr. Georges informing me that he could not accept my offer, nor was he in interested in a counter."

Dex's mouth fell open. "You. You were the other buyer," he said in disbelief. "How? It wasn't even on the market for–"

"I might have made a stop somewhere between you throwing me out and the airport," Briar interrupted.

Dex rolled his eyes at the mentioning of that.

Briar continued. "Benny promised me, should he ever sell, I'd be the first person he'd contact. I couldn't believe it, actually. I guess he saw how much I desperately loved that little place. Then, a few days later I find out that he's selling to a local, at a fifty percent increase from my offer."

Dex remained silent. It only made him sick to his stomach that Briar always planned to return to Argent Falls. The moment she left, he knew he handled the situation poorly, but he couldn't admit that. The damage was done.

"Imagine my surprise when I find out who the bastard is that ripped away something I badly wanted."

"Look, Briar," Dex began, trying to keep his voice level. "I'm not selling that property right now, and I'm absolutely not selling it to you and your…whatever he is."

A smirk came across Briar's face and Dex realized how jealous he sounded with that last part.

"Why did you buy it," Briar asked, ignoring Dex's statement.

Dex would never answer that, especially not to her. With that, he rose from his seat. All Marlee wanted him to do was to meet the buyer and tell them himself that he wasn't selling. He had done that.

"I think we're done here."

Without giving Briar a chance to say another word, Dex was out the door.

He didn't bother trying to find Marlee or her office. He knew the way out of the building, and that's exactly where he headed, attempting to put as much distance between his heart and that relentless girl.

He slammed the front door to the real estate office behind him, and took off down the sidewalk. Chêne was only a few blocks over, and though alcohol solved nothing, after the day he was having, he could definitely go for a cold beer.

Sandy placed the beer in front of Dex and froze. The look in Sandy's eyes gave it all away.

"Just go," Dex growled, already sensing her presence.

"Stop being an asshole and have a conversation with me," Briar spat back. She took the barstool next to Dex.

"Same as him," Briar said to Sandy, and nodded toward Dex's beer.

Dex snapped his head toward Briar, but addressed his words to Sandy. "She's only twenty."

"You do know, it's eighteen in England," Briar said confidently.

Dex wasn't following. "What?"

"The drinking age. It's eighteen," Briar repeated.

Annoyed with the mentioning of England, "Fine. Then go back to England and get a fucking beer."

Sandy ignored the two and hesitantly placed a beer in front of Briar.

She wasn't about to tell Dex, but she didn't drink. At this point, she only wanted to put him in his place for his comment about her age.

"Why," was all she said.

Dex knew what she was referring to, but he couldn't answer truthfully. If he did, she'd know that he never got over her. Looking back, he was stupid to ever think that he could.

"I saw it as an investment opportunity," Dex finally answered.

Briar scoffed. "It's been over a year. You haven't done anything with it, not even rented it out."

"I've been busy," is all he gave her.

"Dex, I've made a generous—"

"You and your little sweetheart can find somewhere else to make chocolate," Dex coldly interrupted.

Wanting to poke the sleeping bear, Briar sighed happily. "Henrik is a sweetheart."

The sip of beer going down Dex's throat suddenly tasted like he was swallowing his own vomit.

"Glad you found what you were looking for."

"Right? I mean…someone who's never weak, but always strong…to protect me, and defend me…whether I'm right or wrong…to open each and–"

Dex aggressively put his half empty bottle down on the bar, silencing Briar and turned his stool toward her. "You can stop. I got it."

Briar chuckled, realizing that Dex recognized the words.

He couldn't believe her. She definitely had more fire in her than he had ever seen, which only reinforced that pushing her away had been the best thing for her.

"Bob fucking Dylan," he murmured under his breath.

After a few more passing minutes, "Can we talk about the property?"

Dex ignored Briar and took out his wallet. He placed a ten-dollar bill between his empty beer and Briar's full one, paying for them both. "Thanks, Sandy."

"So, what? You're just going to ignore me," Briar shouted at Dex's back outside of Chêne.

"Depends. You going to keep following me?"

Dex felt a jerk on his upper arm and allowed his body to turn with the pull.

"I need to talk to you."

Dex took a step forward and watched Briar's eyes widen at their closeness. It was the closest they had been in years.

"There isn't a damn thing you can say that will make me sell that place to you and Henry."

"Henrik," Briar corrected.

"Whatever. I think it's in your best interest to go back to wherever–"

"Are you jealous?"

Dex took a step back.

Briar laughed, which only made the crack on Dex's heart widen.

"Oh, come on, let's not pretend that you haven't had someone keeping your bed warm all this time. I think I'm entitled to–"

He couldn't stand to hear her finish her statement, and blurted out the words before he knew what he was saying.

Briar's mouth fell open. That couldn't be. She didn't hear him correctly. For the first time since she stormed back into his life, Briar was speechless.

"You're joking," she finally managed.

Dex felt his heart pounding. This wasn't a conversation to be having on the sidewalk in downtown Argent Falls. "No. I'm not."

"Coming from the man who brought home the first woman he could find when I kissed him, I don't believe that."

Dex brought himself closer to Briar and towered over her. "Believe what you want. Believe whatever you need to so that you feel happy with your little prissy prep school boyfriend."

Ignoring the mentioning of Henrik, "Why?"

"Why, what," Dex asked, not understanding what her question was directed at.

"Why haven't you been with anyone else?"

"Don't ask questions you know the fucking answer to."

An eerie feeling of déjà vu came over Briar. That response wasn't going to be good enough this time.

"Maybe I'm asking because I don't know the answer." She didn't mean for her voice to rise in anger and annoyance the way it had, but that was very much the emotions running through her. How could he tell her something like that? "Enlighten me," she pressed. "How is it that the sexiest single guy in this town hasn't been with a woman in years?"

Dex ran his hand through his hair. He was teetering on the edge, near combustion, to vomiting everything that needed to stay buried.

"Aww. Are we shy now? Suddenly, Mr. I-Say-Whatever-The-Fuck-I-Want can't answer a simple question?"

"Don't," Dex groaned.

It was a warning. Briar knew his warnings all too well, but she had come to Argent Falls for more than just the shop. She wasn't going to let Dex's stubbornness get in the way.

"No, Dex. I'm asking the question because I don't know the answer, so don't assume that I do."

"But you do! You just want me to say it," he yelled back.

Across the street an elderly couple shot them looks and whispered amongst themselves.

"Then say it!"

Dex threw his hands up in the air. "I fucked up! Okay? I get it. I messed up that day."

Briar fell silent. It wasn't exactly what she planned on hearing, but she knew there was more to come.

"I was angry. I was so upset that you we're willing to throw away your future to stay here, to stay with me," Dex finally admitted.

Briar opened her mouth to protest, but Dex didn't allow her to say a word.

"Stop. Don't say it. I know that's not how you saw it, but that's how it was to me, and I just lost it."

Before Dex could go off again, Briar fought to get another question in. "Why didn't you reach out?"

Dex had thought about that for far too long. "After I read your note and with that fucking check—"

"Which you never cashed," Briar interrupted.

Dex rolled his eyes. She had to be absurd to think he'd ever take a dime from her.

"The note was so…I don't know." He wasn't good with words. "Cold and to the point, like we were distant friends at most, never lovers."

"Well, after what you had said to me before that, what did you expect?"

"You're right. I thought about reaching out, but I didn't want to hold you back in any way. There are way better men out there for you than me, and you deserved to get to experience that, without being tied to this place or me." He couldn't believe his next words. "After all, you met Henrik, and he seems to make you happy. Everything worked out the way it was supposed to."

Briar was livid at what Dex was saying, and the fact that he still managed to say all that and avoid answering why he hadn't been with anyone else.

"No, Dex. You're wrong."

Dex's right brow shot up in confusion.

"Henrik and I aren't together," Briar clarified.

Dex said nothing, but tightly folded his arms over his chest, watching the playful glimmer in green eyes he never wanted to stop staring into.

"But he—"

"Kissed me on the cheek and called me love? Yes. He does that with *every-one*. He has a job lined up at a restaurant in New York and made the trip here to see where I wanted to open my business. He's *just* a friend."

Dex rarely got embarrassed, but he could feel the heat licking his face.

Feeling bold and in control of the conversation, "Now, will you stop telling me what I've grown to assume over the years and answer why you supposedly haven't so much as touched a woman?"

"So, you're not in a relationship," Dex asked, still rather confused, yet still avoiding her question.

"Are you fucking serious," Briar screamed.

Dex bit his lip to keep from smiling. Briar rarely cussed when he met her, but something about her outburst just now made it attractive as hell.

"Okay, you want to pretend to be a dense asshole? You're the only man I've ever truly been with, ever wanted to be with, ever loved. There. Happy? I can give you what you need to hear, but you can't do the same for me."

Without thinking, only operating on instinct, Dex wrapped one arm around Briar's waist and the other at the base of her neck, but before their lips met, she pulled away.

Oddly, that sent a rush of elation through him. She had in her a fire that he always knew was simmering beneath the surface.

"You don't get that privilege," Briar began.

Dex smiled and shook his head before bringing his eyes up to meet hers. "You're right."

It was another phrase Briar didn't expect from Dex.

"I couldn't move on. Actually, couldn't is the wrong word. I didn't want to move on." Dex rubbed a hand over his face. "This is going to make me sound like such a damn sissy," he grumbled. "After being with you, sex with another woman felt...wrong. Every time someone wanted to set me up...I just..." Dex stopped and pointed in the area of his heart. "It hurt. It physically hurt."

Briar couldn't take it anymore and took swift steps toward Dex until she was pulling him down by the collar of his shirt.

"Say it," she demanded.

"I love you, and–"

Before he could say another word and risk messing up the moment, Briar pressed her lips to his.

CHAPTER 53

"I can't believe I'm going to say this," Dex managed, as he breathlessly tore his lips from Briar's and slammed the door to his apartment. "I think we should slow down."

"You're right. I wanted to hate you a little longer," Briar said with a sinister smirk.

Her body was already betraying her words as she stepped closer to Dex and ran her hands up his chest.

Dex lowered his head and breathed into her neck, knowing that was a weakness for her. "You're not helping the situation."

"Look, I know I'm supposed to tell you that we need to talk. Too much time has passed for this to be happening. Everything is still raw. We should take baby steps. Whatever else I'm expected to say…"

Dex grabbed her hips and both pulled her into him, yet held her firmly in place to keep her from latching on to him.

"You can say whatever you want."

Briar turned serious and wrapped her arms around Dex's neck. "After hearing you say words that I've needed to hear for the last two years, I don't care about what I'm supposed to say or do. I just want you, all of you." Then, feeling playful, she added, "I can hate you later."

Dex knew he'd never live down that day, but he could make sure that he'd never push her away again. He'd let her know every day how loved she was, for as long as she'd allow him.

It took every bit of restraint on both to eventually end up making it to the bedroom. Once they did, the kiss was broken as Dex effortlessly tossed Briar on the bed.

"Bathroom," was all he said, as he rushed out of the room.

Briar took the shortest of moments to glance around the room she missed every night. Aside from the new comforter, hardly anything had changed.

She scurried up the bed toward the nightstand and pulled open the drawer, rummaging around for a condom.

Very little was in the drawer, and as she shifted things around a familiar letter caught her attention. She wanted to smile and cry at the same time when she saw that Dex had kept that.

"Dex," Briar shouted. "I can't find the…"

Her words trailed off when she came across a different box, one that most definitely didn't have condoms. Needing to feed her curiosity, she opened it, her heart and head already telling her what she'd find inside.

To say that it was beautiful was an understatement. It was absolutely perfect. Yellow gold. One large oval diamond, probably somewhere around two carats. And two smaller round ones to the left and right of the main one.

"You can't find what," Dex asked, entering the bedroom.

All he could see was Briar's back at first. It wasn't until she turned to face him that he saw tears in her eyes. Then he saw what she held in her hands.

He swiftly crossed the room and yanked the box away from her, throwing it back in the drawer without even bothering to close it.

"I…I'm sorry…I was…looking for condoms. I didn't mean to pry…I just…"

"I don't have any."

All Briar did was nod. She couldn't care less about condoms right now.

She had never gone through Dex's personal things. Seeing an engagement ring in his nightstand brought back a conversation long ago that she remembered with Alyssa.

"At least this year at Thanksgiving, I won't have to listen to her describe her perfect engagement ring."

Briar dabbed at her eyes and ceased any more tears from falling. She wasn't sure what the protocol was after that. One thing for certain, sex was off the table. Feeling the awkwardness with the silence, leaving was her only option.

Briar rose from the bed, and without looking Dex in the face, "I should go."

"Sit," was his immediate response.

The commanding tone in his voice had her body obeying before she even realized what he wanted her to do.

She stared at the floor and waited for him to say something, anything. Instead, she felt the bed sink beside her.

Dex placed his hand just above Briar's knee and sighed one time too many. "Briar…"

"It's fine. I get it," she immediately responded.

"Get what?"

"I knew you were with her for a long time. I'm sure the two of you contemplated on marriage. I mean Alyssa told me that–"

Dex interrupted Briar with a laugh she hadn't heard in ages. A genuine and rare Dex laugh.

Briar quickly shut her mouth, not finding one thing humorous about the situation. She could feel Dex looking at her, but kept her eyes glued to the floor.

"Briar," he repeated, although this time he dragged her name out.

He squeezed where he had his hand on her leg and only then did she give him her attention. His cold and crystal blue eyes stared into hers, captivating her, locking her into place. It wasn't until then that she saw something past the tiredness in them. Amusement.

Dex saw that she was on pins and needles, waiting for him to say something, to confirm her suspicions, no matter how ridiculous they were.

At first, he was a little upset that she found that box. It wasn't something he wanted anyone to know, aside from the fact that both Rusty and Sandy did know his intentions all that time ago.

A part of him was actually scared to correct her. Telling her that he loved her was already a monumental admission. That, Briar could deal with. It was obviously what she wanted. Knowing that he once thought about proposing after only knowing her for roughly six months?

"The ring was for you," he finally blurted out.

Briar's face went flat, unreadable.

Seeing the look on her face, Dex realized that maybe he should have lied, told her the ring was for Lexi, his once on and off again girlfriend of two years.

Finally, "Please don't tell me it was going to be that day."

A saddened and forced chuckle came from Dex. He didn't bother confirming that. The fact that she asked the question meant that she already knew.

"When I found out about the school thing, I realized I couldn't. Then, another part of me doubted whether I'd ever be good enough for someone as perfect as you."

"I'm far from perfect," Briar corrected.

"Anyway, it's not that I didn't love you then. Obviously, I did. I mean hell, I wanted to marry you. I know you're upset about that day and how I handled everything, but you have to know, I only ever wanted the best for you," Dex stressed.

He didn't expect the flood of tears that started streaming down her face. His words just tumbled out so easily. He tried to think if there was something in them that would have further upset her.

Briar knew. It had taken a lot of sleepless nights for her to realize that Dex did what he did for unselfish reasons. By then, too much time had passed for a simple phone call.

"Then you have to know," she began, mimicking his words. "*You* were always the best for me."

Dex leaned in while bringing his hand up, cradling Briar's neck, and placed the softest kiss on her lips, knowing that after everything, it wouldn't be enough. It would never be enough.

After the sweet kiss turned deeper and more passionate, Briar fisted Dex's shirt, pulling him down with her on the bed.

Breaking the kiss and hovering over Briar, Dex was forced to remind her. "Condoms…"

"Birth control," Briar responded, while attempting to pull Dex back on top of her.

"What?!"

Briar shook her head, already knowing where Dex's mind went. "One, stop being jealous. The last person I slept with was you. Two, do you really want to talk about my female *stuff* right now?"

Dex clenched his eyes shut at the mentioning.

"Good point."

He then lowered his mouth to Briar's neck, and lightly swirled his tongue over the spot that drove her crazy. Briar lifted her hips, attempting to grind into Dex, in response.

Dex quietly chuckled, but Briar could feel his vibrations going from her neck straight to her core. She vigorously began working at the buttons on her shirt.

"Stop teasing," she insisted as she rose just enough to get the sleeves off.

Before she laid back down, Dex reached behind her and unclasped the lacy white bra, slowly sliding the straps down her arms, allowing her breasts to spill out.

"What makes you think I'm teasing," Dex playfully teased.

He briefly pulled away and allowed her to remove her pants, which she did in record time.

Briar's hands then flew to Dex's belt and he did nothing to stop her, relishing at the fact that she wanted this just as much as he did. She could see that clearly by the erection straining against his jeans.

382

Once she had the zipper down, Dex helped, until he was only in his boxers and shirt. Briar reached for the base of his shirt, but for some reason Dex stopped her. Just as she was about to protest, his hand drifted up her thigh, immediately distracting her.

Briar's hands gripped the comforter beneath her when Dex's finger dipped inside her panties.

Dex let out a hiss. "So fucking wet."

Briar thrust her hips upward, needing more than just a finger skimming through her folds.

"You have no idea how many nights I dreamed of you touching me again."

After so long, Dex wanted to take their first encounter slow, but both their bodies were screaming for release, and he fully intended on having Briar come at least once before he had his way with her. That needed to happen fast, because ever since she mentioned being on the pill, and he realized he'd get to come inside her, mark her, claim her, with no restrictions, he was near combustion.

Briar cried out when not only did Dex enter her with two fingers, but his mouth landed back on that spot on her neck. Him sucking that spot alone could get her near an orgasm.

Dex picked up speed, roughly thrusting two fingers deep inside her while using his thumb to rub circles over her clit.

He held her tightly to his chest when a moment later, her body shook, writhing in euphoric sensations as her orgasm hit hard.

"Fuck! Yes! Dex," Briar cried out.

Her nails dug into his shoulders and her pussy clenched tightly onto his fingers begging for every last bit of pleasure they could give.

"Wow. That was fast," Dex chuckled as he watched Briar attempt to catch her breath.

Dex brought his fingers to his mouth and sucked off the dripping juices, and Briar groaned in embarrassment. He brought himself down to whisper in

383

her ear, noting that she'd most definitely have markings of their encounter on her neck for days to come.

"Don't worry. It's only bad if it's the guy…And…As much as I hate to admit this, once my dick gets a taste of you, I can't promise it won't be the same for me," he growled.

Briar once again reached for Dex's shirt and he, yet again, pulled away; however, this time she wasn't distracted.

She looked at him curiously as his eyes fell from hers and he slowly began working on the buttons. It wasn't until he was nearly done that Briar saw something on his chest peeking out.

Briar froze and her throat closed up, unable to speak, swallow, breathe, when Dex removed his shirt. Her eyes roamed over the markings on his left side. They were ones she had never seen before.

She reached up to the spot where he was shot and felt the slightest bump along his skin. Though she felt it, and knew it was there, the ink kept it concealed, hidden beneath its surface.

Dex shuddered as her delicate fingers trailed along the thorny vines of light pink flowers, until her hand reached his heart, where a single rose was painted.

"They're…" She stopped herself from saying another word. She didn't know what to say, she was speechless.

"Briar Roses," Dex managed, already knowing that she knew.

Briar kept her hand over Dex's heart while her eyes continued to admire the markings. He could have gotten something, anything, small to cover up the scar from the gunshot. The fact that he got this, and that it ended at his heart, spoke volumes to her.

Had he never told her that he loved her, this alone was confirmation of it.

Dex held Briar's naked body against his, sure that her cheek could feel his heart pounding out of his chest.

"That was," Briar began.

"Amazing," Dex finished, quite surprised with himself for not exploding the second he entered her.

Briar's arm snaked around his torso and pulled herself closer, if that was even possible.

Dex couldn't help but melt at the gesture, and held her tightly. He was never good at relationships, but he finally found someone who all he wanted to do was make happy. Whatever she needed or wanted, he'd give her.

He was made aware of that after the aftershocks of sex wore off and Briar rose from the bed and ruffled through his closet for a shirt.

"There is something that I still need to talk to you about," she began, after pulling on a t-shirt of his and walking back toward the bed.

She handed Dex his boxers, which he reluctantly pulled back on. Briar seemed serious all of a sudden, so he figured right now wasn't the time to tell her he'd be good to go in another two minutes.

Briar sat on the bed cross-legged, facing Dex head on. "It's about the property."

Dex immediately saw the conversation as pointless, and brought himself closer to Briar so that he could place a hand on each side of her face. He didn't want to waste time talking about something in which there needed to be no discussion of, so he bluntly put it out there.

"It's yours. It's always been yours."

That was another thing she didn't expect Dex to say that day, and it made her heart soar.

"Really," she gasped. "I…I mean…I'll pay you for–"

"Absolutely not," Dex cut her off.

He pulled her into his arms and gently kissed the top of her head.

"I can't believe you would consider throwing away most of your inheritance for some little shop in Argent Falls," he laughed.

Briar pulled back and their eyes met, happiness from one sinking through to the other.

Briar nervously brushed back her hair and bit at her bottom lip, a smile forming across her entire face.

"About my inheritance. I didn't tell you everything…"

EPILOGUE

Six months later.

"Everything is fine," Dex said for what seemed like the millionth time.

"It cannot be fine! It needs to be perfect," Briar stressed.

Dex watched as she reorganized the display counter for what also felt like the millionth time.

Her shop didn't open until the following week; however, she had put in calls and arranged for an early sampling for food bloggers and at least three magazines throughout the state. Just to ease her nerves, she had invited several friends and acquaintances in Argent Falls.

Dex came up behind Briar and placed his hands on her shoulders. "Relax," he whispered in her ear. "Just breathe."

A smile slowly came to Briar's face. Dex's presence was always so comforting and calming.

"I just want this to work," Briar sighed. She reluctantly pulled away from Dex and went around the counter to one of the bistro tables, beginning to play with a vase of flowers.

"Look, why don't you take a break, go get ready, and then—"

Briar spun around with a gasp, interrupting Dex's words. "I am ready," she squawked, gesturing over her outfit.

"Oh...I meant..." Dex realized he was in trouble with the way his words came out.

"This dress was a bad idea, wasn't it?"

"No, the dress looks fine."

The look on Briar's face told him that he was only digging his grave deeper.

"Fine? Seriously, Dex?!" Briar smoothed over the black and green patterned fabric. "It's missing something," she mumbled to herself, before turning back to straighten another vase of flowers. "Maybe I should have worn the sash that came with it."

"Maybe jewelry? A necklace." Once he said it, he realized that was it; he'd have to go through with it.

Briar scoffed, dismissing Dex. "You know I don't wear jewelry."

"We should change that."

Something in Dex's voice was different, giving Briar pause.

Dex didn't say another word, all he could do now was wait, and knowing Briar's curiosity, it wouldn't be long.

As she slowly turned around, "Briar Stone, will you–"

"Are you serious," Briar gasped.

"Uh…"

Briar knew that one day Dex would take a step forward in their relationship, especially considering that two months ago they moved out of the apartment and into a house, a home, together.

"I'm sorry," she began, covering her face in embarrassment, catching Dex off guard. "Shit. No," she quickly corrected. "I don't mean I'm sorry the answer is no. I mean I'm sorry for messing this up. I didn't expect you to actually get down on one knee," she rambled on. "I thought…I don't know I guess you'd just one day say something like…Hey, want to get married? I just…this…"

Dex stood, and walked to Briar until he couldn't get any closer, forcing her to look up at him. "Breathe," he softly commanded, to which Briar nodded. "Can I finish?"

Briar bit down on her bottom lip to keep from grinning from ear to ear and nodded even more vigorously.

Dex took her nervous and shaky hands into his surprisingly warm and calm ones. "Will you marry me," he asked simply.

"Yes," Briar shouted as Dex's words still hung in the air.

When he slipped the ring on her finger, it was then that she noticed it wasn't the same one she found in that drawer many months ago. Though she knew very little about jewelry, she knew for a fact that he had upgraded what she thought was already a beautiful ring.

As if reading her thoughts, "You already saw the other one, and I didn't know if that's some bad omen or anything. Do you like it?"

"I love it," Briar exclaimed. "But I don't care about the ring. I didn't even need one."

"Would have been nice to know before I wrote out that check," Dex teased.

Briar threw her arms around Dex. "I just need you, always you."

Dex pulled her in tight and pressed his lips to hers, already knowing that a simple kiss wouldn't be enough. Just as expected, Briar bit at the bottom of his lip, silently begging for something deeper, which he was happy to oblige, until he realized where they were.

Dex pulled away and pressed their foreheads together. "I love you."

The smile on Briar's face was enough of a response, but hearing her say those words back sent every good feeling there was straight through him.

Briar knew Dex was right when he insisted that they'd have to celebrate their engagement later that night.

Despite the fact that an influx of people would soon be arriving, a large amount of them very critical at that, Briar no longer felt nervous. She felt strangely at peace, and simply put, happy.

This wasn't the life she ever imagined growing up. In her short time on earth, there were many things in her life that she could never have foreseen, never thought possible. At one point, she didn't ever see herself making it this far, as giving up seemed so much easier.

But life isn't always easy. With all the bad also came all the good.

While her dreams changed over the years, she realized that she had found a place, and was building something, with someone she loved, surrounded by people she loved, that she would always be able to call home.

The End.

Made in the USA
Middletown, DE
12 January 2022

58400772R00231